SONG OF THE BRONZE STATUE

David Wingrove is the Hugo Award-winning co-author (with Brian Aldiss) of *Trillion Year Spree: The History of Science Fiction*, and co-author of the first three *Myst* books – novelizations of one of the world's bestselling computer games. He is also author of *The Roads to Moscow* trilogy. He lives in north London.

SONG OF THE BRONZE STATUE

DAVID WINGROVE

Song of the Bronze Statue was first published as part of *White Moon, Red Dragon* in Great Britain in 1994 by New English Library.

First published in trade paperback and eBook in Great Britain in 2022 by Fragile Books.

A CIP catalogue record for this book is available from the British Library.

Trade paperback ISBN: 978-1-912094-74-5
eBook ISBN: 978-1-912094-76-9

Printed in Great Britain by 4edge Limited.

Fragile Books
5a Arundel Square
London
N7 8AT

www.fragilemedialtd.com

CONTENTS

For John Patrick Kavanagh, brother in arms, dedicated B52 pilot and all round fine fellow. "Give 'em a dollar!"

SONG OF THE BRONZE STATUE

Book Thirteen

'Open wide the door of heaven!
On a black clould I ride in splendour,
Bidding the whirlwind drive before me,
Causing the rainstorm to lay the dust.'
—*Ta Ssu Ming*, 'The Great Master of Fate'
From the *Chiu Ko*, the 'Nine Songs' by Ch'u Yuan,
2nd century **BC**

'Before me floats an image, man or shade,
Shade more than man, more image than shade;
For Hades' bobbin bound in mummy-cloth
May unwind the winding path;
A mouth that has no moisture and no breath
Breathless mouths may summon;
I hail the superhuman;
I call it death-in-life and life-in-death.'
—William Butler Yeats, from *Byzantium*, AD 1930

PROLOGUE   Forgotten Words

WINTER 2215

Where can I find a man who has forgotten words?
He is the one I would like to talk to.
—Chuang Tzu, 6th century BC (*Writings*, xxvi, II)

FORGOTTEN WORDS

Ebert stood on the lip of the crater, looking across the ruined city towards the distant sun. It was early morning and a rime of frost covered the iron-red rocks, making them glisten. Below him, in the deep shadows, he could discern the twisted shape of the struts that had once curved half a *li* into the air, supporting the dome of the greatest of Mars' nineteen cities.

He crouched, placing a gloved hand on a nearby rock, conscious of the sound of his own breathing inside the helmet. Behind him, five paces back, the woman and the boy waited silently.

It was here that the dream had ended, gone in a single night, burned up in a violent conflagration that had taken the lives of more than twenty million people. Dust they were. Dead, like the planet that had never been their home, only a prison, a resting place between two darknesses.

He shivered, understanding. The chain had been broken here, the links scattered. That was the message the great Kan Jiang had offered in his poems. Mars was not the future, Mars was a dead end, a cosmic cul-de-sac. If they tried for a million years Man would never make a home of this place. No, they had to go back, back to earth – to Chung Kuo. Only then could they move on. Only then might there be a future.

And the Osu? Did *they* have a future?

He turned, looking back. The woman was watching him, her face behind the thick glass of the helmet like carved ebony. Beside her, resting in the crook of her arm, the boy looked into the distance, dreaming as usual, his eyes far off.

Ebert smiled. It was a year ago that he had first met her, in one of the northern settlements.

In his desire to become a sage he had renounced the flesh, holding that darker part of himself in abeyance, yet, when she had come to him that night, his body had remembered. She had been with him ever since.

It was as Tuan Ti Fo had said – desire took many forms, and sometimes renunciation itself could be a kind of desire. Best then to be at peace with oneself; to have and not to want.

He stood, putting out a hand to her.

"Come."

Then, turning back towards the setting sun, he began to make his way down into the darkness.

He woke in darkness, the nightmare still close – so close it seemed he might reach out and touch it.

Yes, he could sense it, there behind the night's dark skin, the pulse of it still warm, still real. For a moment longer it was there, and then he felt it slip from him, leaving him gasping on the cold, bare floor of the tent, emptied by the vision.

The woman lay beside him, sleeping, her breathing soft, almost inaudible. From outside, the muffled sound of the air-vent's hiss was like the noise the wind makes in the southern deserts during the season of storms. Here, at the bottom of the crater, one of the old air-generators was still partly operational, spewing pure oxygen from a single vent.

He went out, sealing the tent-flap after him. It was an hour until dawn and the darkness was intense. From where he stood the sky was a ragged circle framed by the black of the crater walls, seven stars, shaped like a scythe, blazing in the centre.

He climbed, following the path through the twisted ruins from memory. On the lip he paused, turning to look back across the crater's mouth. The blackness beneath him was perfect. To the east, on the horizon, was the tiny blue-white circle of Chung Kuo.

He shivered, remembering the nightmare. He had had it before, many times, but this time it had seemed real.

He looked down at his right hand, flexing the fingers in the glove, surprised to find it whole. Two of them – his father's men – had held him while another splayed his fingers on the slab. He had struggled, but it was no use. There'd been a flash of silver, then he felt the thick-edged blade slice through the sinewy joint of the knuckle – his nerves singing pain, his hot bloody pumping into the air. He had heard his own high-pitched scream and scuttled like a ghost from out of his flesh. There – usually – it ended – there, thankfully, he had always woke, but this time it went on. He felt his spirit turn, away from the tormented shrieks, following a servant who, bloody bowl in hand, made his way through flickering corridors of stone towards a brightly-lit chamber.

There, at the operating bench, stood his father, cold-mouthed, dead these eight years, his work apron tied neatly about his massive chest. His dead eyes watched as the servant brought the bowl. He took it, spilling its bloodied contents on to the scrubbed white surface.

The old man's mouth had opened like a cave, words tumbling forth like windblown autumn leaves, dust-brown and crumbling.

"The design was wrong. I must begin again. I must make my son anew."

There had been laughter, a cold, ironic laughter. He had turned to see his mother looking on, her ice-blue eyes dismissive.

"Zombies," she said, reaching past her dead husband to lift the severed finger from the bowl. "That's all you've ever made. Dead flesh. It's all dead flesh."

She let the finger fall, a chilling indifference in her face, then turned and left the room.

No warmth in her, he thought. *The woman had no warmth...*

Setting the bowl aside, his father had taken the finger, stretching and moulding it until the figure of a man lay on the bench before him.

Hans had stepped forward, looking down into the unformed face, willing it not to happen, but the dream was ineluctable. Slowly the features formed, like mountain ranges rising from the primal earth, until the mirror image of his face stared back at him... and sneered.

He jerked his head back, gasping.

"Efulefu..."

He swallowed back his fear, then answered the voice that had come up from the darkness.

"What is it, Hama?"

Her figure threaded its way up through the shadows just below. "Are you all right, husband? I thought I heard you groan."

"It is nothing, Hama, only tiredness."

She came to him, reaching out to take his hands. "The boy is sleeping still."

"Good," He smiled, enjoying the sight of her face in the star light, the dream defeated by the reality of her. "I was thinking, Hama. We must call a gathering."

"A gathering? Of the *ndichie?*"

He shook his head. "No, Hama. Of everyone. Of Elders, Tribes and settlers."

He gazed past her at the distant earth, noting how small, how fragile it seemed in all that emptiness. "It is time we decided what to do. Time we chose a path for all to follow."

The Machine blinked, then looked again. One moment there had been nothing, and the next...

"Tuan Ti Fo? Do you see what I see?

The air before the Machine shimmered and took form. Tuan Ti Fo sat cross-legged before the open console, bowing his grey-haired head in greeting. *"What is it that you see?"*

"I see..." The Machine strained, staring into the intense darkness, using all its powers to try to penetrate that single spot where it was blind. "I see... nothing."

Tuan Ti Fo chuckled softly. "You see *nothing?* Then, surely, there *is* nothing?"

"No. Something landed on the surface of the planet north of Kang Kua. I can sense it. It *is* there. Its very *absence* reveals it. And yet it conceals itself."

The old man tugged at his beard thoughtfully. "And your camera probes?"

"Cannot penetrate it. It's as if there is a shell surrounding it. A shell of..." It hesitated, a hesitation that in a man might seem normal, yet in the great Machine revealed the existence of billions of rapid calculations. "Something unknown," it concluded, a strange hesitancy in its normally toneless voice.

Tuan Ti Fo stared at the console a moment, then nodded. His mood was suddenly more sober. "I see."

The Machine fell silent. It was thinking. For more than five million years Mankind had striven upward out of the primal dark towards the light, and from that quest had come itself, the ultimate flowering of mind: one single, all-encompassing intelligence.

Intelligent, yet incomplete. Within its mind it pictured the great swirl of things known and unknown, like a vast *t'ai chi* of light and dark, perfectly balanced. Within that half which was light was a tiny circle of blackness – a pin-point of occlusion, which it knew to be Tuan Ti Fo. And now, within the darkness of those things unknown lay a single point of light.

"If it's a craft," Tuan Ti Fo said, "then it must have come from somewhere."

"But there's no trace," the machine began, then checked itself, realising that, like the absence that revealed something, there was a line of occlusion through its memory; an area of tampering – a no-trace that paradoxically revealed the passage of the craft.

"It came from the System's edge. From the tenth planet."

Yet even as it spoke, it questioned that.

"Something alien?" Tuan Ti Fo asked.

It considered the notion, surprised that for once it was dealing in uncertainties. "No..."

"But you have a hunch?"

"A calculated guess."

"Then you had best send someone."

"Send someone?"

Tuan Ti Fo laughed, then stood, brushing down his silks. "Why, to look, of course." He turned, his figure shimmering, slowly vanishing into the air, his words echoing after he had gone. "Send the boy, He'll see. Whatever it is."

"Nza?"

The voice came from the air. At its sound the boy turned sharply, his body crouched defensively, then he saw the tiny, glittering probe hovering like a silver insect in the air above his head.

"What is it?" he asked, keeping the fear from his voice.

"Where is Ebert?"

The ten-year-old turned, pointing back into the shadows. The probe moved past him, drifting into the darkness – a moment later it returned.

"Come," it said, hovering just above his head, no bigger than his fist, its surface smooth and rounded like a tiny shaven skull.

Nza shivered and then obeyed.

The Machine watched the boy approach the nullity; saw him put out his hand, then withdraw it sharply, as if he had been stung.

"Can you *feel* anything?" it asked, the sensation of curiosity almost overwhelming.

The boy nodded, then put out his hand, tracing what seemed like a smooth, curving slope in the air. But still it could see nothing, sense nothing.

It watched the boy move slowly round, testing the air with his hands, defining more accurately the area of nothingness the Machine's probes had sensed.

Nza turned, his eyes wide.

"What is it?" he asked. "Did you see anything?"

Nza shook his head. "Efulefu... Get Efulefu."

It was light when Ebert got there. He crouched some fifty *ch'i* from the unseen presence, perfectly at rest, watching the shadows shorten as the sun climbed the sky. The wind blew fitfully, and when it did he noted the patterns the sand had made around the nullity.

After two hours he stood and motioned to the boy. Nza went to him and stood there, looking up at him as he mouthed something through the glass of his helmet. It was cold, bitterly cold, and already two of the Machine's six probes had ceased functioning. But Ebert seemed unaware of it.

The cold. It would kill them all one day. Machine and men alike.

Nza stared a moment longer, then nodded and, with that curious loping run of his, scuttled across to the nearest of the probes.

"What is it?" the machine asked, but the boy simply shook his head and pointed to his mouth. It watched, reading the boy's lips.

There's something there. He sense it. He thinks it watches us and listens. And something else.

It waited as the boy ordered his thoughts, realising what Ebert had told him.

He says... when he closes his eyes... he sees a face. An old, familiar face.

It knew, even before the boy's mouth stretched twice to form the word. So he was back. DeVore was back on Mars.

DeVore stood at the view window, looking out across the wind-blown surface towards the crouching figure, then turned to the monitor again. Ebert's face filled the screen, his eyes behind the helmet's glass a deep reposeful blue.

So you survived, old friend. And now you consort with those ugly sons of the night. Swell, stranger things have been known.

He laughed softly, then clicked his fingers, summoning one of his guards.

"Find out how it's going. We've been here too long as it is. I want us gone by nightfall."

The soldier bowed low and backed away. DeVore turned back to the screen, pushing out his chin reflexively. Hans Ebert had been but a child when he's first met him. A spoiled and wilful child. But now, looking at him, *studying* him, he saw how much he had changed. It was there in his eyes, ibn the perfect stillness of the man.

Impressive, he thought, But also dangerous. Hans Ebert was no friend of his – he understood that now. At any other time he'd stop to kill this exiled prince, but right now it was more important to get back to Chung Kuo as quickly – *and as discreetly* – as possible.

He cursed silently, angry that they had had to set down and determined that, once repairs were effected, he'd kill that bastard Hooper himself. As an example to the others.

He crossed the room and tapped into the craft's log. Things were getting slack. Already they had lost two days. As it was, even a week's delay wouldn't affect their cargo, but any longer...

He cleared the screen. That would be one advantage of getting back to Chung Kuo. For too long now he'd had to rely on the services of second-raters. Once back, he could dispense with them and buy some better men.

DeVore smiled. He would enjoy that day. It would be a day of rewards. A day when all of these second-rate fellows would find themselves grinning.

Grinning bone-white before the wind.

There was a sound in the doorway. He turned, noting the guard there.

"Well?"

"Nine hours, Master Hooper says."

"Good." He waved the man away, then went to the window again. Ebert had not moved. He seemed rooted there, part of the dust of Mars.

"I shall come back for you, Hans Ebert," he said quietly. "Once other wars are fought and won. And then..." he laughed, then turned away, imagining the sight.

And then I'll see you dance on the gibbet like the commonest low-life there ever was.

Late in the day he felt it go. There was a change in the air, a lessening of the pressure, and then... nothing.

"It's gone," Ebert said, getting up, his limbs stiff from inactivity and cold.

"I know," Tuan Ti Fo said, appearing beside him. "I felt its passage in the air."

"Where has it gone?"

"Inwards. Back to Chung Kuo."

Ebert nodded. "We must call a gathering. Tonight."

"It is done."

Ebert smiled. "And my intentions? You know those too?"

Tuan Ti Fo's laughter was light, infectious.

"You mistake me, Tsou Tsai Hei. The woman, Hama, spoke to me."

He stared at the old sage, surprised. "You speak with her?"

"Sometimes."

"Is there anything you do not know, Master Tuan?"

Tuan's eyes, normally so calm, so clear, for once looked away, troubled.

"Many things. But only one that bothers me. I do not know what that man wants."

"DeVore, you mean?"'

Tuan Ti Fo nodded. "This world – this *reality* – is like a game to him. He plays his stone, and then awaits an answer. Why, the King of hell is but an apprentice beside him. He has made malice into an art. Some days I think the man is old. Older than the frame of flesh he wears."

"Older than you, Master Tuan?"

Tuan laughed. "Don't mock my grey beard, Worthless One. Time will find you too."

"Of course. But tell me, Master Tuan. What do you mean?"

"Only this. That I think the true nature of the man has been masked from us. DeVore... what is he? Is he a mortal man? An orphan, raised to high office in the T'ang's Security forces? Or was that too merely a guise? A mask of flesh put on to fool mere human eyes? Copies... Think of it, Hans. Why does the man love copies so? He duplicates himself and sends his copies out to do his bidding. Now, is that self-love or some far deeper game?"

Hans considered a moment, then shrugged. "Why did the Machine not destroy his craft while it was here?"

"Destroy it? How? How can one destroy what is not there?"

He laughed. "*Something* was there. I sensed it. With my eyes closed I could *see* it."

"Maybe. But what I said still goes. It was not there. It was... *folded* in somehow: a negative twist of nothingness. The Machine has a theory about it. It thinks the craft exists within a probability space quite near to our own, the atoms of which have been... *vibrated*, like a plucked string."

"There but not there."

"Like your dream."

Hans stared at the old man, startled. "I told Hama nothing of the dream."

"I was there but not there."

"And you?" Ebert asked, passing his hand slowly through the old man's chest as his silk-cloaked figure shimmered into nothingness again. "Are you here, or are *you* folded in?"

They gathered at the long day's end, as the last light of the sun bled from the horizon and the red became black. Hans Ebert, once heir to the great GenSyn Corporation of Chung Kuo, traitor to his T'ang and patricide, known also as Efulefu, "the Worthless One", and Tsou Tsai Hei, "the Walker in the Darkness", climbed up on to the table rock and turned to face the thousands who had come.

He looked about him, noting who was there. Just below him were the *ndichie*, the elders of the Osu, their white curls hidden within the tall domes of their helmets. Beyond them, standing in loose family groups, were members of all the northern tribes, sons and daughters of Mother Sky. To his right, forming a tight knot beside the escarpment, were two or three hundred of the new settlers. They looked on suspiciously, clearly ill at ease, disturbed to see so many of the tribes gathered there. Hans wondered what arguments Old Tuan had used to bring them out so late and so far from their settlement.

He raised a hand then spoke, his voice carrying from his lip mike to the helmets of everyone there.

"Brothers, sisters, friends and respected elders... thank you all for coming. You have been patient, very patient, with me. Twice Mars has circled the sun and still I brought no answer. But finally I see what must be done."

"Speak Efulefu," one of the *ndichie* called, speaking for them all. "Tell us what you see."

"I see a time when the supply ships no longer come. When Chung Kuo no longer looks to Mars with caring eyes."

"What of it?" someone called.

"We do not need their food, their medicines," another, deeper voice shouted from further back. "Let the ships stop. It makes no difference!"

"That's right!" another yelled. "We want nothing from them!"

"No?" Ebert shrugged. "When a father forgets his son... when he casts him off, is that nothing? When a mother casts her unwanted child into a stream, to sink or swim, is that nothing? When a great thread is cut, is *that* nothing?"

He moved forward until he stood on the very edge of the great rock, then leaned towards them. "The poet Kang Jiang was right. This planet isn't home, it's exile. There is no life for us here, only the certainty of eventual extinction. Not now, perhaps, not for a thousand years, but one day. One day no human eye will wake to see this world. One day only our dust will blow about the circle of this place."

"It is fate."

Ebert looked down at the elder who had spoken.

"Fate, Jaga?"

The old man lifted his hands in a gesture of emptiness. "What can we do, Efulefu? There is nowhere else for us. We were cast off two centuries ago. To be Osu... why, it is to live in exile!"

"Maybe that was so," Ebert answered, more gently than before. "But now that must end. We must build a ship."

"A ship!" The surprised words echoed back from all sides.

Ebert nodded. "That is so. Oh, not a huge thing. Nothing that is beyond our means."

There was a furious murmuring. Ebert waited, then raised his hand again. Slowly the noise subsided.

"We must go back... a few of us... and claim a place."

"They would kill us!" someone yelled.

"They will kill *you*," the elder, Jaga said, pointing a gloved hand at Ebert's chest.

"Maybe. Yet we must try. A ship. First off we need a ship. And then men. Eight volunteers. Eight men of honour... eight black-faced heroes to offer to Li Yuan."

He laughed, seeing it clearly now, recalling the day twelve years before when the two gifts of stones had been given to the young prince on his betrothal day.

"It has been foreseen. One has gone on before us. And we must follow. For if we fail, *all* fails."

He stepped back, hearing the great murmur of debate begin, his own part in it done.

Yes, and it was true what he had said: DeVore had gone on before them to place the first white stone upon the board. But he would follow hard upon his heels – he and his eight black stones.

The game... the game had begun again.

He looked down, flexing his ring finger within the glove, remembering the moment in the dream. It was time to be re-joined. Time to play his proper role in things. He knew it now. Knew it with a clarity that filled him. His exile was coming to an end. It was time to return. Time to emerge into the light again.

Song Of The Bronze Statue

SPRING 2216

'Gone that Emperor of Maolin,

Rider through the autumn wind,

Whose horse neighs at night

And has passed without trace by dawn.

The fragrance of autumn lingers still

On those cassia trees by painted galleries

But on every palace wall the green moss grows.

As Wei's envoy sets out to drive a thousand li

The keen wind at the East Gate stings the statue's eyes...

From the ruined palace he brings nothing forth

But the moon shaped disc of Han,

True to his lord, he sheds leaden tears,

And withered orchids by the Xianyang Road

See the traveller on his way.

Ah, if Heaven had a feeling heart, it too must grow old!

He bears the disc off alone

By the light of a desolate moon,

The town far behind him, muted its lapping waves.'

—Li He, '*Song Of The Bronze Statue*', 9th century AD

CHAPTER 121

IN HEAVEN'S SIGHT

Colonel Karr crouched in the tunnel behind his lieutenant, the light from the flatscreen on the man's back casting a pale glow over his face and chest. His helmet hung loosely about his neck, his gun – a heavy automatic with twin clips – rested against the wall. Beyond him, squatting to either side of the unlit tunnel, a thousand men waited.

It was the four hundred and nineteenth day of the siege, and still there was no sign that Tunis would fall. *Not this year*, Karr thought, amazed by its resilience, by the sheer stubbornness of its defenders.

The image on the screen was a familiar one. It showed Tunis from a distance, sat like a giant rock upon the plain, the sea beyond it; an imposing block of part-melted ice, its surface dark, like rough pitch. They had cleared the surrounding stacks long ago with ice-destroying chemicals, but the defenders had coated the rest with diamond-tough bonding; a bonding that seemed to resist all but their most destructive weapons. Close up it had a blistered, burned appearance, like the toughened hide of some deep-sea creature.

They had spent the best part of a year chipping away at it, to little real effect. And what inroads they made were generally short-lived. Nor had their blockade – the keystone of Rheinhardt's plan – had been totally effective. Ting Ju-chang, the local Warlord, had the backing of the Mountain Lords, and despite Karr's best efforts, their ships had managed many times to slip through and supply the City-fortress.

Even so, things had to be bad inside. The defending force was more than three million strong. Add to that a further fifty million – all of them crammed into a space designed for a tenth their number – and it took no genius to imagine the problems they faced. If rumours were true, they were eating one another in there.

The thought made Karr shudder; made him question once again the sense of Rheinhardt's strategy. There had been a good reason for hitting Tunis. For a long time Ting Ju-ch'ang as front man for the Mountain Lords – had used Tunis as a base from which to attack the southern coast of Li Yuan's City, and there was no question they needed to do something about it. That said, there had been no need to capture it. As Karr had argued several times in Rheinhardt's presence, they had merely to contain Ting's activities. To capture a well-defended City was – as he knew from experience – almost an impossibility, especially when, as here, he found himself in hostile territory, outnumbered, his supply lines stretched, and harried at his back all the time.

The truth was, Rheinhardt knew they couldn't win, yet he'd become obsessed with it. To withdraw would be, for him, a severe loss of face. After all, he had promised Li Yuan he would take it, and to go back on that promise was – for him – unthinkable.

And so here we are, Karr thought, *crouched in a tunnel beneath the City, waiting for the signal to attack. While back in City Europe a far greater threat to our security grows and grows, like a fat white grub, feeding upon its fellow grubs.*

Lehmann...

Yes. Lehmann was the problem, not Ting Ju-ch'ang.

Karr stretched his neck, then turned, smiling at the men closest to him reassuringly. He glanced down at the timer inset into his wrist, then raised his hand. It was almost time.

He heard the whisper go back into the darkness, then turned back, feeling the familiar tension in his guts. Up ahead his teams were in position. In less than a minute, as his cruisers mounted a diversionary missile attack on the western gate, they would begin.

He lifted his helmet and secured it, making sure the seal was airtight, the oxygen supply satisfactory, then reached for his gun. Behind him he could hear the scrape and click of hundreds of helmets being secured, the clatter as a gun fell then was retrieved.

Fourteen seconds...

He waited, counting in his head, seeing the first wave of cruisers flash across the screen, their missiles streaking towards the rock-like wall of the City-fortress. Even as they hit – even as he felt the judder from above, there was the *whummpf-whumpff* of mortars being fired further down the tunnel, followed immediately by the piercing, banshee whit of the shells as they spiralled towards their targets.

He turned, looking down the line, noting face after familiar face, under-lit by their helmet lights. These were good men. His best. They'd been with him a long time now and knew exactly what to do.

Who this time? He wondered, seeing how each one met his eyes and smiled. *Whose widow will I be speaking to tonight? Whose grieving mother?*

But there was no more time for that. Scrambling up, Karr began to run, half-crouched, following his lieutenant towards the gap, his men close behind.

In his head he had been counting. Now, at fifteen, he stopped and crouched again, as the blast came back down the tunnel at them. Behind him, he knew, his men would have done the same.

Instinct. It was all instinct now. They'd been fighting this war so long that there was nothing he could tell them that they didn't already know.

He stood, then ran on, making for the breach his suns had made in the City's underbelly.

Up ahead, pre-programmed remotes were picking off most of the defending mechanicals, their lasers raking the sides of the great shaft they were about to infiltrate, exploding any mines. They would clear a path. But it would take men – with their heightened instincts – to get any further.

Karr passed the mortar positions. Some ten *ch'i* further on, just above them and to the right, was the breach. He went through the jagged opening and stepped out into the base of a huge service shaft, looking up into a haze of mist and lights. The mortar shells had contained a mixture of strong hallucinogenics and tiny pellets which, when they exploded, burned with a searing, blinding light. Right now Ting's forces were in temporary disarray – the watch guard blind and half out of its collective skulls – but that advantage wouldn't last long. They had two minutes, maybe four at the outside, before fresh forces were drafted in. After that...

Karr stood beside the breach, waving his men through, urging them on, watching them fan out around the edge of the shaft and begin to climb, proud – with a father's pride – of their professionalism.

Wasted, he thought, angry suddenly that all of their talent, all of their hard-won knowledge should be squandered for so little reward,

We should be dealing with Lehmann. Clearing the levels of the scum who thrive under his patronage.

Yes. But as long as Rheinhardt had Li Yuan's backing there would be no change. Tunis... Tunis would be the rock upon which a million mothers' hearts would be broken.

He swallowed, then, knowing there was a job to be done, turned and, clipping his gun to his back, began to climb.

Pei K'ung, wife of Li Yuan and Empress of City Europe, snapped her fingers. At once the servant standing beside the great, studded doors hurried across, his head bowed. Two paces from her desk he stopped, falling to his knees.

"Mistress!"

"Tsung Ye," she said, not looking up from the document she was reading. "Tell Master Nan I'd like a word with him. Meanwhile, send in the maid. And have the doctor standing by. I want his full report on the new intake of girls."

Tsung Yet hesitated, in case there was anything else, then backed away, hurrying from the room.

Pei Kung looked up, bracing herself for the interview ahead. Her husband had seemed particularly happy this morning. She had heard him whistling below her window, and when she had gone out on the balcony to look, it was to find him walking among the flower beds, , sniffing the dew-heavy roses, more like a love-sick boy that a great T'ang. Of course, it was possible that the beauty of the morning had made him so, but she suspected it was more to do with the company in his bed last night.

She sighed. Last night they had argued, for the first time since they had wed, two and a half years ago. He had turned on her and shouted her down, his face burning with anger, then stormed from the room. And later, when she had gone to him, he had refused point blank to see her.

She had slept little, going over every last event in mind, trying to establish just what had sparked his anger, but she was still no wiser. He had simply snapped, as if something deep within him – something dark and hidden from her – had surfaced, like a carp going for a fly.

She shivered, then got up from her chair, making her way to the far side of the room. A massive silver mirror, its mahogany frame embellished with peacocks and dragons, stood there between two pillars.

She stood there a while, studying herself, knowing there was no way to change the image that the mirror returned to her. Plain she was, and old – eighteen years older than her husband Yuan. It was little wonder that he chose to spend his nights with serving maids. Besides, it had been a condition of their marriage – that there were to be no heirs to the union, no physical side to their relationship. At the time it had seemed a small priced to pay, but now...

There was a knock. Pei K'ung turned, setting her thoughts aside. Slowly, measuring her pace, she returned to her desk and sat. Then, after a calming breath, she turned to face the door.

"Enter!"

The maid came in slowly, her eyes averted, her chin tucked into her neck, her whole body hunched forward as she pigeon- stepped towards the huge desk. It was clear that she found the great study – and Pei K'ung at the centre of it – immensely daunting.

And so she should, thought Pei K'ung, for she had the power of life or death over the girl; a power her husband has granted her on the day of their wedding.

"Stand before me, girl. I want to see you clearly when you answer me."

"Mistress!"

The girl shuffled forward, out of the shadows that obscured the far side of the room and into the sunlight that spilled in from the open garden windows. A pattern of cranes and lilies, white, yellow and black, skirted the edge of the turquoise-blue carpet on which she stood.

Pei K'ung studied her, coldly, clinically almost, as a horse-trader might study a horse, searching it carefully for flaws. She was pretty, of course – they were all pretty – but it was something else that marked her out. Not her age, for they were all much of a muchness – fifteen, sixteen, never old – nor her figure, which was petite but well rounded, but something in the way she stood.

"My husband was he pleased with you last night?"

"I I think so, Mistress."

"You *think* so?"

"He..." She hesitated, a faint colour appearing at her neck. Pei K'ung noted it. A strong neck she had, and strong bones. Peasant bones. But pretty none the less. Very pretty indeed.

"Well, girl?"

The maid swallowed. One hand smoothed the pale lemon silk of her *chi pao*. "He seemed... agitated at first. Angry about something. I had to soothe him. I..."

Pei K'ung waited, sparing the girl nothing.

"I kissed him," she said finally.

Pei K'ung's eyes were like an eagle's, piercing the girl. "*Kissed* him? Where? On the mouth?"

The girl's head dipped an inch or two lower. "No, Mistress. Lower than that... You know."

She almost laughed. How in hell would *she* know? She had never even seen her husband naked, let alone...

"You kissed his penis, you mean?"

The girl nodded.

"And you liked that?"

"I... I didn't mind. If it gave him pleasure."

"And did it?"

The girl's discomfort was quite evident now. "He seemed..."

"Did he reach his climax that way?"

The girl looked up, her eyes wide open. "Mistress?"

"The moment of clouds and rain. Did it happen while he was still in your mouth?"

The girl looked down, the colour speaking to her cheeks. "Only the first time, Mistress."

"Ah... and the second?"

Her answer was almost a whisper. "That was much later."

"And between times. Did you sleep?"

She shook her head.

"Not at all?"

"He... would not let me, Mistress. He was..."

Pei K'ung stiffened slightly, waiting to see how the girl would finish the sentence. Insatiable? Like a tiger? Tireless?

The girl looked up again, a surprising tenderness in her eyes. "Very gentle."

Pei K'ung felt something strange happen deep within her. It was almost physical, yet she knew it wasn't. It was to do with those last two words, with how the girl had looked back at her when she had said them, her dark eyes sparkling with an inner light. *Gentle.* She had heard Yuan called many things, but never gentle. Not even with his son.

She forced herself to speak, to keep on asking questions.

"How do you mean, gentle?"

The girl's smile, like her words, made her feel something new – something she had never felt before. She did not recognise it at first, but them, with the suddenness of shock, she understood. Envy. For the first time since she's married him she felt envy.

The girl's eyes seemed to drift back to the night before; to widen with pleasure at the memory of it.

"I felt... well, I felt he only really got pleasure when he was giving pleasure to me. At first I was uncomfortable. I pleaded with him to relax and let me see to his needs, but he would not have it, Mistress. He..."

Again there was that flush at neck and cheek, that same, strange smile of inner satisfaction. "He said he wanted to make me happy. To make me cry out. To..."

She stopped, as if she sensed some change in the woman facing her. Her head went down once more, the chin tucked in tightly, the eyes averted.

"And *did* you cry out?"

The girl nodded.

"Ah..." Her mouth was dry, her heart beating strangely. Even so, she had to know. "What... what did he do?"

The maid glanced up, as if to gauge her Mistress's mood, then spoke again. "He kissed me, Mistress."

"*Kissed* you?"

Even as she said it, she heard the echo of her earlier words. How often had she sat here going through this obscene litany? Eight, nine hundred times? And never – *never* – until this moment, had it meant anything to her. She shivered, only half listening as the girl spelt out just how thoroughly Li Yuan had pleasured her. And as the words went on, she closed her eyes, imagining him doing that to her – for the first time allowing herself to surrender to the thought.

"Mistress?"

She opened her eyes. The girl was watching her, surprised, her mouth open like a fish.

"Forgive me," Pei K'ung said, angry with herself; conscious that she had let her guard slip. "I am tired. If you would go now."

"Mistress!"

The girl knelt, touching her head to the floor, then backed away.

Anger, she told herself. It was all connected to his anger. But how? And why had he not been cruel to the girl? Why had he not taken out his anger on *her*? Or was that the way of it? Was something always converted into its opposite? Was his strange tenderness a product of that anger?

She shuddered, then stood, going across to the window. He was out there, standing beside the carp pond, talking to two of his advisors. She could go to him right now if she wanted and ask him – ask him how it felt and why last night, of all nights, he had been different. Yet she knew it was impossible. As impossible to ask as to put herself there in his bed beside him.

Beneath him, she thought, and was surprised by the silent words.

Do I want him? Is that it?

For if it was she had best banish the thought, for it was – it truly was – impossible. Had she not, after all, put her name to the contract they had made? Even so, the suddenness, the strength of that newly-discovered need, surprised her.

She had thought herself safe: had thought that her plain-ness, her age, precluded her from such feelings. But drip by drip these interviews had worn her down, until two words and a tender smile had breached her.

There was a knock. A heavy, purposeful knock that she recognised as Nan Ho's. She turned, calling on him to enter.

"Mistress," he said, coming two paces into the room and bowing to her. Behind him his two assistants did the same, like living shadows of the man.

"Master Nan. I wanted your advice on something. If we could speak alone?"

"Of course," he said, dismissing his assistants with a gesture. "How are you this morning, Mistress?"

"I am..." She almost lied, almost gave in to politeness, yet caught herself in time. "I am disturbed, Master Nan," she said, moving across the floor until she stood beside him. "Li Yuan was in a foul mood last night. He raged at me for no reason. And yet this morning he is like a child."

Nan Ho looked down, then cleared his throat. "These are difficult times for him, Pei K'ung. Much is happening. Sometimes..."

She interrupted him. "Straight answers, Master Nan."

He looked up, meeting her eyes, respect and amusement in them. He was a good twenty five years older than her and a man; even so, they had established a relationship of equals right from the start.

"Straight answers?" he laughed softly. "All right. I'll tell you. We're planning a new campaign."

She frowned. "South America?"

He shook his head. "No, no... *Here*, in Europe. In the lowers. Your husband wants to take control again. He feels it's time. The African campaign has reached a stalemate and the feeling among the Three is that we should withdraw. The problem is what to do with our forces once we've withdrawn them. To have them sit idly at home is not an option any of us wants to consider. Things are bad enough without that."

She nodded, understanding. "And the meeting this morning?"

"Is to sound out all parties."

"I see. And if they're all in agreement?"

Nan Ho shrugged. "That is not my decision, Mistress."

She smiled. *No. Yet you will have the greatest influence over what he decides, neh?*

He bowed. "If that is all, Mistress..."

"Of course." Yet as he turned to leave, she called him back.

"Nan Ho?"

"Yes, Mistress?"

"My husband... when he..." She took a breath, steeling herself to ask. "When he lost his virginity – how was that done?"

Nan Ho smiled, the smile strangely, disconcertingly like that the girl had offered earlier. "He was but a boy and curious in the way boys are. He had begun... you know... night dreams. It worried him. So I sent one of the maids to his bed. Pearl Heart, if I remember correctly. She... *taught* him. She and her sister, Sweet Rose."

He nodded to himself, as if satisfied, then added. "It is the way. His father, Li Shai T'ung, always said that..."

"Thank you," she said, interrupting him. "I was interested, that's all."

"Of course." Nan Ho bowed again. "If that is all?"

She nodded, letting him go, then returned to the window, watching as her husband paced slowly in the sunlight by the pool.

"Pull back! Disengage and pull back!"

Karr's voice boomed momentarily in every helmet then cut out as the defenders jammed the channel, but it was enough.

"*Aiya…*" he whispered softly, watching from his place beneath the breach as his men withdrew, clambering down the pipes and service ladders overhead, then dropping the last few *ch'i* and scrambling for the gap.

The floor of the shaft was littered with bodies, friend and foe indistinguishable in death.

They knew, he thought, touching each of his men briefly on the arm as they moved past him into the safety of the tunnel. *The fuckers knew!*

There was no doubt about it. The counter-attack had been too quick, too well organised for it to have been a matter of chance. Someone had leaked their plan. Someone in the inner circle of command.

Karr grimaced, pained by what had happened. They'd be lucky if a quarter of their number got out. It had been a massacre. Then, seeing how one of his men had fallen on the far side of the shaft, he hurried across, helping the wounded man, half-carrying him back, oblivious to the laser fire from above.

As he handed the man through, a runner pushed into view.

"Sir!"

Karr glanced at him, annoyed to be bothered at such a crucial moment. "What is it, man?"

"New orders, sir. From the General himself. He says you are to withdraw."

"Withdraw?" Karr laughed bitterly and looked past the messenger at his men. Their eyes, like his, were dark with the knowledge of the betrayal. His voice, when he spoke, was heavy with irony. "Tell General Rheinhardt that his forces have anticipated his request."

The runner, noting Karr's mood and perhaps intimidated by the giant, took a step backward. "Further, he says you are to leave here at once and report to Tongjiang."

Karr turned, staring at the man, surprised. "Tongjiang? To the Palace, you mean?"

The man nodded. "The General says you are to go direct. The T'ang himself wishes to see you. He says it is a matter of the most extreme urgency."

Karr nodded. Then, recollecting himself, he waved the man away. "Tell the General I will come. Tell him... tell him I will come once my men are safely away from here."

"But sir..."

Karr turned back, glaring at the man. "Just tell him!"

Then, turning away, he went back inside, to try and salvage what he could.

The news from Tunis was good. The latest attack had been beaten off, the great T'ang's forces scattered. Fu Chiang, "the Priest", Big Boss of the Red Flower Triad of North Africa, folded the paper and smiled, then looked about him at the banquet chamber, his hazel eyes taking in the lavish silverware, the ornate red and gold decorations. Briefly he hesitated, as if about to criticise, then backed hurriedly from the room.

Good, he thought, satisfied that all was finally ready, then turned away, drawing his dark red silks tighter about him. As little as a week ago he would have considered such a meeting impossible, but curiosity was a powerful incentive – it had achieved what neither common sense nor coercion had previously managed.

His 'cousins' – "Mountain Lords", Triad Bosses like himself – were waiting in the next room. He had known them in bad times, in those years when Wang Hsien had ruled City Africa with an iron glove, but now they were Great Men – men whose power had grown enormously this past decade, insect-like, feeding upon War and Change. Between them they controlled almost two-thirds of City Africa's lowers.

He smiled, then went through.

They were standing before the dragon arch, the fight-pit beyond them, its galleries climbing up out of sight. In an hour those galleries would be packed with his men, their bodies tense, their eyes wide with blood lust. Right now, however, the pit was dark and empty like a hollowed skull, the galleries silent.

"Cousins," he said, greeting them. If one knew no better one might almost laugh at the sight of them. A giant and a dwarf, a fat man and a one-eyed hermaphrodite! But appearances were deceptive. Any one of them was as deadly as a hungry viper, while together...

"Are you sure he's coming?" the tiny, almost doll-like figure of Mo Nan-ling, "the Little Emperor" asked, his fingers toying with the thick gold chain about his neck.

Fu Chiang smiled benevolently. "He will be here any time, Cousin Mo. I have tracked his craft over the mountains. He comes alone."

"Into the tiger's mouth," the big man at Mo Nan-ling's side said, cracking his knuckles. "The man must be a fool."

Fu Chiang stared at the giant, his face pensive. "So it seems, Yang Chih-wen. And yet that cannot be. Our cousins in City Europe underestimated him, and where are they now? Dead, their kingdoms smashed, the sacred brotherhoods destroyed."

Yang Chih-wen shrugged. He was almost three *ch'i* in height and heavily muscled. "The bear" they called him and the likeness to that ancient, extinct animal was uncanny, from the long, thick nose to the dark hair that sprouted from every pore.

"They were weak and careless," he said gruffly, as if that were all there was to say, but Hsueh Chi, Boss of the southern *Hsien* and half-brother of the great Warlord, Hsueh Nan, stepped forward, scratching his ample stomach.

"Forgive me, but I knew Fat Wong, and he was neither weak nor careless. Caution was his by-word. And yet Li Min proved too cunning for him. He waited, building his strength, biding his time, then took Wong Yi-sun on when he least expected it – *against the odds* – and beat him. He and his fellow Bosses. So we might do well to listen to what our cousin Fu says. It seems to me that we must act together or not at all."

Yang Chih-wen laughed dismissively. "You talk as if he were a threat, Hsueh Chi, but what kind of danger does he really pose? Ambushing Fat Wong and his allies was one thing, but taking Africa..." He shook his gear, bear-like head. "Why, the full might of Li Yuan's armies cannot shake our grip. What then could this *pai nan jen* – this 'pale man' – do?"

There was an air of challenge, of ridicule, in these final words that was aimed directly at Hsueh Chi. Noting it, Fu Chiang hurriedly spoke up, trying to calm things down.

"Maybe my cousin Yang is right. Maybe there *is* no threat. But it would be foolish to repeat past mistakes, surely? Besides, we need decide nothing here today. We are here only to listen to the man, to find out what he has to say. And to judge for ourselves what kind of a man this 'White T'ang' really is."

While the talk had gone on, Sheng Min-chung had gone pout onto the balcony. For a while he had stood there, his hands on the rail, looking down into the dark, steep-sided pit. Now he came back into the room.

"We will do as Fu Chiang says."

Yang opened his mouth as if to debate the matter further, but at a glance from Sheng he closed it again and nodded. Though they were all 'equals' here, Sheng Min-chung was more equal than the rest.

The Big Boss of East Africa was a strange one. As a child he had been raised by an uncle – touched, some said – who had dressed him as a girl. The experience had hardened Sheng. Then, at thirteen, he had lost his right eye in a knife fight. Later, when he had become Red Pole of the Iron Fists, he had paid to have his remaining eye 'enhanced', leaving the other vacant. Ever since it was said that his single good eye saw far more clearly – and further – than the two eyes of a dozen other men.

One-Eye Sheng moved between them, his long silks swishing across the marble floor, then turned, facing them.

"And *ch'un tzu*... let us show our friend, Li Min the utmost courtesy. What a man was born, that he cannot help, but what he becomes, through his own efforts," his one eye glared at Yang Chih-wen, "*that*, I would say, demands our respect."

The bear-like Yang stared back at Sheng a moment, then nodded, and Fu Chiang, looking on, smiled broadly, moved by Sheng's words.

Respect. Yes, without respect a man was nothing. To gain and hold respect, that was worth more than gold. Whatever transpired today and in the days to come, much would depend on establishing a common trust – a solid bridge of mutual respect – between themselves and Li Min.

Fu Chiang smiled, pleased that he, of all of them, had been the one Li Min had chosen, for to him would be given the credit for this momentous event. He turned his head, looking about him, pride at his own achievements filling him. Ten years ago he had been nothing. *Nothing*. But now he was Head of the Red Flower, a Great Man with the power of life and death over others. Sheng Min-chung had spoken true. It was not what a man was born, it was what he became.

Fu Chiang, "the Priest", Big Boss of the red Flower Triad, puffed out his chest, then looked to his fellow Lords, gesturing for them to follow him through into the banquet hall.

"*Ch'un tzu…*"

Rocket-launchers swivelled automatically, tracking Lehmann's cruiser as it came in over the *mountains, while from the cockpit's speakers came a constant drone of Mandarin.*

"Impressive," Lehmann said tonelessly, looking past the pilot at Fu Chiang's fortress. Beyond its sturdy walls and watchtowers the Atlas Mountains stretched into the misted distance, while beneath it a sheer cliff dropped four thousand *ch'i* into a wooded valley.

Visak , in the co-pilot's seat, took a brief peek at his Master's face, then turned back, swallowing nervously.

"You know what to do?" Lehmann asked.

Visak nodded. He was to do nothing, not even if they threatened Lehmann. He wanted to question that – to say "Are you sure?" – but Lehmann had given his orders and they were not to be questioned or countermanded. Not for any reason.

The pilot leaned forward, flicked one of the switches on the panel in front of him, then nodded. "Hao Pa…" *Okay.* He looked up at Lehmann. "We've got clearance to land. You want to go in?"

Lehmann nodded, watching as the massive stone walls of the fortress passed beneath them.

He gets off on this! Visak thought, stealing another glance. *He actually likes risking his life!*

Slowly, very slowly, they moved out over the drop.

Visak took a long breath. *If they shoot us now we'll fall five li.* That was, if there was anything to fall.

The pad came into sight, further down the ragged crest of the peak. Five sleek, black cruisers sat there already, between the oval pad and the fortress a transparent lift-chute climbed the sheer rock face.

Impressive's an understatement, Visak thought, certain now that they'd made a mistake.

If he got out of this alive he would quit at the earliest opportunity. Get his face changed and leave Europe on the first flight out. Away, far away from this madman and his insane, life-endangering risks.

He flexed his hands, realising he had been clenching them, then looked up again. Lehmann was watching him.

"You okay?"

He nodded. Through the screen of the cockpit the rock face came closer and yet closer. For a moment the whine of the engine rose, drowning the chatter of the speakers, and then, with the faintest shudder, the craft set down.

The engines whined down through several octaves then fell silent. A moment later there was a sharp click and the doors hissed open.

"Okay," Lehmann said, patting his shoulder, "Let's do business."

It was a small courtyard, no more than five *ch'i* to a side, set off from the rest of the palace and reached through a moon door set into a plane white wall. Shadow halved the sunlit space, its edge serrated, following the form of the ancient, steep-tiled roof. In one corner, in a simple rounded pot with lion's feet, was a tiny tree, its branches twisted like limbs in agony, its tight leaf-clusters separate, distinct from one another so that each narrow, worm-like branch stood out, stretched and melted, black like iron against the background whiteness. In the centre of the courtyard was a tiny fountain, a *shui shih*, its twin, lion-headed jets still – two tiny mouths of silence.

Gregor Karr stood there in full colonel's uniform, waiting for Li Yuan, conscious of the peacefulness, the harmony of this tiny place. A leaf floated in the dark water of the fountain's circular pool like a silver arrowhead. Karr looked at it and smiled, strangely pleased by its presence. Sunlight fell across his shoulders and warmed the right side of his face. It was an oddly pleasant sensation, and though he had often been outside the City, he had never felt so at ease with only the sky above him.

He was looking up, his eyes tracing the shape of a cloud, when Li Yuan stepped through the great circular space of the moon door and came into the courtyard. The T'ang smiled, seeing the direction of his colonel's gaze, then lifted his own face to the sky.

"It is a beautiful day, neh, Colonel Karr?" And Li Yuan laughed, his face momentarily open, unguarded; a side of him Karr had never seen. Then, more soberly. "However, we are not here to discuss the weather."

Karr waited, silent, not presuming upon that moment's openness, knowing his place. For a time Li Yuan did nothing, merely looked at him, as if weighing something in his mind. Then, abruptly, he put out his hand.

"Give me your badge."

Without hesitation, Karr unbuttoned his tunic and took the badge of office from where it rested against his left breast, handing it to his T'ang. Then he stood there, at attention, his head lowered respectfully, awaiting orders.

Li Yuan looked down at the badge in his hand. It was more than a symbol of rank, it was a means of identification, an instrument of legal power and a compact store-house of information, all in one. Without it, Karr lost all status as a soldier, all privilege. In taking it from him Li Yuan had done what even his general could not do, for it was like stripping such a man of his life. He looked back at Karr and smiled, satisfied. The man had not even paused to question – he had acted at once upon his Lord's command. That was good. That was what he wanted. He handed the badge back and watched as Karr buttoned up his tunic. Only then did he speak.

"Tomorrow I plan to appoint a new general. Tolonen would have had me have you, young as you are, inexperienced as you are. But that cannot be. However loyal, however right you might be for the task, I could not have you, for the post is as much a political appointment as a strategic one."

Karr kept his face expressionless and held his tongue, but between them, none the less, was the knowledge of Hans Ebert's betrayal years before – of the political appointment that had gone badly wrong. Even so, Karr understood what his T'ang was saying. His family was new to the Above and had no influence. And as general he would need much influence.

"I called you here today for two reasons. First to let you know that, were it possible, I would have had you as my general. And one day, perhaps, I shall. But for now there are other things I wish you to do for me."

Li Yuan paused. "I took your badge from you, Gregor. Did you think it some kind of test?"

Karr hesitated, then nodded. "Afterwards, *Chieh Hsia*. I..."

Li Yuan raised a hand. "No need to explain. I understand. But listen, it was more than a test. From this moment you are no longer commander of my Security forces in Africa."

This time Karr did frown. But still he held his tongue and, after a moment, bowed his head in a gesture of obedience.

Li Yuan smiled, pleased once more by Karr's reaction, then stepped closer, standing almost at the tall *Hung Mao*'s shoulder, looking up into Karr's face, his dark, olive eyes fierce, his mouth set.

"This is a new age, Gregor Karr. New things are happening – new circumstances which create new demands on a ruler. Even among those close to me there is, it seems, a new relationship."

The young T'ang smiled sourly and turned away. When he turned back his features were harder. He stood beside the miniature tree, the fingers of his left hand brushing the crown absently.

"You are to be given a new role. I need a new *Ssu-li Hsiao-wei*. Do you think you can do the job, Colonel Karr?"

"*Chieh Hsia!*" Karr laughed, astonished. After General, the post of *Ssu-li Hsiao wei* – Colonel of Internal security – was the most prestigious in the whole Security service. It meant he would be in charge of security at all the imperial palaces, in command of the elite palace guard and responsible for the personal safety of Li Yuan and all his family wherever they went. It was a massive responsibility – but also a huge honour.

He considered a moment, then bowed his head. Beside him, in the dark circle of the fountain, the leaf turned slowly, like a needle on a compass. Inside he felt excitement at the challenge: more excitement than he had felt for years. Looking across at Li Yuan he saw how carefully the T'ang watched him and realised, with a sudden, almost overwhelming sense of warmth, what trust his Lord was placing in his hands.

On impulse he knelt, offering his neck ritually to his Master.

"I would be honoured, *Chieh Hsia*."

Li Yuan stepped forward, then placed his botted foot gently but firmly on Karr's bared neck.

"Good. Then you will report to me tomorrow at twelve. We shall discuss your duties then."

"So tell us, Li Min. Just why *are* you here?"

Lehmann looked up, then pushed his plate aside, surprised by the suddenness of the query. For two hours they had played a cautious game with him, avoiding anything direct, but now, it seemed, one of them at least – "the Bear", Yang Chih-wen – had tired of such subtleties.

He glanced at Fu Chiang, then met Yang's eyes.

"The two Americas have fallen. Likewise Australasia. Asia – both west and east – is a snake-pit overseen by jackals. And Europe..." He picked a miniature fruit from the nearby bowl, chewed at it, then swallowed. "Europe is but a shadow of its former self. Which leaves Africa..." He smiled coldly. "I am told that Africa is the world's treasure chest."

"And is that why you are here? To plunder that treasury?"

Lehmann shifted his weight and turned so that he faced Yang Chih-wen full on. The man was big, it was true, but he had faced bigger men. Yes, and killed them too.

"Does that *disturb* you, Cousin Yang?"

Yang shrugged, as if unconcerned, but his eyes told a different story. "I'll lose no sleep over it."

"That's good. A man needs his sleep, neh? And what better tonic than to know that one's neighbour is also one's friend."

That brought a spate of glances – tiny, telling exchanges that confirmed what Lehmann had suspected. For all their swagger, these men were deeply insecure. The collapse of their City and the war that had followed had given them their opportunity, yet their rule was tenuous. They would only fight him if they must.

He lifted his hands. "Besides, when you talk of plunder you mistake me, cousins. I am not here to talk of plunder. I am here to talk of trade. Trade between equals."

"*Equals?*"

It was Mo Nan-ling, the Little Emperor, who spoke. He wiped at his mouth delicately, then leaned towards Lehmann, his fine gold necklace tinkling as he did. "You talk of trade, Li Min, but your words presuppose that there is something we should wish to trade with you."

Lehmann sat back a little, gesturing for him to expand on that.

"What I mean is this, *cousin*. Africa is indeed a treasure chest and we Mountain Lords have had rich pickings these past few years. Our coffers are full, our foot soldiers happy. What could we possibly need that you might offer?"

Lehmann nodded, as if acceding the point, then turned and signalled to Visak, who came across at once, placing a hardshell case in front of his Master.

"Has that...?" Mo Nan-ling began, but Fu Chiang raised hand and nodded. It *had* been scanned – four times in all – but still he had no clue as to what it held. He watched now, his curiosity naked in his eyes, as Lehmann flipped the latches then turned the case about, opening the lid.

There was a murmur of surprise.

"*Drugs?* You want to trade in *drugs?*" Yang Chih-wen's voice was incredulous. He pushed away from the table, his face scornful. "Are you *serious* Li Min?"

But Lehmann seemed not to hear the insult in the Bear's voice. He leaned forward and carefully picked the six tiny golden ingots from the depressions in the smooth black velvet, then looked across at Fu Chiang.

"Forgive me, Fu Chiang, but may I draw my knife?"

Fu Chiang hesitated, looking about him, then nodded.

"Thank you."

Lehmann tipped all the ingot-shaped capsules into Visak's open palm, then stood, reaching down with his left hand to unsheathe the pearl-handled knife from his boot.

Yang Chih-wen moved back a fraction, his hand resting on his own hidden blade.

"You talk of drugs, Cousin Yang," Lehmann said, facing him again, "yet the term covers many different things, neh? Some cure diseases. Some enhance performance, others intelligence. Some keep the penis stiff when stiffness is a virtue, others liberate the mind or entertain. These…" he smiled a death's-head smile then drew the razor-sharp blade across his right arm, just below the elbow.

A great gash opened up, blood pumping from a severed artery.

Lehmann threw the knife aside, then took one of the ingots from Visak's palm and squeezed its thick golden contents over the open wound. It hissed and steamed and then, astonishingly, began to move, as if a tiny golden creature burrowed in the gash.

"What in the gods' names…?"

But Fu Chiang's words were barely out when he fell silent, staring open-mouthed. Where the flesh had gaped, it was now drawn in, the wound raw and scabbed. Then, even as they watched, the scabbed flesh shimmered and – like a film run backwards – disappeared, leaving the skin smooth, unblemished.

The silence had the quality of shock. It was Sheng Min-chung who finally broke it.

"GenSyn," he said, authoritatively. "There were rumours of regenerative drugs."

Lehmann have a single nod.

"And this is what you're offering to trade?"

Lehmann shook his head, then took the five remaining ingots from Visak's open palm and began to hand them around.

"No. This I'm *giving* you. What I'll trade is information."

Waving the guards aside, Li Yuan pushed through the doors and went inside. A dozen men stood at the balcony's edge, watching what was happening below. They had been training and wore only breech-cloths or simple black one-pieces. The scent of sweat was strong.

Hearing the door close, two of them turned and, seeing their T'ang, bowed low and made to leave, but Li Yuan signalled them to stay and went across, joining them at the rail.

He looked down. Kuei Jen, his seven-year-old son, was standing in the middle of the floor, at the very centre of the fight circle. About him, facing him east, north, west and south, were four burly adolescents, Lo Wen, his shaven-headed, middle-aged instructor, stood to one side, his face inexpressive, his arms folded before his chest.

All five combatants were breathing heavily, Kuei Jen, at the centre of it all, turned slowly, eyeing his opponents warily, his body tensed and slightly crouched., his weight balanced delicately on the balls of his feet. The boy was naked to the waist and wore only the flimsiest of breech-cloths – more strong than cloth. His hair was slicked back, his body sheathed in sweat, but his eyes...

Li Yuan smiled. The boy had fighters' eyes, like his dead uncle, Li Han Ch'in. Eyes that watched, hawk-like, missing nothing.

Two of them moved at once – from east and west. As quick as a fox, Kuei Jen ducked and turned, swinging his right leg low, then twisted on his hips and straight-punched – right left, right left – in quick succession.

Two of the youths were down, groaning. Between them stood Kuei Jen as if nothing had happened, his breath hissing through his teeth. Looking on, Lo Wen exhibited not even the slightest flicker of interest.

Li Yuan felt the hairs on his neck rise. There had been a low murmur of satisfaction from the men surrounding him, nods of respect.

The third boy backed off a pace, then, with a blood-curdling yell, he threw himself at the young prince. As he did, the last of them took two quick, quiet steps forward.

He wanted to cry out – to *warn* his son – but knew it would be wrong.

Kuei Jen's first punch connected cleanly, his fist striking his opponent squarely in the breast bone, knocking him back. But even as he drew his arm back from the second, decisive blow, the other was on his back, pulling him down, a wire cord looped about Kuei Jen's throat.

Li Yuan cried out, unable to help himself. Yet even as his cry echoed in the hall, Kuei Jen flipped backward, the unexpected movement tearing the cord from his assailant's hands. There was a blur of movement and the youth was down, winded. Kuei Jen turned from him, took a single step, and punched, finishing the third of them.

He turned back, looking calmly at the wheezing youth, and, moving closer, put out his foot and delicately – using only his toes – toppled him onto his back.

There was a great roar from the balcony. A storm of applause. Li Yuan, amazed, joined in.

As it faded he called down to his son.

"Kuei Jen!"

The young prince span round and looked up, astonished to find his father there. He bowed low, a colour at his neck.

"Father..."

About him, the four youths scrambled to present themselves, tucking themselves into a kneeling position, two of them coughing, their shaven heads bowed towards their T'ang.

Lo Wen, like a statue until that moment, stepped between them and, bowing to the waist, addressed his Master.

"*Chieh Hsia*... I did not know..."

Li Yuan waved it aside. "What he did just then... you *taught* him that, Master Lo?"

"I did, *Chieh Hsia*."

"I am much pleased, Master Lo. A student is but as good as his teacher, neh?"

Lo Wen bowed, pleased by his Master's praise.

"And you, young men... you played your part well. You will have a bonus for this morning's work. A hundred *yuan* apiece!"

"*Chieh Hsia!*" they cried, almost as one, delight in their voices.

Li Yuan stood back slightly, gripping the rail tightly, his pride in his son immense. He was about to say something more – to praise the boy before them all, when the doors behind him opened.

"*Chieh Hsia...!*"

He turned. It was Hu Ch'ang, his Chancellor, Nan Ho's Principal Secretary.

"What is it, Secretary Hu?"

Hu came through and, kneeling before his T'ang, placed his forehead to the floor. Rising slightly, he answered LI Yuan.

"It is your cousin, Tsu Ma, *Chieh Hsia*. He is calling from his palace in Astrakhan. He says he needs to talk to you urgently."

"Then I shall come."

He turned back, looking to his son, who awaited his father pleasure, head bowed, perfectly still, and gave the boy a small bow of respect.

"You did well, Kuei Jen. Very well. Come to my study later. After lunch."

Then, turning away, he swept past the kneeling Hu Ch'ang, heading for his study.

She had just come from her bath and was sitting in the chair by the window, having her hair brushed by the maid, when Li Yuan rushed into the room, unannounced.

"Pei K'ung... you will never guess what!"

She stared at him, surprised by his animation, by the great beam of a smile he was wearing. Pulling her silk robe tighter about her, she stood, dismissing the maid.

"What is it, husband? Have our armies won some great victory in Africa?"

"Victory?" He laughed, then came across to her. "No, no... nothing like that. It is Tsu Ma. He has decided to marry!"

She stared at him, astonished.

"It is true," he went on, then laughed again. "It seems he has chosen the girl already. Her family has been approached and they are to be betrothed within the week."

"But the rituals..."

Li Yuan raised a hand. "They will be fully carried out. Ah, but it is an excellent idea, don't you think, Pei K'ung? An imperial wedding! Why it could come at no better time."

She saw that at once. Even so, for Tsu Ma to marry so late in life might cause almost as many problems as it solved.

"Was this a... *sudden* decision, husband?"

Li Yuan shrugged, becoming more serious. "It seems the matter has played upon his mind for some time. But what forced him to the issue, who knows?"

He went to the window and stared out across the garden as if looking for someone. "All I know is that the time must be ripe."

She went and stood by him, studying his face. "And is that how you chose me, Yuan? When the time was ripe?"

He turned his head and looked at her.

"Five wives I've had, Pei K'ung, and still I do not understand why *this* should be or *that*. To be married... for each man and every woman, it is a different thing, neh?"

She nodded, but still she held his eyes. "And for Tsu ma? Does he marry simply to beget sons?"

Li Yuan hesitated, then shrugged. "It would seem the obvious answer."

"Then why not before? Why wait until now?"

He looked away.

She watched him, feeling – and not knowing why – that something strange was happening inside of him. "Husband, tell me this. Why did he not marry before now?"

He looked back at her, his eyes stern suddenly. "A T'ang does not need to answer such a question."

She held her ground. "I did not ask Tsu Ma. Nor would I be so impertinent. I asked *you*, husband. If you have no idea, simply say so and I shall be quiet. But I am curious. Tsu Ma is a handsome man. A man much enamoured of women and – from what I've seen – a good uncle to his nephews. Children... I would have thought he'd have had many children by now."

Li Yuan huffed out a breath, clearly troubled by the direction of this conversation. He considered things a moment, then waved a hand vaguely in the direction of the east – as if toward Tsu Ma himself.

"Something happened. Long ago. He... he was betrothed once. In his teens. And the girl..."

"The girl died."

Li Yuan looked at her and nodded. But it still seemed he had not given up all he knew.

"Was there... something else?"

His answer was immediate, almost brutal. "No. Nothing else."

She shivered inwardly, surprised – no, *shocked* – by the anger he was containing. Anger? Anger at Tsu Ma? For what? Or had she read things wrongly? Was there still something she didn't understand?

"Did he love the girl?"

"I... I am not sure. I guess he must have."

"And his father... did his father not insist that he be betrothed to another? If he was the eldest son..."

Li Yuan turned on her, his anger open now. "You do not understand, Pei K'ung. Tsu Ma was like me in that. He had an elder brother. His nephews... they are his elder brother's sons. Tsu ma was not born to rule. And as to how he has chosen to live his life... well, enough talk of it, Pei K'ung. You understand?"

She bowed her head obediently. "I understand." But deep down inside her curiosity was burning like a coal. Something *had* happened. Something between Tsu Ma and her husband. What it was she couldn't guess, but she would find it out. Yes, she would seek it out and know it, were it the last thing she did.

Tsu Ma stood on the balcony of his summer palace in Astrakhan, looking out across the moonlit Caspian. It was a clear night and at this hour – just after two – it seemed like the whole world was sleeping. He alone could not sleep; he alone was plagued by the demons of restlessness.

His foot was sore tonight and troubling him. Tiredness had made his limp more exaggerated. He reached down and scratched at the joint, getting some relief.

No good, he thought, *it'll only make it worse.* But he couldn't help himself. He had always been the same. Impulsive. Give him an itch and he would scratch it. He laughed humourlessly.

Yes, and maybe that's the root of it.

Far out – two, maybe three li out from the shore – the lights of an imperial cruiser skimmed the water as it made its regular patrol.

Protecting me, he thought. Yes, but who would protect him from himself? Maybe that was why he was getting married, finally, in the hope that he would change.

A young wife. Children. If anything could change a man, then surely these could do it. Why, he had seen how Li Yuan was with his son…

Yes, but he was not Li Yuan.

So why was he doing it? Why now, when he was so settled in his ways? Or was that it at all? Was it not, perhaps, some kind of punishment?

He turned from the rail, angry with himself, looking back into the darkness of the room where, on a bed of silk, lay one of his maids.

To change himself. It was a forlorn hope. Yet try it he must, or die an old goat, his grave untended.

There had always been time. Always a tomorrow. An infinity of tomorrows. But slowly he had used them up. Days had passed like dying cells and he was slowly growing older.

Yes, there had always been time.

He sighed. Wasn't it strange how young men thought they were like the sea, ageless and eternal. So he had been. Tsu Ma. The Horse. He had out-run, out-drunk, and out-fucked every last one of them. But now…

Now time weighed heavily on him and the seas in his veins ran slow and sluggish.

Time was he had been a child, carefree, a full *ch'i* smaller than his eldest brother. That same beloved brother whom he had seen fall from his horse like a mannequin and who had bled to death in his arms, the assassin's crossbow bolt in his neck, the black iron shaft of it poking obscenely from the bloodied flesh. He had promised himself he would never love anyone that much again and had fled into debauchery as if that might stop the hurt or end the dreams that came to him, night after night. But never is a long time, and then Fei Yen had come. Fei Yen, his cousin Li Yuan's wife.

He shivered, then held on to the door, a sudden weakness taking him. For a moment he clung on, as the blackness swept over him, then he let out a breath. He was okay. It was nothing. He had had several of these spells of late and he put them down to over-exertion. It was simply his body telling him to ease off. There was no point mentioning them to his surgeon.

I should eat something, he thought, taking a long, calming breath. Or maybe sleep. After all, he was no longer as robust as he had once been.

He stepped inside, closing his eyes briefly to catch the young girl's scent. He moaned softly, his senses intoxicated by the sweet perfume of her, then, opening his eyes again, put his hand out, feeling for the edge of the bed. He could hear her now. From the soft regularity of her breathing he could tell she was sleeping.

His hand searched among the silken covers until it felt something warm and smooth – her leg.

He sat, kicking off his slippers, his hand caressing the young girl's thigh, tracing the smooth contours of her body.

As he did she woke.

"*Chieh Hsia?*"

"Quiet, girl," he said, his hand finding her face in the dark. She nuzzled it, kissing it softly, wetly, making his sex stir.

Tomorrow, he thought, pushing her down then untying the sash of his sleeping robe. *I shall reform myself tomorrow.*

CHAPTER 122

BREATHLESS MOUTHS

Kim stirred, then turned abruptly on the bed, like a fish on a hook, mouth gasping, left hand reaching for the ceiling.

"A-dhywas-lur! A-dhywas-lur!"

He woke, his dark eyes blinking, staring up into the camera lens, the narrow band about his neck pulsing brightly in the darkened room. Silence, then: "What is she doing?"

It was the first question he asked, today and every day.

"She's awake," the Machine answered, the soft Han lilt of its voice filling the tiny room. "Right now she's eating breakfast. Would you like to see her?"

Each day the same struggle within him; each day the same answer.

"No."

Its circuits made a shrugging motion, unseen, unheard.

Ward sat up, then twisted about, planting his feet firmly on the uncarpeted floor. One would have thought that today of all days something else would have been on his waking mind, but no, the young man was Machine-like in his obsession. Not an hour went by without some reference to her.

Kim turned, looking up at the lens. "And her father? The Marshal? Will he be accompanying Li Yuan?"

"He is part of the T'ang's official party, so I assume..."

Kim's raised arm silenced it. It watched him cross the bare cell-like room and enter the bathroom, a second lens above the shower watching him step up into the unit.

"Hot or cold?"

"Cold."

At once the water fell, bracingly cold, a touch of northern ice in its needle-sharp flow. It watched the young man grimace and then shudder in a kind of pained ecstasy.

Why did he continually punish himself? What inner need drove him to such extreme? Or was the young woman, Jelka, the answer to that also?

"Enough!"

It cut the flow. At once warm air-currents filled the cubicle, drying the young man's body. Again there was that movement in his face; again that faint, almost indiscernible shudder.

Kim stepped from the shower and went over to the sink, popping a calcium pill to clean his mouth and teeth. As it dissolved he hummed a tune to himself – an air from the time before the City; a song of love and loss and constancy.

"Any messages?"

It would have been easier to have tapped them direct into the wire inside his head, but Kim had forbidden it. For some archaic reason he preferred this quasi-human form – this question and answer in the air.

"Only two. Reiss and Curval."

Kim slid the cupboard door open and took a pale red lone-piece from inside. It was all he ever wore these days – a succession of crisp new lab-suits, each one burned at the end of the day, as if in some constant ritual of self-purification.

"When does Reiss want to meet?"

Not "What does Reiss want?" – he knew what Reiss wanted: to settle the terms for the renewal of his contact – but "When?" As ever, Kim wasted no time with what was already known.

"Lunch, if possible. This evening if not. He seemed quite concerned."

As he ought. Kin four weeks he could be losing the services of the greatest scientist in Chung Kuo. That was, unless he could come up with a deal enticing enough to make Kim Ward stay with SimFic.

Unconscious of the gesture, Kim touched the glowing band about his neck. "It'll have to be this evening. Book dinner at eight. At the Hive. But Reiss only. None of the other monkeys!"

"He thought you'd say that, but he wants to bring someone along with him – a young executive named Jack Neville. Says you'd understand."

Kim stepped into the one-piece, zipped it up, then turned, looking up at the camera.

"Okay. And Curval?"

"He called half an hour back. Wanted to know if you'll need him for the trial run. To be frank, I think he just wants to be there."

"Then tell him I'll expect him, ten o' clock in the main lab."

He sat on the edge of the bed, reached underneath, then pulled on a pair of worn slip-ons. "And our game?"

In answer it placed a hologram in the air beside him – a life-size image of a wei chi board, the black and white stones of a half-completed game covering two-thirds of the nineteen by nineteen grid. As Kim looked a new black stone appeared two down, six in from the top, right hand edge. It glowed for the briefest moment then grew dull.

Kim smiled. "Interesting."

It said nothing, merely watched, knowing that for that single moment they were alike, he and it – simple mechanisms that thought and calculated. Then Kim looked up, the faintest glimmer in his eye, and it knew the moment had passed.

"What is she doing now? Is she walking in the garden?"

Jelka stopped on the tiny bridge at the centre of the Ebert Mansion gardens, looking toward where her father crouched, playing with the boy. Laughter filled the morning air, the boy's high-pitched shrieks threading the old man's deep laughter, like a young bird fluttering in the branches of an ancient oak.

She smiled. Who would have imagined, three years back, when he'd first taken on the role of protector to the boy, that it would have come to this. Back then he had positively loathed the child; had raged, calling him "that half-caste little bastard," but now...

She watched him scoop the boy up and hold him high, his craggy face filled with an unusual lightness, his eyes drinking in the young lad's laughter. So he'd been with her; father and mother to her, for more than twenty years. She shivered, then went across to join them.

"Father?"

Tolonen set the boy down and turned, smiling, one arm out to her in welcome. Beside him, the boy waited, his arms at his sides, his head bowed politely, as he'd been taught; every bit the little soldier.

"How are you, Pauli?"

He looked up at her shyly through his dark fall of hair and nodded. It was the most she ever got from him. Whether she frightened him or whether, as her father said, he was half in love with her, she didn't know, but when she was there he clammed up totally.

She smiled inwardly, but outwardly she kept her face stern and serious, walking slowly around him as if inspecting a young officer. Satisfied, she nodded.

"You've done all your schoolwork?"

He nodded, his eyes careful not to meet hers.

"Good." She permitted herself a smile, then reached out and ruffled his hair. Han... there was no doubt that the boy was Han, yet something of his father's blood – of Hans Ebert's Saxon stock – had shaped that young face, giving it a curious strength. With or without the great trading empire he would one day inherit, Pauli Ebert would be a force to reckon with when he was older.

She turned, looking to her father. "Oughtn't you to be getting ready?"

He glanced at the timer set into his wrist, then made a face of surprise. "Gods, is that the time?"

She nodded, amused by his pretence. These days he would even keep Li Yuan waiting if it meant an extra ten minutes play with his ward.

"Still, there's not much to do," he said, making no move to leave, his eyes resting fondly on the boy. "Steward Lo has already laid out my uniform. I only need to shower, and that won't take a minute."

"Even so..."

She paused as Steward Lo himself appeared in the doorway leading to the West Wing. Her father, noting her attention, turned.

"What is it, Lo?" he asked, suddenly more formal.

Lo bowed. "You have visitors, Master."

"At this hour?" A flash of irritation crossed his face, then he nodded. "All right. Show them into the main Reception Hall. I'll see them there. Oh, and tell them that have fifteen minutes of my time, no more. The T'ang himself is expecting me."

When Stewart Lo had gone, Jelka stepped closer. "Who is it?" she asked quietly.

His face was hard, his eyes troubled. "Oh, it's no one..."

She laid her hand on his arm – his flesh and blood human arm. "Father?"

He laughed gruffly at her admonishment, but still his eyes were troubled. "It's them again. Wanting, always wanting."

"Ah..." She understood at once. By 'them' he meant the small group of powerful businessmen, who – when Hans Ebert had ordered his bastard child terminated – had saved the boy and raised him secretly for his first four years.

Jelka shivered. "What do they want now?"

A sourness filled the old Marshal's face. "Who knows? Favours. The usual thing."

"And you give them what they want?"

His laughter was almost ugly. "No. Thus far I've delayed them, fobbed them off, but they're becoming more insistent, their claims more outrageous."

She squeezed his arm. "Tell them you owe them nothing."

He looked at her, then shook his head. "I wish I could, but it's not so simple. As the world perceives it, the boy owes them a great deal, maybe everything."

"But legally..."

He looked away. "Leave it, please, my love."

She stepped back, obedient, bowing her head, while beside her, his dark eyes taking in everything, the boy frowned.

"Well? What do you want?"

The two men got to their feet abruptly, surprised by the sudden presence of Tolonen in the room, shocked by the hostility in his voice.

"Forgive us for intruding at this hour," began the first of them, a small, rotund man in pale lemon silks, "but this matter..."

Tolonen cut in. "You'll forgive me if I'm less than polite, Shih Berrenson, but I'm not accustomed to being dragged from my breakfast for ad hoc meetings. I am a busy man – a very busy man, and should you wish to make an appointment with me it can be done through my Private Secretary."

Berrenson looked to his partner, Fox, then ducked his head slightly, as if at the same time agreeing and disagreeing with Tolonen.

"Forgive me, Marshal, but that is exactly what we have been trying to do for the past six days. A dozen times we've approached him to arrange an audience with you and each time your man has put us off. In the end we were left with no option…"

"But to come knocking on my door like tradesmen…"

Berrenson's face stiffened. Beside him, Fox looked indignant. "Tradesmen?"

Tolonen stepped right up to him, then tapped his chest with the fingers of his golden, artificial arm.

"Tradesmen. Wheeler-dealers. What do you want me to call you? *Ch'un tzu*?" He laughed coldly. "No, gentlemen, let's not hide the fact with pretty words. I know what you want."

Berrenson stared at the golden fingers pressed into his chest then met Tolonen's eyes again. "Whatever your personal feelings are in this matter, I feel it would be best…"

"*Best?*" Tolonen shook his head. "What would be best would be for you to go away and stop pestering the child. He is grateful, certainly, but your attempts to turn such gratitude into financial advantage are – and let me make this *absolutely* clear – becoming tiresome."

Berrenson took a long breath, then looked to his colleague again. "I see we are wasting our time here. It seems that the Marshal has no understanding of how things work in the realm of finance. Not that that's surprising. He is, after all, a mere soldier…"

The insult was barely out before Berrenson found himself sprawling backward. He sat up, groaning, blood dripping from his nose and from the gash in his top lip. Fox looked on, astonished.

"Nothing," Tolonen said, standing over him threateningly. "You shall have nothing. You or any of your pack of jackals."

Berrenson dabbed at his broken nose with the collar of his silks, then glared up at the old man. "You'll regret this, Tolonen. Before I'm done GenSyn won't be worth a fucking five yuan note!"

Tolonen laughed. "Is that a threat, *Shih* Berrenson? Because if it is, you'd better be prepared to carry it out. But let me warn you, you loathsome little insect. If I find you've said one word that's detrimental to the company or made one deal that could harm my ward's interests, then I'll come for you… *personally*, you understand me? And next time it won't be just your nose I'll break, it'll be every bone in that overweight tradesman's body of yours." He leaned in close, pushing his face almost into Berrenson's, "*Understand me?*"

Berrenson nodded.

"Good. Now go. And don't ever bother me again."

Kim waited as the door hissed back, then stepped through, his breath warm in the protective suit. This was a secure area and as the door closed behind him, sealing itself airtight, a fine mist enveloped him, killing any bacteria he might have brought in from outside.

Inside, beyond the second airtight door, was the garden he had had built at the centre of the labs. There, beneath a fake blue sky that was eternally summer, were the two dozen *special rose bushes he had planted in the rich, dark earth that covered the whole of the* thirty by thirty area to a depth of three feet.

As the second door slid back, Kim stepped inside, the micro-fine filters in the helmet allowing him to smell the sweet scent of the roses. He paused a moment, eyes closed, enjoying the early morning warmth, the strange freshness of the place, then moved on, making his way down the lines of bushes.

SimFic had spent more than fifteen million *yuan* building this place, simply to humour him. The thought of that – of the sheer waste of it – had worried him at first, but then he had begun to see it from their viewpoint. Here he could think – here, undisturbed, he could put flesh to the bone of speculation. And thinking was what he was paid to do.

Yesterday he had watched her spin this web, making first the spokes and then the central spiral. A broader 'guide' spiral – a kind of scaffolding – had followed, and then the great spiral itself, the 'bridge lines' as they were called. He had watched, fascinated, as she wove and gummed the threads, her tiny rounded body balanced on the scaffolding as she plucked the gummed line to spread the tiny droplets equidistantly along its length.

When he had first seen it he had thrilled to the discovery, recognising once more the importance of the laws of resonance and how they governed the natural world – from the largest things to the smallest – and it had brought back to him a moment when he had witnessed a great spider-like machine hum and produce a chair from nothingness.

So long ago, that seemed, yet the moment was linked to this, resonating down the years. Memories. They too obeyed the laws of resonance.

He moved on. Beside the orb web spiders he had others – scaffold-web spiders like *Nesticidae* that had settled in a tiny rocky cave he had had built at the far end of the garden, and triangular-web spiders like *Hyotiotes*. But his favourite was the elegant *Dinopis*, a net-throwing spider with the face of a fairy-tale ogre. How often he had watched her construct her net between her back legs and then wait, with a patience that seemed limitless, to snare any insect foolish enough to pass below.

Insects had long been banned from City Earth. The great tyrant, Tsao Ch'un, had had them eradicated from the levels, building intricate systems of filters and barriers to keep them out. But here, in this single airtight room, he, Kim Ward, had brought them back.

Using stored DNA, GenSyn had rebuilt these once common species especially for him; these and their prey – ants and beetles, centipedes, ladybirds and flies, silk moths and aphids.

It had not been easy, however. He had first had to get Li Yuan's permission. A special edict had been passed, co-signed by all three T'ang, while SimFic, for their part, had guaranteed that there would be no breaches of the strict quarantine procedures. Not that that was really a problem.

Kim looked about him, feeling a brief contentment. Here he had mused on many things: on the physical nature of memory; on the ageing of cells and the use of nanotechnology to induce the rapid healing of damaged tissue; on the duplication of neurons; and, most recently, on the creation of a safe and stable intelligence-enhancement drug. Each time he had come here knowing no answer, and each time the tranquillity of the garden had woven its magic spell, conjuring something from the depths of him.

But now it was almost done, his time in exile finished.

In four weeks he could walk from here, a free man again, the pulsing band gone from around his neck. If he chose.

He reached out and brushed the delicate, dew-touched petals of a blood red rose with his gloved fingers, watching the pearled drops fall. It was all one great ballet – a cosmic dance, governed by immutable laws, and he the key, the focus of it all. He saw how it all worked, how it could be shaped and used. And yet some part of him held back – some dark and quiet part of him *refused* to use that knowledge.

He expelled a long, slow breath, then looked about him again, as if seeing it all for the first time.

Thus far he had but scratched the surface of the real. SimFic had asked

and he had answered, But their questions had been small and insignificant...
unimaginative. It was as if they couldn't see the possibilities of this, whereas
he...

Kim frowned, not liking the shape of his thoughts. Yet it was necessary
to face the truth. Intellectually he was their superior. That made him
no better than them – not in simple, human terms – but it did make him
different, and he was convinced that that difference had been granted him
for a reason. The twists and turns of his existence – his very survival – all of it
meant something. He had been raised up out of the darkness for a purpose,
and now it was time, perhaps, to discover just what that purpose was – to
ask himself the big questions: the questions that only he – from up here on
his intellectual mountain top – could frame.

He crossed the room and stood before the long metal cabinet that was
attached to the wall. Taking a long-stemmed key from the belt of his suit he
fitted it into the lock and turned it twice. There was a moment's delay and
then a series of tiny metal doors in the inside of the cabinet clicked open.

Kim stood back, watching the insects tumble out in a spill of darkness.
They were freshly fashioned, their neutered forms made for a single purpose
– to be eaten by his spiders. It was a disturbing thought. Like so much else
that he had created they were little more than toys – distractions from the
real business of life.

He watched them flap and whirr and scuttle and felt his inner self curl up
in aversion.

They lived, yet they were dead.

"Kim?"

He looked up at the camera lens overhead. "Yes?"

"Curval wants to speak with you about the new figures."

"Tell him I'll be with him in a while."

He looked down. The real reason he had come here this morning was
to see if he could focus himself for long enough to make a decision about
whether he should stay with SimFic in some capacity or go his own way.
But, as ever, there was too much to do, too many things to be attended to,
to allow him time to think it through properly. The decision, when it came,
would be of the moment. They would ask and he would reach inside himself
and... well, it would be there, on his tongue.

Until then he didn't know.

Kim retraced his steps. As the door hissed closed behind him and a faint mist enveloped him, one final thought came to him.

Does she still think of me? Does she even remember me?

Jelka had heard her father shouting; had heard the commotion in the entrance hall as the two men left. But it was an hour before he emerged from his rooms, wearing his Marshal's uniform, his face composed, as if nothing had happened.

She greeted him in the atrium at the front of the Mansion, walking around him to inspect him, just as she'd done to the boy. It was unnecessary, of course – Steward Lo would never have let him leave his rooms unless he were immaculate – but it had become almost a ritual between them.

"Well?" he asked.

She touched his arm. "You look very smart, father. It's not often you wear full dress uniform these days. What's the occasion?"

"I..." He looked down at his wrist-timer then shook his head. "Gods! Is that the time? Look, sweetheart, I have to go. I'm late already."

She kissed his cheek. "Go on. Hurry now. I'll see you when you get back."

He smiled. "Look after Pauli, neh?"

She nodded, then sighed, watching him disappear through the open doorway, but a moment later he was back, smiling apologetically.

"I almost forgot. The final guest list for the party... it's on my desk. If you'd check it to make sure we've not left anyone out."

"I'll make a start on it at once."

He returned her smile. "Good.... Later then, huh?"

She watched him go then turned, gazing down the hallway towards the big picture window at the end with its view of the gardens at the centre of the Mansion, then shook her head. How she hated this place.

Five years she had lived here now and still she felt like an intruder. Not that she had ever liked this house, with its dark walls and its heavy furnishings, its monumental statuary and its thick, oppressive tapestries. No. The ghosts of the Ebert family still presided here and their fleshy imprint lay on everything. This was their place, like the lair of some strange, half-furred, feral creatures. And for her there was the further memory of her betrothal to the son of the House, Hans Ebert.

Jelka shuddered. It had been just here, in the Great Hall, just to the right of where she stood. She walked across, then stopped in the doorway, looking in.

Nothing had changed. The jet black tiles gleamed with polish, while between squat red pillars, on lush green walls that reminded her of primal forests, hung the same huge canvases of ancient hunts that had hung there on the day she had been betrothed to him.

She closed her eyes, remembering. In the half dark the machine had floated towards her like a giant bloated egg, silent, two brutish GenSyn giants guiding it. Its outer surface had been like smoked glass, but a tightly-focused circle of light directly beneath it had glimmered like a living presence in the depths of the floor.

Jelka had stood there, as in a dream, rooted with fear, watching kit come, like Fate itself, implacable and unavoidable.

She made a small movement of her head, surprised by the vividness of the memory. So much had happened since that distant day. So many had died or been betrayed, yet she – Jelka Tolonen – had survived.

She had danced her way to life.

Turning, she noticed that the door ton her father's study was open. Steward Lo was inside, tidying up after his master.

Looking up, Lo saw her.

"*Nu Shi*..."

She went across, looking about her as Steward Lo finished his chores. Even here there was little sign of her father. He had changed nothing. Bookshelves filled three walls, but those had been there before he'd come and the leather-bound books that lined them had been undisturbed for twenty, maybe thirty years, the Ebert crest stamped into the title page of each one. Only the personal items on the huge desk that filled the far corner of he room were her father's.

She sent across and began searching for the list.

There were letters from old friends and bulky files with the S-within-G logo of GenSyn stamped into their bright blue covers, a note from General Rheinhardt about the next Security Council meeting and her father's desk diary, open at today's page.

She searched a moment longer, surprised to find nothing, then stopped, her eyes caught by the final entry in the diary.

She shook her head, then read it once again.

No. She hadn't been mistaken. There it was, in his own handwriting – *SimFic Labs with Li Yuan. 12 pm. Kim-Ward and Work In Progress.*

He hadn't told her. He *hadn't* told her!

She eased back, an unfocussed anger gripping her. Then, clenching both fists, she called for inner calm and slowly, very slowly, it came to her.

So... it was still going on. Seven years – seven long years he had kept this up. But now it had to stop.

She let out a long breath then looked across the study. Steward Lo was watching her.

"Are you alright, *Nu Shi?*"

She let her voice project her inner calm. "I'm fine, Steward Lo. It's just that my father said he's left a list... a guest list for my Coming-Of-Age party."

"Ah..."

Lo came across and, with a bow to her, reached past her and took a slender file from among the GenSyn papers.

"Here," he said, dusting it off and handing it to her, bowing again. "It is not long now, neh, *Nu Shih?*"

"Not long," she answered, nodding her thanks. Then, moving past him, she hastened from the study.

Back in her room, she sat on the edge of her bed, the file in her lap, letting her thoughts grow still. They would all be here, of course – all of those important names from Above society one might expect to turn up for the Coming-Of-Age party of the Marshal's daughter, but there was only one name she was interested in.

She counted ten then opened it, scanning the list quickly with her finger.

Most of the names were familiar – Security mostly – but some, she knew, were there because one could not hold such a party and not invite such people. She would have to go through it more carefully later on, but for now...

She came to the end. Nothing. There was no sign of his name.

So it was true. He really was keeping his word. Very well. She should not really have expected other of him. But this was *her* party, *her* Coming-Of-Age, and there was one person, more than any other, she would have there on that day.

Kim Ward,

She went through to her study and sat at her desk, leaning across to take the ink brush from its stand. Inking it, she tried to remember the last time she had seen him, after the Wiring Operation. Seven years had passed since that day, and never, in all that time, had she stopped thinking of him, wondering about him, *preparing* herself for him.

She took the list and wrote in his name, there between Wang Ling, the Minister for Production, and her father's friend, Colonel Wareham.

There! She thought. Yet even as the ink dried, she knew it would not end with that. He would fight her over it, she knew, for it was the one thing they had *always* fought over.

Damn you, you old bugger! She thought, angry at him yet loving him all the same. *Why can't you want what I want just this once?*

But she knew it was no good wishing. Her father was like a rock, impervious to time and good opinion. She would have to face him out on this. Tonight, perhaps, or tomorrow.

Jelka shivered, frustration and anger threatening to drive her to distraction. Then, controlling herself again, she switched on her desk-top comset and turned to the front of the list, determined he would have no other reason to find fault with her.

Tolonen gazed out of the window of the cruiser then looked back at his T'ang, answering him finally.

"I don't know, *Chieh Hsia*. I think you should try other means before taking such drastic action."

Li Yuan gestured wearily. "I wish I could, but time is against us. Each day sees the man grow stronger at my expense. The situation in Africa is worsening and my armies there are restless. If I do nothing, things will simply deteriorate until... well, until Li Min will merely have to raise his voice and the whole thing will come tumbling down."

Tolonen sighed, troubled by such talk. "Forgive me, *Chieh Hsia*, but surely things are not so bad? We have had *peace* these past three years. The House has been docile, food rations have increased..."

Li Yuan huffed out a breath, exasperated. "Can't you see it, Knut? The peace you talk of, it's a fragile, *brittle* thing. No. Time is running out. Our options are dwindling. We must either fight the bastard now or hand the City over to him."

"Then send Karr to negotiate with him, as I suggested. Have him offer Li

Min a temporary peace – something that will give us time to draw up a proper plan of campaign. To fight him now – without preparation–" Tolonen made a bitter face. "It would be madness!"

Li Yuan sat back, smoothing his chin nervously.

Tolonen, watching him, saw the gesture and looked down, reminded of the young man's father, Li Shai Tung. So the old man had looked in those months before his death – his eyes haunted, his face made gaunt with worry. And maybe Yuan *was* right – maybe things *were* worse than they seemed – but to hit out blindly, simply for something to do...well, he had said it already: it was madness.

Tolonen sighed. "Besides, there's always Ward. If *he* delivers the goods..."

Li Yuan nodded distractedly, then met Tolonen's eyes again. "I understand you had some visitors this morning."

"Ah, *that*."

"Is there a problem, Knut? Something I can help you with?"

Tolonen gave a short laugh. "Nothing I can't deal with, *Chieh Hsia*."

"No..." Li Yuan stared at him a moment, then laughed. "I doubt there's anything you couldn't deal with."

They were both silent a while, then Tolonen spoke again.

"Do you think Ward will sign up again?"

"For SimFic?" Li Yuan considered a moment, then shrugged. "It's hard to say. One thing is for certain, he doesn't need the money. I'm advised he's worth close on four hundred and fifty million, and with royalties on SimFic products he's had a hand in, that's likely to treble within the next five years. If In were in Reiss's position I would be looking beyond financial incentives."

Tolonen stared at his hands, uncomfortable suddenly. "He's a strange one, neh?"

Li Yuan nodded. "It must *be* strange, being as he is."

Tolonen hesitated then looked up. "What do you think of him as a person?"

Li Yuan frowned. The question was unexpected.

"I... respect him. His talent is formidable... frightening. I can't begin to imagine how he thinks. It's as if he's thinking in a different *direction* to the rest of us. Like Shepherd in his field."

Tolonen was leaning forward now, his face set, waiting.

"But as a person?" Li Yuan shrugged, then pulled his silks about him, as if suddenly cold. "I don't know. I cannot make him out. There's something... *dark* in him. I've tried to like him, but..."

Tolonen nodded, understanding. It was how he himself felt – at one and the same time awed and repelled by the boy.

Boy? He laughed inwardly at the slip. Why, Ward was a man now... a young man of twenty-five years, but still he thought of him as a child, perhaps because Ward still had thebody of a child – an effete yet threatening child.

He shivered. If the truth were known he thought Ward an ugly, stunted little creature and what his daughter had ever seen in him he couldn't imagine. Clayborn he was, and like all of the Clayborn there was something deeply, intrinsically repugnant about him.

Tolonen sat back, then locked his fingers together in his lap, gold metallic fingers alternating with pink-white flesh. He had not seen Ward since he's come back from America – in truth he had hoped never to see him again. When America had fallen he had believed the boy was dead – had thought it done with for good and all. But Ward had got out – SimFic had protected their investment and shipped him out on the last flight – and he, hearing the news, had felt a bitter disappointment.

A curse. Ward was a curse on him. An evil spell. Always coming between him and his daughter.

He felt the cruiser begin to bank, the engine tone change, and knew they were approaching their destination. Looking back at Li Yuan he saw he was staring out of the window, yet his hazel eyes were looking inward, his mind worrying over some problem of State. Tolonen, seeing him thus, felt his own worries dissipate. They were nothing beside his Master's. To serve his T'ang, that was – had *always* been – his prime directive, and whatever he felt about Ward, he must let none of it come between him and his duty.

To serve... Tolonen nodded, then straightened in his seat, pushing out his chest and placing his hands firmly, decisively on his knees... it was the very reason for his existence.

Kim leaned in to the screen, tracing the slow, descending line of the graph with his index finger, his worst fears confirmed.

"There's no doubt, is there?"

Curval, beside him, stared a moment longer then shook his head. "No. These performance figures bear out what we've suspected for a while now. There's a definite memory drain."

"Any guesses as to why?"

Curval glanced at Kim, then shrugged. "I've no idea. But it's happening. At this rate the whole of the implanted memory core will be gone in... three months? Four at the outside."

"And the body's good for sixty, maybe eighty years."

"Bit of a problem, neh?"

The two men laughed.

"So what are we going to do?" Curval asked, smoothing the polished dome of his skull.

"Start again? Re-design from scratch?"

"Li Yuan won't like it."

"But if there's no other option..."

Curval considered. "What if we were to create back-ups? Make more than a single implant? Maybe it's simply a question of reinforcement? After all, the human brain makes copies of all new memories and distributes them, so maybe that's what's lacking. Maybe we're over-simplifying."

"Maybe," Kim said thoughtfully. "Then again, maybe we're not being simple enough. I've the feeling that the answer's there, staring us in the face, only it's so obvious, so glaring, that we just can't see it."

"You think do? If you ask me there's a fault in the materials we've been using."

Kim shook his head.

"Then what? There's got to be an answer. This..." Curval tapped the screen. "This oughtn't to be happening."

"And yet it is. Which means something basic is going wrong – something so integral to the process that we're going to have to take the whole thing apart, piece by piece, before we can understand what it is."

"That'll take time."

"I know."

"And we haven't got time."

"I know."

"So what are we going to do?"

Kim smiled. "First we're going to see the T'ang and show him what we've got."

The tests were over. Li Yuan watched them lead the man-like morph away then looked down at his hands.

In some ways it was impressive, much more impressive than anything GenSyn had thus far managed to produce. The creature's feats of memory and mathematics were breath-taking and there was no doubting its mental agility. Physically, however, it was disappointing. Oh, it was fit – super fit if the performance figures quoted could be trusted – and its coordination was excellent. Moreover its vision and muscular strength had been enhanced; even so, it was not what he had envisaged.

He sighed and looked across at Tolonen. The old man smiled back at him, but he looked tired, as if the whole thing had been too much for him. Seeing that, Li Yuan relented a little. They had all worked hard – Tolonen included – to get this far. And maybe he was simply expecting too much. After all, three years ago there had been nothing. Nothing but the rumour that DeVore and Hans Ebert had been working on something like this. That and the 'manufactured' brains they had discovered in North America.

He was used to synthetic beings. He had grown up surrounded by them – tank-grown creatures, the products of GenSyn's bio-engineering programmes – but this was different. The skin, the eyes, they had been grown in GenSyn's vats – special 'nutrient reservoirs' feeding the living, self-replicating parts; doing the jobs other cells would normally have carried out – but the rest... the rest had been *built*. Beneath the human form that presented itself to the eye was a machine; a machine that – however crudely – thought for itself.

He turned, looking to Kim. "There's one thing I don't understand. Why does it make those lists?"

Kim hesitated, glancing at Reiss, then answered him.

"It makes lists because it's autistic."

"Autistic?"

"You saw how easily it remembered things. It's like a blotting paper, soaking things up. And once shown it never forgets. But what it lacks is the ability to ascribe a meaning or purpose to things – especially to people and places. It has no *structure* to its existence, you see. There's a gap there where it ought to be. So to plug that gap it fills its life with lists."

"Ah…"

"In humans the problem is rooted in the cerebellum – that's where our sense of 'self' is to be found."

Kim laughed.

"I've heard that the Temple of the Oracle at ancient Delphie had an inscription carved into the stone over the entrance. 'Know Thyself' it read. Unfortunately that isn't even an option for our android friend. The Brain structure we've developed for this model is simply too crude, too simple to allow self-consciousness."

"And nothing can be done about that?"

Kim shrugged. "Possibly. But there are other problems we have to solve first. At present the brain in this model is quite small – like the ones the Marshal brought back from America. The reason for that's quite simple. An ounce of nerve tissue uses up far more calories in the process of thinking than an ounce of muscles burns up in exercise. In fact. The brain uses up a quarter of our body's energy. We've tried to accommodate this fact by providing extra power to our models, hence the two storage packs in the small of its back. But we can only do so much. Being aware is actually very hard work. To make that model more aware we would have to increase its cranial capacity considerably, and that would mean increasing its body size and weight proportionately. What you'd have, in effect, would be a giant."

Li Yuan leaned back, his disappointment deeper by the moment. "I hoped we would be able to improve on things somehow."

Kim smiled apologetically. "Maybe we shall. Given time. At first I considered doing something new – designing something that was completely different from the basic human blueprint – but ultimately I had to concede that there was nothing wrong with the old model. Tens of million years of evolution can't be bucked. The brain is as it is because that's how it *has* to be."

"I understand. But tell me… why did it take so long to recognise. Even you. It seemed almost not to see you until you spoke to it. I thought its vision had been enhanced."

"It has, But the model is essentially prosopagnosic. That is, it can't recognise faces. Not at once, anyway. Retinas, yes, voices too – from the inflections – but a whole face takes much longer. It has to check a number of different elements – shape of nose, colour of eyes, distance between forehead and mouth – against a pre-programmed list of the same elements and tick off each item. It doesn't take long, but there's a definite delay. Like many of its behavioural traits, it's a crude analogy of how a human functions, not a perfect copy."

"I was surprised by how human it looks," Li Yuan confessed. "I was expecting something more..."

"*Brutal?*" Kim shrugged. "I toyed with the idea of making it look very different; of enhancing it even more and making it like some sleek custom-designed machine, but in the end I decide it would be best to work with something that looked as unthreatening – as *normal* – as possible. After all, if it's simple *threat* you want, you already have GenSyn's half-men, their *Hei*. My thinking was what if this project had any purpose, it was to produce something that would fool our enemies. Its very normality is, I feel, its greatest strength."

"Is it safe?"

Kim laughed. "Safe? It's positively docile. In fact, one of the problems we've been having with this model is its passivity. It'll make decisions, but only when it's *asked* to make decisions. Most of the time it'll just sit there."

"I see. And there's no way to alter that?"

Kim hesitated, then glanced at Reiss, who had remained by the door, looking on.

Li Yuan turned, a faint hope growing in him. "Is there something I should know, Director Reiss?"

Reiss bowed his head. "*Chieh Hsia*... I..."

"Just tell me."

Reiss swallowed. "There's a... a second prototype."

Li Yuan raised an eyebrow. "A *second* prototype?"

"Yes, *Chieh Hsia*, except..."

"Except we've been having problems with it," Kim said, interrupting him.

Li Yuan turned. "What kind of problems?"

Kim smiled then put out an arm, inviting Li Yuan to accompany him. "I think you'd better see it for yourself."

Li Yuan stood beside Kim in the tiny room, staring at the creature sprawled on the narrow bed. The first prototype had seemed more than a complex marionette, like the golden bird in the poem Ben Shepherd had sent him. But this... He felt a strange thrill – of fear? excitement? – run up his spine. This was something special. He could see that at a glance.

"So what *is* the problem?"

"Can't you see?"

Li Yuan made to step closer, but Kim touched his arm. "Forgive me, *Chieh Hsia*, but no closer. It's... erratic."

"Dangerous?"

"It hasn't been, but... well, I'd hate to be proved wrong."

"Should we... ?" Lin Yuan gestured to the door.

"No. It'll ignore us if we keep our distance. Usually it..."

"Usually it *what*?"

The creature turned its head and stared at them, its eyes dark with intelligence.

Yes, Li Yuan thought, his breath catching in his throat, *this* was more like what he'd expected!

It turned and slid its legs over the edge of the bed.

"How are you today?"

It ignored Kim's question, staring at Li Yuan as if to place him.

"What do the latest figures show?" it asked.

"The same trend."

The creature nodded, then, in a gesture that was peculiarly human, combed its dark hair back from its eyes. "So what will you do?"

"I can re-implant."

"No good. If you do that I lose what I am. All I've been. Already..." It grimaced painfully. "Already things are slipping from me."

"Has it a name?" Li Yuan asked.

Kim turned, surprised, as if he had forgotten that the young T'ang was there. "Ravachol... I called him Ravachol."

"A Slavic name. Interesting. He looks Slav."

Kim nodded, but already his attention was back with the creature.

"What do *you* want me to do?"

Ravachol looked away, pained, its every action revealing some deep inner torment. "I... I don't know. Some new technique, perhaps? A drug?"

"But there *are* no drugs."

It stared at Kim once more, then shrugged. "So how long do I have?"

"Three, maybe four months."

It nodded. Then, smiling suddenly, it leaned towards Kim. "I had another dream."

"A dream? Tell me. Was it the same as before?"

Ravachol hesitated, concentrating, then shook its head. "No... I don't think so."

Kim spoke to it softly, as if coaxing a child. "So?"

It frowned fiercely, as if struggling to recall the details, then began, its voice faltering.

"It began in the light. A fierce, burning light. It *seared* me. I was *consumed* by it. Caught up within a great wheel of incandescent light. And... and then it focused. I was... I *felt* new-made. I stepped out from the centre of the light and... it was as if I was stepping into an airtight cube of glass – of ice – a place of stillness. Perfect, immaculate stillness."

It sat back, its face beatific, and sighed.

"I could hear nothing. Feel nothing. Smell and sense nothing. It was... *strange*. The silence was both within me and without. There was no pulse in me, no beating in my chest. It was like I was dead, and yet I was conscious. I could turn my head and see. But there was nothing to be seen. Even the light... even *that* had gone. Not that it was dark. It was just..."

Ravachol stopped, its muscles locked, its eyes staring at Kim as if it had been switched off.

"And then?"

The way it came to again was eery, frightening, like a time-piece clicking into motion on the hour. Li Yuan felt a small shiver of fear pass through him. Yes, he could see now what Kim meant. The thing was mad. Totally, unequivocally mad.

"I can't remember. Something happened, but I can't remember what it was. It's like a piece of cloth where the edge has frayed. I get so far and then there's nothing left."

It stared at Kim, mouth open in a perfect O of surprise.

"Okay," Kim said, "you'd better rest. If you dream the dream again write it down. Or speak of it to the camera, before the edges fray."

It nodded, then, with a curious meekness, allowed itself to be tucked in beneath the thin white sheets. It lay there, passive, eyes open, staring at the ceiling. Then, with a suddenness that was shocking, its eyelids clicked shut.

Outside again, Li Yuan stood at the view window looking in.

"What does it mean, all that?"

"The dream?" Kim scribbled something in a small notebook then slipped it into the pocket of his bright red one-piece. "It's the same every time, detail for detail. It's not really a dream – not as you and I have them – more a symbolic landscape of its self-consciousness... a tacit recognition of its basic non-existence. It *knows*, you see. Knows what it is and how it was made. It even knows what's wrong with it. The dreams... they're a kind of anxiety outlet. The only one it has. Without them it would cease to function."

"I see." Li Yuan shuddered, feeling a strange pity for the creature. He was silent for a time, then he sighed. "I hoped we'd be further along."

"We've come a long way."

"I know. It's just..."

"Time?"

Li Yuan nodded, then turned to face Kim. "Time. It's the curse of kings and emperors." He laughed wistfully. "When I was a child, I thought there was all the time in the world – that things would be the same for ever. Time was like an old friend, unalterable, unending. But it isn't so. My father knew it. The day I was born, they say, he had a dream. A dream of the darkness to come."

Kim traced a circle on the one-way mirror. "You think collapse is inevitable, then?"

"Inevitable? No. But likely. More and more likely every day. Unless we take preventive action."

"And this?" Kim tapped the glass, indicating the sleeping android. "Do you *really* think this is any kind of solution?"

"You don't, I take it?"

Kim laughed, "You are the T'ang, *Chieh Hsia*."

Li Yuan smiled. "So when will it be ready?"

"A year. Six months if we're really lucky."

"Lucky?" Li Yuan raised an eyebrow. "I thought your science was a *precise* thing."

"Oh no, *Chieh Hsia*. Far from it. Luck plays a huge part in things. But the problems we've been having with the prototypes have stemmed mainly from the pace of development. We've come from nothing to this in less than three years. That's fast. Too fast, perhaps. If we were dealing with a single, homogenous bio-system it would be relatively straightforward – we could locate any errors as and when they occurred – but we're not; we're dealing with a dozen, fifteen different bio-systems at any one time, and those systems aren't discrete, they're dependent on each other. One goes wrong, the whole lot go wrong. And the trouble is the systems have had no time to evolve properly – to grow together. We've had to rely on guesswork most of the time, and our guesses have sometimes been wrong. But why something doesn't work – whether it's this system we've got wrong or that – well, it's difficult to say."

Li Yuan raised a hand. "I understand. But a year... a year should do it, right?"

Kim nodded.

"Good. Then it's time, perhaps, to make the thing specific."

"Specific?"

"Facial details, build, height and weight. That kind of thing."

"Ah..." Kim digested that a moment, then looked back at Li Yuan. "Who is it?"

"I think it's best you don't know."

"Who *is* it?" Kim insisted. "I have to know."

Li Yuan stared at him, surprised, reminded briefly of Ben Shepherd, then took the envelope from within his silks and offered it to Kim.

"He's a killer. A man named Soucek. But that information is classified, right? Four men died getting those details."

Kim studied the sheaf of papers a moment longer, then nodded. "I understand. But why him?"

"He works for Li Min. His right-hand man. He has *access*."

A shadow passed over Kim's face. "Ah..."

"You want to pull out?"

Kim shook his head. "I didn't say that. But I needed to know."

"A year? At the very most?"

"A year."

"Then let us pray that we *have* a year, neh, my Clayborn friend? Let us pray to all the gods we know that time, this once, does not outrun us!"

Soucek sat in a chair to one side of the magistrate's desk, his legs crossed casually, his long, pock-marked face inexpressive. Two guards stood at his back – big, brutal-faced thugs, heavy automatics held across their chests. Behind the desk, Old yang, the magistrate, cleared his throat then tugged nervously at his wispy beard.

The hall was packed. People stood at the back and along the side walls or crouched in the aisles, talking and fanning themselves indolently. There were over two dozen cases to be heard this session and this was only the third of them. Already they had seen two deaths and there was a mounting excitement now that this case, too, was coming to a head.

From where she stood against the back wall, Emily looked on apprehensively. How many times had she seen this in these last two years? How many times had she had to stand and watch this dumb show of justice? *Far too often*, she thought, her fingers tracing the shape of the gun beneath her jacket. But today... today would be different.

The accused – a young Han male of seventeen years – stood in the blood-spattered space in front of the dais, his hands bound behind his back, his head bowed. His scalp had been crudely shaved and was flecked with cuts. A leather thong had been tied around his head, over his mouth, holding down his tongue to keep him from speaking. Two bare-chested tony members stood behind him, butchers' cleavers in their belts, ceremonial black sashes about their brows. The arresting tong officer's testimony had been read, the security camera evidence shown. All that remained was for the Magistrate to pronounce sentence.

The evidence seemed conclusive. They had a Security film of the boy – a non-tong member – purchasing a knife from an unidentified criminal, and the sworn statements of "friends" that he had been boasting about what he was going to do with it.

The matter appeared clear cut. He had committed a crime for which the penalty was death. But the evidence was faked, the boy innocent.

She had seen the parents yesterday and listened to their story, then had checked out the details for herself. The father was a local market trader and the couple had three children: two boys and a girl. A week back he'd had an argument with one of the local tong officials – what it was about she hadn't managed to get from him, but it had to do with their fourteen-year-old daughter. The two men had exchanged sharp words. The old man had thought that that was it, but the official had not let the matter rest. He had bought evidence – faked film, the "word" of several worthless youths –

and had had his cousin, the officer responsible for security in these stacks, arrest the boy.

The circumstances were not unusual. She had evidence now on more than eighty such cases and knew that these represented only a small part of what was going on throughout the Lowers. For two years now the White T'ang had run the tribunals down here, imposing his "Code of Iron" on these levels. But what had at first seemed like justice had quickly revealed itself as just another means for tong members to lord it over the common citizens. It was a stinking, corrupt system, administered by bullies, cheats and murderers.

Like this case here.

She sighed, her anger mixed with pain. This wasn't justice, this was arranged murder, with the victim denied even the right to speak for himself. And Soucek – Soucek was the architect of it all, the administrator and chief executioner. It was he who let the sewers run with filth.

But today... Today she would strike a blow for all those who had suffered under him.

As the Magistrate began to pronounce sentence, those who were crouching stood, craning their necks to see, an electric current of anticipation running through the crowded hall. Emil stood on her toes, noting where the guards were standing, then began to move through the press of bodies, making her way towards the front.

Old Yang was shouting now, berating the youth in a shrill, ugly voice, calling him the vilest of names and insulting his family. Then it was done, the sentence pronounced.

There was a murmur of anticipation.

Emily slowed, looking about her. She was still some way from the front. She would need to get closer.

At a signal from Soucek, one of the tong members behind the youth stepped up and kicked the youth hard just beneath his left knee. With a groan the boy went down. As he got up on his knees the arresting officer came across and drawing his gun, cocked it and placed it against the boy's head.

The hall was silent now, a tension in the air like that before a thunderstorm. She edged nearer.

The shot was like a release. Heads jerked, mouths opened. A great sigh ran round the hall.

It was done. The White T'ang's word meant something. But for Emily there was only anger. Her hand covered her gun. She was only five or six from the front now. She could see Soucek clearly, see how calm – how hideously calm – he was as he turned to speak to one of the guards.

There was a wailing to her right. *His mother*, she thought, slipping her hand inside her jacket pocket and cocking the gun. Then, shockingly, there was a gunshot.

She turned her head, anxious, trying to see where it had come from. A small cloud of smoke was rising from the crowd to her right. As she saw it, another shot rang out. There was screaming, the beginnings of panic. Tong guards were converging from all sides. For a moment she didn't understand, then, as the crowd parted, she saw. It was the youth's father. He was standing there, his face distraught, holding a gun out at arm's length. She saw his hand tremble as he tried to fire again, and then one of the big automatics opened up and he jerked back, bullets ripping into him, the gun falling from his hand.

As if at a signal everyone got down. She did the same. But as she did she saw, up on the dais, one of the guards crouched over Soucek.

He's hit! She thought, exultant. *The old man got the bastard!*

Yet even as a half dozen tong thugs scrambled up onto the dais to surround him, she saw Soucek get up and, shrugging off the guards' hands, pushed past the men and vanish through the door at the far end.

She looked down, disappointed. Soucek was bleeding. From the look of it one of the old man's shots had hit his right shoulder and broken the collar bone. But he had survived. She would have to wait for another opportunity to get to him.

Yes, only it wouldn't be so easy next time. After today they would be sure to take greater precautions.

She got up. Old yang was slumped in his seat, dead. All about her people were moaning and whimpering. To her right it was a scene of utter chaos. Chairs were scattered everywhere. A dozen or more people were down, dead or wounded.

As the guards began to clear the hall, she let herself be herded with the rest, letting the gun slip down her leg onto the floor then peeled the flesh-thin gloves from her hands and then dropped them casually.

There'll be another time, she promised herself. *The bastard can't always be so lucky.* Yet she felt sick at heart and bitter --- and angry. More angry than she'd ever felt before.

Kim stood before the mirror in his room, adjusting his silks, He was due at The Hive in an hour, but still he hadn't made up his mind whether to sign again or not.

"Well?" he asked, addressing the air. "What did you see?"

"He hates you."

Kim turned, startled by the words. "*Hates me? Li Yuan?*"

"No. I mean Tolonen. He wishes you dead. There is such anger in him. Such unexpressed violence."

Kim let out a breath. "I hoped things might have changed. I hoped..."

"She's with the boy," it said, anticipating his next question.

"The boy?"

"Pauli. Her father's ward. He can't sleep and she's gone to his room to comfort him."

"Ah..." Kim grimaced at his reflection than turned away. "And Reiss?"

The machine was silent a moment, then, rather than answering his question, did something it had never done before and offered him advice.

"You should go and see her."

"*See her?*" Kim laughed uncomfortably. "Now why should I do that?"

"Because you ought."

Kim turned, looking up into the camera's eye. "It's unlike you to be so vague."

"Alright," Kim said, faintly disturbed. "I'll think about it."

"You should buy yourself a mansion."

"A *mansion?* Are you alright?"

The Machine's voice was hesitant. "You don't see things. The obvious things. Your vision... it's so narrow."

Kim stared, astonished.

"Maybe you should talk to Reiss about it. Insist on it as a term in whatever deal you make with him. After all, you need a home, Kim - somewhere to build from. This... this is no good for you."

Kim stood there a moment longer, then, with an impatient, dismissive gesture, he left the room.

"It makes good sense," the Machine said, its voice following Kim down the corridor. "If you were to have children..."

Kim stopped then turned, angry now. "Matters logical, they're your province. As for matters of the heart... well, what would you know of those?"

He waited, expecting an answer, but the Machine was silent. Kim walked on, troubled, thinking about what it had said.

"Kim... so there you are!"

Reiss got up and came out to greet Ward as he approached the table. The Hive was packed, as it always was this time of evening, but Reiss had paid to have the four tables surrounding his kept clear. He embraced Kim then turned, introducing his companions.

"Kim, this is Jack Neville. Jack... this is Kim ward."

"Pleased to meet you," Neville said, stepping round Reiss and offering his hand. He was a slender, brown-haired man in his early thirties with a plump, almost boyish face.

"I'm sorry I'm late," Kim said, taking a seat across from them. "There was something I had to do."

Reiss smiled. "No matter. I understand things went rather well after I'd gone."

Kim smiled apologetically. "I'm sorry about that. I know what you said about the second prototype. But I was sure Li Yuan would see it our way once things were explained."

Reiss took the menu the Head Steward was offering, then smiled back at Kim. "And you were right. Nan Ho was onto me only an hour back. It seems Li Yuan has decided to extend the programme for a further year!"

"Excellent!" Then, understanding why Reiss was not quite so enthusiastic, Kim gave a soft laugh. "We'd best resolve this, neh? As it is... well, I'm finding it hard to work."

Neville, watching the two, raised an eyebrow, then looked to Reiss, who nodded. "You want to hear our offer before you eat or after?"

Kim took a menu, scanned it, then set it aside. "Let's order, then you can tell me what you've got in mind."

"Okay." Reiss looked to the Head Steward. "My usual, Chang, medium rare, and a bottle of Golden Emperor. A magnum. The '98 if you have it."

"I'll have the same," Kim said, "but rare. And just water for me, thanks.

No offence, but I'll get nothing done tomorrow if I drink tonight."

"I understand. But you don't mind…"

"No." Kim smiled broadly. "Some people can take their drink. Me…" He laughed. "Anyway, Jack, what are you having?"

Neville looked up, surprised and somewhat flattered to be addressed by his first name.

"I think I'll have the rainbow trout. I don't think I've ever tasted it." He laughed. "In fact, I didn't know it still existed."

"It doesn't," Kim said, as the Steward withdrew. "At least, not the real thing. That's been extinct some two centuries now. But it's as good as, so they say. GenSyn have been making great strides these past few years, bringing back a lot of the old species. You've seen the ads."

Neville nodded, surprised that Kim kept up with such things. "Does anything escape your notice?"

Kim laughed. "Not much. I like to keep abreast of developments. It makes my task easier if I know I'm not duplicating things. And I like to keep up with the latest media trends. I'm told you're something of an innovator in that field."

Neville looked down, a faint flush at his neck. Reiss, behind him, beamed with an almost parental pride.

"He's a good man," Reiss answered. "We expect much of him. That' why I asked him to come up with a package we could offer you."

"I see." Kim sat back, surprised that the Machine hadn't told him. In fact, now that he came to think of it, the thing had been behaving very strangely these past few weeks. Almost as if it were conscious.

Kim shook his head, no. That wasn't possible. He'd seen just how difficult it was to create even the most basic functioning intelligence in a machine. It simply wasn't possible that a machine – however large, however complex – could develop consciousness. Not on its own.

Neville was watching him, fascinated. "What is it?"

Kim laughed. "Sorry. I was doing it again, wasn't I?"

"Doing what?"

"Thinking."

"Ah…" Neville nodded, then, with a glance at Reiss, he leaned toward Kim. "You want to hear our offer?"

Kim nodded, strangely relaxed now that the moment was here.

"The bad news..." Neville grinned. "The bad news is that you're no longer to be an employee of the Company."

Kim laughed. "And the good news?"

Neville reached beside him and took a slender folder from the empty chair. He handed it across.

Kim hesitated, then opened it.

"You don't have to give your decision now," Reiss said, sitting back as the waiter placed the ice bucket on the table and lifted a magnificent-looking golden bottle from within. "You'll want to think things over, I'm sure."

Kim nodded. "I see." He scanned the two sheets quickly, then put the folder down, watching as the waiter uncapped the honey-gold bottle and poured an ice-chilled glass for Reiss.

"And if I were to ask you for a mansion?"

Reiss smiled and lifted his glass. "You have one in mind?"

Kim looked back at the folder. His own company, that was what they were offering. A subsidiary of SimFic, yet big enough to compete on its own terms in the market. He shivered inwardly. Once before he had been in such a position. Once before he had tried to make a go of it on his own – and failed. But this time it would be difficult. This time he would have the giant SimFic company at his back, protecting him, keeping him from being swallowed up. Yes, and this time there would be no circle of Old Men trying to pull him down and destroy him.

It was a tempting proposition.

He watched Reiss sip and then grunt his appreciation. The waiter pulled again, filling Neville's glass. Neville nodded his thanks, then lifted his glass, toasting Kim.

"To you, Kim, whatever you decide!"

CHAPTER 123

WIVES

Pei K'ung had opened only a dozen or so letters – placing each unread into the tray beside her – when the handwriting on one made her frown and pause. She turned the single sheet over, then, seeing the signature, the family seal at the foot of the page, caught her breath. She sat back, her face drained.

Tsung Ye stared at her, alarmed. "Mistress? Are you alright?"

She waved him away, then turned the page, reading it from the top right column, concentrating fiercely on the neat, handwritten Mandarin.

"The nerve..." she said, after a moment, giving the paper an impatient rustle. Why, she had a mind to call the bitch right now! How *dare* she write to him?

Fei Yen... the letter was from Li Yuan's first wife, Yin Fei Yen.

She brought her fist down hard, making everything on the desk jump, then stood, her whole body trembling now with anger. Crossing to the window, she summoned her secretary to her.

Tsung Ye half ran into the room, then hurried across, his face troubled by the sudden change in his mistress.

She lifted her left hand against the cool, rain-beaded glass and took a calming breath, looking out across the Eastern Gardens toward the stables. It would not do to act too hastily. No, She must act correctly or not at all.

She looked down at the paper in her other hand and shook it angrily. Why, the woman had even had the impudence to mention her bastard son!

After all she'd done!

Pei K'ung shuddered. She felt like burning the letter or ripping it into tiny shreds, but that was no solution. No. It had to be answered. There was no peace for her until it was.

She stopped, staring at the letter again, struck suddenly by the familiarity of its tone; the presumption of a friendship, and felt herself go cold. What if this wasn't the first letter Fei Yen had written him? What if the wording was a pretence – a kind of code between them? What if they often met?

Her throat was suddenly dry, her heart beating fast.

Nan Ho. Nan Ho would know. Yes, but even if he did...

She crumpled the paper into a ball and let it fall. Was he still seeing her? When he went away on business, did she go to him then? Did she still sleep with him?

Pei K'ung closed her eyes, tormented by the thought, even as she told herself just how unlikely this was. Or was that true? Who would tell her, after all? Nan Ho? His secretary, Chang? The men who travelled with him? No, they would say nothing. Indeed, they would see it as their sacred duty to keep it from her.

Besides, did she really know her husband? Did she know his thoughts, his innermost desires? No. Not at all. Oh, she had tried to know him – had tried to get close to him – but there was still a part of him he kept from her, an inner core which she had never penetrated.

She bent down to retrieve the letter, un-crumpling it. As she did so she realised that Tsung Ye, her secretary, was still there, his head bowed, awaiting her instructions.

"Tsung Ye, I'm sorry. I..."

She saw him blush and cursed herself, knowing what her husband had said about never saying sorry to a servant. But it was hard sometimes. Empress she might be, but she was only human after all. Gathering together the shreds of her dignity, she returned to her desk and sat, spreading the letter out and smoothing it several times. For a moment she sat there, staring at the carved jade ink block and at the cop of Nan Ho's seal which lay beside it, then nodded to herself, her decision made.

"Tsung Ye, I have a letter I want delivered in the utmost confidence. It must be delivered by hand directly to the recipient. No one else must know of it nor learn of its contents, you understand me?"

Tsung Ye bowed low. "I shall do as my Mistress asks."

"Good." She reached out and took a clean sheet of her husband's paper, lifted a fine-pointed brush from the stand and began to write.

The woman's screams filled the tiny cell and echoed down the corridor outside, carrying into the nearby living quarters where two guards, playing cards at a table that doubled as a security barrier, paused, looking up uneasily, then carried on with their game.

Back in the cell, Lehmann turned from the naked body on the bench and placed the fine-tipped iron back on the white-hot grid. The smell of burned flesh and faeces was strong in the room, mixed like an obscene cocktail of pain and suffering. Overhead a camera captured it all. The film would sell for over five hundred *yuan* on the black market.

As Lehmann turned back to her, her eyes followed his every move – wide, terrified eyes, the pupils contracted to a tiny point by the drugs she'd been given to enhance the pain. She was bound to the four spikes at the corners of the bench by crude metal bands which, as she'd struggled, had cut into the flesh. The metal glinted in the spotlight, slick with blood.

She was young - early twenties, twenty-five at most – and unlike most of the women you found down here in the Lowers, she was well fleshed, no signs of malnourishment about her. It was that which had tipped his man off, That and the sidearm they had found in her rooms when they had searched them.

It was clever. He had known for some while that Li Yuan was infiltrating his organisation, but this female angle was a new one. She had been hired as a whore at one of his establishments and had proved very popular with many of his Above contacts. But whatever she had found out would die with her now.

Whores... he'd have them all checked out now that they'd discovered this one.

He moved closer, lowering his face until it was only a hand's width from hers, then blew his breath across her face.

"Are you ready to talk?"

She swallowed then shook her head.

"Brave girl. I'll make sure your master gets a copy of the tape. Maybe he'll give you a promotion... posthumously, of course."

Her eyes glared at him defiantly. She gritted her teeth against the pain, then spoke, her voice a whisper.

"Go to hell."

He turned away, then took the iron from the grid and studied the tip. There, delicately carved into the white-hot iron tip was the tiny Mandarin character Si. Death.

He looked at her and laughed; the coldest, emptiest sound she'd ever heard, then positioned the iron carefully. Cupping her right breast almost lovingly, he leaned in to her, pressing the white-hot tip to the nipple.

"There..." he said when she was silent again. "A matching pair. Now... you want me to start lower?"

Her skin was beaded with sweat, her eyes delirious. He could see that she was close now. One more tiny push.

"Okay," he said softly, placing the iron back on the grid. "Let's start again. Who sent you?"

There was a knock. Lehmann turned, a flash of anger – pure, like lightening – passing through him. He had told them not to disturb him. If this was something trivial he would have them on the bench in her place. Controlling his anger, he went to the peep-hole and peered out.

Hart! What the fuck did Hart want? And who was the fat man with him?

He slid the bolt back then pulled the door open.

"Forgive me, Stefan," Hart said, beginning to come in. "I..." He stopped, taking in what was going on. "Kuan Yin... I... look, I didn't know. If you want me to come back?"

"No. Come in. I'll be done in a while. But be quiet. I'm taping this."

Hart glanced at the camera uneasily, then went to the far side of the room, out of the camera's line of sight.

"This is Berrenson," he said, waving his companion across. "He's a businessman."

Berrenson went across, staring all the while at the naked woman, a lewd smile playing on his lips.

"Hey! What's going on here?" he began, almost cheerfully, but Hart put a hand over his mouth then drew him closer, whispering into his ear hurriedly. Slowly, Berrenson's face clouded over. He nodded then swallowed deeply.

Lehmann locked the door, took the heated iron from the grid, then returned to the bench, as if the two men weren't there.

"Okay. Who sent you?"

She was trembling, her eyes fixated on the iron's glowing tip. Unable to present it, she began to piss herself again.

"I'll ask you one last time. Who sent you? Rheinhardt? Tolonen? Nan Ho?"

Her mouth moved, her tongue licked drily at her lips, then she shook her head.

"Who then?"

"The... the hand."

He had moved his face closer, now he drew it back, but still the iron hovered above her, at a point just below her navel.

"The *Black* Hand?"

She nodded.

Lehmann was silent a moment, thinking, then he turned and set the iron back on the grid. Seeing that, she closed her eyes, relief flooding through her.

He stood over her again, then leaned in close, his face almost touching hers once more, his eyes directly above her eyes.

Her eyes were wide open again – afraid to blink; petrified in case she missed what he was doing.

"You did well," he said gently, caressing her face with his long, pale fingers. "You did very well. But I need one more thing. I want the name – the *real* name – of your cell leader."

There was a strange movement in her eyes – a sudden realisation that, whatever she did, whatever she said, there would be no end to this. Not until she was dead.

She shook her head, her whole face creased with pain, knowing the torment to come. Vainly she began to call out and struggle.

Looking on, Hart felt himself go cold. He had never seen anything like it. *Never.* He shuddered then closed his eyes as the woman's screams began again, while beside him, Berrenson looked on with a sickly fascination.

Later, in Lehmann's offices, Berrenson sat there silently, sipping iced-water and chewing at a knuckle while Hart spelled out what it was they wanted.

Lehmann sat casually in his chair, listening patiently, turning the tiny white cassette between his fingers, time and again, staring at it thoughtfully all the while. As Hart finished he looked up at him and nodded.

"I'm glad you came to me, Alex. You did the right thing. But I think you are going about this the wrong way. Killing Tolonen... well, it would give a lot of people – myself included – a great deal of pleasure, but it would solve nothing. To begin with, it would make Li Yuan angry, and I don't want that. Not yet. Moreover, he would only appoint an even more intractable protector for the boy. Rheinhardt, perhaps. And where would you be then? No. We need to be more direct."

"*More* direct? But killing Tolonen..." Hart laughed. "What could be more direct than that? Besides, it would justly avenge your father."

The look Lehmann gave him made him fall silent, lowering his eyes.

"Listen," Lehmann said coldly, looking to Hart and then to Berrenson. "I'll say this only once. I don't want Tolonen killed. It doesn't fit my plans. There is, however, a different way. Berrenson, your people took the boy from the Ebert Mansion once, am I right?"

"That is so, but..."

"But nothing. If it was done once it could be done again. We'll take the boy and hold him. And if Tolonen still refuses to come to terms, then we'll kill him."

"But the Marshal..."

Lehmann glared at Berrenson. "You will leave it to me. And you will tell no one about this meeting – not your wives, nor your friends, and certainly not your business associates."

He leaned towards them threateningly, the tape held up between his fingers. "Remember what you saw this morning. Remember it well. Because if there's one thing I won't tolerate, it's indiscipline."

Swallowing nervously, the two men bowed their heads. The interview was over. They hurried away, the screams of the dying woman echoing ghost-like in their ears.

Li Yuan dismissed his three advisers then turned to the twin screens facing him.

Once there had been seven of them, meeting in council twice a year to discuss matters of state and formulate policy, but the years had slowly pared the Seven down. Now there were just the three of them.

"Tsu Ma... Wei Tseng Li..." he said, greeting his fellow T'ang. "You have heard what Marshal Tolonen and General Rheinhardt had to say, and I am sure you have taken your own specialist advice on the matter. Now, however, we must decide on a course of action, something all three of us are happy with."

Tsu Ma was first to speak. "Tolonen talks sense. Africa has become a luxury we can ill afford. The cost of policing it, both in manpower and in funding, exceeds any benefit we derive from keeping it. Moreover, we all have more pressing problems at home, neh? While there was a shooting war in Africa our presence there at least distracted men's minds from domestic worries, but these last twelve months things have been quiet and the people have grown weary of the struggle. What's in their bellies worries them more than whether Africa is won or lost. And rightly so, perhaps. My vote is to get out."

"And you, Cousin Wei?"

Wei Tseng-li was his father's third son and had inherited only after the murder of his elder brothers. For a time he had been Li Yuan's personal secretary and, when stationed on Li Yuan's floating palace, *Yangjing*, had saved Yuan's son, Kuei Jen, from certain death. As such there was a strong bond between the two young men. In many respects they were more like brothers than cousins. Just now, however, Tseng-li was deep in thought, his smooth, beardless face pale. The problems of state sat heavier on him than on the other two, and he had been ill these past months, though his surgeons could not trace the cause.

"I hear what my cousin Ma says," he began, speaking slowly, every word considered. "And whilst what he says makes sense, I am still loath to throw away what we have fought so hard to keep. History teaches that, once lost, territory can never be regained so easily. So with Africa. Withdraw and we withdraw for good. Chung Kuo will be diminished. Not only that, but it will be seen by all to be a sign of weakness. A sign so large that even the most myopic of our enemies might read it, therefore my counsel is against withdrawal. I say we should persevere. Until times turn to our favour once again."

Li Yuan sat back.

"I hear you, Cousin, and, were it merely a matter of withdrawal, would agree with you entirely. It would not do to display any sign of weakness. And that is why I am suggesting that we make of this necessity a virtue."

"How so?" Tsu Ma asked.

Li Yuan smiled. "Can we meet?"

"In person?"

"It would be best."

Tsu Ma frowned. "Forgive me, Yuan, but is that wise, given the climate of the times?"

"It must be so. For what I have to say is for the eyes of we three alone. The days when we could trust such distant communications as this are past. We must assume that every call is monitored, every communication suspect."

Wei Tseng-li nodded. "I, for one, agree."

"Then so be it," Tsu Ma said with a sigh. "We shall arrange a time and place to settle this for good and all. Until then, may the gods preserve you, cousins."

"And you," Li Yuan said, breaking contact.

Tsu Ma was right, of course. It was dangerous for all three of them to meet in person. Extremely dangerous, given the circumstances, but there was no option. He could not go ahead without their consent, and for his scheme to work absolute confidentiality was needed. So they would have to meet. But where? And when?

Li Yuan smiled. The answer was staring him in the face. Tsu Ma's betrothal ceremony! What better opportunity for an informal meeting? Why, they could have it here, at To, and then Karr could look after the security.

Yes, and maybe it would prove a turning point – the first step on the long road to recovery.

Li Yuan nodded to himself, then, taking a brush from the ink stand began to pen a memorandum for his Chancellor.

Karr slipped the coded key into the lock, let the scanner register his retinal imprint then slid the door back quietly, listening for sounds from within.

It was silent. He set down his pack and turned, looking about him. Nothing had changed. Even the smell was how he remembered it. For a moment he closed his eyes. Six months it had been since he's last stood here. Six months.

He slid the door closed then went through. The door to May's room was open. He stood there, looking in, bewitched by the sight that met his eyes.

The three-year-old lay on her back, her mouth open, her legs splayed carelessly in sleep. Beside her lay his wife, his darling Marie, her back to him, her long dark hair spread out upon the pillow.

He felt his heart go out to them both, felt all the longing, the heartache he had suffered, being away from them, well up in him again.

Home. He was home.

He made to step back, when she turned, drowsy-eyed, and looked at him.

"Gregor?" Then, suddenly more awake. "*Gregor!*"

She sat up, rubbing her eyes, then, with a brief glance at her sleeping child, came across to him.

They embraced, long months of denial shaping the passion of their kisses. It was eight weeks since she'd last visited him in Africa.

She drew back, breathless. "Gods I've missed you!"

He stared back at her, her beautiful face only inches from his own, as it was every night in his dreams. "And I've missed you."

"How much?" She reached down, then giggled. "Oh, *that* much, neh?"

He grinned. "Here?"

She shook her head then pulled May's door across. "No. In the shower. I've dreamed of it. Dreamed of you and me in there together."

He laughed. "You think I smell?"

"Like a pig, but I don't care. Come on, I need you right now."

He followed her into the shower unit, his hand never leaving hers. Then they were undressing frantically, his hands caressing her, his eyes drinking in her lovely nakedness.

"Marie... Oh, Marie."

As the water fell, shockingly cold at first and then hot, he entered her, her gasp, the look of pained delight in her eyes making him shudder and come instantly.

"Aiya!" he said, grimacing, pinning her against the wall as he thrust into her again and again and again. And then she was crying out, unable to help herself, pressing against him so tightly it seemed she wanted to breach him. He shuddered, then let his face fall against her shoulder. And still the water fell.

They were still for a moment, silent, and then she reached up and turned his face, making him look at her.

"What's happened?"

He laughed, almost making some wise-crack, then grew serious. "I've a new appointment. A promotion."

Her eyes widened. "A *promotion*? But I thought..."

"No." He laughed. "Not Rheinhardt's job. Not yet, anyway. I'm to be *Ssu-li Hsiao-wei*!"

She frowned. "Colonel of Security? But..." Then she understood. "Li Yuan! You're to be Li Yuan's own colonel!"

He nodded, his smile mirroring that on her face now. "I've to report to him tomorrow. We're moving, my love. Moving to Tongjiang!"

Tsu Ma reined in his horse and leaned forward in the saddle, looking out over the edge of the cliff. Far below him the sea boiled about the dark and jagged rocks as the water sucked back. A moment later the next huge wave crashed against the granite, throwing a fine spray high up the cliff face. The grass beneath his horse's hoofs was slick with salt, the air misted, sharply cold.

He turned and watched as his young nephews caught up with him. Breathless they drew alongside, their horses' heads pulling against the bit, afraid of the drop only a pace or two away. Their finely braided coats steamed in the cold air, their hoofs dragging impatiently at the hard earth after their headlong gallop.

Tsu Ma laughed, seeing how his heirs were watching him uncertainly, their eyes going briefly to the steep drop then returning to his face. They said nothing, yet heir expressions were eloquent.

His brother's sons.

Resting one arm on the pommel, he leaned forward, studying each in turn. The eldest, Tsu Kung-chih was like his father, taller than Tsu Ma and – though only nineteen – broader at the shoulders. His physical presence was misleading, however, for in his features he had inherited all the weaknesses of his maternal grandfather – a certain limpness in the mouth, an absence of muscle in the jaw, a softness to his nose and narrow brow. His eyes – which seldom met those of his uncle – were the eyes of a salesman, calculating but somehow unambitious. Small, petty eyes. All in all it was a face that few would trust – the face of a vassal, not a prince. Seeing that face steeled Tsu Ma in his purpose and made him put all feeling from his heart.

Beside Kung-chih sat a smaller, lither boy, Tao Chu. Tsu Ma smiled as he looked at him and saw how the fifteen year old smiled back, all the while smoothing his horse's neck to calm it.

Tao Chu was very much his mother's son, half-brother to Kung-chih, yet Tsu Ma saw something of himself in the boy. Tao Chu had nothing of his half-brother's awkwardness, but was direct and open – was in every way a natural ruler, a T'ang with a T'ang's generosity of spirt. There was strength in his laughter and power in his smallest, subtlest action – a restrained power that only Tsu Ma seemed to recognise in him. Wing gusted through his fine hair, spilling its neat-cut strands across his brow.

The boy shook his head and looked away a moment. For him this would be a lot easier. He, after all, had never thought to rule. Even so, Tao Chu was fiercely loyal to his undeserving half-brother and would feel this disappointment keenly on his behalf.

Tsu Ma straightened and, raising his voice against the sound of wind and wave, spoke.

"Nephews... I am to be married."

He saw how Kung-chih's face struggled with the words; how he turned to look at Tao Chu, as if the younger boy might explain it to him, but Tao Chu was watching his uncle carefully.

"When?" he asked, and Tsu Ma could see that he had weighed it all at once – as if he had prepared himself for this moment.

Tsu Ma smiled sadly. "The betrothal ceremony is to take place this very week."

Kung-chih was still watching his half-brother, his face stiff with shock. Then, slowly, he turned to face Tsu Ma, the severity of his disappointment open in his face. For a moment he stared back at his uncle, his mouth half open, then, abruptly, he turned his horse and galloped away. Tao Chu stayed a moment longer, then, with a bow to his uncle, he turned his horse and raced after his brother.

Tsu Ma watched until they were tiny figures in the distance, then turned his horse and followed the cliff's edge, staring down at the raging sea.

It was done.

Tsu Kung-chih's dream of inheritance had been shattered. Tsu Ma lifted his face and stopped his mount, looking out across the sea's grey, uneven surface. He had left this too long and now it seemed a kind of cruelty. This marriage would win him few friends in his immediate family.

"Well... so be it," he said softly, the words torn from his lips by the wind.

So be it. But he was determined now. He would do what he had refused to do before this day and settle down; have sons and watch them gro. Sons like Tao Chu, or like his friend Li Yuan. And, in his old age, they would rule in his place; strong, wise, decisive – sons he could be proud of.

Unbidden, a tear came to his eye. Turning away, he forced the horse into a gallop, heading back across the open fields towards the estate, thinking of the one woman he had love.

Of Fei Yen... and of the boy, Han.

Fei Yen stood at the window of her room, watching the imperial cruiser land behind the hangar on the far side of the lake, nervous anticipation making her stomach cramp.

She had sent the letter two days back when she had been at a low ebb. There had been arguments with her eldest brother over her son, Han Ch'in, and then, out of the blue, her latest lover had packed his bags. She had written it only an hour after he had gone, filled with remorse and self-loathing, and had had a messenger deliver it at once. But in the clear light of morning she had panicked, bitterly regretting her action, and praying to the ten thousand gods that he would never see it, never even – perhaps – get to hear of it. But now it was clearly too late. The presence of his cruiser said as much. Now she would know what he thought of her.

She went to her wardrobe and searched for something to wear to greet his messenger. Something simple and yet sophisticated. Something that might suggest she was a woman in control of her life, contented with her lot. She took gown a simple red *chi pao* then put it back. No. Red was the wedding colour – the colour of happiness and celebration. Black, *then? She hesitated a moment, then, realising she hadn't any time, took it down and,* peeling off what she was wearing, hurriedly pulled it on.

There was no time for maids and lengthy preparations. Besides, it was only a messenger. If he was anything like most men he would scarcely notice what she was wearing. Even so...

She stood before the mirror, combing her hair quickly, then put it up in a bun. Yes, that was it. That was the look she was trying for. She smiled, practicing courteous phrases to greet him, hen, satisfied, she turned and hurried from the room.

She met him at the front door, standing dutifully behind her brother as he went through the rituals of greeting.

As he introduced her, she bowed low, making herself the very picture of demureness.

"Well, Tsung Ye," her brother said, inviting the man inside. "How can I be of assistance?"

Tsung Ye, however, stood his ground, a polite smile on his face. "Forgive me, Prince Yin, if I decline your most generous offer, but my instructions are clear. I am to escort your sister, the Princess Yin Fei Yen, back to Tongjiang without delay."

Hearing those words, Fei Yen felt faint. Tongjiang! She had never meant *this* to happen!

He had sent for her. Li Yuan had sent for her.

"You have *instructions*?" Yin Sung asked, puzzled.

"Here, Prince Yin," Tsung Ye said, taking a sealed letter from his pouch and handing it to him.

Yin Sung studied it a moment, noting the Chancellor's wax seal, then broke it open. He read it quickly, then, frowning, handed it to his sister. "Do you know what this is about?"

Fei Yen shook her head, conscious that she was blushing. "I have no idea, brother. Why, I…"

"Forgive me," Tsung Ye interrupted, "but my instructions…"

"Of course."

Yin Sung gave a bow, acknowledging Tsung Ye's status as his Master's messenger, then turned and summoned one of the house servants. "Bring Lady Fei's cloak. She must leave at once."

Then, looking to his sister, he took her arm, speaking more gently than before, "you will tell me if you know me, neh?"

"Yes, eldest brother."

"Good. In the meantime I shall make sure Han Ch'in is well looked after."

She bowed, keeping all the worries she was feeling at that moment – for her son and for herself – from her face.

"Good," he said again. "Then go. Chancellor Nan expects you."

Yes, she thought, letting the servant put her cloak across her shoulders, then hurried down the path after the T'ang's messenger.

The Great Hall at Tongjiang was cold and dimly lit, the huge space between the pillars empty, the flagstones black with age. Torches flicked in iron baskets hung about the walls, the shadows of the pillars wavering like the dancing limbs of giants, but in the centre it was almost dark. There, at that centre point, on a ceremonial chair that had been set down by an honour guard, sat Fei Yen. She had sat there for an hour now, alone in the silence, waiting.

On a narrow balcony overlooking the hall, Pei K'ung looked on from behind a lattice screen, studying the figure in the chair. Her husband had once loved the woman – loved her to the point of distraction… and beyond. If rumour were correct he had once in anger killed all her horses while she, in answer, had told him that the child in her belly was not his.

Pei K'ung gave a small, shuddering sigh. Maybe it was just the time of the month, but for the last few days her emotions had been in turmoil. She had thought herself beyond such juvenile feelings, but it seemed it wasn't so. That feeling she had experienced on reading Fei Yen's note to her husband – she recognised it now. It was jealousy. She was jealous of what this woman had once had with her husband, and afraid – no, terrified – that that feeling still existed between them.

Agitated, she fanned herself then turned away, slipping quietly from the balcony, her servants following after. She was tempted to send the bitch straight home again – but that would solve nothing. She had to speak to her.

And if it was as she feared?

She pictured herself confronting her husband; saw him laugh and turn from her, dismissing her without a word, returning to his men as if she were not there. She shivered, forcing herself to walk on, to show nothing of her inner turmoil. Could she face that? Could she live with that rejection?

Of course she would. After all, that was the deal, wasn't it? To be a wife in name alone, while he…

She stopped dead, her servants almost stumbling over her.

Maybe that was what she should do. Maybe she should put the woman in his bed, to show him that she knew. To prove she was no fool.

Yes, but what if she were wrong? What if her husband *hadn't* been meeting Fei Yen secretly? What if her action proved the beginning of a reconciliation between Fei Yen and he?

She whirled about, heading for her rooms.

No. Li Yuan must not even know she had been here. She must meet the woman and dispense with her. Threaten her, if necessary. After all, it was she who had the power now. She who was Empress.

Yes, but if Li Yuan loves her still...

She stopped, groaning softly, reaching out to steady herself against the wall. At once her servants rushed to her and held her up, as if she were ill, but she brushed them off angrily.

"Leave me be!"

"But Mistress..."

She turned on Tsung Ye, who had spoken, and glared at him. At once he bowed his head low.

"Tsung Ye. Let her sit there another hour, then bring her to my study. And let no one go to her or speak with her. Understand?"

Tsung Ye nodded, then backed away.

She took a long breath, calming herself, then walked on. An hour. She nodded savagely. Yes, let her wait. It would do the bitch good to stew for another hour. In the meantime she would bath and change her clothes. Then she would deal with this matter. Deal with it once and for all.

Fei Yen waited outside the door as Tsung Ye went inside, her mouth dry, her heart racing. It was more than five years since she had last seen Li Yuan, that day in the Great Room at the estate in Hei Shui – the day after his wives had been killed. Then, astonishingly, he had asked her to come back to him; had begged her to try again, but she had sent him away once more, pride and anger, and fear perhaps of his discarding her again, keeping her from saying yes.

The years had passed and no further word had come. Li Yuan had married again, immersing himself in his work. And the Great Wheel had turned, and slowly, very slowly, she had grown older. Older, yes, and ever less content.

Aiya! she thought, looking down at her hands. *What am I doing? What madness brought me here?*

Was it love that had brought her here? Or was it simple bitterness? Bitterness that her dreams had not come true?

"Princess Yin..."

Tsung Ye stood there with his hand on the open door, his head bowed, waiting for her. Swallowing, she brushed her palms against her sides, then stepped past him into the room.

"Yin Fei Yen..."

She heard the door click shut behind her and squinted into the sunlight on the far side of the room, where, behind a huge desk by the window, someone sat.

For a moment she did not recognise the voice. She hesitated, confused that it was not Li Yuan, not understanding what was happening.

"Please, Lady Fei, come closer to the desk."

This time she understood. Pei K'ung! It was his wife, Pei K'ung!

Fei Yen bowed her head then slowly crossed the room, a small knot of fear at the pit of her stomach. Was this *his* doing? Was this his way of humiliating her?

That thought dispelled the fear, replacing it with anger.

She stopped, two paces from the desk, her head held defiantly aloft, her eyes boring into those of the Empress.

"Am I not to see Li Yuan?"

Pei K'ung stared back at her uncompromisingly, her eyes hard, her whole manner stern, like a mother-in-law.

"Li Yuan is not here. He is away on business."

Fei Yen took that in, trying to assess the significance of it. Was that deliberate on his part? Was this all – the summons, the two hour wait, and now this – simply an elaborate snub; his way of getting back at her for her rejection of him? She bristled with anger at the thought and held herself straighter. She was worth ten of this aged fish-wife. Why, if rumour were to be believed, Li Yuan did not even sleep with her. And who could blame him? Ugly was perhaps too strong a word for it, but for certain the woman was plain.

"I am sorry to hear that," she answered, as if it were of no importance. "I had hoped to give him my regards."

Pei K'ung stared at her a moment longer, then looked away, a short, sardonic laugh her only comment.

Fei Yen waited, wondering what this woman wanted – what she had been instructed to do. Whatever it was, she was determined not to be belittled by her. Whatever the woman said, she would give as good as she got. Besides, who knew whether what she had said were true. For all she knew, Li Yuan was in the next room, watching it all.

She studied Pei K'ung a moment, noting the elegant cut of her silks, the sophisticated way she had put up her hair, and wondered if that had been done specially for this meeting. Whatever, they did little to allay the severity of her features. To be frank, there was something almost masculine about the Empress. Her nose was too long, her hands too big, her ears... She almost laughed. Why, without the expensive silks the woman would have looked little better than the coarsest peasant's wife. The thought of it gave her confidence.

"Am I to be granted an audience?"

Pei K'ung looked back at her. "An audience?" Her voice was scathingly dismissive. "No, Lady Fei. This is the closest you will ever get to seeing my husband. I will not allow him to be distracted over such a... *trivial* matter."

The words made Fei Yen reassess the situation. Li Yuan didn't know! He wasn't even aware that she was there, in Tongjiang! Yet if that was the case, why had Nan Ho not summoned her?

Her eyes quickly searched the desk and found what she was looking for. There it was, beside the elaborate jade ink stand. Nan Ho's spare seal. She recognised it from former days.

Fei Yen felt herself go still. She had got it wrong. She had thought Li Yuan himself had summoned her, using his Chancellor as a go-between, but it had been Pei K'ung. For some reason the Empress had wanted to see her face to face. But why? Was it, as she said, to keep her husband from so-called 'trivial' distractions? Or was there another, deeper reason?

She met Pei K'ung's eyes again and laughed. Saw how her laughter lit some inner fuse of anger. Anger, yes, and something else.

"What are you afraid of, Pei K'ung?"

"Afraid?" Pei K'ung's laughter was humourless. "I am not afraid, Yin Fei Yen. Certainly not of you. You forget who you speak to. I am the Empress and my powers..."

"Are your husband's powers. No more, no less. You forget who you speak to. You forget that I once sat where you now sit. Yes, and shared my husband's bed."

She had regretted it as soon as it were uttered, yet she had not been wrong. Pei K'ung had started at the words. Now, her manner much stiffer, she leaned towards Fei Yen.

"Yes, and he *divorced* you. Do you forget *that*, Lady Fei?"

"He was but a boy."

"And wayward, as boys are. He should never have married you. You were his brother's wife."

No more than you are Yuan's she thought to say, but this time something held her back. It was true. If Li Han Ch'in had not been killed, she would be Empress now. If he had not been killed then none of this would have happened. She shivered and looked down.

"What did you want?" Pei K'ung asked after a moment, her voice more neutral than before. "What did you think to achieve after all these years?"

Fei Yden looked up and shrugged, feeling suddenly less hostile towards the woman. Was it her fault Li Yuan had married her? And was it her fault that he preferred to have much younger women in his bed?

"To be honest, I was hoping for some advancement for my son. Han Ch'in is eight now... nine this September... I thought..."

Pei K'ung's answer was blunt. "Is the estate at Hei Shui not enough for you? Nor the pension you and your son receive? Why, considering the circumstances..."

Furious, Fei Yen grasped the edge off the desk and leaned towards the other woman, shouting at her now.

"He owed me that! That and much more. It was *his* neglect, *his* indifference toward me!"

"Yes, and *your* betrayal!"

Fei Yen moved back slightly, shaking her head. "No. He betrayed me, long before I even thought to stray. It was he who cheated me. Cheated me first of my rightful place in his bed, and then of my son's rightful birth-right!"

"His *rightful* birth-right?" Pei K'ung sat back, laughing scornfully. "Why, your son's a bastard, Yin Fei Yen... yes, and no better than any gardener's son, I bet!"

Fei Yen stood up straight, her anger cold now and unforgiving. "If you but knew the truth of it, Pei K'ung." Then she turned and walked slowly, with great dignity, to the door, then looked back at Pei K'ung. "If you but knew."

Pei K'ung sat there after she'd gone, staring at the open door.

Now what in the gods' names had Fei Yen meant by that? *Cheated? How cheated?* No. There had been tests to ascertain the boy's father. Why, if there had been any doubt, Li Yuan would never have divorced her.

Her mouth fell open. No. It wasn't possible. Fei Yen would have contested it.

But what if she hadn't known? What if Li Yuan had kept the knowledge secret?

No. It made no sense. If Han Ch'in *were* Li Yuan's son and Fei Yen had known that – known it for certain – then she would have moved heaven and earth to have him made heir. No mother would have done less. But she had done nothing.

So what *did* Fei Yen mean? Why had she been so angry at the suggestion of her son's low origins?

Mystery. It was all shrouded in mystery. But the truth was in there somewhere and she would find it out.

And Fei Yen?

Fei Yen was beautiful. There was no denying that. Still beautiful enough to turn a prince's head. Or a T'ang's.

Pei K'ung shivered, knowing that for all she had said the matter was far from settled. Far from scaring the Lady Fei away, she had merely made her more determined.

Yes, she thought, but I shall win in the end, for though you are beautiful, Time is on my side. The days, which rob you of your beauty, shall slowly make me indispensable to my husband.

Beauty. Pah! She would show them how littler beauty meant! Why, she could fill her husband's bed with a thousand dumb beauties and still he would depend on her.

She laughed, determined on it, knowing now what had to be done, then rang the bell to summon Tsung Ye, keen to begin the task.

CHAPTER 124

SECRET LANGUAGES

K im?... Kim! Wake up!"

The young man turned, gasping, his left hand reaching for the ceiling, then woke, his dark eyes blinking.

"*Pandra vyth gwres?*"

The Machines' voice answered him, soft, reassuring in the dimly-lit room. "It's Curval. There's an emergency."

Kim sat up, rubbing at his eyes. "What time is it?"

"Four seventeen. Now get dressed. You're needed."

Kim didn't argue. He pulled on his one-piece and went out into the corridor.

Alarms were sounding distantly and he could hear shouts and running feet.

Kim began to run, heading for the source of the sound. At the first turn he almost cannoned into Curval, coming to get him.

"What's happening?"

Curval was breathless. He raked his fingers across his bald pate, getting his breath, then answered. "It's Ravachol. He escaped from his cell. He took one of the guards by surprise. Stole his knife."

"Gods..." Kim thought quickly. "Where's Ravachol now?"

"The guards have got it hemmed in on the far side of the labs. It's been breaking everything it can get its hands on!"

Kim nodded, pained by what he was hearing, then touched Curval's arm.

"Alright. Let's get over there."

They could hear the smashing of glass long before they turned the corner and came out into the main laboratory area. Ravachol was on the far side of the benches, going from one store cupboard to the next, pulling whatever he could from within and hurling it across the floor. A dozen guards crouched behind the nearest benches, stun guns levelled at the android. As Kim came into the room, their captain came across.

"I've done what I can, *Shih* Ward, but it's in danger of damaging itself. Some of the chemicals it's throwing down..."

"I know," Kim said, anxious now that he'd seen how agitated the creature was. Something had pushed it over the edge. Something or someone...

"Ravachol!" he called, walking towards it. "Come now. You've got to stop that."

The android stopped and turned, staring at him, the knife held out threateningly. Kim made to take a further step but the captain grabbed his arm and pulled him back.

"No, Sir. I can't let you. Director Reiss..."

Kim shrugged himself free, but the captain took his arm again, more firmly this time.

"I'm sorry but I've orders, *Shih* Ward. It's too dangerous. If you should be hurt..."

"He's right," Curval said, coming up beside him. "Look at it. It's gone. Look at its eyes. It doesn't even recognise you. It's what we feared. Its neural matrix has destabilised completely."

Kim stared at it. It had been stable this past week, but Curval was right; it had degenerated badly. Even so, he wanted to go to it – to try and reason with it.

"It's dangerous," the captain said. "I've already two men in hospital. If it comes at us, my men have orders to stun it, but that may not be enough. It's very strong and its nervous system may not respond the same way as a human's."

Kim nodded, understanding what the captain was really saying. He didn't want to take any risks. He wanted to kill it, before it did any further damage.

"What else did the Director say?"

"That he'll be here within the hour. Let *him* sort this one out."

Kim shook his head. "No. I can't do that." He sighed, then turned to the

Duty Officer. "Give me your gun, captain. *I* made it. *I'll* destroy it!"

The captain stared at Curval a moment, then un-holstered his pistol and handed it to Kim, who weighed it in his hand for a moment, then, looking directly at the creature, began to walk towards it.

"Ravachol! Do you know who I am?"

It stood there, perfectly still, watching him approach. When Kim was only ten *ch'i* from it, it raised a hand, shielding its eyes, as if it were staring into brilliant sunlight.

"Kim? Is that you?"

"It's me."

It opened its mouth, hesitated, then shook its head. Looking down, it frowned, as if it didn't understand what had caused the mess that surrounded it. Its feet were leaking blood and there was a faint sparking down one side, the slightest hint of burning.

"It's growing dark," it said, looking back at Him, bewildered. "I can't..."

It seemed to freeze, then, with a tiny jerk, began to move again. Its eyes blinked violently, his left hand juddered, dropping the knife.

"You're not well," Kim said quietly. "You keep forgetting."

It nodded, but it was as if it only half understood. Curval was right. It had gone. There was nothing they could do for it now. Nothing but end its misery.

Kim raised the gun.

"What are you doing?" it asked tonelessly. "What is that?"

Release, Kim thought, and pulled the trigger.

The detonation shocked him. It was much louder than he'd imagined. He stared at his hand, then traced a line to where Ravachol had been standing. He was gone. No, he was down, there beside the bench. Kim stepped closer, then stood over the creature, setting the gun down beside it.

Where the bullet had hit its chest was a jagged hole through which a strange amalgam of wiring and organic matter could be glimpsed, silver and pinkish red. Locked into some obsolete programme, its left leg made climbing movements in the air, while its eyes stared straight ahead. The smell was stronger now – the scent of burnt plastic mixed with burning flesh.

Kim crouched over it, pained by the sight, wanting to hold the thing and comfort it in its final moments, but something stopped him. It wasn't dying. You couldn't say that it was dying for it had never really been alive. It had only *seemed* alive. But for once, that distinction seemed meaningless. Ravachol had been more than a machine – more than a simple thing of wires and flesh.

Kim hesitated, then, conscious that the others were watching him, put his hand out and brushed the hair back from the android's forehead,

It was warm, just as a dying man was warm. And all its memories...

Even as the thought formed, Ravachol's eyes blinked and snapped shut. There was a tiny tremor through the body then it was still.

Gone. But where? Where did the soul of a machine depart to?

The thought disturbed him. Darkened his thought. For just as he was conscious of having made Ravachol, so he was conscious that something – some force or creature greater than himself – had fashioned *him*. For the first time, he had a strong, clear sense of it.

Copies, he thought, nodding to himself. *We are all copies of some greater thing.*

He stood, then walked back to where Curval was waiting.

"Are you alright?"

Kim shrugged. "I don't know. I'm not even sure if I want to think about it."

Curval smiled sadly. "Maybe you should take the day off. Have a break from it."

"No. We have to begin again. This morning. I want the body in the autopsy room by seven. We can take scans, slices – find out what went wrong. And next time..." Kim took a shivering breath. "Next time, we get it right."

Curval nodded, then briefly touched his arm. "Okay. I'll get things moving straight away."

At first light Emily went down to the market on Fifty-One, walking through the echoing openness of Main as stallholders set up their barrows and old men sat on benches listening to the caged birds sing.

It was the time of day she liked best, the time when anything seemed possible. Each day was new, filled with possibility, and no matter how many times she had been disappointed, she had always welcomed the dawn, fake as it was.

Yu I, the proprietor, saw her and came across, smiling his gap-toothed smile and bowing to her, as if she were a princess, his hands tucked into his voluminous sleeves.

"Ra-chel," he said, his old eyes twinkling playfully. "It is a long time since you come."

"I've been busy, *Lao jen*. I only came back last night. But I've missed this place. Your *ch'a* is renowned for fifty stacks."

Yu I bowed again, delighted by her compliment. "And what will you have, *Nu Shih*? A Sparrow Tongue, perhaps? Or a water fairy?"

She smiled broadly. "A T'ieh Lo-han would be nice, Master Yu. A large *chung*. And some *chiao tzu* if you have any."

"*Nu Shih*..." He nodded, then backed away, hurrying off to fill her order.

From rails overhead more cages hung – elaborate things of painted wire. She looked up at them, listening to the birds, watching a tiny chaffinch puff out his chest. How he sang, that small bird – so full of joy... or was it avian pride?

She smiled, then sat back, looking about her from her high vantage point.

At a nearby table, a young shaven-headed boy sat beside his grandfather. He was staring at her in that pure, unembarrassed way children have, his dark eyes big and round. Emily smiled at him then looked away.

Pockets of normality... that was what it was all reduced to these days. Brief moments – like this – of sanity before the mayhem began again.

A young waiter came across, setting a pale lavender *chung* beside her. He produced a rounded ball and polished it on his sleeve before setting it before her.

"Thanks."

The young man nodded and turned away. Apart from Yu I, few talked to her here. They were mainly Han, she *Hung Mao*, a big-nose barbarian. So it was these days. Tolerance was the most she might expect.

She poured, then lifted the mock-porcelain bowl, cupping it in both hands, enjoying its warmth, the strong scent of the "Iron Goddess of Mercy," reminding her of her youth – of those times she had sat beside her father in places like this while he talked with his friends.

Was that why she came here? To renew that simple memory? To keep in touch with that earlier, kinder self. Or was it for the peace she found here and nowhere else?

She sighed, then took a long sip of the *ch'a*, swilling it about her mouth as the Han did, enjoying the simplicity of it.

The great world changed, yet these smaller, simpler things persisted.

Small things.

Emily nodded to herself, thinking of the horrors she had seen, the deaths she had been witness to. Yes, though Empires fell, small things – those intensely human things – remained unchanged. A thousand years might pass and great Emperors turn to dust in their tombs, but still in some small tea-house in some corner of the world the old men would meat beneath the caged songbirds and sip *ch'a* and talk away the day.

The thought brought her comfort. Yesterday she had gone to see the gutted deck, had seen with her own eyes just how cruel and indiscriminate the White T'ang's justice was.

The bastard! She thought, remembering the stink of the place, the pictures she had seen from the leaked security video. It had been awful, unbearable to watch. But necessary. For now, she knew for certain that there was no option. She had to kill him. *Had to.* For the sake of them all. The only question now was how.

She sipped once more, then set the bowl down. Yu I was coming across again, a large plate of the delicious dumplings in one hand, a small bowl of spicy sauce in the other.

"*Chiao tzu,*" he said, grinning at her again. "If there is anything else, *Nu Shih?*"

"No, *Lao jen,* that's fine." And she handed him a ten *yuan* chip and closed his hand about it. "Buy your grandson something."

Yu I grinned, nodding his thanks.

Alone again, she picked up one of the meat-filled dumplings with her chopsticks, savouring the delicious smell of it. As with the *ch'a,* this too was part of the ritual – this too she had first tasted with her father.

So it began, she thought, suddenly heavy of heart. *Yes, and so, perhaps, it ends.*

Killing Lehmann, Some said it was impossible. Only nothing was impossible. She laughed and took a second dumpling from the plate, dipping it in the sauce, then popped it into her mouth, enjoying the mixture of pork, cabbage, and onion, even as she thought the problem through.

No. Killing him would not be hard – what was impossible was surviving the attempt.

She cleared the plate then sat back. It had been good. She had forgotten how good. She turned, meaning to order another plate – to indulge herself for once – and saw that Yu I and his waiters were gathered beneath one of the big media screens, staring up at it.

From where she sat, she couldn't make out what the picture was, but after a moment a small cheer went up from the men, their faces suddenly lit up and laughing.

Yu I, seeing her, came across again. "You want more, *Nu Shih?*"

She handed him a five *yuan* chip. "Yes, but tell me... what was all that about? You seemed very excited."

The old man grinned and nodded, his delight evident. "It was good news, *Nu Shih*. Very good news indeed. It seems the great T'ang, Tsu Ma, is to be married."

The announcement was a simple one. *Liang K'o Ting chih nu Shu-sun lin wei Luang-hou* – "Shu Sun, daughter of Liang K'o Ting, is hereby created Empress."

The imperial rescript was read out on the media channels and posted throughout the levels of City West Asia.

At Tsu Ma's palace at Astrakhan, there was a small ceremony. The prospective bride's father, Liang K'o Ting, approached Tsu Ma and knelt, pressing his forehead to the floor. Tsu Ma looked down at him from his throne and smiled, watching as he went through the *san kuei chiu k'ou* – the three kneelings and nine strikings of the head that was required before a Son Of Heaven.

As Old Liang straightened up, Tsu Ma looked past him at Shu Sun, wondering how such a stick of a man had bred such a voluptuous daughter.

Shu Sun noticed his attention and let her head fall slightly, blushing. She was eighteen years old and fresh as a peach. Just looking at her made his blood race, and when she looked up at him and smiled...

He turned his attention to Old Liang again. The man was thanking him for the honour of elevating his daughter to the imperial dignity. He listened, hearing the old man out, then bestowed on him the button of First Rank, given by right to the *hou-fu*, the father of the Empress, appointing him an officer of the imperial bodyguard. And then it was done, the great Family seals placed upon the betrothal agreement, all speeches made.

There was laughter and raised glasses, yet at the back of the Hall, unnoticed by Tsu Ma or his future in-laws, a young man slipped away, crossing the Great Hall swiftly, silently.

At the doorway, Tsu Kung-chih turned, looking back at the smiling group surrounding the throne, his eyes burning with resentment. Then, his face set, his right hand gripping the handle of his dagger, he strode out and ran down the echoing corridors to his rooms, slamming the door behind him.

Tsu Tao Chu reined in his pony at the cliff's edge and sat forward in the saddle, looking out across the calm sea's surface. Shen, his mount, moved his long head restlessly, then bent to crop.

The youth reached down to smooth its long, sleek neck before straightening up again, sighing heavily, thinking of the ceremony that morning. It was here, only a week ago, that Tsu Ma had spoken to them. Here that his half-brother, Kung Chih's sickness had begun.

He dismounted, then sat at the cliff's edge, his legs dangling over the drop. Far below, the water slopped over and around the tips of jagged rocks. It was high tide and the sluggish movement of the current seemed like the shallow breath of a sleeper. The water was thick and glassy green and the dark, vague shapes of rocks beneath the surface seemed more like shadows than hard realities. Tao Chu took a handful of stones from the bare patch of earth beside him and sprinkled them over the edge, watching the diffuse pattern of ripples spread on the rising, falling back of the water.

He looked down at himself. Dust was spattered across his knee-high boots. He raised a leg to brush the earth from the dark leather, bracing a heel against a large, up-jutting stone. Then, taking a white silk handkerchief from the pocket of his riding jacket, he spat on it and began to rub the shine back into the leather. He had just leaned forward to breathe on it when the stone moved, and he tilted forward.

There was no time to save himself. Where his foot had been the cliff had fallen away and he found himself tumbling headfirst toward the water, his arms flailing the air. He made a sound, more of surprise than fear, then hit the surface hard, all breath knocked from him, the sudden, shocking coldness of the water making him gasp and try to take a watery breath, but some flicker of reason made him choke back the instinct.

He struggled upward, his mind dark, in turmoil, his lungs on fire, a searing pain in his side, then broke water, coughing violently, and, floundering against a rock, held on for dear life, the waves washing over him.

It was some while before he came fully to his senses. He was still coughing and the pain in his side had grown worse. His teeth were chattering now, and he realised that if he didn't get to shore soon he would die from exposure. He turned in the water, trying to make out where best to swim for, but as he did the pain grew so severe he had to close his eyes, almost blacking-out.

Carefully he felt beneath the waterline, tracing the wound tenderly with his fingers. He shuddered. It was bad. Very bad. But he wasn't helping himself by staying here. Gritting his teeth, bracing himself against the pain he knew would come, he began to swim, leaning over to one side, doing a kind of lop-sided doggy-paddle that took the strain off his injured side.

Several times on that long and painful swim he thought of giving up, of relaxing and letting himself be sucked down beneath the surface of the cold, clear water, but something kept him from succumbing to that, kept him doggedly pressing on, until, at last, he crawled up onto the beach, the outward wash forming long ribbons of silver laced with red at the side of his legs. Slowly, feeling close to exhaustion now, he pulled himself up out of the water, then turned to examine the gash properly.

The wound looked smaller than it had felt, and not so deep. Miraculously it had missed the bone. The rock had sliced into the flesh of his left-side between the edge of the pelvis and the outer cage of the ribs. The sea water had washed it clean and the flow of blood from it had eased.

He had been lucky. Very, very lucky.

For the first time in what seemed an eternity, Tao Chu smiled. Somehow he had missed the rocks. Somehow, he had fallen between those hard, cruel points of darkness. As he rested there, taking long, sweet breaths of the salty air, a sense of elation, of pure joy at having survived his own stupidity, washed over him.

He laughed.

He was still laughing when a call came from the rocks overlooking the small bay he had swum to. Awkwardly, still in some pain, he turned and looked. Three men, servants of his uncle, were standing there. One of them waved, calling out his reassurances as they began to hurry down the slanting, rock-strewn face towards him.

Tao Chu let them lift him and carry him carefully back to the cliff's summit. There one of them examined the wound again, wincing to himself, and removed his jacket, tearing it into strips which he then bound about Tao Chu. Then they began to carry him again, hurrying now. They were halfway across the long, flat stretch of grass that led to the orchards when Tao Chu saw his mount.

"Stop!"

They set him down, then made some small murmurs of protest when he told them to catch and bring his pony. There was a moment's muttering between them, then one of them scurried off and, after some trouble, brought the reluctant, skittish pony back.

Tao Chu stared at the beast, delighted. "Now help me mount her," he ordered, struggling up into a sitting position.

This time there was open protest from the men, but Tao Chu insisted, his voice taking on the tone of command. The three men looked among themselves again, then shrugged. One held the horse steady while the others helped Tao Chu into the saddle.

Fresh blood stained the bindings at his side, but Tao Chu felt strangely better now that he was mounted. He smiled fiercely, doing his sixteen-year-old best to ignore the pain that was now a horribly nagging ache. Seated thus he let them lead him on, one drawing the horse by its harness while the other two walked either side of him, ensuring he did not fall, their hands supporting him in the saddle.

Coming into the courtyard of his uncle's palace, he saw his half-brother, Kung-chih over by the stables. He made to call tom him, then stopped, frowning. Kung-chih was standing with his back to him, talking to a small, bald-headed man.

Kung's presence in the stables was not unusual, nor was the fact that he was talking to a servant, but this servant was neither groom nor stable-hand, he was Hwa Kwei, one of Tsu Ma's most trusted men, the Chief Steward of his bedchamber. What was the eunuch doing talking to Kung-chih? And why here, in the stables? Kung-chih made a furtive gesture with one hand and Hwa Kwei scuttled away. Then Kung-chih himself strode purposefully across the cobbled space and into a side door, far from the one Hwa Kwei had taken.

Concerned, Tao Chu looked down at the men surrounding him, but they seemed to have noticed nothing. He grimaced, the pain starting up again more fiercely than before.

"Help me down," he said quietly.

When Kung-chih came to see him later, Tao Chu said nothing of what he'd seen. Tsu Ma was sitting in the room with them, concerned for his favourite nephew. Tao Chu had told him everything, omitting nothing, and had seen his uncle frown and then laugh with pride as he told him about mounting his horse and riding home.

"That is indeed how a prince should act!" Tsu ma had said, delighted. "And do not worry, Tao Chu, I shall not punish the men for your obstinacy!"

But Kung-chih was quieter, somewhat less attentive than he might usually have been. He had said little since that day on the cliff tops – had made no threats nor shown any disrespect to Tsu Ma. He had been kind, almost his old self, yet in small ways he had changed. He no longer confided in Tao Chu, no longer shared his hopes and fears with his young half-brother. He had become insular and broody and subject to sudden moods. Seeing him with Hwa Kwei had therefore awoken Tao Chu's suspicions. He was sure that Kung-chih was up to something.

"How are you, little brother?" Kung-chih asked on entering the room. "I hear you have been swimming."

It was an attempt at the old banter that had once existed between them, but now it fell strangely flat.

"I was stupid," Tao Chu said, sighing. "I ought to be dead. I'll not be so lucky twice in my life!"

The comment was no meant to carry any other meaning, yet as Tao Chu looked up into his brother's face, he saw how Kung-chih's eyes moved away sharply, as if stung by the words. There was a momentary sourness in his expression, but then he looked back at Tao Chu and, softening, smiled. "Still... I'm glad you're safe"

Are you? Tao Chu thought, seeing that all-too-familiar face in a different light, as if with new-created eyes; seeing the softness, the weakness there. But it was an unworthy, uncharitable thought and he felt guilty, knowing that, for all his half-brother's self-preoccupation, his love was genuine enough. Reaching out, he took his hand and pressed it gently.

"I know," he said, and in his mind added, *because you need me, Tsu Kung-*

chih, *Need me to save you from yourself. To keep you from falling.*

That was, if it wasn't already too late.

Jelka looked up from the screen and rubbed at his eyes. She had been working on the tapes most of the day, selecting and editing those parts he'd find of interest, determined that she would finally get them done.

She had frozen the tape at an image of Titan she had taken when they'd been heading back on the *Meridian*. The orange surface of the moon was hazed in cloud, the dark red collar in its northern hemisphere showing up strongly. Beyond it, seeming to spear it, Saturn's rings swept in a glorious arc through the star-spattered blackness, the great gas giant itself just out of shot. The sight of it had taken her back to that moment, sending a strange thrill through her.

If only you could have been there with me, Kim. If only you could have seen it as I saw it.

She turned, looking across at the picture of her in her spacesuit taken on the steps of the *Meridian*. It was strange how comfortable she had felt in it – odd how something in her had responded to the icy cold of the outer planets.

She turned back, stretching, nodding to herself, then took a print of the image. She would have it blown up and hung on the wall behind her desk. The rest... the rest was for Kim.

She let the film run, listening to her own voice as she repeated for the camera what she had been told, facts and figures flowing from her tongue effortlessly. This was the last of them – the last of a dozen eight-hour tapes she had compiled for him from what had been months of material.

For almost a year now she had spent at least an hour a day preparing them, but now they were almost done. Another few hours at most.

And then?

She wasn't sure. Wasn't sure whether to send them or hand them over herself. After all, what if he had forgotten her? What if there was someone else?

Titan receded slowly, the bulk of Saturn moving into shot, dwarfing the tiny moon, the swirling striations of its northern hemisphere filling the screen. It was beautiful Breath-taking. She let it run, knowing that whatever else happened, he, at least, would get to share this much of her experience.

So small our world is. Like a tiny speck of dust in a vast, echoing hall.

Slowly the image of Saturn shrank, slowly the darkness filled the screen again. She shivered, frightened by the sheer intensity of her feelings.

He had promised he would wait. Seven years, he'd said. Seven years.

There was a knock. She leaned forward and pressed HOLD, then turned back to face the door.

"Come in!"

"Jelka?"

Her father took a step into the room and looked about him. "Can you spare me a few moments?"

"Sure." She turned back, pressed SAVE, then blanked the screen. She could finish it later.

"How's Pauli?" she asked, going across to him and kissing his cheek.

Tolonen grinned. "Oh, he's fine. He's resting now. That new tutor of his makes him work. Sometimes I wonder if he's not a bit too hard on the child."

"He's a good boy," she said, taking his arm and leading him out of the room. "And a bit of discipline won't harm him, will it? You forget how strict my tutors were with me."

"I guess so. But then, you were always a tough one. Headstrong, too." He laughed. "Still are, I guess."

They went into his study. While he sat, she walked about the room, picking books from the shelves, then putting them back.

"So what is it?"

He looked up from his papers and grunted. "Just, er... a few details to sort out. For the party."

"Ah..."

The invitation to Kim – that was what this was about. Steeling herself, she went across and sat, facing him across the desk.

"Here." He took a small pile of bright red envelopes from his tray and handed them to her. "You'd better check them before they go out."

She took them, nodding to him, afraid to look.

"I was wondering about the music," he said. "I've booked the *Chi L'ing* Ensemble. I've been told they are very good. But maybe you feel they're a bit too... conventional."

She would have laughed, but for the tension in the pit of her stomach.

"It's all right," she answered, her voice small. The *Chi L'ing* will be fine.

His smile was business like. "Good.... Then that's settled."

She stared at him, trying to read his face, while her fingers sorted through the pile, counting the cards. Eleven. There were only eleven. But she had made twelve additions to the list. She wetted her lips, then spoke.

"There's one missing."

"Pardon?" He looked at her, then, understanding, gave a brief laugh. "Oh, I see... Old Joss Hawkins is dead, I'm afraid. Died a good eight, nine months back. I thought you'd heard."

She stared at him, mouth open, then looked down, flicking through the envelopes.

There! Six down. She stared at her father's handwriting on the envelope, surprised. "Kim Ward" it said, then gave his address at the SimFic labs. She looked up again. "I thought..."

"You thought?"

She shook her head. "It doesn't matter."

"Good, Then let's look at the catering. I've been thinking that maybe we should change a few things."

After she'd gone, Tolonen sat there deep in thought. It was just as he'd suspected. No... as he'd *feared*. He had seen it in her face. He had thought it finished with, but it wasn't. She was still obsessed with the Clayborn – still determined on being with him.

He sighed, then sat back, steepling his fingers beneath his nose.

Rich or not, genius or not, it could not be countenanced. His daughter and a Clayborn! No, it was unthinkable. His family would be a laughingstock, his daughter's chances at a real marriage destroyed for all time. He had to do something. Defying her was no good – he knew that now. But there were other ways.

He sat forward and pulled his diary towards him, opening it at that day's entry. The card he had been given lay there where he had left it. He picked it up and stared at it, then, grimacing, drew the comset across to him and tapped in the number.

It rang once, twice, a third time.

I'll try later, he thought, about to put it down. But then the signal changed and a voice answered him.

"Hello... Madam Peng here...Can I help you?"

He cleared his throat. "Madam Peng... it's Marshal Tolonen here. A friend of mine gave me your number, I... I have a problem I hope you can help me with."

Kim stepped from the sedan and looked about, taking in the breath-taking opulence of the place. The Mansion was a big, three-storey building in the Han style with sloping tiled roofs, but the gardens too were expansive, with a small river and an orchard on the far side of an ornamental bridge. Fake clouds drifted slowly across the blue of the ceiling, fifty *ch'i* overhead, while the walls gave views of distant mountains. He had seen its like before, but he had never thought to own such a place.

Reiss had called him just over an hour back and told him to go and see it. If he liked it, it was his, whether he signed the new deal or not. If not, well, there would be others.

"*Shih* Ward!"

He turned as a middle-aged Han in dark green business silks strode towards him down the gravel path.

"I am Chang. ... Hiugh Chang from Supernal Property." He bowed and shook Kim's hand at one and the same time, then turned, indicating the Mansion. "Beautiful, isn't it? It's rare for one of these really big Mansions to come on the market, but Director Reiss asked me to look out for something and notify him first. So here we are. I understand you're interested in acquiring something *special*."

Kim stared at the man a moment, irritated by his bullish, over-familiar manner, then answered him.

"I haven't really thought about it."

"But I thought..."

"Just show me," Kim said, moving toward the house. "I want straight answers to my questions. And don't try to persuade me to buy it. If I like it, I like it. If not..."

He swept past Chang, imagining the look the man gave him behind his back. But right now, he didn't care. It had been a bad day – a very bad day so far – and even this could not really lift his spirits. Losing Ravachol had been a body-blow, and though he had set to the task again at once, it was more to disguise his feeling of loss, of alienation from the task at hand, than to seriously solve the problems that had come up.

The truth was, he felt like giving it all up. Like calling Reiss back and saying no, keep your Company, I want none of it. At the same time, he recognised that it was only a passing mood, and that however bad he felt now he would feel better in a day or two. Well enough, perhaps, to start anew.

As he approached the huge double doors to the main house, two guards stepped forward to bar his way, then backed away hurriedly as Chang waved them aside.

"Security is tight, as you see," the man said, coming alongside Kim as they went into the shadowy hallway. "There are six guard towers in the wall and special security barriers at both lifts – as you saw on the way in. We've recently installed a special electronic tracking system for the perimeter walls and emergency seal doors inside the house itself."

Kim glanced at him, surprised. "Is that normal?"

Chang shrugged. "You know how it is these days. No one's safe. Not even up this high. Not unless they've got all this stuff."

"And the people who owned this?"

"They took great precautions. In the eight years they were here there wasn't a single breach of security."

"So what happened to them? Did they get tired of living like this? Or did they buy something even bigger?"

"Like... a stack?" Chang laughed, then grew serious again. "No. You want a straight answer, right?"

"Right."

"Okay... They were killed. Butchered in their sedan. They'd gone to a charity ball run by that new group, you know, the New Conscience Movement. Seems like they were targeted. A terrorist cell took them in their lift coming up. The death by a thousand cuts. Very messy, so I'm told."

Kim nodded, sobered by the story. He looked to the right up the broad main stairs, then turned, looking through to the kitchens. It was all very dour and ostentatious. It simply trumpeted its wealth, Moreover, the place was huge. One could have a hundred children here and still not fill it. Even so, it didn't have to stay like this. With a little imagination he could make something of it – turn part of it into a research centre, another of the wings into a lab complex. After all, money was no object now. He could do pretty much as he wanted.

Yes, he thought, *but what would Jelka say? What does she want?*

For a moment the absurdity of his situation almost made him laugh. Here he was, looking at a First Level Mansion – a place worth, what? A hundred, a hundred and fifty million *yuan?* – that was his, gratis, if he said yes, and the only thing stopping him was whether a young woman he hadn't seen in seven years – and who he couldn't be sure even remembered him – would like to live there.

He huffed out a breath, exasperated with himself, then looked at Chang again.

"Okay, I'll take it. But I want to make changes. That's possible, I assume?"

Chang beamed. "As far as we're concerned, *Shih* Ward, you can burn the place down and start again from scratch. What you pay for is the deck itself. The Mansion... He made a dismissive gesture. You could replace this for... oh, twenty million?"

"As little as that, huh?"

Chang nodded, unaware, it seemed, of the irony in Kim's voice. "Naturally, should you wish to make changes, we could put you in touch with the very best construction technicians. Craftsmen, they are. Why..."

"Thank you, Chang, but I think I've seen enough. Draw up the papers and send them to Director Reiss. If I wish to see the place again I'll know who to speak to, neh?"

Chang smiled, then handed Kim his card. "Just press the reverse and it'll put you in direct contact."

Kim studied it with a professional interest, then pocketed it. He was about to turn away, when it came back to him what he'd meant to ask earlier.

"By the way... about the previous owners. What group was it that attacked them?"

The smile went from Chang's face. "It was the hand. The Black Hand. No one else is so audacious. Why, I'm told..."

He stopped, realising he had overstepped the mark, then bowed. "Forgive me, *Shih* Ward. I don't want to keep you."

Kim nodded, then walked out and across to his sedan. Yet as he climbed inside, he was thinking of all he'd heard recently. There was no doubting it, they were living in troubled times. Society had changed. Once it had been driven by the simple mechanics of the levels – of aspiration and demotion.

Life had been a giant game of snakes and ladders. But now... now society was fear driven. All of these guns and guards and laser-tracking devices were signs of a deeply paranoid culture. So paranoid that it was now quite normal to assume the worst – to assume that your enemies would come and get you in your bed.

Or your sedan...

He sat, feeling suddenly heavy-boned and tired. Paranoia... it was the philosophy of the Clay, of the place from which he'd come. Upwards he'd climbed and ever upwards, until he'd found himself here, at the very top of the City, beneath the roof, like a bird in the loft of an old house, fluttering about, trying to get out. But there was no way out. And slowly, very slowly, the darkness was climbing after him. Up and up it came. And what guns and trackers would keep it out? What precautions would ever be enough?

As the sedan lifted, he sat back, shaking his head angrily.

It was Ravachol's death that had made him think all this. That and Chang's foolish prattling. So a few rich people had died... hadn't that always been that way? Wasn't history filled with such instances? Yes, but that made it no more comforting, for the signs were clear- there for the dullest man to read.

The sedan shuddered slightly, then began its swaying motion.

Li Yuan was right. They had to act now or go under. But what action could prevent the coming crisis? What measures might assure their children's futures?

Yes. That was the nub of it. For what was the point in loving someone – in pursuing and marrying them – if it were all to come to nothing? If society were to crumble away and the species end itself in a frenzy of bloodlust?

Why take the risk of loving and having children when the risks were so high, the rewards of love so tentative? Why make oneself a hostage to the times?

Because you have no choice, Kim Ward. Because you love her and want her and... and because if you don't try, you'll never forgive yourself.

And because nothing else mattered. Nothing.

"Rachel?"

Emily gave a little start then turned, regaining her composure. For a second, she had forgotten who she was – had been thrown by the use of her assumed name. She had been daydreaming: thinking about Michael and wondering where he was, what he was doing.

"What is it?" she asked half-challengingly, staring back at the tall, pock-faced *Hung Mao* who stood there, an arm's length from her.

Pasek smiled coldly, then moved past her, looking out from the balcony across the ragged awnings, the packed mass of unwashed and shabby humanity that crowded the floor between the stalls, dismissing what he saw.

"I thought we ought to talk."

She felt her stomach muscles tighten with aversion. "Talk?"

"Sure. We need to clear the air between us."

She fell silent, uncertain what to say.

Pasek's smile was like a sneer. "You don't like me, Rachel DeValerian. I know that. I can see it even now. But that doesn't matter. What matters is that we don't let it get in the way of things."

"I don't see..."

He raised his pale, thin hand, interrupting her. "There are going to be changes."

She stared at the dark leather band about his wrist. On it was a copy of the symbol he wore on a silver chain about his neck. A cross within a circle.

"Changes?"

His smile evaporated. The eyes were brutal now.

"It's already happening. A purge. Those we can't trust. I've ordered it."

"You..."

She fell silent, understanding. He had had Chou Te-hsing killed. Yes, and all his deputies. All except her. She looked up, meeting his eyes. "Why?"

"Because it was time. We were drifting. We needed a new direction. Chou had no idea. He had to go."

She nodded, not because she agreed, but because she saw it all clearly now – saw why he'd pressed to have his men placed in key strategic positions; why he'd held his tongue in the last council meeting, when Chou had spelt out the new programme.

You planned this, he thought, all of her instincts about the man confirmed in an instant. He'd known then that it didn't matter what Chou said or didn't say at that meeting; knew then that, come this morning, Chou would be dead, his power base in the Black Hand destroyed. Pasek had taken over. He *was the Black Hand.*

"What do you want?"

His hand went to the cross hanging about his neck. "I want you to join us. Become one of the sealed."

She made to answer him, but he spoke over her. "Oh, I know you don't believe. That doesn't matter. Not now, anyway. Right now what matters is that we consolidate. Make sure the hand doesn't tear itself apart. There'll be a lot of ill feeling. Chou had a lot of support at grass root level. People respected him. Wrongly, as it turns out, but that's by the by. As for you, Rachel, you're respected too. Rightly so. I've watched you for a long time and I like what I've seen. There are no illusions about you. You get on with things. It's as if you've seen it all before. Nothing shocks you. Even this. I saw how quickly you understood how things stood – how quickly you accepted the situation – and I like that. I'd be sorry to lose you."

She felt a faint shiver, not of fear, but aversion, ripple through her. "So that's it, is it? I join you – become one of the sealed – or I die?"

He shook his head. "If I wanted you dead, you'd be dead. No. It has to be your choice. If you choose not to work with me you can go into exile. Africa, maybe, or Asia."

"And if I stay?"

"You get to help formulate policy."

She laughed, astonished, then frowned, searching his eyes for some kind of explanation. "I don't get it. I want what Chou wanted."

"No. I've *watched* you at those meetings. I've *seen* the doubt in your face, the frustration at some of the decisions. You want what I want. Not all of it, but enough for us to work together. To make the Black Hand not just another shitty little faction but a genuinely important force. A force for change. You want that. I know you do. I've seen it in your eyes."

Emily looked away. It was true. The last eighteen months had been nothing *but* frustration. But to work with Pasek... It was on her lips to say no, to tell him to go to hell, but something stopped her.

"I need to think about it."

He looked her up and down, then nodded. "Okay. Twenty-four hours. That's all I can give you. We're meeting at noon tomorrow. At the White Mantis. If you're with me, be there. If not... well, good luck."

She watched him go. Saw his tall, spiderish figure vanish into the crowd, then shivered, chilled by this sudden turn in events, Twenty-four hours. It wasn't long. And if she *didn't* turn up?

She didn't know. For once her instincts failed her.

Well? She asked herself, sighing heavily. *What are you going to do?*

She turned, placing her hands on the rail of the balcony, leaning her full weight on them as she looked across the crowded marketplace. She knew what she wanted – at least, she thought she did. But Pasek... could she work with Pasek?

Twenty-four hours. It wasn't long. But maybe that was how it always was.

Emily pushed away from the rail, then turned, hurrying away, pushing through the crowded corridor urgently, hastening toward her room, conscious of the seconds ticking away.

Tao Chu looked round the door into his half-brother's suite of rooms, then took a step inside. "Kung-chih?" he called softly. "Are you there, brother?"

The study was in shadow, the last of the evening's light blocked off by the closed slats of the huge window. On the far side of the room, the door to his brother's bedroom was open. Tao Chu went across, one hand pressed to the bandage at his side.

"Kung-chih?"

There was no answer. The room was empty, the bed made up. Tao Chu turned, looking back into the study wondering where Kung-chih could have got to.

A sharp pain stabbed through him, taking his breath. Making his way across slowly, he eased into his brother's chair and sat there until the pain had subsided.

He looked down. There was fresh blood on the bandage. Surgeon Tung would be angry with him and would no doubt speak to his uncle, but that didn't matter right now – he had to speak to Kung-chih. To find out what was going on.

"Curse him," he said quietly, his anxiety for his beloved half-brother outweighing any concern he had for himself. "Curse his stupid pride!"

He leaned forward, searching the desktop with his eyes, looking for some clue as to where he might be, but there was nothing. Kung-chih was probably out walking in the grounds somewhere – in the orchards, maybe – or riding in the woods to the south of the palace.

Brooding, probably. Yes, he'd seen the way he had looked at their uncle,

Ma; seen the resentment in his eyes, the hurt. But Kung-chih had to come to terms with that. His life – his expectations – had changed and he must live with that. He could not more about forever.

He was about to get up and return to his room when he heard voices outside, coming closer. His brother's voice and...

Tao Chu frowned, surprised. It was Hwa Kwei again – Tsu Ma's Chief Steward of the Bedchambers. What in the gods' names was Kung-chih doing talking to him twice in one day?

There was a murmured exchange, a curt dismissal, and hen Kung-chih came into the room. He switched on the lamp, and turned, then stopped dead, his mouth open, seeing Tao Chu there at his desk. For a moment there was a look of guilty shock on his face, then anger.

"Tao Chu! Why aren't you in your bed? And what the hell are you doing here?"

"I..."

Kung-chih came and stood over him, glaring at him fiercely. "Did Uncle Ma send you to spy on me? Is that it?"

Tao Chu shook his head, hurt by the accusation, but Kung-chih went on.

"Why, you fucking little sneak! I thought I could trust you, but just as soon as my back's turned you were in here, weren't you? Poking about to see what you could find! But you won't find anything, *brother*!"

Find what? He wanted to ask, but the question made no sense. He hadn't come here to poke about, he'd come here to talk to him, to warn him about associating with the likes of Kwa Wei.

He closed his eyes, the ache in his side suddenly worse, but Kung-chih went on, his voice savage now, unrelenting. "You little worm! You snivelling little worm! All those words of consolation and all the while you're fucking lapping it up. That's the truth, isn't it? You loved seeing Tsu Ma humiliate me. You just loved it!"

"No..." Tao Chu said, crying now, unable to believe that this was Kung-chih talking to him this way. What had he done – what had he ever done – to deserve this?

"Fuck off! Go on, just fuck off! Next time I find you poking around my rooms I'll kick you from here to Africa!"

Slowly, every movement an effort, Tao Chu pulled himself up. For a moment he stood there, swaying, his vision swimming, then it came clear again. Kung-chih stood there close by, less than an arm's length from Tao Chu, yet so far away it seemed like a whole world separated them.

"Brother," he said, his eyes pleading with Kung-chih, his right hand reaching for him, but Kung-chih brushed his hand off angrily, then leaned in close, his words spat out into Tao Chu's face.

"*Brother?* No, Tao Chu, you have it wrong. You're not even a friend!"

Ravachol lay face down on the operating table, naked under the pale blue light. They had finished the dissection and had begun to tidy up. Kim stood back, weary now, letting his assistants finish off.

After extensive scanning they had taken sample slices from different areas of the android's brain, running a number of tests on them. All had shown the same thing – a severe deterioration of the brain tissue, almost as if it had been burned away.

What could have done that? He wondered, puzzled by the phenomenon. Was Curval right? Was the organic material they were using sub-standard? Or had something more sinister taken place?

Later, as he showered, his mind toyed with possible explanations. Synaptic burn-out of some kind? A virus? Or maybe – just maybe – some form of neuronal poison?

There was no physical evidence for it. Its food had been strictly vetted and there had been no signs on the body of an injection, but the more he thought about it, the more certain he was. Someone had got to him. Someone – an agent of one of their business rivals? – had made sure the experiment would fail.

I wasn't wrong, he realised with a start. *The brain's structure was sound.* But someone had been tampering with it. Someone who had access.

The thought was chilling. At any other time, he would have dismissed it as a product of the late hour and his depressed mood, but this was not paranoia. The more he considered the history of its deterioration, the more he saw how false, how *unscientific* it had been. No... it hadn't been a natural decay. All along they had floundered for explanations for what was happening, not wanting to face the obvious.

But who?

He stepped from the shower and shook himself, not wanting to wait for the warm air-currents to start up, then padded across to the terminal in the corner of the room.

"Who was it?" he asked. knowing that if anyone knew, it knew. "Who poisoned Ravachol?"

The Machine was silent.

"You know. I know you know. So why won't you say? You see *everything*. If it happened, you saw it. Why, you could even show me, I bet!"

"The screen," it said tonelessly. "Watch the screen."

Kim watched, fascinated at first and then horrified as he saw who it was. When he spoke again his voice was small and frightened.

"Why didn't you say? Why didn't you show me this before?"

"You didn't ask."

"But..."

Kim leaned against the terminal, feeling suddenly more tired than he'd ever felt. He had thought it was over, thought himself cured, but here was proof that it was still going on, unknown to him.

"Run it again," he said, forcing himself to watch as, on screen, he slipped from his room and, creeping stealthily past the guards, went to the android's cell. There, crouching beside the sleeping creature, he took a small pouch from his pocket and gently brushed some of its powdery contents onto Ravachol's lips.

As the figure on the screen turned, the lens zoomed in, catching for a moment the dark malevolence of its eyes. Kim shuddered, recognising it from his dreams.

It was Gweder, his mirror self.

Gweder and *Lagasek* – 'Mirror' and 'Starer, his two halves, the dark and light of his being, their names from his Clayborn past.

A-dhywas-lur, he said softly, a ripple of pure fear running down his spine. *Up from the ground*. Then, more practically. "What did it use?"

"Something it stole from you. Something you made and then forgot about."

"But I don't forget."

"No?"

The images ran. Again and again he saw himself slip from his room and make his way to the android's cell. Again and again he saw himself administer the poison. And never once had he suspected. Never once had he had even the faintest idea what was going on.

"Where's the pouch now?"

"In your room."

Kim gave a laugh of disbelief. "It can' be. I would have seen it."

"No. He doesn't let you."

"How…"

Kim stopped, frowning fiercely, then rubbed at his brow. "How do you know this?"

"You forget. I have all your files. I saw you through Rehabilitation. I know things about you that even you don't know."

"So what else do you know?"

"I can't tell you."

"Why?"

"Because…"

Kim gave a small yelp of frustration. "Why?"

It was silent a moment, then, in a voice that seemed as old as the rocks, it spoke to him again. "Get dressed now and go to bed. We'll talk in the morning. I'll tell you then what you need to know. And Kim…"

"Yes?"

"Don't blame yourself. You are what you are. Without him – without Gweder – well, I think you probably understand."

Kim nodded, then, sighing deeply, he turned away from the screen and took a fresh one-piece from the pile, slipping it on.

"Tomorrow?" he asked, looking up into the camera's eye.

"Tomorrow."

CHAPTER 125

CAGED BIRDS

L i Yuan's son, the Imperial Prince, Kuei Jen, sat in a tall official's chair facing the three old men, his back straight, his eyes staring straight ahead. The Old Men – distinguished-looking greybeards – sat some twenty *ch'i* from the prince, wearing the flowing saffron robes of New Confucian officials, no sign of rank displayed anywhere about them. Yet these were not simple priests, these were the *San Shih*, the three priest-Scholars – princes themselves, honoured sons of the Twenty Nine, the Minor Families – and they were here to test the young prince on his knowledge of the Five Classics.

Li Yuan and his Chancellor, Nan Ho, sat to one side, looking on. While the examination was in progress they could not interrupt. So it was. So it had been for two thousand years and more, since the time of the great Han emperors. With one difference. Kuei Jen – at seven – was probably the youngest ever to sit the oral examination.

A long white banner hung to one side of the hall. On it, painted in large red pictograms, was Kang Hsi's famous *Sacred Edict* with its sixteen injunctions exalting the twin virtues of filial piety and brotherly love. Copies of it hung throughout the Cities of Chung Kuo and were recited twice a month by teachers and pupils alike.

Just now they were questioning Kuei Jen on the *Ch'un Ch'iu*, the Spring and Autumn Annals of the State of Lu.

The *Ch'un Ch'iu* was the earliest historical record of the Han people, covering the period from 722 BC to 481 BC, when the fifteen major feudal states of the North China Plain had first formed a loose confederation called *Chung Kuo*, the 'Middle Kingdom'. Though it was some while since he himself had ready it, Li Yuan could still remember how he had felt as a boy, knowing how deeply rooted – how *ancient* – those traditions were.

Looking on, he knew that this was Kuei Jen's favourite area of study – one that not merely interested him, but excited him – yet the boy's answers, couched in fluent Mandarin, were strangely hesitant, stilted almost, as if he spoke from rote.

"Ch'i was the first of the Five Hegemons – the *Pa* – followed by Sung, then Ts'in, then Ch'in, and finally Ch'u, before authority was returned to its rightful owner, the Son of Heaven."

One of the Old Men leaned towards Kuei Jen, his voice, like those of his fellow *San Shih*, filled with the authority of his position.

"And the lord-Protector, Ch'i… tell me about him, Kuei Jen. Who was he Lord of and where was his capital?

Again, Kuei Jen hesitated, trying not to let his father down, resisting the temptation to turn and look at him.

"Lord Ch'i was Prince of Ts'i, and his capital was the powerful and wealthy city of Lin-tsu in Shantung Province. The Lord Ts'i could trace his ancestry thirteen generations to the kings of Chou. His daughter married the Emperor."

The old man nodded, then glanced at his fellows, clearly pleased by the answer. As he sat back, another of hem leaned forward.

"You speak well, Prince Kuei, but tell me, what event caused the Lord Chi to take up arms at the request of his Lord, the Emperor."

Li Yuan frowned, surprised by the question, trying to recollect what he knew of the House of Ts'i and its history. Lord Ch'i had eventually been assassinated, but as to why he had taken up arms in the first place.

Kuei Jen shifted uncomfortably, then, as if mirroring the old man, leaned forward slightly.

"Was it to do with what happened in 894 BC?"

"Go on…"

"Well, in that year one of the Emperor's advisers had counselled that he should have the Lord of Lu boiled alive, which the Emperor did. Two hundred and four years later, one of Lu's descendants launched an armed attack on the descendants of the adviser, and the Lord Ch'i was commissioned by the Emperor to act on his behalf in bringing Lu to justice."

"Very good. Now tell me..."

And so it went on, question following question, unrelenting, until, after almost four hours, it came to an end.

Li Yuan stood, pleased - profoundly pleased – and proud of his son's performance. To fail would have been no disgrace, for exactly the same examination was taken by men four times young Kuei Jen's age, yet he had answered every question, most of them with a detailed knowledge that, he suspected, was rarely shown, even by much older candidates.

As the *San Shi* backed away, to consult among themselves and prepare to give their verdict, he went across to Kuei Jen. What he wanted to do was pick the boy up and hug him, he was so proud, but as ever the eyes of his servants and officials watched his every move, constraining his actions.

Later, he promised himself, seeing how awkwardly Kuei Jen stood there, how nervous he was even now, after it was over.

"You did well," he said, bowing stiffly to his son, honouring him by the gesture. "Whatever the *San Shi* say, I am very proud of you, Kuei Jen. Your answers showed not merely a sound knowledge of the texts but also a profound understanding of their meaning. You are a good son, Kuei Jen. The very best of sons."

Kuei Jen blushed then bowed his head. "Father..."

"*Chieh Hsia?*"

He turned. "What is it, Master Nan?"

"Forgive me, *Chieh Hsia*, but it seems your wife, Pei K'ung, has been waiting these past few hours to speak with you."

"Does she say why?"

"It seems it is a personal matter, *Chieh Hsia*. She will speak to no one but yourself."

Li Yuan huffed, exasperated. What with this, he was already behind with his work, and there would be no chance to catch up, for he must leave at six to fly to meet Tsu Ma at his palace in Astrakhan.

"Tell her I shall come, Master Nan. Tell her... tell her I must finish here. She'll understand."

"*Chieh Hsia.*"

He turned back, puzzled as to why Pei K'ung should wish to see him so urgently. Maybe her father was ill. Maybe that was it. Maybe she wanted permission to visit him.

The *San Shi* returned, bowing as they entered the hall again, then came across, presenting themselves formally to their T'ang.

"Well, *ch'un tzu*," he said, nervous himself now that the moment of decision had come. "Give me your verdict."

"The Prince spoke well," Old Luo began. "He answered confidently and, for the main part, correctly. His tutors are to be commended."

Li Yuan felt himself stiffen, hearing the unspoken "but" behind the old man's words.

Luo continued. "His knowledge of the texts was good for one his age, though more work needs to be done on both the *Shih Ching* and the second book of the *Li Ching* where his knowledge o though correct – seems fairly thin."

"However..." Li Yuan said, impatient now.

The Oldman bowed his head slightly. "However, it is the feeling of all three of us that, while the Prince exhibit a good knowledge of the *form* of the *Wu Ching* – of the words and events set down in the texts – he is nonetheless if an age when... well, perhaps the *substance* is not so strongly rooted in his being."

"Put bluntly, you think him too young."

"Not too young, *Chieh Hsia*, merely... inexperienced."

Li Yuan felt his anger welling and beat it down, maintaining a calm and stately demeanour.

"Inexperienced?" He turned away, taking a pace or two, as if considering the idea, then turned back, staring directly at Old Luo.

"You think my son is too young, and you think, because I am a grown man, that I should agree with you. Well, *ch'un tzu*, let me say this. When my brother Han Ch'in was assassinated, I was but eight years old. Only nine months older then Kuei Jen is now. Some men forget what they were like at that age, but I cannot. How I was that day – how I felt, what I thought, what I had *experienced* – is etched unforgettably in my memory."

He turned, looking back at Kuei Jen.

"You look at my son and you see only a child – a precocious little boy who has learned his lessons well. But when I look at him, I see myself as I was, and remember what I was like at his age."

He confronted the three ancients again.

"You talk of form and substance, yet you forget the lessons of the Tao, What is a child but the seed of becoming? And if the seed is not sound, how will the tree grow straight?"

"So it might be, *Chieh Hsia*, yet it is our feeling..."

"Oh, *damn* your feeling!" Li Yuan yelled, losing his temper. "Get out of here, *Lao Jen*! Now! Before I lose all patience with you!"

Luo blanched, then, looking to his fellows, backed away, his bow stiff and angry.

When they were gone, Li Yuan turned, looking to his son. Kuei Jen stood there, his head down, his face and neck scarlet with embarrassment.

"Kuei Jen?"

The young prince swallowed then looked up at his father. Tears were welling in his eyes. "Call them back, father, *please*. They are great men. Influential men. Besides, maybe they are right. Maybe I *am* too young to be made a scholar."

"Nonsense! Luo Ye is an old fool! You answered all his questions perfectly!"

He shuddered with indignation, looking about him, defying anyone to gainsay him.

"Why, the nerve of the man! I am of a mind to..."

"*Father!*"

Li Yuan looked at Kuei Jen and frowned, noticing for the first time the tears that were coursing down his cheeks.

"Kuei Jen... what is it?"

"Please, father. Call them back and make peace with them. Before it's too late. Before any more damage is done."

Li Yuan sighed, his anger tempered by his son's obvious distress. "All right," he said. "But only because you want it so."

He turned, summoning the nearest of his retainers.

"Hu Chang... go fetch the *San Shi*. Tell them I shall speak to them privately, in my study."

Then, turning to Kuei Jen, he smiled and reached out to brush away the tears.

"You are right, my son. It does not matter what the old men think. You and I know what you are. And maybe you are wiser than the *San Shi*. Much wiser, neh, my boy?"

Pei K'ung sat on a chair in the corridor, facing her husband's rooms, her hands clasped together tightly in her lap. Nearby stood her secretaries and, beyond them, a group of guards and minor officials, all there at their T'ang's command.

The old men – the *San Shi* – had been in with him for more than twenty minutes now and she had heard raised voices more than once.

Dangerous, she thought, remembering how Li Yuan had lost his temper with her that evening and how she had felt. Yes, but she was only a wife – only the helpmeet of the T'ang. Those old men... well, to alienate *them* was much more serious, for they were leading figures in the New Confucian hierarchy, and without the whole-hearted support of the New Confucians Li Yuan's position was *greatly weakened.*

The door clicked open and the three greybeards backed out, bowing like comic figures in an opera. As the door closed they began to talk urgently among themselves, then, seeing her, fell silent.

She rose imperiously from her chair and gave them a tight smile, then went to the door and knocked.

Inside, Li Yuan was seated at his desk, drumming his fingers on the surface impatiently.

"Husband," she said, dropping to her knees and lowering her head.

"Get up, Pei K'ung," he said, motioning him across. "What is it? Is your father ill?"

"My father?" She frowned then shook her head. "No. But I am angry."

He raised an eyebrow.

"I visited the imperial library."

"And?"

She drew herself up straight, the full weight of her indignation in her voice. "And the old man sent me away as if I were a common serving maid!"

Li Yuan gave a shout of laughter and leaned towards her. "Chu Shi-ch'e, you mean?"

She bristled with anger. "I don't see what is funny. You should punish him for his impudence!"

"Punish him? *Punish* Chu Shi-ch'e? Why, the man is ninety if he is a day! If I punished him, it would kill him, and I am loath to do that, Pei K'ung.

Besides, what did he say?"

"He said I could not look at the family archives. That I needed your permission."

He smiled. "So?"

She stared at him, astonished. "You mean… it's true?"

She let out a shuddering breath then turned and went to the door.

"Pei K'ung…"

She stopped, her hand on the door's thick edge.

"Come here, Pei K'ung."

She turned and went across, her whole manner set against him now.

"Yes, husband?"

He took a pen and inked it, then wrote a note and signed it, pressing his seal to the bottom of the paper.

"There," he said, handing it to her. "But let's have no more talk of punishment. The *Pi-shu Chien* is one of our finest servants. He served my father and my grandfather before him. Sixty-eight years he has filled that post and there is no man in the whole of Chung Kuo who knows more about or is more loyal to our family. Use him well, good wife, but do not anger him. Chu Shi-ch'e can be a cursed old crow when he'd angered."

She laughed, surprised, then, with a bow of thanks, turned and left.

Outside, she stopped and stared at the permission letter then shook her head, Why, he hadn't even asked what it was for. He had simply signed it, trusting her.

Trusting her.

The thought was sobering. Yet what had she expected?

I expected him to say no.

She stood there a moment longer, then, the letter held out carefully at her side, she began to walk, heading back towards the library, her two secretaries falling in behind her as she went.

Lehmann sat on the sofa in the corner of the room, his booted feet on a low table, staring at his Financial Strategist, Cao Chang, who stood, head bowed before him.

"Well, Cao Chang? What will it cost us?"

Cao Chang hesitated. "Is this the place to discuss this, Master?"

Lehmann waved aside the objection. "Our guests are busy, Chang. We are as safe talking here as anywhere. So tell me. What would it cost us to depose the T'ang?"

Cao Chang gave a bow, then took a tiny cassette from the breast pocket of his black silk *pau* and slid the thin domino-shaped tape into the slot behind his ear. His eyes glazed a moment than came clear. He was suddenly more alert, his speech more hurried, as if it sought to keep up with the accelerated pace of his thoughts. "Our analysis shows nine main elements. Three of these – recruitment, training and weaponry – might need to be adjusted upward should our policy in Africa prove unsuccessful. For my calculations, however, I have assumed a training period of six months and a total figure of two million, eight hundred thousand men, including a mercenary force of half a million."

Lehmann nodded. "Good. Now outline the other six elements."

"One," Cao began, enumerating each point on his fingers. "The cost of fermenting revolt in Li Yuan's African armies. Important in preventing Li Yuan from using those forces directly against us. Two. The cost of our pacifying our Triad friends in Africa, important in ensuring that they do not take the opportunity to step in and take over our South European operations. Three. The infiltration of Li Yuan's European Security forces and the purchase of a minimum of two thousand top-level officers, Important in undermining the efficient operation of Li Yuan's forces in the first hours of our attack. Four... the purchase of *tai* at Weimar in the weeks running up to our operation. Important in helping to create a mood of popular dissent. Five. The funding of terrorist factions in both East and West Asia. Vitally important if we are not to find ourselves fighting not merely Li Yuan but also Tsu Ma and Wei Tseng-li. Six. The cost of destroying major GenSyn installations in the hours before our attack, particularly the five Hei garrisons."

"And the costings?"

There was the briefest flicker of hesitation, then the figures spilled from Cao Chang's lips.

"For recruitment and training, forty-seven point six billion. For weaponry, sixty-eight point eight billion. To pay off the African armies, twenty-four point five billion. To pacify our Triad friends, fifty-six billion. For the infiltration of Li Yuan's security forces, sixteen point four billion. For the purchase of *tai* three point five billion. To fund terrorist factions in the Asian Cities, fifty-two billion. To destroy major GenSyn installations, twenty-two point two billion. Which comes to… two hundred and ninety-one billion. Add to that a wastage factor of twenty per cent and the final figure is three hundred and forty-nine point two billion *yuan*."

Lehmann nodded. It was a huge sum, but no more than he had anticipated.

"Thank you, Cao Chang. You have done well. Relax now. Take a girl if you want."

Cao Chang gave a deep bow, then turned away, vanishing through the bead curtains on the far side of the room.

Lehmann took his feet from the table and sat forward, staring into space. Though three hundred and fifty as a massive sum – the equivalent of three years' profits from all his ventures - raising the money wasn't the problem. The problem would be keeping details of his scheme secret from Li Yuan. Not that he had any illusions about that. Both he and Li Yuan knew now that a war must come. Both had begun their preparations. But when and how it would be fought, *that* was the nub of it.

Time was everything.

He sighed, then sat back, looking about him at the plush décor of the foyer, feeling a natural aversion to its silk-cushioned opulence. He had had the House of the Ninth Ecstasy gutted and rebuilt, much as it was when Mu Chua, its legendary Madam, had been running it.

Not only that, but he had had Mu Chua reconstructed too, using visual records to recreate a GenSyn duplicate of the woman. Fifteen million she had cost him, all told – including the fees of the assassins he had sent to cover his tracks – but it had been money well spent; perhaps the best fifteen million he had ever spent.

Whatever he personally felt about such places, there was no denying their usefulness. In the eighteen months since he had rebuilt it, the House of the Ninth Ecstasy had regained its former prestige as a watering-hole for above merchants wishing to do business 'down-level,' its reputation spreading far and wide. All sorts were attracted here, lured by rumours of what could be had in the Madam's famous 'red room' – Security officers and Company heads, Minor Family princes and sons of the rich and famous, Representatives from the House, and even, once, a Junior Minister. Through Mu Chua she snared them all. Drew them all into his cage.

Like birds, he thought, and stood, stretching his long, pale limbs, feeling the power there in every movement. He smiled: a bleak, corpse-like rictus.

It was time to use those connections: to make the small birds flutter in their cages.

Tolonen travelled up to Lubeck shortly after lunch. Madam Peng was waiting for him at the door to her First Level salon, her eight assistants lined up behind her to greet their prestigious visitor.

Rotund and bird-like, as her name, Peng, suggested, the Madam hovered anxiously as the eight pole men set the Marshal's sedan down.

She had entertained many prominent citizens in the thirty-four years she had been in business and prided herself on the quality – the *exclusivity* – of her clientele, but never had one so elevated or so powerful entered through her doors.

"Marshal Tolonen," she said, bowing low, her eight assistants kneeling just beyond her, four to the left, four to the right, their foreheads scraping the thickly-carpeted floor.

"Madam Peng," Tolonen answered, stepping forward to take her gloved hand and gallantly kiss it. "I am grateful you could see me at such short notice."

"Not at all, Marshal," she said, a smile splitting her heavily rouged lips. "You honour my humble salon with your presence. Please come through. I have cancelled all other engagements to see you."

"You are most kind," Tolonen answered, inclining his head, then moved between the twin ranks of assistants.

"Forgive me if I sound impertinent, Marshal," the Madam said, hurrying to catch up with him, "but might I say how well you look."

Tolonen nodded, clearly distracted by his thoughts. Yet it was true. The old man looked closer to sixty than eighty-one. He had kept himself supremely fit and though his stubble-length hair was the colour of snow, his eyes were clear and strong. Even in his casual silks he looked exactly what he was – a leader of men – and seemed a match for any man half his age.

Double doors opened automatically before them and the two stepped through, into the Madam's "boudoir." Here she did all her business. Here, surrounded by her bright silk wall-hangings, across the low, black, antique table that dominated the centre of the richly-decorated space, she had made her reputation as City Europe's leading match-maker.

Showing the Marshal to a sturdy chair that had been imported specially for the occasion, she plumped herself down on a sofa facing him, her ample figure settling into the big silk cushions like a brightly coloured bird into its nest.

"Well, Marshal," she began, her ancient and thickly-powdered Han face grinning broadly – almost obscenely – as a servant approached bearing a tray of wines and sweet-meats. "How exactly can I help you."

It was not unusual for an old man to want a young wife, especially as they came to realise that their grip on mortality was growing daily more tenuous, yet somehow, she had never thought Tolonen the type. Still, she was prepared, and had spent an hour that morning selecting a handful of special girls that might well suit his profile. Tolonen waved away the offer of a drink and leaned towards her, his grey eyes troubled.

"It is my daughter, Jelka, I..." He looked at the servant, reluctant to say more. At once Madam Peng dismissed the man.

She sat up slightly, smiling reassuringly. "All that is said between us here is absolutely confidential, Marshal. But forgive me... when you spoke to my yesterday, I thought... well, I thought you meant to take a bride yourself."

"A bride? Me?" Tolonen laughed, but his eyes seemed horrified at the notion. "Gods, no, Madam Peng! It is my daughter, Jelka, I am worried about. She..." Again, he seemed ill at ease broaching the subject. "Well, to be blunt with you, she has a crush on an awful little fellow – a Clayborn by the name of Ward. He..."

She put her hand out, her face all sympathy now. "You need not say another word, Marshal Tolonen. I *quite* understand. Why, even the thought of it is absurd, neh?"

Tolonen smiled weakly.

"No, you were absolutely right to come to me."

She leaned forward, her fingers brushing a pad on the desk in front of her. At once a screen came up out of the surface, facing her. She tapped in a few words, then eased back, smiling at Tolonen once again. "It's true what they say, neh, Marshal? Clay is Clay. It cannot be raised."

He nodded, comforted, it seemed, by her understanding.

"Now, your daughter is..." she studied the details on the screen, "twenty-four I see. So your principal worry is, I guess, that she will do something silly after her Coming-Of-Age in three weeks' time."

Tolonen swallowed. "That is so."

"Then we must act quickly, neh? We must find a way to break this former attraction. And what better way than creating a new one?"

She leaned forward, tapping at the keys, the huge golden rings on her fingers glittering in the spotlights. She paused, watching the data come up, then, satisfied, sat back, the screen lowering into the table's surface once again.

"You know your daughter well, Marshal Tolonen?"

"Well enough," he said from the darkness where he sat. "Her mother died giving birth to her. I raised her from a child."

"Ah..."

"If it helps, she was engaged once. To Hans Ebert."

"Ah yes, I recall that now. She was... *reluctant*, am I right?"

Tolonen sighed. "She hated him, if the truth be told. I tried to force her into the marriage. I... Well, I do not wish to make the same mistake again, Madam Peng, let me make that clear. She must choose her own mate, but not *him*! Not Ward."

There was a vehemence to those last few words that made Madam Peng reassess the situation. If he was so worked up about it then there was clearly a very *real* danger that his daughter would marry the Clayborn. That made her own task more difficult; made it essential that she knew everything there was to know about the matter, for to fail in this, her most prestigious case – well, it was unthinkable! As unthinkable as the Marshal's daughter marrying a Clayborn!

"This Clayborn..." she began, trying her best to be tactful. "This Ward... What is it, do you think, that attracts your daughter to him?"

The old man's laugh was sour. "The Gods alone know. Oh, he's clever enough, there's no doubting that, and he has the T'ang's ear in matters scientific, but... well, as to what attracts her physically..."

"I see," she said, after a moment's awkward silence. "And yet there is an attraction? You're quite sure of that?"

"Oh yes. She wanted to *marry* him! She defied me openly, in front of old friends who'd come to dinner! Why, I had to send her away to prevent it."

Madam Peng sighed silently. The more she heard the less she liked this commission, but it was too late now – and she had committed herself the moment she had invited the old man to come and visit her. If she turned him away now it would get out – for rumour had a vicious tongue in her circles – and her reputation would be damaged.

Then again, it was far from certain she could do anything meaningful in the circumstances. If what she'd heard was true, the Marshal's daughter was a headstrong, independent young woman.

"Okay," she said, her voice betraying nothing of her thoughts. "Let us try to build up some kind of profile of what she finds attractive in a man. This Ward... I assume he's the usual type... big head, bulgy, staring eyes, stunted body?"

Tolonen grunted, his discomfort evident.

"So, My guess is that it's not actually something physical your daughter is responding to, but some...*inner* quality. You say he's very intelligent."

"Perhaps the most intelligent young man on the planet, Ben Shepherd aside."

She brightened, letting her voice grow more animated. "Then that's it! What we need to do is look for a young man who is not merely good looking, but bright with it!"

"Maybe..." the old man said uncertainly. "And yet Ebert was bright."

"Yes, but look at what a foul piece of work *he* turned out to be! Why, it wouldn't surprise me if something in his manner *alerted* your daughter!"

Tolonen laughed. "I'm beginning to understand just why you have such a good reputation, Madam Peng. It was as you say. But tell me, who do you have in mind?"

He heard the tap of her fingers on the keyboard. There was a brief delay and then the hazy red glow at the centre of the table began to intensify and grow.

"I have programmed the Selector to search the files for eligible young men who fit the profile. It will come up with those four that best fit the parameters we've been discussing. Then... well, we'll take a look at them, neh, Marshal Tolonen? And then you can tell me which of them you'd like to pay your daughter a visit over the coming weeks."

The sign flickered fitfully, sending a sweet burning scent into the air. Emily, standing at the rail of the balcony, two floors up, looked down at it, seeing how the giant electronic mantis seemed to spring and trap its prey, its long tongue moving with an inhuman quickness.

Two guards, plainly dressed but carrying Security-issue automatics, stood by the door, moving the curious along.

Inside, Pasek waited for her.

She sent down. At the door they searched her then waved her through. She didn't recognise either of them, yet that was not unusual – the whole of the Hand could have assembled and she'd have known no more than eighty, maybe ninety of them at most.

Or would have, she thought, *before yesterday.*

What she had noticed, however, were the pendants about their necks, the very same as that which hung about Pasek's – the cross within the circle.

Inside, she pulled the curtain aside, then stopped. The White Mantis had been an opulent, bustling place – a gambling and drinking hole the Hand had bought as cover – but now it was silent. All the fittings had been ripped out, the carpets removed, the silk hangings torn down. All was bare now – eerily so.

She walked across and stood in front of the door to the main gaming hall, hearing the murmur of voices from within. She pushed through, then stopped, astonished. She had expected Pasek to be there with a few of Pasek's men; instead, she found herself looking into a room packed with a hundred or more people.

Emily looked about her, recognising faces – some she'd not thought to see again – and understood at once. He had summoned them all – all the hand's surviving cell leaders. Never in the history of the Black Hand, had they met like this – all of them in one place at one time – and something told her it would not happen again.

She walked through, making for the tiny dais on the far side of the low-ceilinged room, conscious that every eye was on her. Many smiled, clearly pleased – reassured – to see her there, and reached out to touch her arm as she passed, but one or two of them scowled, as if her very presence was a betrayal

Coming out by the dais, she found herself facing a line of Pasek's men – his four henchmen, Ashman, Grant, Blaskic and Eyre. For the past four years they had been Pasek's constant shadows; big, well-built men, a good ten or fifteen years younger than Pasek, with strong Nordic features and short ash-blonde hair.

Security types, She thought, meeting their eyes unflinchingly, *Just the kind of empty, soulless type the man attracts.*

"Where's Pasek?" she asked, looking to Blaskic.

"He'll be here," Blaskic answered, the slightest suggestion of a smile playing on his lips. Yesterday he had been out-ranked by her – a lowly minion in the Hand's hierarchy - but today...

She turned, looking about her, making a swift calculation. There were roughly a hundred and fifty people in the room. Of those she knew fifty, maybe sixty at most. The majority of the rest were sure to be Pasek's. All in all, then, it was finely balanced. Pasek had enough support to guarantee the success of his initial coup, yet not enough to make it absolutely safe.

She smiled inwardly, understanding suddenly why she was there. It wasn't just that Pasek 'respected' her, he *needed* her, to hold things together while he consolidated his rule. But only for a time. Things would change – she understood that instinctively – and Pasek would slowly increase his stranglehold until...

Until he no longer needs me.

Emily turned back, knowing now what she had to do; knowing *exactly* how to play her hand. She didn't have long to wait. A gong sounded from the next room and then a door opened at the back of the dais.

Pasek stepped out. He stood there a moment, looking about him as if noting who was there, then nodded.

"Friends," he said, lifting a hand, palm out, to greet them. "You know what has happened, and some of you are... *uncomfortable* with it. In the circumstances I felt we should meet. To clear the air."

His voice was warm, yet his eyes, when he met Emily's, were cold, uncompromising.

"Rachel..." he said, acknowledging her. "Would you like to start?"

She stared back at him belligerently. "Start?"

"I mean, is there anything you want to say?"

She smiled darkly. There were plenty of things she's like to say – like what a callous shit he'd been to have Chou Te-hsing murdered – but that wasn't what he meant.

She looked about her once again. "I'm here," she said, finally, as if that said it all.

"And?"

She almost laughed. And what? That she was his loyal supporter? That she condoned what he had done and was happy with the way things had turned out? No. The truth was, the m lore she thought about it, the *less* happy she was about things. She had joined the Hand because it seemed to her to be the best way of changing things – of achieving some limited form of justice and directly affecting the lives of the common people – but in practice it hadn't worked that way, and now, under Pasek, there was even less chance of that.

She thought back to their meeting the day before. Pasek had been wrong when he'd spoken of them wanting similar things. Wrong, or simply lying. For while she saw the hand as a vehicle for social justice – as a corrective rod to beat corrupt officials and counterbalance the grosser abuses of power - what *he* wanted was to transform it into a society of religious zealots like himself.

Which was fine, only she wasn't going to go along with that. Not without a struggle.

Brushing aside Grant and Blaskic, she stepped up onto the dais, facing Pasek.

"I'll join you," she said, eyeing him defiantly. "But there's one condition."

He stared back at her, confident, it seemed, now that she had given her vocal support. "Name it," he said.

"That you let me take lour Lehmann."

There was an audible gasp from the body of the room, a look of shock on every face. All, that was, except Pasek's. He just smiled – a pale, ghostly smile – and nodded.

Afterwards he spoke to her alone.

"How did you find out?"

"Find lout?" She laughed, "What are you talking about?"

"The tape. I only got it an hour back. How did you hear about it?"

She stared at him. Clearly there was something she didn't know. "Lehmann... we're talking about Lehmann, right?"

He nodded, then, "Look, you'd best come through. You'd best see this before we talk any further."

He had cleared one of the bedrooms at the back of the Mantis and made it into a makeshift office. There was a desk, two simple, ice-cast chairs and –

on the wall behind the desk – a larger version of the pendant he always wore, the cross within the circle.

"Sit down," he said, pointing towards the nearest chair, then went round the desk and took a hand-held from the top drawer.

"Here," he said, handing the viewer to her. "But I warn you. It isn't pleasant."

Pleasant? What *was* pleasant about Lehmann? She stared at Pasek a moment, then looked down at the tiny screen of the hand-held, activating it.

Ten minutes later she understood.

"Who was she?"

"One of our south-eastern operatives, Jane Vierheller, her name was."

"And the man?"

Pasek laughed coldly. "That's your man. That's Lehmann."

"Lehmann?"

Emily brought the screen closer to her face, rewinding until his face came clearly into view. So *that* was what he looked like. She felt a shiver of pure aversion pass through her.

"You still want to take him out?"

She glared at him. "And you don't?"

"Sure. But not just yet. Not until we're strong enough."

"Strong? Look, I don't want to depose him. I just want to kill him."

"I understand. But that won't be easy. To get to him at all we'd need quite a force. They say he's better defended than Li Yuan."

"You forget. I almost got to Soucek."

"Sure. But Soucek's an entirely different matter. He's *meant* to be seen! Lehmann… well, no one sees Lehmann, not unless he wants them to."

She considered that. Then, with a jolt, she realised something.

"The tape! How did he get it to you? How did he know where to find us?"

Pasek leaned towards her. "He didn't. We found it. He meant us to find it."

"I don't understand. How?"

"The woman… Vierheller… was part of a cell of five, Later in that sequence – towards the end of it – she gives Lehmann a name and a location. The name she gives is that of her cell-leader, Wilhelm Dieter, the location is his apartment. Two hours back, when Dieter didn't show for the meeting, I sent Ashman to bring him. Ashman brought him alright, but Dieter was dead.

Lehmann had killed him."

"And the tape was in his apartment, right?"

Pasek shook his head. "You have to understand just what you're taking on. You need to know what Lehmann's like, otherwise..." He spread his hands, palms upward.

"So what do I need to know? He torched a whole desk. Only a monster would do that."

"That's true. But it's useful to know the nature of the monster, no? To know just what he's capable of."

"Torture. Mass death. Are you still in any doubt that we should kill the man?"

"No doubt at all But listen. The tape wasn't with Dieter, it was *inside* him. Lehmann had had him cut open and his innards scooped out like a grapefruit. Then they sewed him up and lay him on his bed, face down. There was a message burned into the skin of his back."

Emily swallowed. She had known Dieter. Not well, but enough to know that he had been a good man. She hoped it would have been quick; that he hadn't suffered the way the woman, Vierheller, had suffered. She shuddered, then forced herself to ask.

"What did it say?"

Pasek sat back, lacing his fingers together. "You can look for yourself, if you want. His body's in the next room."

"Just tell me."

"He's very direct, our friend, Lehmann. He knows what he wants."

"Cut the shit. What did he say?"

Pasek's smile disturbed her.

"Just four words," he said. "'*Don't fuck with me.*' Effective, wouldn't you say?"

Emily looked down, staring at the frozen image on the screen – at that pale, albinoid face with its awful slit of a mouth and its cold, un-emotive eyes. Monsters. The time bred monsters. But this one surpassed them all.

She met Pasek's eyes again. "So what are we going to do? Just how *are* we going to get strong enough to take this bastard out?"

Pasek's smile broadened. He leaned toward her conspiratorially. "We're going to do what we should have done years back. We're going to make sure that the Hand's the coming force... the *only* force in the land. You understand?"

"War," she said quietly. War against the myriad other terrorist organisations; that was what he was talking about. A war to make the Black Hand not merely dominant, but supreme.

"That's right," he said, nodding slowly, his eyes gleaming at the thought of it. "And then you can have that bastard, I promise you, Rachel. On my mother's memory..."

The door was locked, the room in darkness. For hours now, Pei K'ung had sat there, hunched forward, her hands gripping her knees, watching the holograms flicker in the air above the table – so real and yet so distant. She had seen her husband as a child, playing in the orchards of Tongjiang with his elder brother, Han, his round face laughing as he ran between the trees; had watched him on the day of his coronation as he stepped down from the Temple of Heaven, resplendent in his silks of imperial yellow, like a young god sent among them; had witnessed his grief at the news of his wives' deaths, then watched him clasp his baby son, Kuei Jen to him, his face filled with disbelief and joy after the floating palace of Yangjing had been destroyed; had spied on him in his bridal bed and looked one as he stood at the window of his study, his face wistful as he watched the young maids play ball in the gardens.

So much she had seen. So much she had forced herself to witness.

Pei K'ung sighed then clapped her hands. At once the room's lights came up, the hologram vanishing like a wraith. She stood, the blood pulsing at her temples, and reached out to steady herself.

Too much, she thought, "*I have seen too much.*"

She closed her eyes, trying to shut it out, to push it far away, but she could not help herself: she kept seeing it, time and again, Fei Yen lying on the bed beneath him, her arms opening to him, her tiny breasts like offerings, and his face...

She took a sharp intake of breath, *Stupid*, she thought, angry with herself, not merely that she had succumbed to the temptation, but that she'd acted so... *predictably.*

"It's over," she told herself, with more confidence than she felt. "It was over long ago. Those were just images. Fading memories."

Yes, and yet the sharp clarity of those images seemed to belie that fact.

Looking at them, she had felt her stomach tighten with jealousy – as if it had been only yesterday.

She went to the mirror and pointed a finger at herself accusingly.

"Stupid, Pei K'ung…. How could you be so stupid!"

She should not have let the woman's taunts get to her. But now it was too late. Now she was infected by Fei Yen's image. She could not turn her head nor close her eyes without seeing the woman there in her husband's bed, there, moving slowly and sensuously beneath him, then, as he climaxed, smiling triumphantly back at the recording lens, as if to mock her over the years.

"Damn you!" he said, not sure whether she meant Fei Yen or herself.

She felt like punishing the woman, humiliating her in front of her servants, yet even a cast-off wife had her rights, her *status*, and besides, she would need Li Yuan's permission before she did such a thing, and how could she possibly do that?

She turned and went quickly to the door, unlocking it and throwing it open.

"Mistress?" the waiting steward asked, bowing low.

"Send my maids," she said. "I shall bathe before dinner."

She went back inside, composing herself. Li Yuan had already gone – he would be at Tsu Ma's within the hour – but still her duties claimed her. With her husband gone, she would sit at the head of the table, entertaining whichever of his guests remained. But there was almost two hours before then.

She heard footsteps in the corridor outside. A moment later both of her maids stood before her. They curtseyed breathlessly.

"Mistress!"

"Run a bath," she said, imperiously. "And lay lout my clothes. Then leave me."

There was the briefest of glances between them, for they were used to seeing to her every need – then, without a word, they set to work.

Pei K'ung went to the table, looking down at the golden cases of the holograms and shaking her head. When she had married him, she had thought it would be simple, never guessing – never even suspecting – what he would awake in her.

He had not meant to be his mate, merely his helper. Her sexuality had been neutered by their marriage contract; she herself rendered into a fake male – a female eunuch.

She shuddered.

I should have stayed where I was. I was contented there. I knew my place. Whereas here…

She went over to the bathroom, watching one of her girls pour scent into the water, then strew the surface with rose petals.

Here I know nothing anymore. Only that I've changed.

Finished, he two maids bowed and backed away. She heard the door click shut, then spun round and went to her desk, activating the intercom.

"Tsung Ye?"

She waited and then a voice came over the speaker.

"Mistress?"

"Come to my rooms, now."

"Mistress."

Pei K'ung took her hand from the pad and straightened up. She was no longer young and she had never been beautiful, but she *was* Empress!

As she made her way back to the bathroom, her fingers reached up, unfastening the top button of her *chi pao*.

She stretched her neck, relived to be free of the tight-fitting collar, then felt for the button at her collar bone, pushing it through the eye.

There had been a brief time in her adolescence when she had hoped to be a bride, to be a woman in the fullest meaning of the word, but the years had passed and no suitor had been found, and she had resigned herself to the fact that she would never have that other, secret life that most women had.

She let the *chi pao* slip from her, then stepped from her silk briefs, turning to face the mirror, naked now.

Forget that face, she told herself, knowing how horse-like and masculine it was; *look at the body.*

She stood there a moment longer, studying herself, reaching up to cup her breasts, then tracing the broad swell of her hips.

Not bad, she thought, *considering.*

She turned, looking at herself side-on, when there was a knock on the door.

"Mistress? It is Tsung Ye!"

Pei K'ung looked across to where her silk bathrobe hung from a silver peg, then, smiling nervously, encouragingly to herself, she stepped to the edge of the huge, sunken bath and slipped in beneath the rose-scented water.

She flexed her muscles, trying to calm herself, to still the trembling in her limbs, then turned her head, facing the door.

"Come in, Tsung Ye!"

She heard the door open; heard it click shut.

"Mistress?"

"In here."

She heard him come part way and then hesitate; knew he had seen the discarded *chi pao*.

"Come here, Tsung Ye, I need your advice."

She waited, staring directly into the mirror, watching the reflection of the doorway, as slowly, with extreme reluctance, Tsung Ye edged into the room, his discomfort more than evident.

"Mistress?"

She turned to face him, lifting herself slightly in the water so that her breasts came into view. He was staring at her now, wide-eyed, his mouth fallen open. The sight of that gave her more confidence. After all, he was a mere servant, she an Empress!

"Well, Tsung Ye?... what are you waiting for? Come in and scrub my back."

"Mistress?" There was an edge of panic in his voice now, almost of pleading.

"You heard me, Tsung Ye. Het those clothes off and join me here. But be quick now!"

He swallowed, not believing what he was hearing, then stammered a reply.

"I... I... am se-secretary, Mistress, I..."

Slowly she stood, letting him see that she was indeed naked, aware that he could not keep his *eyes from her. That knowledge gave her power; gave her voice a new-found resonance.*

"In here, Tsung Ye, at once, or my husband will hear you have insulted me!"

Li Yuan stopped at the top of the steps, looking down into the Great Hall, five thousand heads turning to look up at him. Long banners of bright yellow silk and huge red lanterns, all printed with the characters *chang shou* – long life – hung over the heads of the great and mighty who had gathered. He smiled, then turned to meet Tsu Ma's eyes.

"It is your last evening as a single man, Cousin Ma. It seems almost a shame to spend it thus."

Tsu Ma laughed softly, then leaned heavily on his jade-handled cane. "That is our fate, neh, Cousin Yuan. Common folk can get drunk and play the fool, but we... we must perform like actors before an eager crowd. Come, let us go down. There will be time later to share a quiet moment."

They went down, the great mass of courtiers and ministers, soldiers and aristocrats, company heads and politicians, bowing as one before the two T'ang, then moving back, like the sea parting before the bow of a great ship.

Relieved of any official obligations, Li Yuan looked on, at ease in his cousin's court, yet also somewhat wistful, remembering the night before his own brother's wedding when, in the Great Hall at Tongjiang, they had held a similar reception.

Then, as now, there had been peace. Then, as now, beneath the calm surface of courtly ritual, things had been in flux.

And tomorrow it begins again, he thought, wondering for a moment how Karr was spending this evening – his last before he took on his official duties. Was he at home with his wife and child? Or was he out celebrating with his friends and colleagues?

With his family, Li Yuan decided, smiling at the thought. *A good man, Karr. Reliable. And honest, too. Honest as the day is long.*

He had not told Tsu Ma yet, but there would be time later, once Wei Tseng-li was here. When the three of them were alone.

Smiling, he accepted a drink from one of the stewards and took a large sip, steeling himself, then turned in time to greet one of Tsu Ma's senior ministers.

The hours passed. Just after ten, Wei Tseng-li arrived, the young T'ang greeting his fellows with a laugh and a smile, as if the moment had no significance, yet each of them knew what lay behind this meeting. The last time all three had met had been thirty months before, at Tongjiang, that same day when Wang Sau-leyan, their fellow T'ang and cousin, had sent his elite troops against them in an attempt to wipe them out. Two Sons of

Heaven had died that day, including Tseng-li's elder brother, Wei Chan Yin. But they had survived, and Wang, in time, had been brought to account for his treachery.

"Cousin," Tsu Ma said, embracing Wei Tseng-li, then holding him at arm's length. "Why, you've put on weight! Is this what three wives has done for you?"

Wei Tseng-li laughed heartily, his dark eyes twinkling. "And you, Cousin... is it *anticipation* of marriage has bloated you so?"

Tsu Ma roared with laughter – laughter that was taken up by all those surrounding him until the Great Hall rang with it. He nodded, pleased by the rejoinder, then looked to Li Yuan. "So here we are," he said quietly. "Like the Three Old Worthies."

Li Yuan smiled. "Old, Tsu Ma?" Then, looking past Tsu Ma, he touched his arm lightly. "But hush... here comes your bride."

Shu-sun stood beside her father at the top of the steps, resplendent in a full-length dress of jasmine edged with lavender, her pretty face framed in delicate yellow flowers.

Looking up at her, Li Yuan felt his heart grow heavy, once more reminded of the day before his brother's wedding.

If I had but known what was to come.

He looked down sharply, tears welling in his eyes.

What would you have done? He asked himself. How could you have prevented Han Ch'in's death? And if you had, how would you have stopped the next attempt, or the one that followed that? Could you have kept your brother safe - safe until his last breath, until you stood over him, an old man in his bed, a dozen great-grandchildren weeping silently in the death chamber?

No, came the answer. *No, for it was willed otherwise.*

But even if you had – even if the gods gave that day to you – how could you then have lived, knowing that she was his? How could you have looked at her, day after day, and not have your heart break within you, knowing she was not yours?

As she came down, a look almost of awe in his eyes.

"She is like the dawn, neh, Yuan? Like Spring's first shoot."

"She is very beautiful," he answered, determined to set aside all troublesome memories. "May you have many sons!"

Tsu Ma chuckled but did not look at him, his eyes snared by his betrothed.

"And I shall call the first one Yuan..."

Fei Yen climbed from the bed and crossed the room, her fingers reaching for the door. She could hear the man's soft snoring in the darkness, could still feel his weight on her, smell the sickly perfumed scent of him, and shuddered, despising herself. Kisses and flattery, that was all it ever was; crude disguises for some darker, baser need. Why could she never see that? Why was she always tethered to her senses, like a hawk on a leash, circling the lure? Where in the gods' names was her pride, her dignity?

She took a gown from the peg outside the door and pulled it on, then slipped lout into the corridor.

A nigh light flickered in a wall bracket to her left, some twenty *ch'i* along, above the stairwell. Across from it a servant slept atop a lacquered chest, his knees up under his chin, his mouth open. Wrapping her gown tightly about her, she went to the right, hurrying down the broad, carpeted hallway, heading for her dead father's rooms, her feet making no sound.

Inside, in the silent darkness, she rested, her back against the door, her eyes closed, letting her heartbeat slow, the faint musty scent of the room filling her lungs.

The evening had been awful. She had drunk too much, laughed too much, and hen... gods, the things she had let him do! The awful, degenerate things!

She gritted her teeth. The *Wu*... she must consult her father's diviner – his *Wu* – and have him cast an oracle. But first she must wash that foul man's scent from her.

Finding her way in the dark, she crossed the room and pushed the bathroom door open.

"Light," she said, speaking to the House Computer. At once the room was bathed in artificial sunlight from the panels in the ceiling.

"Gentler..."

The light softened.

Since her father's death four years back, no one had used these rooms, yet the servants maintained them as if he were due back at any moment. Solid gold fittings sparkled under the crystal lights, marble surfaces gleamed. In one corner a green jade fountain, carved in the shape of a rearing dragon jutted over a circular pool, its tiled floor decorated like a huge *Tai Chi*.

She went to it and, activating the controls on the panels between its wings, stood and watched as a steaming jet of water spewed from the dragon's mouth, describing a glittering arc in the air.

"Cooler..."

Throwing off her gown, she went down the steps, into the swirling current of the slowly-filling pool.

The fierceness of the spray against her skin was exhilarating. She turned slowly in the glittering fall, her arms out, feeling the water drum against her face and breasts and back, cascading down her flanks and between her legs, cleansing her, washing all memory of the man from her skin. And as the disgust passed from her, that feeling of anger and indignation she had had in Pei K'ung's office returned. She was still young, her body trim and firm, her beauty undiminished. How dare the woman treat her like a servant? How *dare* she?

"Enough!"

At once the jet of water died. At once warm air-currents played over her body, drying and caressing it.

She knew, of course, just why she had got drunk. It was the news – those hideous images from Tsu Ma's palace in Astrakhan. She had seen the way he looked at his bride – seen how his eyes drank in the youthful beauty of her.

Just as he had once looked at her.

"Wake the *Wu*!" she said, climbing the steps, then stooping to pick up her gown. "Send him to my study. I'll see him there!"

The *Wu* looked up from the fallen yarrow stalks and met her eyes.

"Heaven above water... it is *Sung*... conflict,"

Fei Yen nodded, but she was disappointed. She had hoped for something clearer. Conflict – of course there would be conflict.

Old Fung turned to his book and picked it up, beginning to read.

"Conflict. You are sincere

And are being obstructed."

"Yes," she said, impatient now. "Go now, Fung, I need to think."

The old man bowed and backed away, knowing his Mistress's moods, not even bothering to gather up his things.

Lightning, she thought, gathering up the stalks and letting them fall on to the table once again: *from the sky into the sea. Yes, I shall be like the lightning falling on them.*

And her son? What would happen to Han if she did as she proposed?

Better, perhaps, to ask what would happen if I did nothing: if he had to live out his life in the shadow of my bitterness.

Maybe... yet it stayed her hand. It had *always* stayed her hand. But no longer. If she could not get satisfaction from Li Yuan, she would go to Tsu Ma and tell him direct.

Han was his son. *His.* She would prove it before the world.

She shivered, indignation singing in her blood – then swept her arm across the table, clearing it.

Conflict... she would give them conflict. Whether they wanted it or no.

CHAPTER 126

THE WHITE T'ANG

Pei K'ung looked up from the corner desk in which she sat, trying to keep the impatience from her voice.

"Yes, Master Chu, what is it now?"

The old man bowed – more a slight leaning forward than a proper bow, he was so bent already – then placed four gold-bound cases in front of her.

"Ah..." Her eyes lit up. "I thought..."

"Your husband's permission covers everything, it seems."

She smiled, then drew the cases toward her, her fingers tracing the embossed shape of the *Ywe Lung,* the Wheel of Dragons.

"Thank you, Chu Shih-ch'e. I am sorry if I was... *tetchy* with you earlier. But if you would leave me now."

"Mistress."

The old man inclined his body slightly and backed away, but Pei K'ung's attention was already on the tapes. If these showed what she thought they showed...

She gathered them up and went across. At the centre of the room was a circular black lacquered platform, some six *ch'i* in width, its surface carved with the symbol of the *Ywe Lung,* the whole thing resting on seven golden dragon heads. Setting the cases down beside it, she went to the window and pulled at the thick silk cord that hung there. At once, massive blinds, each slat a full *ch'i* thick, began slowly to descend, shutting out the daylight.

She returned to the platform, then knelt, taking the first of the discs from its case.

"I'm right," she whispered to herself, her hands trembling with anticipation. "I *know* I am."

Leaning across the platform, she carefully placed the disc on to the spindle at the bug, then moved back. Slowly the room's lights faded. A faint glow filled the air above the platform.

"I am Pei K'ung," she said, "Wife of Li Yuan and Empress of Ch'eng Ou Chou."

"Welcome, Mistress," the machine answered, accepting her voice recognition code, its own voice soft, melodious. "What would you like to see?"

"The stables," she said, her heart beating faster. "The royal party, setting out to ride."

"Mistress..."

The air shimmered and took shape. As ever, she found herself surprised by the sharpness, the crystalline clarity of the image. It was so real she could almost smell the horses.

She watched, fascinated, her suspicions confirmed. She saw the horses being led from their stalls, their breath pluming in the cold December air; saw Tsu Ma wave the groom aside and help Fei Yen into the saddle, his hands lingering over-long on her waist. And then that smile – a smile that said it all.

Lovers... yes, they had been lovers.

Closing her eyes, she let out a long sigh. She ought to have felt satisfaction that her guess had proved right, but all she could think of was Li Yuan: of how hurt he must have felt, how *damaged.*

"Enough!"

The air-show died.

"You wish to see something more, Mistress?"

"No... No, I..." She made a gesture of dismissal.

Slowly the lights came up.

So now she knew. Bending down, she picked up the empty casing, studying the date. Like the other three, it came from a four-week period in December 2206- the month Fei Yen had conceived her son.

Pei K'ung shivered, wanting to hate the woman for what she had done to her husband – for the suffering she had caused him, and for being so weak, so impulsive a creature – but it was no longer possible. Not after last night.

She sank onto her knees, letting her head fall forward, remembering. So sweet it had been. So deliciously sweet. And his body. *Aiya,* his body... once more she shivered, desire welling up in her, making her place a hand against her breast, gently, tenderly... as he had done.

She hadn't known. She simply hadn't known. But now she understood. What had been dark was now light. What had been hidden was now revealed to her. She smiled. Yes... so many things had come clear in the night.

It was then, lying there in the dark beside him, listening to his soft breathing, his flesh pressed close and warm against her own, that she had begun to think it through.

If it were not Li Yuan's child, then whose was it? Who had had the opportunity? A servant? One of the house musicians, perhaps? A groom? Or had it been someone greater than that? Someone whose very power and nobility had been enough to rob Fei Yen of her senses?

Rising at dawn, she had gone straight to the library and, getting Old Chu from his bed, had consulted the family records for that month. Searching through the Imperial Itinerary for the palace, she had found that on four separate occasions Tsu Ma had visited Tongjiang, each time when Li Yuan was away.

She should have left it there. Should have contented herself with that, but she had had to know for certain.

There was a knock. She turned towards it, frightened, then, quickly gathering up the cases, stood.

"Who is it?"

There was a moment's hesitation, then a young male voice answered her. "It is I, Mistress. Tsung-Ye..."

She felt her heart flutter, her stomach tighten. Calming herself, she set the cases down, then faced the door again.

"Come in, Tsung Ye."

The door eased open slowly. The young secretary took a pace into the room then stopped, his head bowed, unable to look at her.

"What is it?" she asked, as if nothing had happened between them.

"You are wanted, Mistress," he said awkwardly. "Your cruiser is prepared. You must leave within the hour."

"Ah..." Pei K'ung turned her head, looking at the old clock that hung on the far side of the study above the racks of gold-bound cases, then nodded. She hadn't realised it was so late. "Thank you, Tsung Ye. I shall come and prepare myself at once."

He gave a little bow, beginning to step away, but she called him back.

"Tsung Ye... close the door."

"Mistress?" His eyes flew up, alarmed.

"You heard me. Then come here. We need to talk."

He swallowed, then turned and closed the door, then went over and stood before her.

"Listen," she said softly, laying a hand on his arm. "What happened last night – you will keep quiet about it, neh, Tsung Ye?"

He nodded, trembling slightly.

She leaned closer. "It is not that I am ashamed, you understand. Nor that my husband would be angry. Far from it. He has instructed me to find my own amusement. But the staff must not know. You understand, Tsung Ye? My husband must be Master in his own house. No man must have cause to mock him. We must be... *discreet.*"

"Discreet?" He looked at her directly, his alarm quite open now.

She squeezed his arm and smiled. "Hush now, Tsung Ye. No harm will come to you. Besides, it was good, neh? You were..." She leaned close and gently kissed his neck. "Very sweet."

He stared at her, direct, eye to eye for a moment, then looked down. "I will do whatever you ask, Mistress."

"Good." She let her hand rest on his shoulder, then trace the shape of his arm, finally lacing her fingers in his own. "And Tsung Ye... you are not obliged to love me. Only to make me happy. And if you make me happy... well, a talented young man can go far, neh? Very far indeed."

There was a banner over the gate, the Mandarin characters burning white on the jet black background. Karr halted, ignoring his escorts, looking up at it, translating it in his head.

If only there is persistence, even an iron pillar will be ground into a needle.

Karr studied it a moment longer, then shrugged. Was it meant as a statement of intent? A rallying cry? Or had it simply been left there from another occasion?

The last was unlikely. Everything he had seen had been put there for him to see. He was a witness, after all. What he saw would be taken back and spoken of. And not to casual ears, but to the ears of a T'ang.

He nodded to himself. To be honest he had been surprised by the opulence, the industry of these stacks. Much had changed in the past two years. Lehmann had come a long way since he had last been down here.

As the doors swung back, Karr had a glimpse of a huge crowd of people – uniformed, drawn up in massed ranks – and felt a moment's misgiving. What if it were Lehmann's purpose to humiliate him? And, through him, to send a message to Li Yuan?

Then why any of this? Why such display if the only reason for the meeting was to kill the T'ang's representative?

Because, came the answer, *he might want to send a message to his own people too.*

He straightened up, dispelling his fears, then stepped through, beneath the gate that led into the very heart of the White T'ang's territory, looking about him with a cold disdain, knowing how impressive a sight he – a single man - made in their eyes.

Karr strode slowly between the massed ranks, conscious of them watching him. Once he had been a 'blood' in these levels. Once he had fought the Master, Hwa, to the death, becoming champion.

Against the odds, he thought, remembering how the Marshal had come and asked him if he would serve the T'ang.

Facing him at the far end of the Main, stood three men. Tall, leprous figures, the central one dressed from heads to toe in white, the Han colour of death.

He smiled inwardly, recognising them from the last time he was here. The one in white was Li Min, the "Brave Carp," otherwise known as Stefan Lehmann. Either side of him were his henchmen – *Niu T'ou* and *Ma Mien*, as Karr secretly called them, Ox-head and Horse-face, the Lieutenants of Hell – real names Soucek and Visak.

Twenty *ch'i* from them, he stopped, lifting a hand in greeting – "Ch'un *tzu...*"

Lehmann studied him a while, then stepped forward. "It's been a long time, Colonel Karr. I hear you've been promoted. *Ssu-li Hsiao-wei...* that's a rare honour for a *Hung Mao.*"

Karr blinked, astonished. Only a handful of people knew of his appointment. Why, he hadn't even told his adjutant!"

"And Marie… is she well?" Lehmann came closer, until he stood an arm's length from him, looking up into his face, an arrogance to his stance emphasising that the difference in their size meant nothing to him.

His stomach muscles had tightened at the mention of his wife. "Marie is well, thanks for asking."

"That's good… and young May? It will be good for her to have a sister."

Karr stared at the albino, then answered him quietly. "I'm afraid you are mistaken, Li Min. There is only May."

"Ah…" Lehmann nodded, as if accepting the correction, yet there had been something about his assurance when he'd said it that was disturbing.

"Anyway," Lehmann said. Raising his voice so that all there could hear. "Enough small talk. You did not come here to discuss your family's health, did you, Colonel Karr? You have come here as an envoy, to try and make peace between Above and Below, to bridge that huge gap that exists between the heights and depths of our great City."

Lehmann leaned close, lowering his voice to a whisper. "Forgive the bullshit. We, at least, know why you are here." Then, raising his voice once again. "But come. Let us go through. There is much to be discussed."

The approach to Lehmann's offices was like a rat-run. Walking through the narrow corridors, Karr noticed the false walls and sliding panels and knew it could all be changed in an instant, like an ever-shifting maze. Cameras were everywhere, and laser-weaponry. The best, he realised: NorTek stuff, as good as anything Bremen had.

At the very centre of it all was a single, spartanly-furnished room. Karr followed Lehmann in, impressed despite himself, then stopped, staring at the painting on the wall behind Lehmann's desk.

"You like it?" Lehmann asked, noting the direction of his gaze.

Karr nodded. "I've never seen the like. Who is the artist? Heydemeier?"

Lehmann turned in his seat, studying the painting, taking in the elongated figure of the man, the naked body turned and crouching the face staring back out of the canvas.

"No," he answered, looking back at Karr. "The painter is long dead. Egon Schiele was his name. An extraordinary man."

Karr moved closer, noting the word that was boxed in at the bottom right corner of the canvas. "Kampfer." Is that the model's name?

Lehmann shook his head. "Kampfer is an old German word, from before the City. It means 'fighter.'

Karr nodded again. "I should have known. He looks a fighter."

Lehmann gestured toward the empty chair. "You want to sit down?"

Karr stiffened slightly. "No. I'd prefer to stand. What I have to say won't take long."

Lehmann sat back a little. "As you wish. So... what does your Master want?"

"Peace. An understanding. And some token of your... loyalty."

"My *loyalty*?" Lehmann considered that, then nodded. "And in return?"

"Li Yuan will promise to keep his armies in Africa and not bring them home."

"I see." Lehmann spread his hands on the table, the pale fingers like stilettos. "And when does the Great T'ang want my answer?"

"A week from now?"

Lehmann nodded, then, changing the subject, leaned toward him again. "You killed him, didn't you?"

"Who?"

"DeVore. And Berdichev, too. I've seen the tape."

Karr stared at Lehmann, astonished once again. *No one* had access to that tape. No one but Li Yuan. So either he was lying or...

"You're good," Lehmann said, his pink eyes filled with respect. "They say Tolonen's a fool, but he knew what you were, neh? A killer. A natural-born killer. In that we're alike, neh, Gregor Karr? *Very* alike."

Visak escorted Karr back to the gate. There they blindfolded him again and pushed him toward the waiting sedan. Yet even as he climbed between the curtains, he felt something being pushed into his left hand – felt someone close his fingers over it. He held it tightly, recognising from its shape and texture what it was. A message. Someone had passed a message on to him.

He sat there, silent, as the sedan swayed towards its destination, conscious of the two guards watching him from the seats facing him. He could smell them, hear their breathing. After a while he let himself relax, relieved now it was over and lulled by the movement of the carriage. Even so, he was worried. Lehmann had known far too much. Moreover, he had been too relaxed, too blasé about the whole thing. Why, even Li Yuan's request for some token of loyalty had barely brought a flicker of reaction.

Things were wrong. Things were badly wrong.

They left him at the pick-up point just below the City's roof. Pulling off the blindfold, he opened his hand and, unfolding the paper, read the brief note.

It was from Visak. He wanted a meeting, tomorrow, at noon. Karr nodded. It was just as they'd thought – as their sources inside Lehmann's organisation had told them – things were not as rosy as they seemed. If Visak wanted a meeting...

He folded the note and pocketed it. Then, knowing that time was of the essence, he reached up and pulled down the trap door, reaching for the ladder, hauling himself up into the access tunnel.

On the roof his cruiser waited.

Two hours later he was at Baku Spaceport, transferring to one of Tsu Ma's own cruisers for the twenty-minute flight north along the shore of the Caspian.

Karr sat to the right of the craft, directly behind the pilot, staring out of the cockpit window towards Asia, a sense of deep foreboding growing in him. The more he thought about it, the more convinced he was that Lehmann had 'spies' within Li Yuan's household.

And maybe more than spies. Maybe trained assassins, waiting to be triggered.

The next few days would be critical; he understood that now. Reading the secret briefing Rheinhardt had had prepared, he had realised just how near the brink they were. One thing – one single, crucial incident – could throw them into war, and having seen what happened on Mars and in North Africa, that was the last thing any of them wanted.

Yes, and yet war is coming.

Best then, to do as Li Yuan proposed and bring the armies home from Africa, whatever answer Lehmann gave them. Better break their word of honour than let the world slip into darkness.

He closed his eyes, feeling giddy. *Marie... my darling May...* It pained him to think what might happen to them. Yes, but they were better off in Tongjiang than Europe, that was certain.

He sighed heavily, opening his eyes again.

Down below, the perimeter of Tsu Ma's estate came into view. There was a brief exchange of codes – the high-pitched chatter of computer language – and then silence.

The final days, he thought, remembering the man's pale hands spread on the table like demonic spiders. *These are the final days.*

They circled the palace then descended on to a crowded over-spill pad to the north-east of the main palace buildings. Rheinhardt greeted him as he stepped down from the cruiser.

"Come," he said, hurrying Karr along the path and towards the palace. "The ceremony has already begun, but Li Yuan wants to see you at once." He paused, looking at Karr closely. "Is it good news or bad?"

Karr let the General read the doubt in his eyes and saw the shadow of it reflected back at him. They walked on, silent now, each lost in their own thoughts, brooding on the war to come.

Li Yuan was waiting for them in one of the small halls in the Eastern Palace, a place of shadows and dampness, bare stone and high, echoing ceilings. Tolonen was with him and his Chancellor, Nan Ho. They watched Karr cross the floor to them, their faces apprehensive.

"Well?" Li Yuan asked as Karr rose from his knees.

"He says he will give his answer within the week."

"Ah..."

Quickly he told them what had happened, leaving nothing out, not even the wording of the banner over the gate. When he had finished there was a long silence.

Li Yuan turned away, pacing between the looming pillars, the hem of his silks whispering on the stone flags. Finally, he looked to Tolonen. "Do you still think you are right, Knut? Even after what you've heard?"

Tolonen pushed out his chin, uncomfortable about being put on the spot. "I still think we should wait, *Chieh Hsia.* Let's hear his answer before we act. Things look bad, I admit. His arrogance..." The old man shook his head. "You should have crushed him while you could. Now... "

"You think it is too late?"

Tolonen looked down.

"And you, Master Nan?"

Nan Lo lowered his head. "Nothing I have heard changes my mind, *Chieh Hsia*. We must crush the man. The only question is when."

"And you, Colonel?"

Karr stared back at his T'ang, surprised to be asked his opinion. Recollecting himself, he bowed his head, averting his eyes.

"I… I was not sure before today, *Chieh Hsia*. I thought we could somehow avoid war. Now I know that it is a certainty. Li Min prepares for it. Our delay is to his advantage. And I sense something more. I sense some deeper game of his. He is like DeVore, that one. Shifting, elusive."

Li Yuan waited, then, when Karr said no more, nodded. "Thank you, Colonel. Your first duty as *Ssu-li Hsiao-wei* will be to investigate the possibility that Lehmann has infiltrated our palace at Tongjiang. Until that is completed, we shall stay here with our cousin, Tsu Ma. I shall send for your wife and daughter if it eases your mind. If there's to be any nastiness, it would be best if they were not there to see it, neh?"

Karr bowed low, grateful for his T'ang's concern.

"Then go at once. The sooner done, the…"

Li Yuan stopped, staring past Karr towards the doorway. Karr turned. It was Tsu Ma's secretary, Chiang K'o.

"Forgive me, *Chieh Hsia*, Chiang said, kneeling and bowing his head, "but news has come from Europe. It appears that the Ebert Mansion has been attacked."

Tolonen stepped forward. "Attacked? How do you mean, attacked? Is anyone hurt?"

Chiang looked to the Marshal. "The report mentions six dead and several injured."

"*Aiya!*" The old man looked to the ceiling, his face deeply pained. "Jelka and the boy, Pauli, are they…?"

"Your daughter was away when the attack happened. The boy…" Chiang swallowed and looked down. "I am afraid the boy was taken."

Tolonen shuddered.

Li Yuan stepped across and held Tolonen's arm. "You must go, Knut. At once. I shall explain things to Tsu Ma. Take Karr, Oh, and Knut…"

"*Chieh Hsia?*"

"Do whatever you need to. But get him back, neh?"

Karr watched the old man walk from room to room, disturbed by the vulnerability, the unexpected frailty he glimpsed in that normally rock-hard face. He had always considered Tolonen a cold, heartless man, but watching him crouch over the shrouded body of a female servant, seeing him lift the white sheet and wince, real hurt, real pain in his eyes, made Karr re-evaluate all he knew about him. This had hit him hard. Had shaken him to the core.

Tolonen straightened up, scratching at his neck with the fingers of his flesh and blood hand, then looked across at Karr.

"Where's he gone, Gregor? Where have they taken him?"

Karr shrugged. "We'll know soon. They're obtaining back-up camera material right now. If any exists, that is."

"But Lo Chang..." Tolonen shook his head. "I can't believe that Lo Chang was involved in this!"

It's always those we least suspect, Karr thought, but aloud he said, "We don't know that yet, Marshal. They may have taken him, too. To have someone there that the boy knows. They do that sometimes."

But Tolonen was shaking his head. "The Lo I knew would have died before he let them take the boy. He would have fought them to the death."

Yes, but he didn't. So either he was involved, or...

"Did Steward Lo have any family?"

Tolonen nodded distractedly, then saw what Karr was saying. "I've the details in my study."

Karr followed him through, then waited while the Marshal accessed his records.

"Here," Tolonen said, turning the screen to face him.

Karr studied it, then unclipped his communicator. "It's Colonel Karr. Get me Central Security."

He gave them the details, then looked back at the Marshal. "They'll let me know as soon as they've checked it out. It'll take them ten minutes maximum."

Tolonen looked away, sniffing deeply, clearly struggling to maintain his composure.

"We'll find him," Karr said. "We'll get him back."

Tolonen nodded, but he seemed unconvinced.

Karr hesitated. "Forgive me, Marshal, but we need to put someone in charge of this investigation. How about Colonel Haavikko?"

The mention of Haavikko's name seemed to bring the Marshal back to himself. "Yes... A good man, Haavikko. If anyone can do the job..." Tolonen offered Karr a smile that was closet to a grimace. "Saved my life once." He held up his golden arm. "That's when I lost this..."

Karr nodded, but he was thinking of what the duty captain had said when they'd first arrived. There had been no sign of a forced entry and no alarm had been sent. Which meant that whoever had done this had either been known to the guards on the gate, or...

No. Now that *was* being paranoid.

Tolonen was staring at him. "What is it, Gregor?"

"Security. The men who did this... they were Security. An elite squad. They'd have had proper passes, a reason to be here. They'd have known the lay-out and known how to erase all the security camera tapes.

"No." Tolonen shook his head, but his eyes said yes. After all, who else could have got in so easily? Who but one of the T'ang's own elite teams. His *Shen T'se?*

Karr unclipped his communicator and spoke into it once more. "Central Security? Karr here. Look, were any of the *Shen T'se* teams out this morning?... Two of the, huh? And have they reported in?"

He waited, meeting Tolonen's eyes, both men quite certain now.

"No sign of it, huh? I see. Look, send me full details, Faces, files, psych profiles, the lot. To the Ebert Mansion, that's right. Use Marshal Tolonen's code."

He closed the circuit.

"So," Tolonen said quietly. "All we need to know now is who they're working for, where they've taken him, and what they want."

"Haavikko..." Karr said, feeling useless suddenly. "Let me contact Haavikko."

Tolonen laughed gruffly. "We have to keep busy at times like this, neh, Gregor? It doesn't pay to think too much."

Karr stared back at the old man a moment, feeling a new respect for him, then nodded and made the call.

Jelka arrived back twenty minutes later. In the interim, news had come that Lo Chang's family were gone. They had left home the previous evening and had vanished without a trace.

Tolonen had taken the news badly, but the sight of his daughter at the door, safe but bewildered, brought a broad grin to his face. He went to her, hugging her tightly, almost lifting her off her feet.

"Jelka, my darling! Thank the gods you're safe! For a moment I thought... "

He kissed her face and held her tight again. Then, remembering, he held her at arm's length from him.

"You've heard?"

She nodded.

Slowly, his face collapsed. There was a sudden tremor in his voice. "If he's dead..."

She held him to her, patting his shoulder, comforting him. "He's not dead, Papa. Not our Pauli. We'll find him. You know we will."

She looked past her father towards Karr, who looked down, embarrassed yet also moved by this show of emotion.

"Where were you?" Tolonen asked, after a moment.

"I went to see a friend," she said, her eyes concerned for him. "They must have seen me leave. I couldn't have been gone more than five minutes. If I'd been here..." She looked down guiltily. "I would never have let them in. Not without contacting you first."

"I know," the old man said, caressing his daughter's face.

Karr, however, was staring at her. "You *knew* they were Security?"

She moved away from her father, her blue eyes meeting Karr's clearly. "Who else could it be?"

"*Aiya!*" Tolonen said, staring down at the golden figures of his left hand as if at any moment they might reach up and tear out his throat. "All this betrayal..." He groaned. "Who would have thought?"

But Jelka wasn't listening to him. Her eyes had flown open. She turned to face her father again. "Where's Golden Heart?"

Tolonen reached out to her, his granite face distressed, tears beginning to trickle down his cheeks.

"She's dead, my love. They broke her neck. So Pauli... Pauli is ours now. Ours alone. So we've got to get him back, neh? We've got to bring him home, where he belongs."

"Kim?"

Kim lifted the bulky glasses from his eyes, then looked up at the screen. "Andrew, what is it?"

"You've a visitor," Curval said, smiling down at him. "Name of Neville from Product Development. Says he knows you."

"Sure. I met him a week or so ago. What does he want?"

"He says he wants to speak to you... off the record."

Kim huffed. It would mean going through decontamination again – stripping off one suit and putting on another. For a moment he hesitated, half determined to send Neville away, his tail between his legs, then he relented.

"Okay. Tell him I'm coming out."

Five minutes later, Kim stepped from the tank and, still dripping, made his way through to the reception area. Neville was seated on the far side, reading one of the Company news sheets. Seeing Kim, he got up quickly and came across.

"Kim, I... well, I didn't plan to see you, but I was passing by and I thought..." He stopped, his eyes taking in Kim's condition, smelling the powerful cleansing agents. "Oh, shit...Look, I'm sorry. I didn't know you were..."

Kim laughed. "It's alright. Do you want to come through? I'm afraid I can't spare you long. I'm busy right now. We've begun reassembling the Model B cranium."

Neville's eyes lit up. "Could I see that?"

Kim hesitated, then nodded. "You'll have to suit up. The tiniest trace of infection and we're done for."

"I understand. And look, I'm really grateful. I..."

He handed Kim something. Kim stared at it. It was odd. Tiny, like a domino, and yet heavy.

"Like a scarab," Kim said, looking up. "What is it?"

Neville smiled. "If I'm right, it's going to be the biggest thing in the entertainments industry for the next hundred years. And before you go showing it to everyone, it's embargoed. Only Director Reiss and I have seen it. Oh, and its creator, of course."

"And now me." Kim span the tape in the air and caught it. "Well, thanks. I'm honoured. Whose work is it?"

"Shepherd's. You know him?"

"I've heard of him. Adviser to Li Yuan, isn't he?"

"That's one of his roles. But this... Neville laughed, his face registering awe. "Well, you'll see for yourself. At least, you'll get an idea of it. The real thing is phenomenal. Totally new. We're having to re-design our entertainments hardware to accommodate it."

"I see." Kim nodded thoughtfully. "Anyway, you'd better come through."

Suited up, they went inside, the air-locks hissing shut behind them.

"So what are you trying to do?" Neville asked over the suit mike, a gloved hand pointed clumsily at the exposed brain of the new prototype where it rested in the nutrient tank.

"Right now?" Kim laughed. "Well, right now I'm working on the dopamine and noradrenaline reactions – attempting to extend the time the stuff remains in the synaptic cleft."

"What does that do?"

"Do? It gives the brain a 'high' for a start. Combined with other things – with certain pheremonal responses, for instance – it can trigger a response of... well, of love. Of infatuation and desire."

"You're joking!"

"Not at all. In fact, I've never been so serious about anything. It's where we went wrong before. We tried to tailor its emotional range to fit our criteria of usefulness – criteria which stressed the machine-like, rationalistic aspects of the human mind. In the process we made it... well, effectively we made it mad. Balance, that's what this is all about. Giving our creations balance."

"Maybe so... but *love*? What if it were to develop a crush or something? What use would it be then? Surely the whole idea of developing an android is to create something quite different from us – something free of human emotional weakness."

"Is it?" Kim stared at Neville openly now, a faint amusement in his eyes. "That's what's always been assumed. But what if that's wrong? What if we need to put that full range of emotions in? What if it only works when they're all in there? After all, they've served us humans pretty well over the eons."

"So how *will* your new model be different?"

"It'll be quicker, sharper, *smarter* than the old model."

"Like you, you mean?"

Kim laughed. "Like me." Then, with a nod, he turned back, pulling the bulky glasses down over his eyes.

Neville watched him closely, fascinated, seeing how he 'fine-tuned' the brain, stimulating it with a very delicate-looking wire, injecting it with various chemicals then checking one of the four screens beside the tanks to see what kind of reaction he was getting.

On each of the screens outline skulls – normally a patchwork of blues and greens – lit up with areas of pulsing yellow and burning red. Finally, Kim put the wire down and, lifting his glasses, smiled.

"Okay. I think I'll leave it at that."

Neville nodded toward the screens. "It's certainly colourful."

"Isn't it. It's an old system, but still the most effective for this kind of work. You can see what's happening at a glance." Kim lifted the headset off and laced it on the side, then turned, facing Neville. "Curval said you wanted to talk… informally."

Neville waved a hand. "It's nothing sinister. I just thought it might help you if you had another view on things before you made your mind up about the new deal."

"But you're the one who drew up the contract!"

Neville smiled. "So? That doesn't mean I can't detach myself from things. I mean, I've not got SimFic tattooed on my bollocks!"

Kim laughed. "I'll take your word for it. But let me ask *you* something first."

"Fire away."

"What's Reiss like? You work for him. What's he *really* like?"

Neville hesitated a moment. "Difficult. I guess that's the best word to describe him. Fucking difficult at times, forgive my Mandarin. But he listens. And he's capable of changing his mind. He doesn't tolerate fools, though, nor losers. And he likes new ideas. Thrives on them, in fact. That's why he likes you so much."

"And you?"

Neville smiled. "Me? I don't know you."

Kim returned his smile, pleased by his honesty. "Let's get these suits off, then go through to my office and talk."

Neville sat in the chair in the corner, a bowl of *ch'a* cupped in his right hand, listening.

Kim sat on the edge of his bed, facing him. He had been telling Neville about what had happened in America with Old man Lever and his consortium.

"I failed once," Kim said, finishing his tale. "I don't want to fail again. Next time... well, if it was just myself..."

Neville nodded. "I understand. A man needs a family, neh? And you want security for them, right?"

"Right. But it's not just that. I'm not even talking about myself, really. It's... well, it's what I want to *do* with my talent. I've been given it for some reason - and I want to find out why. Oh. And before you ask, I have glimpses of it, but..."

"You're talking theoretical science, right?"

Kim nodded.

"That's fine. We've been anticipating it."

Kim stared at him. *"Anticipating* it?"

"Sure." Neville drained his *ch'a* and set the bowl down, then leaned towards Kim. "Look, my job is evaluating risks. Big risks and little risks. With a Company the size of SimFic even the little risks could involve the investment of billions of *yuan*. Right now, however, my biggest risk is you. When we talk in that two-page document I gave you of funding you, we mean *funding* - whatever it takes, and however long it takes. It might cost us very little. Then again, it might mean tying up a vast amount of SimFic's capital. And if you died... well, we'd have nothing. On the other hand, if one of our competitors got you..."

Kim stared at him. "Let me get this clear. You're talking about unlimited funding, right? Guaranteed."

Neville nodded. "Fully documented. And guaranteed by Li Yuan."

Kim raised an eyebrow, surprised. "What is the connection? I mean, aside from the fact that SimFic are helping him build the android.

Neville sat back again. "I'll tell you. But it's to go no further than this room, okay?

"Okay."

"Good. Then it's like this. Since the GenSyn Inheritance Hearing six years back, Li Yuan has been busy steering projects away from GenSyn to various other major Companies, SimFic among them. This was done initially to try to make GenSyn less vulnerable while it was under Tolonen's stewardship, but it proved to have a number of other advantages. What it's done, in effect, is to tie in the fortunes of six of the major Companies with those of the T'ang. Now, as far as SimFic is concerned, we've risen considerably these past few years, but we want to build on that – to make ourselves Number One, not only in commercial terms, but in terms of being the trend-setters, the innovators. It's a policy which has Li Yuan's own endorsement."

"I see." Only he had had no idea that this was going on. No idea at all.

Neville smiled. "However... there is one great weakness to this Corporate Strategy, and that's you, Kim. In the past seven years we've become more and more dependent on you as our generator of ideas, of new patents and new directions." He laughed. "Look, I know it must seem a pretty poor bargaining ploy, letting you know just how important you are to us, but... well, what's the point trying to disguise the fact? You know as well as I what you're worth. No. There's only one question we at SimFic have to answer, and that's got nothing to do with money. It's whether we can provide you with the resources to pursue whatever it is you want to do."

"But what if nothing comes of it?"

"Then nothing comes of it. It's not as if we'll be sitting on our hands. Why, it'll take us the best part of a decade to develop some of the stuff you've already given us. And as I said, it would mean our competitors didn't have you."

"So when do I sign?"

"Look, I'm not trying to pressurise you."

"No. I'm serious. If that's the deal, I'll take it."

Neville grinned. "Well..."

There was a knock. Kim stood. "Excuse me a moment."

It was Curval. "Sorry, Kim, but I didn't know if you knew. A package came for you about an hour back. It's in reception. And this." He handed Kim the bright red envelope. "It's Tolonen's hand, isn't it?"

Kim nodded, staring at the envelope suspiciously. The last time he had had a note from the old Marshal it had been to warn him to stay away from his daughter. He turned, looking to Neville. "Forgive me, Jack, but something's come up."

He stepped outside and closed the door, then slit the envelope open with his nail.

"What is it?" Curval asked. "Is the old bastard still playing his stupid games?"

"No." He handed Curval the card. "You said there was a package. Did it come with the card?"

Curval made a noise of surprise, then handed it back. "That's right. The guard said a young woman delivered them. Tall, ash-blonde hair. Sound like anyone you know?"

Kim hesitated, then touched Curval's arm. "Take care of Neville a while, will you? I won't be long."

He walked through to the reception area, trying to keep calm, but feeling all the while that he wanted to run, to whoop and punch the air. It had come. After all these years she had finally made contact again.

He shivered, thinking of her; of the startling blue of her eyes, and her smile. *She was here,* he thought, wondering what she had left him. *She actually came here.*

The guard rose from his chair behind the desk as Kim approached. "Shih Ward..."

He reached down and removed something from one of the drawers, then placed it on the desk in front of Kim. "If you would sign..."

"Of course." But Kim's palms were wet and his fingers were trembling. Steadying himself, he took the stylus and made his mark against the screen, then picked up the package.

It was a simple rectangular box, like a standard tray of samples, wrapped in dark green ersilk paper. Kim shook it gently, hearing a faint rattle from within, and frowned. The guard was watching him.

"The young woman who brought this - did she say anything?"

"Sir?"

Kim waved a hand. "It doesn't matter." Then, making his way across to one of the interview rooms, he closed the door behind him.

He took a long, calming breath, then slit the seal on the side of the box, pulled the paper back and slid out the box.

Tapes. The box held a dozen tiny tapes. He lifted one from its indented slot and studied the hand-written label.

Enceladus, Tethys. Dione and Rhea.

He understood at once. She had recorded it all. All of her travels out there in the System, knowing his fascination with it; knowing he would want to see.

He slotted it back, then picked out another, then another, nodding to himself. It was all there. Everything she'd seen. Everything she'd done. He shivered. She had waited. She had kept her promise. That was what this meant.

He leaned past the box and tapped out an activation code on the desk comset. There was a second or two's delay and then the screen lifted up out of the surface.

"Get me the Ebert mansion," he said as a young Han male's face appeared on the screen. "I'm Kim Ward from SimFic. I wish to speak…"

"I'm sorry, *Shih* Ward," the operator interrupted, "but I cannot take calls for this destination at present. If you would call later…"

"Look, this is important. Extremely important. I…"

The young Han's face shimmered then disappeared, replaced by the face of a high-ranking Security officer in his early forties, his blonde hair cut stubble neat, his eyes as blue as sapphires.

"*Shih* Ward? I understand you've been trying to get through to the Ebert Mansion urgently. I am Colonel Haavikko, in charge of the investigation. Have you any information with regard to the whereabouts of the boy?"

"The boy?" Kim frowned, confused. "I'm sorry, I don't follow you, Colonel. I wished only to talk to *Nu Shih* Tolonen. I…" Kim stopped, what Haavikko had said hitting him suddenly. "What's happened?"

Haavikko smiled tightly. "You have no information, I take it."

"No, no… but look…"

"Forgive me, *Shih* Ward, but time really is tight right now."

"Jelka… is Jelka all right?"

Haavikko had leaned toward the screen to cut connection. Now he sat back again, a weariness in his face. "The Marshal's daughter is fine, *Shih* Ward. Now, please, here's a great deal to be done."

"Of course, and thank you."

The screen went dead. Kim straightened, realising how tense he had been, then let a long, shuddering sigh escape him. For a moment there, he'd thought…

He sat, staring at the box of tapes, The boy. Someone must have taken the boy, Pauli.

"Machine?" he said, addressing the camera overhead. "Just what's going on?"

Lehmann studied the boy through the glass, then turned to his lieutenant, touching his arm.

"You did well, Jiri. But your man..."

"He's dead already."

"Good. Can't have any loose ends, can we?"

Soucek nodded, then. "So what now? Do we tell the old man that we've got him?"

"No. We let Tolonen sweat a while. Two days, maybe three. Then we give him back."

Soucek stared at him uncomprehendingly.

"Trust me, Jiri, I know how to play this. Now go. There's a lot to be done."

When Soucek was gone, he turned back, watching the boy again. Pauli was sitting in the corner once again, head down, his dark hair fallen over his eyes as he chewed the knuckles of his right hand.

That morning's audience with Karr had gone well. The big man had bought the whole package, lock, stock and barrel. All that stuff about having seen the tape of Berdichev's death – that was a lie; an audacious guess based on what he knew of Li Yuan's father. *And an accurate guess too,* he thought, remembering the shock in Karr's face. The rest... well, it had been easy to buy Karr's wife's surgeon.

Yes, and a cheap purchase, too, considering.

It could not have been better timed. With Karr already on his way, word had come that Karr's wife was pregnant – news that even Karr himself had not known.

Lehmann turned from the one-way glass. Information. It was sometimes more deadly than armies, as the great Sun Tzu had known.

Yes, he had planted the seed of paranoia deep. That single truth – gained cheaply – would confirm the veracity of the rest. As Colonel of Internal Security, Karr would embark on a witch-hunt at Tongjiang.

Disruption – maximum disruption, that was his aim. To wrong-foot them and feed them with a stream of misinformation. To play upon their weakest points and milk them. Karr he had touched, and Tolonen. Rheinhardt and Nan Ho would follow. And then Li Yuan himself. One by one he would make them uncertain of themselves.

Yes, for war was not a simple thing of armies and battles: it was a state of mind, a psychological regime. War was not won with bullets and bombs, but with the raw materials of fear, uncertainty and self-doubt.

He laughed - a cold clear laugh – then left the room, keen to get on with things. Why, before he was finished with them, he would make the look before they shat!

The ceremonies had begun before the dawn, as fourth bell sounded across the palace grounds. At that dark hour, Prince Tsu Kung-chih, eldest nephew of Tsu Ma, had stepped from the gate of the Northern Palace, dressed in the gown of the Imperial Commissioner, the *chieh* – a beribboned staff - held out before him. Two torch-bearers lit his way, while behind him came a great procession of courtiers and servants, bearing the betrothal presents on raised platforms, as well as the Golden Scroll and Seal and the *feng yu* – the great bridal chair. They made their way across the gardens at the centre of the four palaces, then stopped before the gate to the Southern Palace, where, on a crimson cushion, Liang K'o Ting, father of the Empress, knelt, awaiting them, as if at the door of his own house.

Once, in ancient times, there had been three great ceremonies of presentation, separated by long weeks of preparation. Now there was only this single, simple ritual. Even so, the servants standing three deep at the windows surrounding the gardens, watched wide-eyed, conscious of the great chain that linked them to the ancient past of their kind.

At the same moment, in a private ceremony in the *T'ai Miao*, the Supreme Hall of Ancestors, Tsu Ma was solemnly reporting the news of his betrothal to the august spirits of his ancestors, their holograms burning brightly as he knelt before them, his forehead pressed to the cold, stone flags.

Twelve hours later, Liang K'o Ting, dressed in his new uniform as an officer of the imperial bodyguard, stepped from the gate of the Southern Palace, heading north across the gardens. Behind him was a procession no less great than that which had set out earlier. This time, however, the *feng yu* was occupied, Tsu Ma's bride, Liang Shu-sun, hidden within, twenty-two bearers moving slowly, solemnly as the drums sounded the "Central Harmony". Fifty servants carried gifts on litters, while a further hundred bore large lanterns and "dragon-phoenix" flags. In the midst of all a dozen men carried two yellow pavilions, holding the Golden Seal and the Golden Scroll, symbols of Shu-sun's authority as Empress, while directly behind the great Phoenix Chair walked the servants and ministers of her household.

At the gate to the Northern Palace, Tsu Kung-ch-ih stood motionless, the *chieh* held out before him, waiting to receive his uncle's bride. Behind him, in the Great Hall at the centre of the palace, Tsu Ma sat on the dragon throne in the full glory of his imperial yellow silks, the nine dragons – eight shown and one hidden – decorating the gown.

As he reached the gate, Liang K'o Ting stood to one side, head bowed, letting the imperial commissioner, Prince Tsu Kung-ch'ih, lead the procession into the Northern Palace, relinquishing his daughter into his care. Inside, surrounding the dragon throne, stood the four hundred members of the *Nei T'ing*, the Inner Court, as well as those invited guests, numbering some fifteen hundred in all. The procession moved between them, then stopped, the great Phoenix Chair being set down below the steps of the dragon throne.

Two bells sounded, one high, one low. The final ceremony began. Tsu Ma stood, then came down the steps, halting before the *feng yu* as eight shaven-headed New Confucian officials, dressed in crimson robes, lifted the red silk curtain that covered the litter, drawing it back over the top.

Within, Shu-sun sat in the Chair, dressed from head to toe in red. The traditional *kai t'ou* covering her face. At a signal from the chief official, Tsu Ma stepped forward and delicately lifted the veil over her head.

Shu-sun's smile was radiant. Taking her hands, Tsu Ma helped her step down, her smile disarming him, making him feel at that moment like the most gauche of schoolboys. As the chants began, he stood there, facing her, disturbed by the fact that at this, one of the most public moments of his life, he was sporting the most enormous erection. As if she knew, Shu-sun's smile broadened, her eyes widening with invitation.

Tonight, he thought, surprised by the strength of his feelings. After all, he scarcely knew her. He had thought himself jaded, emotionally spent, but the simple sight of her inflamed him. Why, the last time he had felt this way had been for Fei Yen.

His sad smile was noted by her. She raised an eyebrow, querying it. So strange it was, for it suggested an intimacy that did not yet exist between them. And yet...

Well, it was as if he knew her from way back – from another cycle of existence.

He watched, unconscious of the words of the ritual, aware only of her face, her beautiful eyes, the light dancing in the darkness of her pupils.

The ceremony was halfway through when sirens began to sound beyond the doors. Tsu Ma turned, looking to his Colonel of Internal Security, Yi Ching and nodded. Yi bowed and turned, running off to discover what was happening.

Heads turned, eyes looked apprehensive, yet no one broke the silent solemnity of the moment. The chants went on, the ritual continued, while outside, echoing menacingly across the empty gardens of the palace, the sirens rose and fell.

Yi Ching rushed into the busy control room, taking control. Voices in his head had apprised him of the situation, yet he spent a moment or two studying the screens, checking for himself before he acted.

The ship was fifty *li*, over the Caspian, coming in fast from the east. Twice they had challenged it for a visual ID and twice it had ignored them. Now they had only two options – to shoot it down or let it land.

He turned to the Duty Captain. "Captain Munk… you're certain about the CGRP?"

"It's a Minor family format, sir, but unspecific."

"Shit!"

No one would blame him for shooting it out of the air, but what if it *was* one of the Minor family princes? After all, it wouldn't be the first time a cruiser's Computer-Generated Recognition Pattern had failed or been wrongly set. Yes, and things were very sensitive right now. To shoot a prince out of the air without warning would cause a terrible stink, no matter what justification there was for it.

Colonel Yi gave a groan of annoyance then banged the console hard with both fists. Now was no time to prevaricate. It would be here in less than five minutes. He leaned forward, barking instructions into the speaker.

"I want two cruisers in the air – *now!* The incoming's communicator may have failed, so make visual contact and head it off. If it ignores you again, blast it out of the sky. And no arguments, right? If it complies, take it south. Land it beyond the perimeter. I'll give further instructions then."

Yi Ching straightened up, voices sounding in the air, giving orders and confirming instructions, the mood of the room changed instantly, everyone happy now that something was happening.

He stared at the flickering point on the map screen and shook his head. Who would be so fucking stupid as to fly into their air-space at such a critical moment? He had a low opinion of the Minor Family princes – they were, after all, the most self-centred, arrogant and stupid people on the planet – but this seemed out of character even for one of them. At the same time, he simply couldn't believe this was a serious attack on the palace. There was no way a single cruiser could get through their defences. It was in the air too long. It made such an easy and obvious target. Unless…

Without a moment's delay, Yi Ching pressed the stud on his right wrist. At once, he was in direct contact with his Lieutenant in the Great Hall.

"Karlgren! Get the T'ang out of there now! Get him into one of the secure rooms and clear the Hall! I think the incoming is a diversion. Oh, and make sure Li Yuan and Wei Tseng-li are safe!"

Yi Ching looked about him, seeing the startled expressions on the faces of the nearby men, but there was no time to explain.

"Captain Munk. Take over here. Make sure my instructions are carried out to the letter."

"Sir!"

Yes, he thought, running from the room, heading back to the Northern Palace, *and let's hope to the gods I'm wrong!*

The sirens had stopped. In the central garden the crowd milled restlessly, the murmur of their voices filling the space between the walls of the ancient palaces. From the top of the steps to the Northern Palace, Prince Tsu Kung-ch'ih looked on, the dour expression he had worn all day replaced by a smile of ironic amusement.

All day he had had to play his uncle's creature, bowing and scraping, acting to *his* order, reading from *his* script, greeting *his* bride, but now – through no effort of his own – he had had the last laugh.

Until he died he would remember the look of anger on his uncle's face, the pure fire of exasperation - of denied expectation – in his eyes as they hustled him away and cleared the Hall, the ceremony unfinished, the woman not yet his bride. And even though it had proved a false alarm, Kung-ch'ih felt it was an omen – a clear sign that this marriage was ill-fated.

You cheated me, he thought, thinking of that day beside the cliff face. *You *led me to believe I was your heir, and then you cheated me. But I'll not relinquish it that easily. Oh no. Not if you take a dozen wives!*

Hearing voices behind him, he turned, in time to see Colonel Yi and the three T'ang coming out from where they had been closeted these past few minutes. Yi Ching backed off a pace and bowed, then turned, letting them move past him.

Tsu Kung-ch'ih straightened up, facing his uncle squarely as he came toward him.

"Nephew," Tsu Ma said, touching his arm gently. "I am afraid we must deal with this matter at once. If you would lead our guests into the Eastern Palace, I shall have Lao Kang arrange refreshments."

"And the ceremony, Uncle?"

Tsu Ma huffed, clearly upset, but the smile he gave his nephew was kind. "I am afraid the ceremony must be delayed until tomorrow, Kung Ch'ih. It would be... *inauspicious* to continue now, neh?"

"As you wish, Uncle," Kung-ch'ih answered, bowing his head low, his face expressing grave disappointment, but inside he was exultant.

The four men stopped just outside the cell, the camera swivelling automatically to cover them, its laser-trackers beading all four of them.

"Are they here?" Tsu Ma asked, pulling at the knuckles of his left hand as if he wanted to strike someone.

Yi Ching hesitated, aware of Li Yuan's presence there beside his Master, then nodded. "The crew of the ship are elsewhere, *Chieh Hsia,* in separate cells. It seems they were acting under orders. However, as far as their Mistress is concerned...

"Their *Mistress?*" Tsu Ma stared at his Colonel in disbelief. "You mean some damned *woman* did this? *Aiya!* I'll have the bitch quartered!"

Yi Ching bowed his head, but glanced uneasily at Li Yuan. "Forgive me, *Chieh Hsia,* but I think you might want to see her alone."

"Nonsense, Colonel Yi. The insult was not to me alone. My cousins deserve an explanation, neh?"

"Of course, *Chieh Hsia.*"

Yi Ching turned, motioning to the guards, who took turns to tap their personal codes into the lock then place their eyes against the retinal-scanner.

The cell door hissed open.

Tsu Ma moved past his Colonel into the cell, then stopped dead, giving a gasp of surprise.

On the bench seat facing him sat Fei Yen, her hands bound, a tracer-necklet glowing faintly about her neck. He turned, in time to see the flash of astonishment in Li Yuan's eyes as he too saw who it was.

"Fei Yen..." he said quietly, his voice incredulous. "What in the gods' names were you up to?"

She stared back at him with dumb insolence, then raised her hands, displaying the restraints.

"Unbind her!" Tsu Ma ordered, then turned to Wei Tseng-li. "Cousin, if you would leave this to us?"

Wei Tseng-li looked from one to the other, not understanding what was going on, then nodded. "As you wish, cousin. If you need me..."

"Of course," Tsu Ma said gently, giving him a troubled smile, then turned back, watching as the guard unclipped Fei Yen's wrist-restraints.

As the door slammed shut, he glanced at Li Yuan, then looked up at the overhead camera.

"Surveillance off!"

At once the red operating light vanished.

Tsu Ma turned, staring directly at Fei Yen, giving full vent to the anger he had been keeping in. "*You!* What the *fuck* do you think you were up to, flying in without proper identification codes? Have you any idea what you've done? *Aiya...* I'd like to know why I shouldn't just have you flogged and executed? You and your whole damned family!"

"I had to see you," she said quietly, her face hardened against his accusations. "Today, before it was too late."

"Too late?" Tsu Ma laughed, exasperated. "Too late for what?"

"For my son."

"Your *son?* What has your son got anything to do with this?"

"Because he's your son too, Tsu Ma."

There was a long silence and then Tsu Ma laughed. But beside him Li Yuan was looking down, his lips pursed.

"No, Fei Yen," Tsu Ma said finally, meeting her eyes, a cruel, unforgiving anger there. "I have no sons."

She looked back at him defiantly. "No, Tsu Ma? You can say that with absolute certainty?"

His chest rose and fell. For a moment it seemed as if he would say nothing, then, with a tiny glance at Li Yuan, he answered her. "I *have* no sons."

"No?" She turned, pointing at Li Yuan. "Why don't you ask your cousin if that's true?"

Tsu Ma turned, looking to Li Yuan, his eyes pained, knowing that a sudden gulf had opened between them - one that perhaps might never be bridged – yet he spoke gently, as if to a brother.

"Is it true, Yuan? Is Han Ch'in my son?"

Li Yuan looked up, a profound sadness in his eyes. In an instant it had all come back to him, all of the hurt he'd felt, all of the bitterness and betrayal. But worse, for now he *knew*. Tsu Ma – his beloved Tsu Ma – had betrayed him.

He shuddered, then answered her, his voice toneless. "You are wrong, Fei Yen. It is as Tsu Ma says. He has no sons."

She stared back at him, disbelief in his eyes, then slowly shook her head, her eyes widening, understanding coming to her. "But... but you *divorced* me!"

He nodded. "I had to. Don't you understand? You were a weakness I could no longer tolerate. A cancer that was eating away at me. To be a T'ang and to be subservient to you... that could not be, Fei Yen. It simply could not be."

"*Aiya!*"

There was pain in her face; pain at the realisation of what had really happened. "Han Ch'in... he's yours, isn't he? Yours. And you knew that, didn't you. Knew it all along!"

Li Yuan shook his head. "No, Fei Yen. Han Ch'in is *your* child. Yours alone. You made your bed, now you must lie in it!"

She stood, angry now and close to tears. "I shall do no such thing! My son..." She swallowed, then lifted her head proudly. "My son will be a T'ang one day!"

He answered her scathingly, his eyes cold. "Your son is nothing, woman. Understand me? *Nothing!*" He took a step toward her, his very calmness menacing. "It was always the way with you, wasn't it, Fei Yen? You could never be content. You *always* had to meddle. To spoil things and break them. Too much was never enough for you, you always had to have more. More and more and more, like a petulant child. But now..." He sighed and shook his head. "Now it must end. You have finally overstepped the mark. You have left me with no option."

Tsu Ma reached out and touched his arm. "But Li Yuan..."

Li Yuan turned, looking down at the hand that rested on his arm, his eyes burning with indignation. "Cousin... don't you think you have already done enough?"

Tsu Ma drew back his hand, then bowed his head.

Li Yuan stared at him a moment longer, then turned back, facing his ex-wife. "As for you, Fei Yen, you shall return to Hei Shui, but this time under guard. You are to speak to no one and see no one. All correspondence between you and the outside world will be strictly censored. And as for your son... your son shall be kept elsewhere, as guarantee of your good behaviour."

She stared at him, then gave a wail of anguish and sank to her knees, pressing her forehead to the floor, her voice distraught.

"*Aiya!* Please the gods, no, Li Yuan! *Please* leave Han Ch'in with me. I've nothing without him. *Nothing!*"

She looked up at him, tearful now, her still beautiful eyes imploring him. "As you once loved me, please do this for me, Li Yuan. Let my son live with me at Hei Shui. I shall do anything, sign anything at all, but let him stay. Please the gods, let him stay!"

He stood there a moment, staring down at her, thinking of the hell she had put him through – of all the bitter blackness he had suffered because of her – and slowly shook his head.

"It is over, Fei Yen. It is finished now. You understand?"

Then, turning from her, he left the cell, Tsu Ma following him out, neither man looking at the other, the screams of the woman following them both as they walked, silent, side by side down the long, dimly-lit corridor.

CHAPTER 127

WHERE THE PATH DIVIDES

Li Yuan returned to Tongjiang at once, taking Pei K'ung and all his entourage with him. There, in the great study that had been his father's and his father's father's before him, he called together all his senior officials, summoning them from whatever duties they were attending to. By five they were all gathered and the Council of War began.

On the journey back he had spoken to no one, not even his Chancellor, Nan Ho, giving no explanation for his mood or actions. Nor, when he opened the great Meeting Of State, did he say a word about what had happened at Astrakhan, though all there, having heard of the alarm during the wedding ceremony, knew that *something* had transpired.

Watching him from the other side of the council table, Master Nan saw the new hardness in his Master's face and wondered what had passed between him and Tsu Ma. He had seen him return from that meeting in the cells – had seen the coldness, the sudden distance between the two great friends – and known at once that something was badly wrong. Then, when Li Yuan had ordered them gone from there, he had known there had been a breach. Nothing else would have made Li Yuan miss his cousin's wedding celebrations. But what had caused it?

For the next six hours Nan Ho had listened as each man spoke, spelling out what stage their preparations were at, yet he knew for a fact that many there, surprised by the suddenness of the summons – were far from as prepared as they claimed. Contingency plans had been drawn up months ago, after the New Year meeting of Ministers, but no one had seriously expected war. Not *this* year.

But things had changed.

When, at long last, they were gone, Master Nan held back, waiting by the door. Normally Li Yuan would call him back to discuss what had been said, but now he just sat there, slumped forward in his chair, his fingers steepled beneath his chin, staring into space.

He closed the door then went across.

"Chieh Hsia?"

Li Yuan looked up, his eyes distracted. "Master Nan. I guess you deserve an explanation."

Nan Ho waited, silent, head bowed.

"I... I have done something that perhaps I should not have done. I have cast off a wife and denied a rightful son."

Nan Ho looked up, surprised. Li Yuan was looking past him, his face muscles tensed against the strong emotions his words were evoking, but his eyes were misted. "I acted wrongly, Master Nan. Yet I too was wronged... both by my wife and my most trusted friend."

Nan Ho felt a ripple of shock pass through him. *So it was true.*

I didn't know," Li Yuan continued. "I didn't really *want* to know, I suppose. Until today." He paused a moment, as if steeling himself against what he was saying, then spoke again. "Today it was all made clear. Today I understood how it was – how it has been all this time."

"Chieh Hsia..."

"No, Master Nan. Let me finish. I should have found out long ago. I should have made it my business to know what really happened. My father said I ought, but my pride was sorely hurt and besides, I... I could just about bear it so long as I didn't know. Knowing - knowing exactly what happened... that would have broken me!"

"I understand."

He stared at his Master, seeing, for that brief moment, the vulnerable little boy he had once had to tend – the young man he had introduced into the ways of the flesh. Oh, if he had only known what love would do to his charge he would have killed Fei Yen with his bare hands long before she ever managed to get her talons into him. He would have gladly sacrificed himself to prevent it. But now it was too late. Now they must learn to exist in the ruins of these relationships. Nan Ho sighed, then uttered the words he knew his Master did not wish to hear.

"You must make peace with him, *Chieh Hsia.* You must set aside your feelings as a man and act as a T'ang... as a true Son Of Heaven would."

Li Yuan studied him a moment, then shook his head. "It is too late for that, Master Nan. To be a T'ang... well, one must know where one stands, neh? One must know who one's friends are and who one's enemies. All I know, right now, is that Tsu Ma is no friend. And if not a friend, then I must count him henceforth as an enemy – as someone I cannot rust to come when I call, asking for aid. I must make my plans dependent on my own strength and follow my own council from here on."

"But *Chieh Hsia...*"

Li Yuan raised his hand imperiously, silencing his Chancellor.

"You are a good man, Master Nan, but do not oppose me in this. Be as a friend and aid me, for I have dire need of friends in these dark times.

"*Nu-ts'ai, Chieh Hsia,*" he said, sinking to his knees and touching his forehead to the ground.

I am your slave, Majesty.

Karr came to him an hour later.

"*Chieh Hsia?*"

"Colonel... please, relax a moment. Take a seat. We need to talk."

Karr hesitated, then sat, facing li Yuan, his huge frame filling the tall-backed official's chair.

"Is there any news of the boy?"

"No, *Chieh Hsia.* I'm fairly certain now that it was one of our own elite teams."

Li Yuan sat back. "I see. And Marshal Tolonen? How is he taking this?"

"Badly, *Chieh Hsia.* He... well, forgive me if this sounds impertinent, but I feel he is close to breaking point."

"Should I send one of my surgeons?"

"It would do no good, *Chieh Hsia.* His daughter tried to get him to rest, but he has refused all sedation. Indeed, I saw him take two Stayawake capsules. He is determined to see this through, whatever the personal cost.

Li Yuan nodded, his eyes pained. "Perhaps I should order him to rest."

"Maybe so, *Chieh Hsia.*"

"And the other matter... your investigations into the household staff. How goes that?"

"Slowly, *Chieh Hsia*. It is difficult to know where to start. I have asked the six most senior members of the palace household to draw up lists of those they would trust implicitly and those they are less certain of."

"And what good would that do?"

"It is my intention to compare the lists and see where they differ, then go back and ask why. At the same time, *Chieh Hsia*, I have set up a team to monitor all contacts between Tongjiang and the outside world. If there's an information leak we shall find it."

"Good. But one further thing before you go. You will have heard that I called a special meeting of my most senior ministers and advisers."

"*Chieh Hsia?*"

"To judge by what was said in that meeting, we would be ready to fight a war at a moment's notice. The truth is very different. My own assessment is that we are weeks, possibly even months from a state of readiness. Would that be your reading too, Colonel Karr?"

Karr smiled. "It would, *Chieh Hsia.*"

"And what would you say was the greatest problem confronting us?"

"Speaking from experience, *Chieh Hsia*, I'd say it was supplies. A war against Li Min... well, it would be even more difficult a logistics problem than the campaign in Africa. There we could at least stake out and clear a stack before each supply drop. Here in Europe... well, it would be a war fought level by level on our own territory. Supplying our own forces while denying our enemies access to those same supplies – that would be an almost impossible task."

"I agree. If, that is, we were to fight a war on that basis."

"*Chieh Hsia?*"

"One last thing. How long would it take to prepare the three Banner armies in Africa for a new campaign?"

Karr considered. "Three days, *Chieh Hsia?*"

"Good. Then that is all."

Karr bowed his head, then, as his T'ang stood, hastened to his feet.

"You have been most helpful, Colonel," he said as he ushered him to the door. "If you would keep me advised on any developments with the boy..."

"Of course, *Chieh Hsia.*"

"Good. I understand your wife is here."

"That is so, *Chieh Hsia.*"

"Then you must see her. Spend the night with her."

"Forgive me, *Chieh Hsia,* but I am on duty."

Li Yuan smiled, placing his arm briefly on the giant's arm. "Go. I order it. I shall have Master Nan arrange cover for you. And make the best of it, neh? I fear you may have few such opportunities in the weeks to come."

As the evening light began to fade, Karr walked slowly back to the guards' quarters, his heart heavy, his mood darkened by what Li Yuan had said. He had known war would come – they all had – but it had always been some vague time in the future, never soon – never only a matter of days away. He should have been ready for it, for he had seen much fighting in the African Campaign, yet somehow this was different. War in City Europe; hand to hand fighting in the levels; all of that disruption, all of that chaos and carnage, the awful, barbaric brutality of it – it was hard to believe that all of that must come now to his homeland.

Marie was in the kitchen when he got there, singing to herself as she unpacked things from one of the big transit-boxes and put them away on shelves. He went across and put his arms about her waist, making her jump with surprise then snuggle back against him.

"Where's May?" he asked, murmuring into her neck as he kissed it.

She turned and leaned back against the sink, smiling at him. "She's out in the gardens with the other children. It's like paradise for her. Why, she doesn't even seem bothered by the insects!"

He looked past her out of the half-open window, hearing the distant shrieks and laughter of the children. It was true. This was like paradise after the confinement of the levels, yet his pleasure at being there was muted by his knowledge of what lay ahead.

"What is it?" she asked, seeing the shadows in his face.

He met her eyes, pained by the simple strength and beauty of her. "It's war, my love. We're going to go to war."

Her breath caught. "Did *he* say that?"

"No, but I could see it in his eyes. He is determined on it. Something must have happened."

The light had gone out of her face. She looked away, then looked back at him, offering a tight smile. "Well, maybe it's best that we're here then. Back there..."

He nodded, then reached out and held her once again, kissing her brow. "I'm off duty tonight," he whispered, smiling at her. "The T'ang has ordered it.

"Ah..." Her face lightened, her eyes widening, yet there was still a darkness at the back of them. War... who knew what War would bring?

"I have some news, too," she said, her smile broadening.

"News?"

"A baby," she said hesitantly. "We're going to have another baby, Gregor."

"That's great..."

Inside, however, he felt himself go cold with fear. He had dismissed what Lehmann had said as idle talk, but the man had been right. Somehow he had known.

"Gregor? What is it?"

"I was *told*. Li Min told me."

She gave a small laugh. "He couldn't have. I only found out yesterday. I haven't told anyone, not even May. I was waiting to tell you first."

"He knew..." he said quietly. "The bastard *knew*." He heaved a sigh, then, "Look, stay here a moment, there's something I want to check."

He made to turn away but she called him back. "Gregor?"

"Yes?"

"Did you... I mean, did you *want* another child?"

Looking at her, he realised suddenly how scared she was, how close she was to tears. He went to her and held her tightly, stroking her back, physically reassuring her.

"Marie... Marie, my darling love, you know I do." He lifted her chin, making her look at him. "It's *wonderful* news, it really is, but..." His smile slowly faded. "Get May in and settle her. Okay? I'll be back in a while."

Outside, in the imperial gardens, the evening light was falling. Walking back to the duty room, Karr ran a dozen different scenarios through his mind, yet he knew, even before Bremen confirmed it. They were dead; the Surgeon and all his staff. Blown into the next world by a bomb planted in some new equipment they had taken delivery of only that morning.

Returning to his rooms, he rehearsed how he would tell her – how reveal to her just how small, how vulnerable they were, but facing her, he found there was no need. She read his face and looked down, nodding.

"Where's May?" he said softly, wearily.

"Asleep. She's tired herself out."

"Ah... He reached for her, holding her tightly once again, squeezing her arms, her back, reassuring himself that she was there, alive and warm – at least for this time longer – knowing suddenly just how easily he could have lost her.

"We'll be safe here," he said, "War or no War, Tongjiang is safe."

And she smiled, as if comforted by his words, yet something in her eyes mirrored back his own growing doubts. Nowhere was safe anymore. Nowhere. Not even Tongjiang.

The moon was full, burning a perfect circle of white in the blackness of the sky. Beside it the mountain glistened, its crooked peak thrust like an ice-pick into the frigid air.

Lehmann stood on the slope on the far side of the valley, staring at the scene, his hood thrown back, his breath pluming in the air. It had been months since he had come out here. Months since he had seen anything so beautiful.

He shivered, more from awe than from the cold, then turned to look to his lieutenant, Soucek, who had just arrived.

"Is there any word yet?"

Soucek rubbed his gloved hand together and shook his head inside the fur-lined hood. "Nothing."

"Ah..." Lehmann turned back, distracted by the news. It was strange. Visak was normally so reliable.

"He's over two hours late," Soucek added, coming alongside. "Do you think something's happened to him?"

He shrugged. For a moment he was silent, breathing in the pure, cold air, letting the inhuman perfection of the place fill him, then he turned, looking back at Soucek.

"It's almost time. You know that, don't you? All these years we've waited, and now... Well, now that it's here I hesitate. We have the means, the will, the *strength* to beat Li Yuan. Even so, I hold back. And I don't know why. That's why we're here, Jiri. To try to see things clearly. To work out if there's anything we might have overlooked."

"It's to be war, then?"

Lehmann nodded, his face mask-like, almost transparent in the moonlight, his eyes sparkling unnaturally, like a demon's. "Are you afraid, Jiri?"

Soucek hesitated, then nodded.

"Good. That's a fighter's emotion. To be afraid and yet to be in control of one's fear." Soucek stamped his feet, the cold getting to him. "It seems a long time since we killed Lo Han. Seven years... You know, I felt *alive* that day. I felt... well, close to something. Something I'd never experienced before. But these past few years, since we defeated Fat Wong and his cousins... well, sometimes it seemed like a dream. As if I wasn't fully awake."

Lehmann turned, looking at Soucek directly, understanding what the other man was saying. He too had missed the danger. Missed that feeling of extending himself – of putting himself at risk. It had all been too easy. Too *safe*.

"You're right, Jiri. We *have* been sleeping, letting events drift when we should have been seizing the moment and shaping it. Playing at being kings when we should have been stoking the fire beneath the dragon throne. But now it's time to change all that."

Soucek had been staring at the tree-line far below. Now he looked back at Lehmann. "What do you mean?"

"I mean we ought to push a little and see what happens."

"Push?"

He turned, looking to the east, as if he could see beyond the mountains, beyond the great sweep of Eastern Europe and the Urals, right to where Li Yuan sat at his desk in Tongjiang. "*Push.* Create pressure in the House. Ferment trouble among the African Banners. Assassinate some of Li Yuan's leading officials. That kind of thing."

"And his offer?"

Lehmann shrugged. He didn't know. He was tempted to say no, to defy Li Yuan and see what he did. But maybe that would be too direct.

"I don't think he wants to go to war. I don't think he has the will. Besides, he'll wait on his cousins – see what they say first. No, the more I think about it, the more I'm convinced we should play a double game. Play loyal subject to his face while undermining him at every opportunity."

"And if we're wrong?"

"Then we fight."

He stopped, looking past Soucek, then relaxed. It was one of his own men.

"What is it, Stewart?"

Stewart bowed his head. "There's no sign of Visak," he said breathlessly. "Not a sign of him since six. He was due to meet some of our people in Osnabruck, but... he didn't show."

"I see." He waved the man away, then turned to Soucek. "What do you think?"

"Think?"

But it was clear what Soucek thought. His eyes gave him away. He thought Visak had gone over – sold them out – and if Soucek thought that then maybe it was true. But he would find out first. Make sure before he acted.

"You know what I think?" he said, looking up at the moon hanging there like a great white stone in the sky. "I think we'd better get back. I think the game's begun."

"Daddy?"

Jelka pushed the door open with her knee, then stepped inside, into the darkness, the tray balanced carefully between her hands.

Her father was sitting in his chair, the holo-viewer on the floor in front of him, the control module in his lap, the golden fingers of his right hand wrapped about it. In the air before him stood a boy, dressed in a miniature of the Marshal's uniform.

She went across and set the tray down, then stood behind him.

It was something they had recorded only weeks ago; part of the great *Kalevala* she herself had set to music. Watching it, she felt once again the sharp pain of Pauli's absence, that awful, gnawing uncertainty of not knowing where he was, nor what was happening to him.

In the projection Pauli stood there, straight and tall and proud, his dark hair combed neatly across his forehead, his whole body lifted slightly on the balls of his feet as he sang, his eyes staring into the distance as he concentrated on the words.

> "Hereupon the bird spoke language,
> And the hawk at once made answer:
> O thou smith, O Ilmarinen,
> Thou the most industrious craftsman!
> Truly art thou very skilful,
> And a most accomplished craftsman!"

> "Thereupon smith Ilmarinen
> Answered in the words that follow:
> 'But indeed 'tis not a wonder,
> If I am a skilled craftsman,
> For 'twas I who forged the heavens,
> And the arch of air who welded.'"

He sang on, his pure, high voice seeming to capture the very essence of those ancient days – of that distant time before the City had been built over the land, before the world had been cloaked in ice. Looking at him, she realised with a start of surprise how very like his father he was – not the Hans Ebert she had known on Chung Kuo, the one who had almost married her, but the one she had met on Mars – "The Changeling" as she liked to think of him. She shivered, strangely moved by the thought. Her father had brought the boy up well. There was nothing spoiled about him, nothing impetuous or soft – nothing *corrupt*. His voice was like a light shining out from deep within, revealing that perfect pitch of his inner being, resonant with innocence and hope. So strange that was, so utterly strange, considering that his father had been a traitor, his mother a madwoman and a whore. But the boy... She listened as he finished, entranced and deeply moved, the ancient tale made new in his song.

The old man froze the image, a tremor passing through him, tears on his cheeks. She laid her hands gently on his shoulders. He turned, looking up at her, then reached up, grasping her hands tightly in his own. She squeezed them, for once not bothered by the cool, metallic feel of his left hand.

"We'll get him back," she said, fighting back the tears. "You *know* we will."

"It's not that easy," he said, his face hardening. "Things are changing by the hour."

He released her hands and stood, facing her, all softness gone from him suddenly. "Things are bad, my love. We could be at war within the week."

She stared at him, shocked. "*War?*"

He nodded. "I asked the T'ang for Karr, but he refused. Things are happening. Pauli... well, Pauli's but a single stone in the great game." His voice faltered, then was strong again. "We must deal with this matter ourselves."

She frowned, not understanding. "Deal with it? How?"

He turned his head, looking at the desk and the tray there. "Is that soup?"

"Yes, but answer me, Daddy. How? *How* are you going to deal with this?"

He looked back at her, a sour look on his lips. "I have not been a soldier sixty years for nothing. I know people..."

"People?"

He looked away. "It's best you don't ask."

Best? She shivered, seeing there, in her father's eyes, a steely hardness, a determination which she recognised from the past – that same determination that had made him defy his T'ang and kill Representative Lehmann before the whole House – that same iron-hard spirit that would wreck a world before it allowed harm to one of its own.

Maybe it is best that I don't know what you are planning, she thought. Then, reaching up, she gently stroked the drying tears from his face.

The cell was dark, the dull red glow of the LOCKED signal above the studded door the only source of illumination. On the bunk in the corner lay the boy, a rough blanket covering his nakedness. Two guards patrolled the corridor outside. He could hear their booted footsteps click and echo in the silence.

Cold. It was so cold here.

He huddled into himself, conscious of the camera somewhere in the dark above him, watching his every move. Infra-red it was – he knew that. Uncle Knut had told him all about such things. He turned over, facing the wall, trying to relax, trying not to cry. He had done so well. Throughout it all he had held his head up and been brave, like he'd been taught. But\ now, alone in the darkness, it was suddenly much harder.

No, he told himself, swallowing hard. *They're watching me, waiting for me to break down, so I mustn't. For Uncle Knut's sake.*

For a moment his thoughts wandered and he imagined himself back in his own bed, back in the Mansion; imagined that the footsteps were those of his servants; then he remembered. The servants were all dead. He had seen them die. Chang Mu and Shih Chih-o, Li Ho-nien and his favourite, Ma Ch'ing, the last in his room, fighting them vainly, trying to stop them from taking him.

He shuddered, trying to control himself, to push back the memories, but they were too powerful for him. Unbidden, a tear trickled down his cheek and then another.

And his mother...

Pauli gritted his teeth, but a low moan forced itself out from somewhere deep inside him.

Be brave, he heard the old man say. *Whatever you have to face in life, be brave and face it squarely.* But it was hard to be brave when no one came, when no one even knew where you were. Harder yet when the memories came crowding back to haunt you.

He ducked his head beneath the blanket and secretly wiped the moistness from his cheeks, then sat up and turned, placing his feet on the cold, earthen floor, ignoring the cold.

Remember the song, he told himself, hearing Jelka's soft voice coaxing him in his head. And, lifting his head, he began, his pure, high voice sounding in the silent darkness, making the guards outside turn and listen.

> "Still the sun was never shining,
> Neither gleamed the golden moonlight,
> Not in Vainola's dark dwellings,
> Not on Kalevala's broad heathlands.
> Frost upon the crops descended,
> And the cattle suffered greatly,
> And the birds of air felt strangely,
> All mankind felt ever mournful,
> For the sunlight shone no longer,
> Neither did there shine the moonlight...."

It was after eleven when Tsu Ma finally left the Council Chamber. He had been loath to call such a meeting, despite what had happened earlier, but the news from his agents in Tongjiang could not be ignored. If their reports were true, Li Yuan was preparing for war, and that would mean trouble in his own City.

He stood in the tiny ante room a moment, alone – for the first time since the dawn, alone – and tried to still his racing thoughts. Too much had happened too fast. That business with Fei Yen...

Tsu Ma let a sigh escape him, then sat, raking his fingers through his hair distractedly. He had always thought that Li Yuan had known; had known but been too tactful, too much a "brother" to ever mention it. Since the day of Li Yuan's coronation, when he had approached him about the child, he had assumed the boy was his: that Li Yuan knew yet had forgiven him. If he had thought for a moment...

"*Aiya...*" he said softly. If he had known what damage that woman could do he would have had her killed. Or was that true? Wasn't he still more than a little in love with her? Hadn't his anger at her today been tempered by some other, darker feeling?

He blew out a long breath, then leaned forward. If the truth were told, seeing her there in the cell, chained and defiant, he had felt that old familiar fire burn up in him again – had remembered, for the briefest instant, how it had been to lie with her. No other woman had ever fired him so. No other had ever made him lie there sleepless with the memory.

Tsu ma shuddered, then stood, realising suddenly that someone was in the doorway, waiting. It was Hwa Kwei, his Master of the Inner Chambers.

"*Chieh Hsia?*"

"What is it, Master Hwa?"

"My Mistress, the Empress, has sent me to ask if you will be coming to her rooms tonight."

His wedding night... He had forgotten. This was, after all, his wedding night.

He stared at Hwa Kwei, then waved a hand at him. "Tell her I shall come in a while. I need a moment's thought."

Hwa bobbed his head. "*Chieh Hsia!* Should I bring something to eat? Some soup perhaps? And something for the Empress?"

Tsu Ma was looking away, staring at the portrait of his father that hung over the fireplace. "That's kind, Master Hwa, but I have no appetite. Bring something for the Empress, however."

"*Chieh Hsia...*"

Alone again, his thoughts returned to Li Yuan and his cast-off son. How could Li Yuan have done that? It made no sense. No sense at all. If he had wanted to deal with Fei Yen, he could have exiled her and married again. There had been no need to divorce her, not if her son was his.

Unless, of course, he had wanted to punish her. And what better way to punish a headstrong, ambitious woman like Fei Yen than by denying her son the right to be a T'ang.

The thought of it quite shocked him. He had thought Li Yuan a less vindictive man. But who knew what passion – what spurned passion – could do to a man?

He looked back at his father's image. "What would you have done, Tsu Tiao?"

But the question, he knew, was an idle one. His father would never have got involved. His father would have cut off his own manhood before he would touch another man's wife. And as for that woman being the wife of a fellow T'ang...

"This is all my fault," he said quietly, bowing his head to the portrait, ashamed of himself. "And I must rectify it if I can."

Yes, he thought. But how? What in the gods' names can I do to make things up with him? His wife. I stole his wife. It does not matter that her beauty blinded me. What matters is the fact that I betrayed him. He who I counted as a brother.

He shuddered, afraid, suddenly deeply afraid of what he had done.

So the wheel turns. So fate catches up with us.

But it was not too late. If he could only speak to him. If he could only humble himself before his cousin.

He lifted his head, speaking to the camera overhead.

"Contact Li Yuan at Tongjiang. Tell him I wish to speak to him. I shall take the call in my study."

While his servants set up the link, he paced the corridor, trying to work out what he would say – rehearsing phrases, trying to find some formula of words that would explain why he had acted as he had.

I love you, Li Yuan. Can't you see that? As I loved my elder brother Chang. As you loved Han Ch'in. It was their deaths that brought us so close. Beside which, this is nothing.

He sighed, then pushed through the doors into his study. If only that were true. If only it *were* in the past. But he had seen Li Yuan's face and had known at once that the hurt he'd felt had never gone away – that, deep inside, the wound had never healed. Was bleeding yet.

Tsu Ma went to his desk and sat, waiting, his fingers interlaced before him, his whole body trembling with a fearful anticipation. He had thought himself fearless; had thought himself beholden to no other man, but now he knew. Li Yuan. He *needed* Li Yuan. As a friend. As a brother and an intimate. Without him... Well, he could not bear the thought of it. To be severed from Li Yuan after all they had gone through together. It could not be. It simply could not be.

A minute passed, and another. Then, with a suddenness that made him jump, there was a knock.

"Enter," he said, feeling his heart thump heavily in his chest.

His Secretary, Tu Fu-wei, took a step into the room then bowed low.

"What is it, Tu Fu-wei?"

"It is Li Yuan, *Chieh Hsia.* He refuses to speak to you. He..." The young man looked bewildered. "It seems he has given orders for the borders to be closed between the Cities."

Tsu Ma stared at his servant, stunned by the news. The last time Li Yuan had closed the borders had been when he had had the plague in his City and had closed the gates to City Africa. Within months there had been war.

He sat back, robbed of words, then shook his head.

"Chieh Hsia?"

There was a blankness in his head. He could not think. For once he did not know what to do.

Tu Fu-wei came closer, looking at his master with alarm now. *"Chieh Hsia?* Are you alright? Should I send for Surgeon T'ung?"

Tsu Ma looked back at his Secretary. "No, I..." He stopped and shook his head, waving the man away, then stood, needing for the briefest moment to support himself against the desk.

The borders. Li Yuan had closed the borders ...

Tsu Ma crossed the room and went out, heading for his new bride's quarters. He had to see her. It was his duty, after all, to see her. Yet all of the joy – all of that wonderful lustful anticipation he had been feeling earlier had gone from him now, leaving him an empty husk, while all the while, his thoughts circled the same point.

He will come round. He's angry now, but that will change. He needs to sleep on it, that's all. Right now he wants revenge. Rightly so. But in a day or two …

No, he thought, stopping outside Shu-sun's door. *For there are some things that can never be forgiven. Some actions which can never be atoned for. Not in a thousand years.*

Then, steeling himself against his new bride's disappointment, he knocked on the door and pushed it open, the rich scent of her perfume greeting him as he stepped into the darkness.

"Hwa Kwei?"

The voice from the shadows was only a whisper. Nonetheless, Tsu Ma's Master of the Inner Chambers stopped dead, giving a small cry of surprise. He had thought he was alone and unobserved.

Stepping from the shadows, Prince Kung-ch'ih took him by the arm and drew him aside, into one of the small reception rooms.

Closing the door quietly behind him, the young prince turned, looking at the tray Hwa was carrying, at the cloth-covered bowl, then met his eyes again. "Have you…?"

Hwa shook his head, then answered the prince quietly, terrified of being overheard. "I couldn't. Her door is locked. It seems the T'ang sleeps alone tonight."

"Alone?" Kung-ch'ih's voice was loud with surprise. "On his *wedding* night?"

Hwa Kwei winced. "Please, Master…"

Kung-ch'ih grinned. "That bodes well, neh, Master Hwa? But we must be sure." He reached down and removed the cloth from the bowl, then sniffed at the soup. "You are sure this will work?"

Hwa Kwei nodded.

"Good. Then make sure you treat our Mistress, the new Empress well, Master Hwa. Make sure she has her bed-time bowl of soup, particularly those nights when my uncle *does* choose to visit her."

Hwa Kwei swallowed then bowed his head. "I shall do as you command, Prince Kung."

Kung-ch'ih straightened up, his demeanour changing, suddenly more threatening. "Make sure you do, Hwa Kwei. Make *very* sure you do."

Li Yuan stood before the carp pool, looking down into its depths, watching the fish drift slowly, dark within the dark, circling like the thoughts within his skull.

It shall be war, he thought, the last shred of doubt gone from him. *I shall recall the armies from Africa and crush the monster in the depths of my City.*

That was the easy part. As for the rest...

The day, now it was done, seemed like a dream. The hurt he'd felt – the anguish and pain – now seemed unreal, like a nightmare he had woken from. Not that they were gone. No. They were still there, in the depths. It was just that he was blank now, emotionally inert.

An hour back, Pei K'ung had sent a girl, thinking it a kindness, but he had turned her away. Throwing on a cloak, he had come here, hoping to lose himself, knowing the silent spell this place wove over him.

He crouched then put out a hand, stirring the water's surface.

Just fall forward, he told himself. *Just let go, Li Yuan, and it will all be done with.*

But he couldn't let go. In spite of everything, some part of him refused to weaken, refused to take that final, irrevocable step. No. They could take it all from him – his brother, his father, his wives, yes, even the one man he had truly trusted; the lone man he had truly loved – and still he would not succumb.

Tired as he was, he was not *that* tired. Hurt as he was, he was not *that* hurt.

Like a brother he'd been...

He let his head droop, let a shuddering breath escape him, then, slowly, he straightened up. His limbs felt leaden, his blood sluggish in his veins.

"Chieh Hsia?"

Nan Ho must have been standing there some while, his head bowed, his arms straight at his sides, like a shadow beside the door.

"What is it, Master Nan?"

Nan Ho stepped forward, his face suddenly half lit, his dark eyes concerned.

"Forgive me, *Chieh Hsia.* I did not mean to disturb you. I just wondered... well, if you were alright?"

Li Yuan smiled wearily. "It has been a long day, Master Nan. I am tired. Very tired."

"Of course, *Chieh Hsia.* I..." He hesitated, stepped back into the shadow, then came forward again. "I did not know, *Chieh Hsia*. I just wanted you to know that. There were rumours at the time – rumours we crushed in the bud, but... well, I did not believe them. Marshal Tolonen and I..."

Li Yuan raised a hand. At once Nan Ho fell silent. The T'ang's eyes were pained, his face muscles tensed. He looked down, composing himself, then looked back at his Chancellor, his face stern.

"I hear what you say, Master Nan, but there will be no further mention of that man within my hearing, nor within the walls of any palace or official building under my jurisdiction. From henceforth it must be as if he does not – and never did – exist."

Nan Ho stared at him a moment, shocked by the coldness he saw in his Master's face, then bowed his head.

"It shall be so, *Chieh Hsia*."

"Good," Li Yuan said. "Then good night, Master Nan. May the gods look after us in these coming days."

Karr woke in the small hours, his whole body beaded in sweat, shaken by a dream in which Lehmann had stolen into their rooms and taken May, replacing her with a perfect changeling – an android copy. Fearful, he had gone to May's room and knelt beside her bed, touching her arm in the darkness to feel the warmth there, checking at her neck for a pulse.

She had stirred and he had sung to her, crooning softly until he was certain she had settled. Only then did he go back.

Marie spoke to him from the darkness, her voice heavy with sleep. "Gregor?"

"It's alright," he said, climbing in beside her. "I heard a noise, from May's room. I was just checking she was okay."

She murmured some vague noise of understanding then cuddled close, placing her head on his chest, asleep in an instant. Normally it would have been enough to soothe him, to calm his fears, but this once he could not get to sleep again. He lay there, tense, disturbed by it – seeing again and again his daughter turn and laugh up at him, her mouth a dark hole within which he could see the full moon burning.

CHAPTER 128

TO THE EDGE

The tower dominated the valley. Inside, heavy wooden blinds had been pulled down over the massive windows at either end of the Upper Hall, leaving it in heavy shadow – a brooding darkness that a shaft of light from a skylight breached, picking out a tiny figure in blood-red silks, standing on the stone flags beside a fountain.

Fu Chiang, "The Priest", Big Boss of the Red Flower Triad of North Africa, stood at the centre of the Hall, looking up through the skylight at the faint circle of the moon in the early morning sky. Behind him, the light glittered off the flowing water of the fountain, making the green-bronze flanks of the running horse shimmer.

He loved this hour, when the air was so clear and cool and the fortress silent. Walking to the door, he pushed aside the blue silk curtain and went out onto the balcony, stepping from shadow into sunlight.

Dismissing the two guards, he went to the parapet and looked out across the valley. From this vantage point, all was below him. To his right three peaks soared into the cloudless sky, their very stillness making him think of Eternity. Dark green pines clothed their flanks, hiding the gun emplacements he knew were there. To his left the land fell away more steeply, the stark, geometric shapes of the lower garrison bunkers jutting from the smooth face of the rock. Far below, a river wound its way into the distance like a black snake coiled in the grass. Somewhere in the middle ground lay two small villages. Beyond them the dark massed shapes of the Atlas Mountains rose once more, stretching to the horizon.

Fu Chiang looked up, taking a deep breath and stared into the perfect blue of the sky. More and more he found himself drawn to this place. More and more he left the day-to-day running of the brotherhood to his lieutenants; to his Red Pole, Hu Lin and his White Paper Fan, Tan Sui.

This had once *been* a summer retreat for Wang Sau-leyan. It was rumoured he had even brought his woman here – the *Hsueh pai.* But that had been some while back now. Fu Chiang had taken it over two years ago, after Wang's death, paying off the local Warlord, Yen Fu.

For now, he thought. *For the day will come when Yen Fu will pay me.*

Yes, but Yen Fu was not a problem. An irritation, maybe, but not a problem.

Li Min... Lin Min was the problem.

Fu Chiang turned, looking to the north, the stone face of the tower climbing into the air to his left. This morning, not long after first light, a cruiser had come from that direction. On board had been Li Min's henchman, Visak.

Fu Chiang pulled at his beard thoughtfully. His *Wu* would be here shortly. He had summoned him as soon as he had learned what Visak wanted, knowing that this was not a course to be entered on lightly. To give Visak shelter – to agree to what Visak wanted – would, if Li Min heard of it, surely make an enemy of the man. On the other hand, to send him back...

He sighed, suddenly impatient. Where *was* the man? Why hadn't he come? He turned and went back inside, hurrying across the Hall and throwing the doors open.

"Guard!"

The man came quickly to his Master's summons and knelt at his feet.

"Find out what's happened to the Wu!"

"Master!"

The man bowed low, then hurried off, calling to others as he went. Fu Chiang stood there a moment, banging his clenched fist against the doorpost with frustration, then went back inside. It would not have been so bad had he been able to trust any of his fellow Mountain Lords, but who was to say which one of them would take advantage of the situation and inform Li Min?

Or was he worrying too much? Could Li Min *really* harm him?

Yes, he thought. Not directly, but the bastard could withdraw his support and fund his enemies, and that could shift the balance of power against him. Unless...

Unless I make a deal — another deal — this time with Li Min's principal enemy.

Fu Chiang laughed. The very thought was outrageous. But why not? Why shouldn't he, a Mountain Lord, make deals with one of the Seven?

After all, the times had changed. And if Visak *was* so important, then maybe Li Yuan would be willing to buy the man.

The more he thought of it, the more he liked the idea.

He turned, hearing voices and running footsteps and nodded to himself. If the *Wu confirmed it — if the signs were right — then he would act.*

And if they weren't?

No. He was convinced of it. The oracle would bear it out. Visak... Visak was the key that would open many doors for him.

Tsung Ye edged to the side of the bed, then, carefully pulling the silken covers aside, slipped out, tiptoeing to the chair where he had left his clothes. Pei K'ung lay on her side on the far side of the bed, naked, her shoulder and the curve of her back visible from where he stood, dressing.

He had waited almost twenty minutes until he was sure she was asleep, knowing that if he woke her he would be there still an hour hence. The thought of it made him lower his eyes and groan inwardly. It was not that his Mistress was a bad lover. Far from it. He was surprised by how passionate, how enthusiastic she was; how quickly she had learned the arts of pleasure. Nor did her age or lack of beauty put him off. It was just that she was so... well, *insatiable.* As if she was attempting to make up for forty years of celibacy in a few brief days.

Tsung ye sat, pulling on his boots, then stifled a yawn. She had kept him at it all night, that last time riding him like a demon, her face distorted so that, for the briefest moment, he had been afraid, thinking she had been taken over by the legendary fox lady. He shuddered, recalling it, then stood, pressing his feet down into the bottom of the soft kid boots she had bought him.

That, at least, was one good thing that had come out of this. The presents she kept showering on him: new clothes, a golden timepiece, silks, jewellery and cloth-bound books. Even so, the situation worried him. One of these days, they would be caught. He knew it for a certainty. And though she said her husband knew, how certain could he be of that? After all, it was not something he could check.

He sighed. Maybe she would tire of him. Maybe, once her passion for him had waned, she would take another to her bed. Until then he must be careful. Until then he must do as she said.

He tiptoed to the door and opened it, checking the corridor, then slipped outside. Pulling the door closed behind him, he hurried away, making for his bed and the sweet oblivion of sleep.

Pei K'ung heard the door click shut then turned and pulled herself up onto the cushions. Stretching, she yawned, then smiled.

Last night had been wonderful, the best yet, but though she felt exhausted, she could not sleep. For a while she lay there in a fitful reverie, remembering what they had done, her hand straying down to touch her breasts, her sides, the soft-haired nest between her legs.

Yes, my little bird, she thought, a sigh of contentment escaping her – *you were right to slip away when you did. Get some sleep. For tonight I shall have need of you again.*

After a while she got up and went through to her bathroom. Squatting there over the bowl, washing herself, she felt a shiver run through her, imagining not Tsung Ye but her husband, watching her.

For a moment she closed her eyes, letting her fantasy run its course, imagining him chancing on her, there where she was, then coming across to throw her down upon the tiled floor and have her on the spot.

The thought of it made her nerves tingle, the hair on her neck stand on end.

Awake, she thought. *After all this time I am awake.*

She dried herself then went back through, not bothering to summon her maids, but searching the great carved wardrobes herself, looking for something that suited her mood. Something light and airy. She decided on a simple wrap of lavender and pink decorated silk butterflies. Laying it on the bed, she went to her dressing table and sat.

"Send my maids," she said, addressing the House Computer.

They were there in an instant. Curtseying in the doorway they came in, then stopped, hesitating as they saw her in the mirror, naked.

She smiled, seeing how they averted their eyes as they came across, then spoke to them, giving them their orders.

"Tiny jade? I want you to put my hair up. You will do something fashionable with it, all right? As for you, Autumn Snow, you must use all your skills to make your Mistress presentable."

"Mistress!" the two maids said together, bowing, then looking to each other with worried glances; glances that Pei K'ung pretended not to see.

"And girls," she said, the familiar authority of her voice tempered with an unexpected tenderness. "Do this properly and I shall reward you well."

Nan Ho stopped outside the Empress's rooms, then, clearing his throat, knocked loudly on the outer door.

There was a faint exchange of voices from within and then the door eased back, a guard staring out at the Chancellor. Seeing who it was, the man bowed his head and stepped back, announcing him.

"Mistress, it is his Excellency, the Chancellor."

Pei K'ung was seated on her throne, the dignitaries of her household surrounding her, as if she'd been expecting him.

"Master Nan," she said, smiling. "To what do I owe this pleasure?"

Nan Ho knelt, bowing his head, then stood, returning her smile. Forgive me, Mistress. But I have just come from your husband. He wishes to see you at once."

She turned, dismissing the dignitaries. As they went, Nan Ho frowned, noting the absence of Tsung Ye, surprised not to see the ever-present young secretary at her side.

He bowed again, letting her pass, then fell in two paces behind her as they went out into the corridor.

"Is my husband better?"

"Better, Mistress?"

She stopped and turned, facing him. "Forgive me for being so blunt, Master Nan – I mean no disrespect by it – but let me have no more bull-shit from you. You *know* what I mean! Yesterday we returned from Astrakhan at a moment's notice, snubbing our cousin's wedding. Today a decree is issued banning all mention of the man's name. It takes no great intelligence to figure out that something happened between my husband and his cousin, does it?"

Nan Ho nodded, conceding the point.

"Moreover, it was noticeable how pale my husband seemed, returning from our cousin's place. So I ask you again, Master Nan. Is my husband feeling any better?

He laughed. "That is something I think you had better judge for yourself." He put his hand out. "If you would..."

She smiled, then turned, walking on at a pace, leaving him to half walk, half run to try and keep up with her.

Li Yuan was halfway through a meeting when she came into his study. Without breaking sentence, he motioned towards a chair, his eyes following her as she made her way across and sat.

Flicking out her fan, she waved it before her face, hiding a yawn, then clicked it shut, studying the senior official who stood, stoop-backed before her husband's desk.

At once she sensed something different. It was not just the tension in the room, though that, of itself, was quite remarkable; nor was it the crowd of advisers and retainers who were gathered in the room; it was something in the words her husband used – in their curt significance and in the underlying menace she sensed in them. Even before he dismissed the man and turned to her, she knew. He had decided upon war.

"*Chieh Hsia*," she said, addressing him formally, anticipating him. "Might we talk alone?"

He stared at her a moment, then waved the rest away. When they'd gone, he stood then came round the desk to her.

"So, Pei K'ung, what is it?"

She met his eyes squarely, as if to an equal. "Yesterday. That business with your cousin. I know you don't want to talk about it, but..."

"But *what?*" There was a hardness in him suddenly that told her she had been right. "Speak then be silent."

She bowed her head. "When I was researching in the Imperial Library, I came upon something. Something to do with your cousin."

"Go on," he said, a note of curiosity entering his voice.

"It was to do with your first wife... with Fei Yen."

She looked up, expecting to find him glaring at her, but to her surprise he was looking away, a muscle at his cheek jumping. To her astonishment a tear dropped from the corner of his eye and rolled down his cheek, falling into the folds of his silks.

She blinked. "Husband, I..."

He turned to face her, then sniffed deeply and wiped away a second tear that had formed but not fallen. "You understand, then?"

She nodded, but at the core of her she was shocked. So it was true. It really was true. And because of it, the two T'ang were not now speaking, and Li Yuan was preparing for war. She shivered and clicked open her fan again, moving it distractedly.

"I have had her placed under house arrest," he said. "As for her son, he is held separately. Without him, she'll do no more mischief."

"Ah..." Again she felt a faint shock of surprise. "She tried to see you," she said quietly.

He stared at her.

"A few days ago," she continued, putting the fan down and holding it stiffly in her lap. "I... I saw her myself. Sent her away. I..." She looked up at him again. "I thought it best. I did not realise..."

"No." He sighed. "You were not to blame, Pei K'ung. The woman..." He shook his head and grimaced. "The woman was always unstable. I was wrong to marry her. It was infatuation... childish infatuation. I see that now."

She nodded. But whereas only three days ago she would not have understood, now she saw it clear. When it came to love and sex the eyes were blind.

"Is it war?" she asked, changing the subject. "I mean, against Li Min?"

"Yes," and strangely, he offered her a smile. "I'm glad, you know. I... I was so lonely. So wrapped up in myself. But now... Well, now it's easier, neh?"

He stared at her a moment, as if seeing her for the first time, then frowned. "You're... *different*, Pei K'ung. Your hair. That dress. It... it makes you look much younger."

Pei K'ung bowed her head, a faint blush coming to her neck. "I... I thought I would try to please you, husband. I..." She looked up again, noting that her eyes were still upon her. "I thought I could, perhaps, come to you tonight. After you had retired. To talk and... well, to help you relax."

He opened his mouth, as if, for the briefest moment, he was going to say no, then, with a curt little movement, he nodded.

Pei K'ung sat there, her heart pounding, her mouth suddenly dry. Then, realising that the audience was at an end, she stood and, bowing, backed away.

May stood in the doorway to the shower, watching while her father washed himself down, her four-year-old eyes taking in his every movement. Glancing at her, he smiled, self-consciously, then turned, facing the stone wall, whistling softly to herself.

"Papa?"

He stopped and turned back. "Yes, little plum blossom?"

"Those marks..." She pointed to the tattoos on his chest and arms, her tiny face creased with curiosity.

"These?" He laughed, then, cutting the flow, stepped out and grabbed a towel. "I had these done when I was twelve. Long ago, that was. Long, long ago. And far away, come to that."

She stared at him, waiting. Shrugging, he towelled his loins dry, pulled on some shorts, then crouched down next to her.

"These," he said, indicating the dragon tattoos on his left arm, "are the red dragon of summer and the green dragon of spring. And this..." He smiled, seeing how her eyes widened at the sight of it, "is the great eagle, symbolising strength.

May reached out, touching and tracing the design.

"But why is it so cruel?" she asked, pointing to the terror-stricken horse, an eagle clutched in each of its steel-like talons.

"Because strength is cruel, perhaps?" He watched her, seeing how she studied the design, and felt a tightening his stomach muscles at the thought of what lay ahead.

What kind of world will you grow up in? he wondered. *A world of eagles and dragons? Or will it be a kinder, safer place?*

The thought disturbed him. He reached out and picked her up, cuddling her, making her laugh, then carried her through into the kitchen, where Marie was preparing breakfast.

"You want a hand?" he asked, setting May down.

She turned from the stove and smiled. "Are you ill, Gregor?"

He laughed. "No. It's just that I'm not used to being waited on. In Africa

I would eat with the men, help prepare the meals. But that's not what I meant. This..." He looked about him. "I wonder if all this will be the same... afterwards."

There was a flicker of uncertainty in her face and then she smiled again, reassuring him. "We'll come through, Gregor. We always do. Besides, you've more than two of us to think of now."

Karr smiled, but the memory of what Lehmann had said lay underneath his joy. Death. Death lay beneath the surface wherever one looked. He went across and stood beside her, reaching past her to take the tiny statue from the shelf by the window. More and more these past few years people had reverted to such things.

"You should be careful," he said, holding it out to her. "It's still illegal."

Marie raised an eyebrow, then took the kitchen god statue from him and set it back. "It's Si Ming," she said, meeting his eyes.

"Ah..." He looked at it again, then nodded to himself. Si Ming was the God of Fate, bestower of life and death. It was he, they said, who determined how long a man's life should be. He shivered then reached out to touch the tiny statue, as if to take some of its good luck.

"Gregor?"

He looked at her, then laughed. "It'll do no harm."

"I thought you made your own luck?"

He nodded. It was what he had always said, but in the days ahead a single man would be like a seed, blown by the great wind. Yes, in the days to come they would need all the luck they could get.

"I..."

Karr stopped, hearing a knocking at the door, then moved past Marie. It had an urgent sound to it.

He threw the door open. A messenger stood there, dressed in the dark green and red of Li Yuan's personal staff. The young man handed him a sealed letter, then bowed and backed away.

Karr watched him go, then broke the seal and took the letter from inside.

"What is it?" Marie asked from the kitchen doorway, wiping her hands on a cloth.

"New orders," he said, looking back at her. "I'm to go to Africa."

"To the Banners?"

He shook his head. "No. I am to meet a Mountain Lord named Fu Chiang.

It seems Lehmann's man, Visak, has fled the nest, and he wants to make a deal."

"Tell me your name."

Light flickered in the creature's eye. The pupil moved to the right, contracting slightly.

It hesitated, searching its newly-implanted memory.

"Well?" Kim asked, adjusting the scope that was set up over the creature's face then glancing at the twin screens beside the operating table.

"I am unnamed," it said finally.

"Good," Kim said, looking across the room to where Curval sat behind the control desk. "Why do you think that is?"

There was activity on the right-hand screen – tiny flares of red and yellow within the dark outline of the skull – and then an answer.

"Because I have not *been* named?"

"Good." Kim peered down the scope again, adjusting the fingertip controls. "And yet it is in the nature of things to be named, no?"

The creature was silent. At the desk, Curval smiled.

"So why does everything – even the smallest, inanimate thing – possess a name and you none?"

Again the flares danced in the outline skull, brighter this time and more intense.

"I... I do not know."

Kim straightened up then studied the left hand screen, where two graphs – one in green, one in yellow – showed respiration and blood pressure. He nodded, satisfied, then looked back at the creature.

"Do you remember your parents?"

It gave a smile of recognition. "I remember them, Yes."

"Good." Kim patted its arm. "So what did *they* call you?"

"Call me?"

"You lived with them, right?"

Flares of yellow intensified into red, faded and then returned. The respiration rate was up – dramatically so.

Kim looked to Curval and nodded.

"You remember them, but you can't remember being with them, is that how it is?"

"There was a look of pain on the creature's face now. Of confusion. It gave a tiny nod, its head movements restrained by the scope.

"Good. And the house you lived in... It was a big house, neh?"

"Very big. There were fifteen rooms."

"Fifteen? That's a lot of rooms for just the three of you. You had no brothers or sisters?

"No..." Again it hesitated. "I... I don't think so."

"Okay." Kim laid its hand on the creature's shoulder, reassuring it. "You can relax now. We'll talk more later."

Kim went out, Curval joining him in the ante room.

"Well?" the older man asked impatiently. "What do you think?"

Kim went to the machine in the corner and punched for a bulb of soup. "I think the implant's taken well."

Curval followed him across. "So what was all that about?"

Kim turned back, handing the bulb to Curval, then punched for another. "You mean, why didn't I programme him properly? Why did I leave gaps?"

"That's *exactly* what I mean."

Kim took the bulb and cracked it open, then sat on the corner of the nearby table. "Because I want to see what it does with them... with the gaps. If my hunch is right, its brain won't be happy with the situation. With there being gaps. If I'm right, it will try to fill them."

"Fill them? How? We'd have to programme it again, surely?"

"Would we?" Kim sipped again, then laughed. "Let's give it half an hour and see what happens."

Curval turned, looking through the glass at the creature on the table. It lay there, inert, like a piece of discarded machinery. "What *could* happen?"

Kim finished his soup then threw the flattened bulb into the disposal. "It might invent something."

"Like what?

"Wait and see," Kim said, going to the machine and punching for another soup. "Just wait and see."

"Tell me your name?"

Light flickered in the creature's eye. On the right hand screen a single flare of yellow brightened and then faded.

"I am Box."

"I see." Kim met Curval's eyes. The older man, seated at the desk again, was sitting forward, astonished.

"Box? That's the name your parents gave you, yes?"

"Yes."

"You remember your parents, then?

"You asked me that before."

Kim smiled. "I did, didn't I?"

"You asked me if I remembered being with them and I said no."

"But now you do?"

It hesitated, then. "Yes. I remember it now."

"Why do you think that is?"

"I... I must have forgotten."

"Of course." Kim loosened the scope arm and pulled it aside. "Sit up, Box. I want to talk to you about what you remember."

Like a waxwork waking into life, it sat up, slipping its legs over the side of the operating table. Its eyes were an intense blue. Kim stood, facing it, dwarfed by it.

"Good." Kim studied it as if looking for flaws. "Now tell me. The house. You remember the house, yes?"

"I remember."

"Fifteen rooms, you said. A big house. The house where Box lived with his parents."

"And my brothers."

Kim nodded, as if it were the answer he'd expected. "Two brothers?"

"Three," it corrected him.

"Of course." Kim smiled. "Your brothers... did they have names?"

"They... Yes. They had names."

"Good. And their names... what were they, Box?"

"One... One was named 'Other'. The second was 'Pole'. The third..." It reached deep inside, its face forming the rudiments of a frown. And then it smiled. The third was 'Square'."

Kim smiled. "Good. That's very good, Box. But tell me... did you play with your brothers? In the garden, for instance?"

"I..." Its hesitation this time was pronounced. "I must have. I... I *think* I remember playing with them."

"Were there trees in the garden?"

It was more confident this time. "Yes. Four trees."

"One for each brother?"

"That's right."

"Okay. We'll leave it now. Rest now, Box. Lay down and rest."

Outside once more, Curval rounded on him. "What's going on, Kim? Where the hell did it get all that stuff?"

"It made it up."

"Made it up?"

"To fill the gaps."

Curval laughed humourlessly. "Three brothers... *Aiya!* It's a pathological liar! We might as well destroy it right now. It's living in a fantasy world!"

Kim nodded. "Sure. But that's exactly what we intended, wasn't it?

"Yes, but..."

"No, think about it, Andrew. What did we set out to achieve with the implant? To give it memories that seemed real. To give it some kind of back-story so that it thought of itself as being more than a simple machine of flesh – so that it could function properly. All well and good. But the trouble is how do we make sure that that story – that 'false history', if you like – is detailed enough? Up to now we've been assuming that what we were giving it was enough. That it would accept the implant verbatim and use it like some kind of theatrical backdrop. But we know now that that assumption was a false one."

"Because there were gaps. Because you didn't name it."

"Sure. But there are *always* going to be gaps. Don't you see that? That demonstration just now – the things I left out of its back-story were glaring and obvious, but they make the point. Whatever we leave out, it will invent. Wherever it finds gaps – however small – it will fill them. That, after all, is the nature of it."

Kim laughed. "You're missing the point, Andrew. What we're talking about here is duplicating a life – the memory of a life – detail for detail. We're talking about a piece of programming so huge and so complex that we could put a thousand men on the job and they would still be working on its fifty years from now."

"Okay. So what *is* the point? Are you suggesting that we should just give up? Is that it?"

"Not at all. What I'm saying is that we need to take this new factor –

this facility it has for filling gaps, for inventing its own reality – into our calculations. We need to re-conceive what we've been doing and to construct the next generation of implants not as backdrops but as mental skeletons. If we can give the new models some kind of coherent framework, they can flesh it out themselves. And if I'm right – if my instinct for this is correct – then we'll not only cure the instability problem we've suffered with previous prototypes but we might even simplify the whole imprinting process."

"So where do we go from here?"

"First we go back to GenSyn. Get them to expedite the release of the new brain matter they've been working on. There have been delays with the paperwork – the usual kind of thing – but I'll get on to Tolonen. See if he can't put a rocket up them."

"And Box?"

Kim turned back, looking at the creature. "We'll let Box run for a week. See how he fills himself, And then... well, I guess we close the lid." He looked back at Curval. "The shame of it is that he'll never know, never realise just what he could have been. Gaps... All he'll ever know are gaps."

Von Pasenow stood in the shadows at the back of the room, waiting while Tolonen took the call. He listened, sensitive to the nuances in the Marshal's voice, to the sudden defensive stiffness of his posture, and knew that the old man's over-polite manner concealed real depths of hostility. Whoever Ward was, he was no friend of the Marshal's.

As the old man cut the call and turned to him again, he straightened, attentive once more.

"I'm sorry about that," Tolonen said, a flicker of distaste crossing his face. "You'd think he'd deal with the appropriate manager! Why he has to pester me. Anyway... you were saying you had news."

Von Pasenow took two steps forward, into the circle of light cast by the hover-globe at Tolonen's elbow, then bowed his head.

"I think we've found them, sir."

"Found them! Why that's excellent!" *Where?*"

He raised his head. Tolonen was leaning forward, staring at him eagerly.

"We've traced them to Cosenza in the south. It looks like they've been waiting to slip away to Africa. My guess is that they're waiting to be paid off, otherwise they'd have gone."

Tolonen nodded, then waved him to continue.

"I've had the surrounding levels and stacks staked out thoroughly. Good men. Reliable, ex-service types. My men are in the transits and at all the barriers. If they even cough I'll know about it."

Tolonen stood. "Excellent. Then let's go there, neh?"

"Marshal?" Von Pasenow stared at the old man, surprised. "But I thought..."

Tolonen came round the desk and placed a golden hand on Van Pasenow's shoulder. "You've done a good job, Major. I knew you would. That's why I hired you. But this is personal. You understand?"

Von Pasenow bowed his head. "Of course, sir. I'll take you there at once."

"Good. And Major... if we have to take containment action, we do what has to be done, neh? I'll accept responsibility for any consequences. But I want at least one of the fuckers alive. I don't care how you do it, but you do it, *right?*"

Von Pasenow swallowed, then bowed his head smartly. "Sir!"

The curtains were drawn, the room in semi-darkness. From the far side of the room, he could hear her soft, regular breathing and smiled. The room was warm, filled with the sweetly-perfumed scent of her. Hesitant, he pushed the door closed and tiptoed to the bed.

Shu-sun lay there, her back to him, a bright red silk wrapped about her nakedness. Gently Tsu Ma sat, careful not to disturb her, then leaned across, his eyes taking in the features of her sleeping face.

He had not been wrong. She was every bit as beautiful as he'd remembered. As he watched, she turned, slowly, sensuously uncurling, her lips parting a fraction, her shoulders and neck stretching. Then, with a lazy motion, her eyes opened, the pupils heavy with sleep. Seeing him, she smiled.

"Where were you?" she asked, her voice a lazy, familiar drawl. "I thought you were going to come, but you didn't..."

He felt a pang of guilt and quickly suppressed it. "I'm here now," he said, placing his palm against her cheek and smoothing it. She took it and slowly led it down her body on to the warm, firm breast beneath the silk.

"I wanted you."

"Wanted?" He felt a tiny shiver of anticipation pass through him. The silken warmth of her inflamed him.

"Want," she said, correcting herself.

She lifted his hand to her lips, kissed it, then, releasing it, drew back her silks, revealing her nakedness. Tsu Ma let a long, slow breath escape him, bewitched by the sight of her, then leaned forward and gently kissed first one and then the other breast, his tongue lingering on the nipples.

His eyes met hers. Or would have, for her eyes were closed now, her whole face lit with pleasure.

He bent again, kissing and teasing her breasts, his hands moving down her body, tracing the smooth young shape of it, eliciting soft sighs from her. Moving back, he shrugged off his jacket and stood, beginning to undress. Her eyes opened lazily, watching him, her smile heavy with desire, her body turning toward him like an offering.

He threw off his shirt and kicked away his boots, then peeled off his leggings. As he moved forward to kneel on the edge of the bed, she sat up and reached out to him, her fingers caressing his stomach and his inner thighs, tracing a circle about his groin, her eyes wide, enjoying the sight of his fierce arousal.

He closed his eyes and groaned as she moved closer, her fingers cupping his balls gently, tenderly while her mouth opened to him. Placing his hands on her shoulders, he began to knead the muscles there, half tender, half savage.

"*Aiya!*" he moaned, unable to keep himself from thrusting at her. "*Aiya!*"

His hands were at her neck now. As she leaned in to him, taking him deeper, he reached up with his right hand and, grasping the point where her hair was gathered into a plait, pulled back her head, as if reining in a horse!

She stared back up at him, her mouth still open, her face entirely changed, a primal savagery staring back at him from her eyes. He shuddered, then pulled her down, his mouth going to hers and crushing it almost brutally, even as her legs parted and her body curled about his. With a gasp he was inside her, the shock of entry making them both cry out, she high, he low. Then, savagely, he thrust at her, as if to destroy her, to annihilate her utterly, her cries, the pained contortions of her face robbing him of all reason. She clung to him fiercely, pushing up to meet each downward thrust like some young animal in its death-throes.

As he came she cried out, convulsing beneath him, thrusting up against him as if to split herself, her hands gripping his buttocks fiercely while he groaned as if he had been speared, forcing his seed deep into her, each thrust now like a dagger blow, his teeth gritted, his whole face contorted in a rictus of pain.

Again! Again! *Again!*

He woke an hour later, his head nestled between her breasts, her arms about his neck and shoulders. For a while he lay there, contented, happy simply to listen to her gentle breathing, to feel the soft warmth of her flesh against his own. *Like Paradise,* he thought. Then, knowing he must get back, he gently broke from her, easing up off the bed.

He stood there a moment, staring at her, aroused once more by the mere sight of her. It would be easy simply to stay there for a day or two. To sleep and make love and damn the world outside. After all, that was a T'ang's privilege. But a T'ang had responsibilities too, and right now the world was a place of threats and chaos. Right now the world would allow him only a few snatched moments of pleasure.

He began to dress. For a moment he had forgotten everything – everything but her. He smiled, remembering. The first time had been fierce, like the violent coupling of animals, the second tender, softly, astonishingly gentle. And between...?

He laughed, surprised by it all. Between times he had fallen in love with her.

Fastening the last button of his jacket, he turned, looking at her again, then went across and, leaning across her, planted gentle kisses on her neck, her cheek, her brow.

"Tonight..." he whispered. Then, moving back, he straightened up, preparing himself to go out and face the greater world once more.

Tonight, he thought, knowing that there was at least this one sweet certainty amidst all else. *I shall come to you tonight, my darling Shu-sun.*

But first there was one other matter to be settled.

They were in transit when it began – travelling south from Milan Garrison, their cruiser flitting less than a hundred *ch'i* above the City's roof, as if across a vast, smooth snowscape.

"What's happening?" Tolonen demanded, leaning across to touch Van

Pasenow's arm.

The ex-Major looked up and grimaced. "It looks like their contact has arrived. They're de-camping. If we don't hit them now..."

"Then hit them," Tolonen said sternly. "But remember what I said, I want at least one of them alive. Tell your men to shoot to disable if they can, not to kill."

"And if they suicide?"

"That's a risk we'll have to take."

Von Pasenow turned away, getting back to his man in Cosenza. They arrived ten minutes later, setting down by one of the security hatches. By then it was all over.

"Let's hope they've left us something, Tolonen said as they climbed down from the cruiser.

"Or someone," Von Pasenow said beneath his breath, fearing the worst.

Down below it was chaos. Someone had shot at one of the *Shen T'se* before the ambush was properly set. As a result more than twenty of their own men had been killed or critically wounded. Of the *Shen T'se*, only one was still alive, and that was because they'd blown off both his arms and one of his feet. He lay in one of the rooms, under heavy guard, his wounds freeze-staunched, his condition kept stable by the Resuscitation Machine he was strapped to.

Tolonen went to inspect the dead first, spending a long time staring at the five *Shen T'se*, murmuring to himself about loyalty and trust and wondering aloud how such men as these could be bought. Eventually he left them and came through, frowning fiercely as he studied the half-conscious man.

"You know him?" Von Pasenow asked.

"I did," Tolonen answered. "Or thought I did. He was a good man." He heaved a sigh, then sniffed deeply. "But then, men are not to be taken at face value any longer."

The Marshal turned, looking directly at Von Pasenow. "It began with that rascal DeVore. From him it was contracted by my erstwhile son-in-law, Hans Ebert. And from there, it seems, it has spread, like some contagious disease. The disease of *seeming*. It hollows a man and replaced him with a shadow, a puppet man, dancing to another's orders. So here."

He went across and stood over the wounded *Shen T'se*, his face pained. "Sergeant Hoff... do you know who's speaking to you?

Hoff's eyes slowly opened. "Marshal Tolonen? Is that you|?"

"Hoff… I need to know a few things and I need to know them now."

Hoff shook his head.

"I'll make it simple, Sergeant. You tell me now and I will kill you. Quickly and mercifully. You know I can do that, don't you?"

Hoff nodded. Suddenly more alert.

"If you keep silent, however…" Tolonen sniffed. "Well, I think you've a good enough imagination, neh, Sergeant? I could keep you alive, what, thirty, maybe forty years? And every day of that you would be in agony, in a hell that would make your present condition seem like bliss. So… what is it to be? A quick death or an eternity of suffering?"

Hoff closed his eyes and groaned. "What do you want to know?"

"Who bought you. Who paid you. Who gave you your orders." He paused, then, leaning closer. "And here's the big one. Where's the boy? Tell me that and I may even offer you a better deal."

Hoff shivered, then opened his bloodshot eyes again, looking directly at the old man.

"Our contact was a man named Ruddock. He's a Minor Official according to his Security file, but in point of fact he's one of the main mediators between ourselves and the White T'ang's organisation."

"Go on."

Hoff grimaced, closing his eyes briefly, then began again. "The paymaster was Li Min himself. As for who gave us our orders, it was Rheinhardt."

Tolonen laughed. "I don't believe you."

Hoff's eyes stared back at him, a cold certainty in them.

"There was a secret meeting, two weeks back, up north. In Goteborg or some place like that. More than two dozen people attended that meeting, our commander and a number of other high-ranking Security officers among them. Rheinhardt chaired it. The purpose of that meeting was to try to assess just who would come out on top in the event of a war between Li Yuan and Li Min."

Tolonen let out a long breath. "You have proof?"

Hoff nodded weakly. "Our commander, Needham, swore a personal oath to Rheinhardt. He had us do the same…" Again he grimaced, the pain returning as the quick-shot medication wore off. "When the order came from on high we did as we were told."

"I see..." Tolonen looked one more time at Von Pasenow. "I couldn't understand it," he said. "A *Shen T'se* unit. Their loyalty is unquestionable. But this, if true, explains it."

He looked back to Hoff. "So where's the boy?"

Hoff swallowed drily, then shook his head. "I don't know. We handed him over at Linz on our way down here. To a tall man with an ox-like face. He had a shoulder wound. Pale, cadaverous face,"

"Li Min's man?"

"I... I guess so."

Tolonen stared at him a long while, conscious of the pain Hoff was suffering, then slowly shook his head.

"You know what? I don't trust you, Hoff. Oh, the part about being in Li Min's pay. That rings true. As for the rest, well... I think you're out to make mischief for Li Yuan. Rheinhardt..." He laughed, his voice suddenly louder, more authoritative. "I *know* Helmut Rheinhardt, and he would as soon slit his throat as think of committing treason against his Master."

He leaned in to the man, placing the fingers of his left hand – the golden, metallic fingers – against the cauterised stump of Hoff's right arm and pressed, gently at first and then with greater and greater pressure.

Hoff screamed.

"Now, Sergeant," Tolonen said, his rock-like face hovering above the sweating man. "Let's begin again from the beginning, shall we? We've plenty of time, after all. All the time in the world."

Fu Chiang stood beside Karr at the rain, looking down into the fight pit.

"It is brutal, I know, but it is also one of the few *pure* things there is. To see them fight..." Fu Chiang smiled and turned to look at the giant, casting admiring eyes over his physique. "It cannot be faked. One wins, the other dies. There is such... *clarity!*"

"I know," Karr said, his look intense. "I was a Blood. I too once fought in the Pit, beneath the lights."

Fu Chiang's eyes widened. "You *fought?*" Then he laughed. "You jest with me, Colonel."

Karr turned to him, his eyes deadly serious. "I fought. Beneath the Net. Eight contests, to the death. And then the Supreme Master, Hwa. He almost beat me." Karr breathed deeply, then nodded. "He was a great man, Hwa."

"And then?"

"And then Tolonen found me, *used* me. Made me the T'ang's man."

Fu Chiang frowned. "I did not know. It... well it strikes me as odd that a Blood should rise to become a Colonel in Security, yet looking at you..."

Fu Chiang put out a hand, touching Karr's chest. It was like touching a warm stone pillar. Karr watched him patiently, neither offended nor pleased by the small man's touch. Fu Chang let his hand fall away and shrugged. "Anyway... to business."

"He's here?"

"Up above, in the Tower Hall. I left him admiring the view."

"It must be beautiful."

Fu Chiang smiled. "It is." Then, "I like you, Colonel Karr. If you ever tire of being in Li Yuan's service."

He left the rest unsaid, then put out an arm, indicating that they should leave. As they walked along they talked, going down corridors and up stairs, moving along passages cut from the stone of the mountainside, guards everywhere.

"You know what to do?" Fu Chiang asked, pausing outside the great doors.

Karr nodded, "You talked of purity back there. Of the clarity that comes when life or death's the issue. But it isn't always so. These days..."

He looked away, troubled, then met Fu Chiang's eyes again. "Deals. That's all there is these days. *Deals.*"

"That worries you," Fu Chiang said; statement not question.

"Yes," he admitted. "But I can live with that, if it means I can serve the moral good."

"The moral good? You actually *believe* that?"

"Not all the time. Yet I know there is a difference. To serve a good man, however bad the system that he oversees, well, it might seem strange to you, Fu Chiang, but I find it better than serving such a one as Li Min."

"You make it sound so simple."

Karr shook his head. "Simple? No. It's never simple. Some days..." He smiled, then took a step back from the edge. "Never mind. Let's see the White T'ang's man – the Traitor's traitor."

Fu Chiang laughed. "The Traitor's traitor. I like that. I take it you do not trust our friend, Li Min?"

"No."

"Nor I..."

"Shall we?" Karr asked, indicating the doors.

Fu Chiang smiled. "Be patient, Colonel. Visak will wait as long as you and I wish him to wait, but this... ah, it is rare to talk without masks. I had almost forgotten how."

Karr raised an eyebrow. "Have you no wife, Fu Chiang? No friend in whom to confide?"

"A wife?" Fu Chiang snorted. "I have a dozen wives! But *trusting* them? Why, I'd sooner trust my bollocks on a butcher's block!"

Karr laughed then grew serious again. "And yet a man cannot live in isolation."

"No?" Fu Chiang considered that, then shrugged. "All my life I have been alone. It is the condition in which I exist. I thought you understood that, Colonel... To be a Mountain Lord... it is not an easy path."

"No..." Karr's eyes studied him, their earlier suspicion changed to empathy. "I understand".

"You understand?" Fu Chiang, half Karr's height, an eighth his size, laughed then met the giant's eyes. "No, Colonel Karr. You do not even *begin* to understand!"

Visak was standing beside the fountain, one hand resting on the horse's flank. Hearing the doors creak open, he turned then hurriedly came across, his nervousness marked.

"What's happening, Fu Chiang? Has Li Yuan agreed to my terms?"

"Your *terms?*" Karr stepped between Visak and Fu Chiang.

Visak took a step back, then, deliberately ignoring Karr, looked to Fu Chiang again. "You know what I said, Fu Chiang. I want guarantees, A safe place. Protection. Twenty million *yuan*."

Fu Chiang looked to Karr and nodded. Karr stepped forward, the quickness of the movement surprising for such a big man. In an instant he had pinned Visak's arms behind his back and bound them.

"No deals," Karr said, moving back. "You're my prisoner now, *Shih* Visak."

Visak glared at Fu Chiang. "You viper. You..."

"You had nothing," Fu Chiang said. "Nothing for yourself, that is. But for me..." He grinned, then turned to Karr. "Tell Li Yuan I am grateful for his patronage. Tell him... tell him I hope my gift helps him snare that monster in the depths of his City."

Visak looked from one to the other and snarled. "You cunt! You fucking...!"

Fu Chiang's hand flashed out, the stiffened fingers catching Visak crisply in the solar plexus. Visak doubled up, gasping.

Fu Chiang turned, meeting Karr's eyes.

"That was good," Karr said, lowering his head respectfully.

Fu Chiang smiled. "Maybe I should have told you, Gregor Karr, but I too was once a Blood. Long ago now. Long, long ago."

Li Yuan had signed the Recall order and was inking it with the Great Seal, pushing down with both hands on the massive chop, when Nan Ho's secretary, Hu Chang, entered the room and, hurrying to his Master, whispered something to him. Nan Ho listened, then stepped forward and spoke up.

"*Chieh Hsia.* It seems Marshal Tolonen wishes to speak with you urgently."

Li Yuan looked up, smiling bleakly. "Put him on. I am sure he will want to hear the news."

He moved back, letting the two Custodians of the Seal ease the great square stamp from the silk-paper page and replace it on the cushion, then turned to face the screen which slid down from the ceiling to the left.

"Knut... what is it?"

The old man's face was bright with joyful relief. "He's back, *Chieh Hsia!* Li Min has returned the boy!"

"Returned?" For a moment he did not understand. "You mean Pauli? Li Yuan has returned him?"

"Yes!" Tolonen laughed, forgetting himself. "It's wonderful, neh? And no strings!"

No strings... Li Yuan felt his heart sink. What was Li Min up to?

"Is he alright?"

"Oh, he's fine, *Chieh Hsia.*"

Li Yuan nodded, forcing himself to smile, to pretend to share the old man's joy. It was good news, yes, there was no doubting that, yet he could not help but suspect the move. One thing he knew about Li Min, and that was that there was a reason for everything he did. This was no act of kindness; this was a calculated strategy. But to what end? What else was Li Min planning?

"Have you.... Have you had the boy checked?"

"Checked, *Chieh Hsia?*"

He swallowed, then, knowing no tactful way to put it, said what was on his mind. "Is the boy... *real?* I mean..."

"My personal surgeon has completed a full examination, *Chieh Hsia.* It is Pauli."

"Good." Li Yuan smiled, relaxing a little. "While you are on, Knut, let me tell you the news. I have recalled the Banner Armies from Africa."

"*Chieh Hsia?*" Tolonen's smile faded. "But I thought..."

"I have made my decision, Knut. Now forgive me. There is much to be done."

Abruptly he cut contact, not wanting to argue the matter out in public with his Marshal.

Li Yuan turned, looking for his Chancellor, but Nan Ho had left the room. Frowning, he beckoned Nan's secretary across.

"Hu Chang! Where is Master Nan?"

Yet even as he asked, Nan Ho returned, breathless, a strange smile on his face. He came halfway across the great study, then bowed low.

"Master Nan?"

Nan Ho straightened, then held up a flimsy piece of paper. His eyes were twinkling, his face almost laughing now. "It has come, *Chieh Hsia!* At the last moment it has come!"

He bowed low a second time, then held out his arm, offering the paper to his Master. Li Yuan came round the desk and took it, beginning to read. He had barely read more than a paragraph when he looked up abruptly, shocked, meeting Nan Ho's eyes.

"But this is..."

"His capitulation, *Chieh Hsia!* He calls you Son Of Heaven and swears his absolute loyalty, offering his neck before your foot!" Nan Ho laughed. "We have won, *Chieh Hsia!*"

Li Yuan shook the paper as kif to demonstrate its flimsiness. "But this means nothing!"

Nan Ho bowed his head, sobered by his T'ang's words. "Forgive me, *Chieh Hsia,* but you have not heard the rest. This document… copies of it are going up throughout the Lowers even as we speak. Millions of copies. Tens of millions! He bows before you, *Chieh Hsia!* He calls you 'Son Of Heaven'!"

"I…" Li Yuan was about to say something more, to question what his Chancellor had said, but the summons bell behind his desk had begun to ring urgently. Wei Tseng-li was trying to contact him.

He returned to his desk and faced the screen once more as his young cousin's face appeared.

"Cousin Wei," he said formally, conscious of the servants in the room with him.

"Cousin Li," Wei Tseng-li answered, an unaccustomed hardness in his face. "I am much worried. Word has come that your African armies are to be mobilised and moved back to Europe.

Word? Li Yuan felt himself go cold. How could word have got to Wei Tseng-li so fast? He had only made the decision an hour back, and the Recall Order… that was less than half an hour old! Who of the twenty or so who knew of this had informed his cousin, Wei?

"Forgive me, cousin," he said, with a gesture dismissing all those in the room, "but may I know from whom you heard this… *rumour?*"

Wei Tseng-li waved the query aside. "Do not toy with me, Li Yuan. I have heard of your quarrel with Tsu Ma. The whys and wherefores I know nothing of, but if you plan to throw your City into a state of war simply to…"

"To *what?*" Li Yuan interrupted angrily. "Cousin… I owe you the life of my son… and much more besides… but I am a T'ang and what I decide…"

"Will affect my City." Wei Tseng-li leaned into the screen, "What is happening, Li Yuan? Come clean with me. If you *are* planning a war then tell me, for I shall need to take measures in my own City. If not…"

Li Yuan sat back. "The Banners stay in Africa. As for war…" He picked up the document and turned it, holding it up so that Wei Tseng-li could see.

Wei read, then laughed. "But Yuan, that's…" He laughed, a boyish laugh of delight that strangely warmed Li Yuan. "That's *wonderful* news!"

Li Yuan nodded, but he was still not sure. Wonderful? *Was* it wonderful? Or was it some trick, some empty form designed to trap him? The truth was he didn't know. The bastard had taken him right to the edge. But for now –

for this brief intermission, at least – it was peace.

He let out a long, sighing breath then laughed, letting himself succumb to Wei Tseng-li's obvious delight.

"Yes, Cousin Tseng, it is. It really is."

CHAPTER 129

LIGHT AND DARK

Kim stood on the verandah outside his new study, looking out across the gardens. There, on the south lawn between the gravel path and the outer wall, they had erected a geodesic dome – a huge structure more than sixty *ch'i* in height, framed by a protective web of high-tensile steel. Beneath its darkened outer layer lay two others, all three manufactured from a specially-toughened variant of ice Kim had devised himself. The inner layers sealed from the outside and accessible only through a single cast-steel tunnel in which were three air-locks. Beside the circle of the outer lock stood T'ai Cho, his tall, senatorial figure making a stark contrast to the workmen who were bowed deferentially before him. Kim smiled, then looked about him, pleased by what he saw. It looked so much better now that they had laid the lawn and removed the diggers. For weeks it had been chaos, but in the last few days it had all come together. Almost miraculously, it seemed.

Thank the gods T'ai Cho is here, Kim thought with a smile, knowing he would have gone mad trying to cope with this and the project at the same time. As it was, the conversion had gone very smoothly. In less than three weeks they had transformed the old Mansion. All that remained now was for the dome's alarm system to be connected and the rose garden transferred from its current home in SimFic's labs.

Just in time, he thought, looking back at the elaborately-wrapped present that lay on the table beside the open door, for tonight was Jelka's Coming-of-Age party. Tonight, after seven years, he would finally get to see her again.

He smiled, then went inside, walking from room to room, past bowing servants, feeling an immense satisfaction at what had been achieved. T'ai Cho had done an excellent job furnishing the house. Gone was the heaviness of the old décor, the oppressive sense of age and mustiness; in its place was something much lighter and simpler.

Yes, Kim thought, stepping into the airy main reception room. *This is more like it. This is a home.*

Home. The very word was alien to his experience. He had never had a home before, only rooms. But this... this had the feeling of a home, of somewhere one could work and live. A place one could venture out from and return to, knowing it would always be there.

A place waiting to be filled with life.

He walked to the great window and looked out. To the left was the east wing of the house and, on the far side of a shallow lake, an apple orchard; to the right the main driveway and, beyond the pale, lace-like stone of a curving bridge, the massive arch of the ornamental gates.

Home, he thought, surprised by the strength of the emotion engendered by that single word.

The Machine was right. I needed to make a home – a place for us to be...

He looked across. T'ai Cho, it seemed, had finished. With a curt gesture he dismissed the men then turned and, gathering his silks about him, began to make his way back to the house.

Kim went out, meeting his old friend in the entrance hall, the great sweep of the stairs to his right.

"Is everything ready?"

T'ai Cho handed the electronic clipboard to a servant, then turned to Kim. "We've had a few problems with the T'ang's Inspectorate, but I think I've smoothed them over. They're going to give the system a trial run. Once that's done we can arrange the transfer."

"Today?"

T'ai Cho shook his head. "The Inspectorate are demanding the very tightest security. They want it done tonight, in the early hours when the levels are clear. And SimFic say they need twelve hours notice."

Kim looked down, disappointed.

"Chin up. It'll make no difference. Besides, it's almost midday now.

Even if we *could* arrange it for this evening, you'd only miss it. Unless, of course..."

"No. We'll wait."

T'ai Cho smiled. "You deserve the best, Kim. I hope it all goes well tonight."

Kim sighed. "It scares me, T'ai Cho. Seeing her again... I... I don't know what I'll say."

"Say what comes to your mind. 'Thank you' might be a good start. For the tapes she sent you."

"Yes..." Kim laughed. "Yes, you're right." He stared at his old friend a moment then stepped across and embraced him. "I'm glad you came, T'ai Cho."

"I'm glad you asked me," T'ai Cho answered, hugging him tightly, moved by the gesture of affection. "I missed you."

Years ago, when Kim had first come up from the Clay, it had been T'ai Cho who had found him, T'ai Cho who had trained him, fought for him when things went wrong and Andersen – the Director of the Recruitment Project – had wanted to have him terminated. T'ai Cho had been his tutor, his protector, the closest he had known to a father, his own having been killed – publically executed by the T'ang, unknown to him. Yet, for the last seven years, T'ai Cho had been almost a stranger to him. He had kept in touch, yes, but his work as a commodity slave for SimFic had more than filled his time. That and the waiting...

Kim put a hand to the warm, pulsing band about his neck.

But now the waiting was at an end. Today Jelka came of age. Today he ceased to be a slave and became an owner. And tonight... tonight he would ask her to be his wife. To share his life.

He felt a strange thrill – a mixture of fear and feverish expectancy – pass through him, then turned, looking at the great clock on the wall.

"*Aiya!* I'll be late!"

T'ai Cho shook his head. "Don't worry. I've arranged everything. Director Reiss is coming here."

"Here? But I thought..."

"You're important to them, Kim. Whatever you want..." T'ai Cho stopped, then laughed suddenly. "I'm so pleased for you. So... *thrilled*. I keep remembering how we had to fight, even to keep you alive. But now..."

T'ai Cho turned, indicating the opulence of the Mansion and its grounds, "the world is your oyster. You want a Mansion? They give you one. Your own company? It's yours. The hand of the Marshal's daughter? ...Well, how *could* he refuse? You are a Great Man, Kim Ward. Today you have finally arrived. Today you take your place in the world."

Kim looked away, embarrassed, then smiled. "I'd best get ready. When is Reiss due?"

T'ai Cho glanced at the clock. "Any moment. I told him noon."

"*Noon? Aiya!*" Kim turned, beginning to climb the stairs.

"Kim?"

He stopped, looking back at T'ai Cho from ten steps up.

"Take your time. He'll wait. They'll *all* wait from now on. You are a Great Man now, remember that! He smiled enigmatically. "You are the golden key that opens doors, remember?"

Kim's eyes widened. "Matyas... You remembered."

T'ai Cho nodded. "But those days are done with now. No one will ever bully you again, Kim. No one. Now go and change. It's time they took that collar from your neck."

Kim touched the glowing band, then nodded and, turning, mounted the steps again, jumping them three at a time. And as he went, T'ai Cho spoke softly to his back.

"No one. You understand that, Kim Ward? No one. Not even the great T'ang himself..."

"Jelka?"

Tolonen popped his head round the door, looking into his daughter's room.

"Daddy?" She looked up from her desk, then got up and came across to hug him. "How's it going?"

He smiled. "It's been madness. Absolute madness! I've hardly dared come out of my rooms. But Harrison seems to know what he's doing."

Harrison had been brought in by her father two weeks ago to oversee the final stages of the party. He was the veteran of a thousand social campaigns; a hard taskmaster and accomplished socialite rolled into one.

"Don't worry, Daddy," she said, seeing the troubled look on his face. "Any problems, he'll sort them out."

"Yes... Yes, I suppose he will." He looked past her distractedly, then gestured towards the brightly-lit screen of the scanner on her desk. "Anything interesting?"

She shook her head. "Nothing really... I thought I'd catch up with my journal."

"Journal?" He looked at her, intrigued. "You keep a journal?"

"Yes... and before you ask, no, you *can't* see it. It's private."

He raised a hand, as if fending her off. "Okay... but make sure you're ready for the first guests."

"Fourth bell. Right?"

"Right." He smiled, then looked past her again. "It's a lovely dress. Your mother..." He steeled himself, then said it. "Your mother would have loved to have seen it."

Jelka turned, looking at the dress where it hung alongside her outer-system suit, and nodded. It was her mother's dress – the same dress she had worn to her own Coming-Of-Age party twenty-six years before. She turned back, then, kissing him gently on the brow, pushed him from the room and closed the door, returning to her desk.

For a moment she sat there, staring into space, thinking of her mother; a mother she had only ever seen in holograms; had only dreamed of, never met, never touched.

Could you love someone you had never met? Could you love them because of what they ought to have been in your life? Love them despite their absence?

She shuddered. Never had she framed it so explicitly, but there it was, the thing that made her different from all her friends; the very thing that made her idiosyncratically herself.

The lack of a mother's love.

She typed it in, then sat back.

The closer it gets the less real it seems.

And what if she found that she didn't like him? What if the years had changed what she felt? What if the thing she had been carrying inside her all these years was only an illusion – the chimera of love?

It frightened her. She, who prided herself on fearing nothing – who had survived three separate assassination attempts – was afraid of this; of meeting the man she loved. Afraid in case his feelings for her had changed. Afraid simply because she had never done this kind of thing before, never *loved.* Not in this way. Not in the way she proposed to love him.

Even the thought of it made her feel odd. She had tried *not* to think of it; had tried to divert her thoughts whenever they fell into that track, but her dreams had tripped her up. In her dreams she had been with him, woman to man, naked with him in that cave on the island where she had seen the fox that time, his dark eyes shining in the dark. Dark, animal eyes that made her shiver simply to think of them staring back at her.

Be brave, she told herself. *Furthermore, be true.*

Seven years. So much could change in seven years. Yet she had waited. She had kept her word to him.

Tonight. She shivered then leaned forward, switching off the screen. Tonight he would be hers.

Madam Peng was waiting for him in his study.

"Madam Peng," he said, smiling tightly as he went to his desk.

She got to her feet hastily, taken surprise by his entrance. "Marshal Tolonen. Forgive me..." She bowed, the young man at her side standing to do the same.

Tolonen sat, moving the papers he had been working on to one side, then looked up, taking in the young man at a glance.

"And this is?"

Madam Peng turned to her left. "This is Emil Bartels. I sent you his file..."

"Ah, yes..." Tolonen nodded to the young man. "You understand why you are here, *Shih* Bartels?"

"I believe so, Marshal Tolonen."

Tolonen's expression softened a fraction. "You're a good-looking young man, Emil. And your family... Very sound, if I recall."

The young man nodded, then glanced at Madam Peng uncomfortably.

"Please sit down, both of you."

Madam Peng sat, smiling, fluttering the fan before her face.

Beside her, the young man sat forward slightly, his hands on his left knee, the fingers interlaced, his face in deadly earnest.

"Forgive me, Madam Peng," Tolonen began, sitting back a little. "As you know, it was my intention to have *Shih* Bartels visit my daughter before tonight. To... *prepare* her for this. But there simply hasn't been time. Besides, my daughter is... *difficult,* let us say. She suspects my motives. I wish only the best for her, of course, but she mistakes my interest for meddling. In the circumstances we must be careful. Her encounter with *Shih* Bartels must seem an accident."

"This is most unusual," Madam Peng began. "To guarantee success in a matter like this…"

Tolonen raised a hand. "I understand. If my daughter falls for young Emil here, all well and good. He looks a fine young chap and his past conduct is exemplary, but you do not understand. I…" He frowned, searching for the right words, then shrugged. "Let's put it this way… If you succeed in distracting her tonight… in *entertaining* her, let's say, and taking her mind from other matters, well, there will be a huge bonus in it for both of you."

Bartels looked to Madam Peng, surprised "But I thought…"

"Oh, don't get me wrong," Tolonen said hastily. "If my daughter wishes to see young Bartels here again, and if that association leads to marriage, I shall place no obstacle before it. But the main aim of this exercise is to ensure that tonight goes… well, without a hitch, let's say."

Madam Peng's fan snapped shut. Her face was now openly suspicious. "forgive me, Marshal. You might tell me that it isn't my business, but does your daughter already have a suitor?"

Tolonen looked down, sniffing deeply, then nodded.

"*Aiya!*" Madam Peng said softly. "Why in the gods' names did you not tell me this?"

"You were paid well, Madam Peng," Tolonen said, an edge of steel in his voice. "And if your young man is successful the world shall know of it. As for this rival… this so-called suitor… I shall deal with *him.* Your job is simple. You have only to do what you have always done – to facilitate the coming together of healthy young men and women of the right social level. If there's a problem with that…?"

Madam Peng stared at him a moment, dumbstruck, then shook her head.

"Good. Then you can begin at once. I have arranged a room for you in an apartment nearby. Whatever you need, ask for it. *Shih* Harrison is in charge. He'll see to all your needs."

Tolonen stood, then came round the desk, offering his hand to the young man. "And good luck, Emil. Do your best for me, neh?"

The young man took the hand and shook it, then stepped back and bowed his head, like a soldier before his commanding officer, while beside him, Madam Peng looked on, her face deeply concerned, the fan fluttering uneasily in her hand.

The news was full of it. A bizarre new cult was killing people – many of them suspected terrorists – by nailing them to huge wheel-like crosses, slitting their wrists and leaving them to die. There had been a few instances before now, but this morning more than fifty had been discovered in the Mids, sign of a dramatic increase in the cult's activities.

Rumour was that it was the work of what had once been called The Black Hand – of a new break-off sect called The Sealed. Whatever the truth, it was a disturbing escalation and most of the media channels had turned their full attention to the new 'trend'.

Kim sat beneath the screen in his study, watching with the sound turned down as the images changed. He was troubled by this new upturn in violence. Down where he'd originally come from, in the Clay, such savagery would have seemed quite normal. Dog ate dog down there. But he had climbed the levels to escape from that nightmare reality, thinking it would be different up here.

He had been wrong. The darkness wasn't down there, it was inside. However high men climbed, the darkness climbed with them. It was there, beneath the skin, there behind the pupils of the eyes. Darkness: It was rooted in the head and in the heart. Darkness, everywhere darkness.

"Enough!" he said. At once the screen went black. He turned. T'ai Cho was watching from across the room.

"What is it?" he said softly, sensing Kim's mood.

Kim shrugged. "It gets worse... Every day there's more of it. And every day it's more extreme. The Clay... it's becoming like the Clay."

T'ai Cho nodded and looked away. He too had been disturbed by what he'd seen.

"It worries me," Kim said after a moment. "What kind of world is this to bring one's children into?"

"Things will get better..."

Kim gave a short, despairing laugh. "I'd like to think so, T'ai Cho, but experience teaches otherwise. We live now on the edge of chaos, of perpetual uncertainty. Look at us. I mean... guards and guns. Whoever would have thought it?"

"It has always been so. From the time of the Three Emperors, men have built walls to keep other men from killing them. So it was, so it is."

"And must ever be?" Kim shook his head. "No, T'ai Cho. There just *has* to be something better than this!"

"And if there isn't? If this is *all* there is?"

Kim stared at him, then shook his head. "Darkness... it can't all be darkness. There *has* to be light. Darkness and light... *balanced*. That's what the great Tao says, is it not?

T'ai Cho nodded. "Yes, but remember what the great sage Lao Tzu said. "The bright way appears to be dark."

"And if it *is* dark?"

"Then be a light in that darkness, Kim. Shine out and *make* things change. Dedicate yourself to it. You have a gift, Kim. *Use* it. Maybe that was why you were saved. Maybe that's why the darkness coughed you up."

Kim laughed. "You make it sound so easy."

"Easy? No, I never said it would be easy. Remember how we began. Remember what a knife-edge we walked back then, you and I. Why, one mistake and I'd have had to gas you in your cell. You were such a tiny, bony creature – more wraith than child. Yet I knew you were different. I could see it, right from the start. And to think how far you'd come..."

Kim stood up, then went to the window. It was true. He *had* come far. Yet how much further the light now seemed above him. How much further it seemed he had to climb. Even so... His hand went up to touch his neck where the collar had been removed. It was his choice now. His choice entirely what he was to be.

"Okay. I'll try. I promise you I'll try."

T'ai Cho came over, touched his arm. "Good. But right now you'd best get ready. You don't want to keep Jelka waiting, do you?"

Kim smiled. "No. I think we've waited long enough."

The madman walked through the market quickly, his head back, his shouts, his manic whoops of laughter carrying above the normal hubbub of the place. Emily, sitting alone at one of the tables in The Blue Pagoda, turned to watch him pass, then frowned and sipped from her half empty *chung*.

A madman was a common sight these days. Then again, it was a wonder they weren't all mad, things being as they were.

She sighed, then looked back at the documents she had been reading. She had seen so many things these past ten years – so many awful, dreadful things – but this was by far the worst. And the most awful thing about it was that it proved the old men – the Seven and their servants – right, for such a thing would never have been thought of before the Edict had been relaxed. Now it was almost commonplace. *Almost...* for, thank the gods, there were still some people with a shred of decency – of humanity – left them in.

Emily closed the file with a shudder. Tonight they would hit the place. *Oberon's*, it was called, a club on the Twenty-Fifth level of the fashionable Augsburg stack, the haunt of the super-elite of the First Level, the "Above-the-Above" as they called themselves, the 'Supernal'.

It would not be easy, for the place had its own guards – ex-Security, for the main part – and a state-of-the-art laser defence system, but it could be done, and they *would* do it, whatever the cost.

She finished her *ch'a* then set the *chung* down, recalling the difficulty she had had getting Pasek to agree. He'd been against it, wanting to carry on with his petty wars against his rivals, but she had put her foot down, insisting on this as a price of her continued loyalty and he had given in. But if she fucked up...

Emily laughed quietly, then looked up, signalling for Yu I to bring more *ch'a*. What did it matter if she fucked up – if she didn't get out of there alive? At least she would have done something. At least she would have sent a warning to these monsters that they couldn't do these things without paying a price.

Her smile faded, the anger burning in her again. They thought their money made them immune. They thought that it lifted them above all human decency, but she would teach them otherwise.

Yu I brought back a fresh-filled *chung* and set it beside her with a bow, taking away the empty. She watched him go, knowing it might be the last time she would witness the sight. The thought didn't upset her. Rather, it lifted her. These past few weeks had been like a dream; she had been going through the motions like a hireling, but now she had a chance to act, to do something real, and that made her feel alive again.

Emily looked up at the cages overhead. The birds were quiet, dozing on their perches, like old men in the late afternoon.

She tensed, feeling a hand on her shoulder. Two men slipped on to the bench either side of her, hemming her in.

"Rachel... We were told we'd find you here."

It was the one to the right of her – middle-aged, male – who had spoken. She turned, meeting his dark Han eyes. "What do you want, Ts'ao Wu?"

Ts'ao Wu smiled unpleasantly, looking past her at his companion, a tall, shaven-headed *Hung Mao* named Peters. Both were Hand. Both were Cell leaders. Both, as far as she knew, were Pasek's men.

"We've had enough," Ts'ao Wu said quietly, his face close to hers, his bad breath making her want to choke. "This new spate of killings... these *crucifixions*, they've gone too far."

"That's right," Peters added, leaning in from her left. "And we want to know what you're going to do about it."

"Do?" She eased back slightly. "I don't intend to do anything. You don't like what's happening, you speak to Pasek... Or leave the Hand."

Ts'ao Wu laughed sourly, his pocked face humourless. "The only way you leave the Hand is through the Oven Man's door. You know that. So I ask again. What are you going to do?"

She looked down at her untouched *ch'a*. "You don't like what Pasek's doing?"

Ts'ao Wu turned and spat on the floor, then looked back at her, raising the middle finger of his left hand. "*That* to his great 'crusade'. *That* to his talk of the One God and Judgement Day!"

"The man's mad," Peters said, his face glowing strangely. "He's gone too far. We have to stop him before he destroys the Hand entirely."

"Or *changes* it?"

Her comment caught them off-guard. She saw them exchange looks and knew suddenly that they were deadly serious. For a moment she had thought this was a trap; an attempt by Pasek to test her loyalty, but that brief exchange of looks – revealing, as it did, their uncertainty, their sudden fear that they had miscalculated – told her that she's been wrong. Setting aside personal dislike, she put her arms round their shoulders and drew them in, looking from one to the other, her voice a whisper.

"I understand. I... *share* some of your fears. But now is not the time. We must plan things carefully. Make soundings. See how deeply the current of mistrust runs.

She saw once again the uncertainty in their faces and squeezed their shoulders, as if to reassure them.

"It will not be easy, but it can be done. You must be watchful, brothers. Sensitive to the moods and expressions of your fellow Han members. And patient, too. You must approach only those whose eyes and gestures reveal their... *unhappiness*."

"But Pasek..."

"Pasek sees only what he wants to see. Likewise his lieutenants. They are like blind men, neh? They see only what he wants them to see, say what he wishes them to say. That is their weakness. We need not fear them. We need fear only ourselves. So go to it. But carefully."

Emily took her arms from their shoulders, then leaned between them to take the file. She stood, stepping out from the bench.

"And you?" Peters asked, both men turning to look up at her. "What will *you* be doing?"

"Me?" Her smile was like a hawk's, fierce and cold. "Don't worry about me, brothers. When the time comes, I shall be there for you. Yes, and Pasek will rue the day he let me live."

If I survive, that is, she thought, turning away. *If I get out of Oberon's alive!*

Jelka stood before the full-length mirror, holding out the voluminous folds of the lilac ball dress and frowning at herself.

It's not me, she thought, wondering what her mother had felt about wearing it. But then, her mother had not been brought up by the T'ang's general. Her mother had had a normal childhood, been a normal woman.

She grimaced at her reflection then, lifting her arms, twirled about, as she had seen dancers do on the trivee.

No. It was grotesque. How could she possibly wear such a thing in front of people? The very thought of it made her want to crawl away and hide!

"Jelka?"

It was her father.

"Jelka? Why is the door locked? Are you alright in there?"

"I'm fine, Daddy. I won't be long."

She could hear his sigh of exasperation though the door.

"Okay," he said, "but don't be too long. Our first guests will be arriving any time now. You ought to be at the door to greet them."

"I'll be there. Just give me a minute."

She listened to his footprints fade, then let out her breath. What was she to do? What on earth was she to do?

If she didn't wear it he would be upset. He would think it an insult to her mother's memory. But if she did...

"*Aiya...*" Why hadn't she tried it on before? Why hadn't she faced this problem weeks ago and settled it then?

Perhaps because she'd known what a fuss her father would make. These past few weeks she had avoided arguing with him, afraid to give him any excuse to cancel the party. But now she had to face it.

"Shit!" she said, making a face at her image. Was this really how she wanted Kim to see her? Was *this* – this garish, silly image of silk and lace and bows – really what he had been waiting seven years to see?

"It isn't me," she moaned softly. "Can't you see that, Daddy? It simply isn't me!"

But he wasn't there to answer her. This one she'd have to sort out for herself. She blew out a long breath. "Shit, shit, shit, shit, *shit!*"

From the front entrance of the Mansion she heard the summons bell sound. The first guests were at the gate. Their sedan would be making its slow way up the drive even now.

Jelka glared at herself, then, turning side on to her image, stuck out her tongue. "If he laughs I'll cut him dead," she said defiantly. "If he dares to laugh..."

The hours passed, the guests arrived, and, after a while, her sense of self-consciousness began to fade, blurring into a kind of numbness in which she laughed and mouthed inoffensive answers to questions from people she barely knew. Yet all the while, beneath it all, some part of her withdrew – was kept separate. Yes, and each time the summons bell sounded she would look to the entrance arch expectantly, her stomach muscles tensed, only for her hopes to be dashed, time after time after time. Now it was just after nine and he still hadn't come.

Where are you, Kim Ward? She asked herself anxiously. *Why aren't you here?*

"Jelka, you look wonderful. That dress... Why, it looks marvellous on you."

She turned, for a moment not recognising the luxuriously-dressed young woman who stood before her. Then she put her hand to her mouth in surprise.

"Yi Pang-chou!"

The young woman beamed and reached out to embrace her, holding her tightly for a moment before she stepped back.

"It's Madam Heng now. I married a Minister three years ago... Or hadn't you heard?"

"No, I..." Jelka laughed, embarrassed, wondering vaguely what had happened to her first husband. "Anyway, how *are* you Pang-chou. It's ages since I last saw you."

"Seven years," Madam Heng said, straightening up. Her peacock blue silks looked fabulously expensive and a small fortune in jewellery rested on her fingers and about her wrists and neck. She had obviously married well second time around.

"And your children? Are they well?"

"Very well, thank you. I have five now."

"Five..." Jelka stared at her, stunned, then nodded vaguely. Yet it made sense. Pang-chou had married and had her first child even before they both left College. So had many of their friends. As she was finding out, the anomaly lay not in them, but in herself. She alone of her school friends remained unmarried, childless.

She turned, glancing at the door.

"Bachman's here," Madam Heng continued. "You remember Lothar Bachman? He's a captain now. They say he'll make Major within the next few years."

Jelka looked back at her. Bachman? Now where had she heard that name? Then it hit her. She stared at Heng Pang-chou, alarmed. "You mean...?"

"Didn't you realise?"

She shook her head. "My father must have invited him. I..."

Bachman. He'd been the cadet officer at the College Graduation Ball who had forced himself on her, trying to kiss her – the young man whose legs and arms she had broken...

Jelka swallowed, then bowed her head slightly. "Forgive me, Heng Pang-chou, but I have to see to something. I'll speak with you later."

She moved away, making for the entrance arch, nodding and smiling as she went, noticing, once again, the young man who seemed to have been shadowing her all night.

Probably Security, she thought. *Something my father has arranged.*

Outside in the corridor it was cooler. Smiling at a pair of guests who had just arrived she went across to the House Steward, Huang Peng, who stood beside the great outer doors, welcoming each guest.

"Has he come yet?"

"*Shih* Ward?" Steward Huang looked across at his assistant, who hastily consulted a list, then shook his head. The Steward turned back to her and bowed. "I am afraid not, Mistress."

"Has he sent a message?"

"We have heard nothing, Mistress. Should I...?"

"No."

She turned away. He was late, that was all. He would be here soon. If he loved her.

For a moment she hesitated, hearing the great swell of voices from the Reception Hall. Ten minutes. No one would miss her for ten minutes. Only she had to know.

As she reached the door she heard soft footsteps behind her. She whirled about.

"You! What do you want?"

"I..." The young man gave a nervous bow, then swept his hair back from his eyes.

"Well?"

He offered her a smile. "My name is Emil. Emil Bartels. I..."

"Did my father send you?"

He hesitated, then gave a nod.

Jelka sighed. A soldier. He looked every inch a soldier.

"Okay. It's not your fault, Emil. Come in. You can wait here. There's something I must do."

She went inside. Back in her study he went over to her desk and sat.

Cursing the folds of her dress, she leaned forward, switching on the comset.

She knew the code. As soon as she'd heard he'd bought the Mansion she had made it her business to discover it. But she had never used it before now. Never dared.

What if he isn't coming? What if he's ill?

But he wasn't ill. She knew that. If he'd been ill he would have sent a message. So what was keeping him? Why hadn't he come?

She took a deep breath then typed out the coded sequence. As the screen emerged from the desk she sat back a little, composing herself.

Her hands were trembling now and her mouth had gone dry at the thought of actually talking to him.

There was a moment's hesitation and then a face appeared. A young, Han face, female, very pretty.

"Nu Shih Tolonen?"

"Yes, I..."

"I am afraid that the number you have called is unavailable. The channel is closed right now, but if you would like to leave a message, we can transmit it once the channel reopens."

She sighed heavily, unable to help herself, then shook her head. "No. It doesn't matter."

She cut the connection, then sat back, her face pained.

Maybe he was on his way. It was even possible that he was here already. Maybe he'd arrived while she was sitting here, fretting. She crossed the room quickly then stopped, seeing the young man standing in the doorway to her bedroom. She cleared her throat.

"Excuse me..."

He jerked round, surprised. "I... I was just looking."

He took a step toward her, his hands out, as if to excuse himself. "I just wondered what kind of girl you were. What kind of things you liked. That's all. Girls' rooms..." He smiled uncertainly. "They reveal a lot about their owners, don't you think?"

She stared at him coldly, then answered him, her voice hard, uncompromising. "What business is it of *yours* who I am or want I like?"

His eyes widened. "You mistake me. I... I didn't mean to pry. I was interested, that's all. If we're to..."

"If we're to what?" She was suspicious now. She took a step toward him, as if facing an attacker. "What are you talking about, lieutenant?"

He gave a brief, surprised laugh. "*Lieutenant?* No. You have it wrong. I'm not a soldier, I'm..."

Bartels swallowed, seeing the look that had come to her face.

"So just what *are* you? And what *do* you want?" She took another step, her body crouched slightly. "Who invited you?"

He took a step back, his hands raised defensively. "Look, I..."

Bartels sighed, his eyes pleading with her now. "Your father said I was to be pleasant to you, that's all. He said..."

Jelka stopped and straightened slowly. Her whole body had gone cold, all of her darkest suspicions suddenly confirmed. *Her father. This was her father's doing.*

That was why there had been no fuss, no arguments, about Kim's invitation. Because he had had no intention of letting the young man step inside his mansion.

Because...

She shivered with indignation, then, sweeping past Bartels, went into her room, slamming the door shut behind her.

"You thought I'd be fooled, didn't you?" she said with a quiet anger, addressing her reflection as she began to peel off the dress. "You thought I'd play the good daughter and not embarrass you."

She kicked the dress away then went across and took the space suit down from its peg. For a moment she hesitated, knowing that if she did this it would be tantamount to an open rejection of her father – that it would mean a breach with him. But that was what he had been counting on: that she would think twice before tackling him head-on.

Well, you were wrong, she thought, angry with him suddenly. Furious that he should use such tactics against her, after all that had happened. Facing the mirror again, she rested the suit against her body, remembering how it had felt out there in the outer system; how at home she'd felt among the cold-worlders. Then, without further hesitation, she pulled it on, the familiarity of the garment – the smell and touch of it – making her shiver with a sense of recognition.

Better, she thought, smiling at this new image of herself. But the hair was still wrong. Hurriedly she took it down and combed it out with her fingers.

Yes, she thought finally. *That's me. Not that other creature of lave and ribbons, but this...*

And if Kim had come? If she'd been wrong about her father?

She laughed, then spoke softly to the mirror. "Then you'll look a fool, Jelka Tolonen, won't you?"

But at least it would be *her* and not some twisted image of her mother – some hideous fulfilment of her father's fantasies.

Seven years she had waited for this day. Seven years. And now, finally, she had come of age.

Today she was her own woman, free to choose for herself.

Yes, but what did that mean – what point had it – if she could not *be* herself?

Smiling uncertainly, Jelka nodded to her image then, steeling herself, knowing what lay ahead, she turned and went to the door.

The masked man stood in the doorway, a big "scatter gun" – a hundred and eighty rounds in its snake-like spiral chamber – levelled at the servants who lay, bound and gagged on the stone floor of the pantry. Their eyes watched him fearfully as, from other parts of the Mansion, strange voices called back and forth. They had seen the symbol on the chain about their necks – the cross within the circle – and feared the worst. If these *were* Hand members then they were dead... sooner or later.

Outside, in the main house, masked men went from room to room, checking they were empty. Finally one of them came down the main steps and went over to a man who sat on the low wall by the drive and snapped to attention in front of him, bowing his head.

"He's not inside here. He must have gone."

Von Pasenow stared at his lieutenant then shook his head. "He's here. He has to be here. What about the dome?"

"It's locked. If he's in there..."

Von Pasenow stood, angry that he had to do the thinking for all of them. "Well, unlock the fucking thing! He's in there. He has to be. He can't be anywhere else, can he? We've watched the transit all day and there's no other way out. So get to it. Use cutting tools if you have to."

"Sir!" The man bowed and backed away, then turned and went back inside, calling men to him as he went.

Von Pasenow glanced at the timer inset into his wrist and swore. Twenty minutes. Twenty fucking minutes! They were supposed to have been in and out in ten, taking Kim with them. But now...

He growled with frustration. Staying here was the last thing he'd wanted. They had to get Kim out of the dome quickly, otherwise they could be into a siege situation, and who knew where *that* would lead?

Fuck you, Knut Tolonen! he thought, kicking at the gravel angrily. *If the shit hits the fan, you can take the blame for this! Yes, and explain it to your precious daughter!*

He had tried to talk the old man out of it, but it had been like talking to a statue. Tolonen was obsessed with keeping Ward and his daughter apart... by any means, it seemed. But he hadn't counted on this!

He watched as two of his men hurried down the steps, carrying a laser cannon.

"Beinlich!"

His lieutenant reappeared in the doorway. "Sir?"

"Drug the servants, then get all but four of your men to the gate. I want to be out of here as soon as possible."

"Sir!"

Von Pasenow let out a breath. Security, when they came to investigate this, would know this wasn't the work of the Black Hand, if only because the Hand left no survivors. But then they were never meant to think that. They were meant to think this was industrial – that Kim had been kidnapped by one of SimFic's major rivals. The make of drugs would be one clue – throwing suspicion on MedFac: suspicion which would be fanned by a whispering campaign over the next few weeks.

Yes, but it won't work. It won't keep your daughter from marrying Ward. Not if she really wants to.

In fact, it might even backfire. Like that whole business of sending her away to the Colonies. If what he'd heard was right, she had spent most of her time pining for the Clayborn!

No. There was only one way to keep those two apart and that was to kill him. But as Tolonen wouldn't go that far...

He walked across to the dome. When he'd taken on the job, he had known very little about Ward, but, scanning the files, he had come to respect the young man, Clayborn or not. In that regard, he didn't share the view of most of the Above. What did it matter where a man came from? It was where he ended up that counted. Too often in his life he had had to put up with arseholes who were his superiors merely through connection. It was nice to come across someone who had risen, like himself, through merit.

If it was he and not the Marshal whose daughter was in love with Ward, he would have given the match his blessing. After all, Ward was one of the richest men in City Europe. And this Mansion... He nodded to himself, impressed. No, he would have no qualms about a daughter of his marrying a Clayborn. Not if the Clayborn were worth six hundred million *yuan*!

By the time he got there they had set up the laser and were already cutting into the steel outer door. There was the sweet smell of burning in the air. He put up a hand to shield his eyes against the glare, then turned, looking back at the magnificent great house.

No... no qualms at all.

Slowly, careful not to make a noise, Kim edged further into the darkness, wriggling his whole body forward a fraction at a time, his head forced to the side by the narrowness of the space between the ceiling and the floor.

The light was just ahead of him now and he could hear the murmur of voices down below. If he was right he was directly above the kitchens. On the far side there was a service hatch, leading down. If he could somehow twist about and get into it.

He rested, inhaling the warm scent of the new pine floor he'd had put in only a week ago. If he hadn't watched them – if he hadn't witnessed how they'd laid the narrow planks – then they'd have taken him for certain. In all probability he would be dead by now, and Jelka...

Jelka would have been widowed even before she was married.

He closed his eyes, wondering what she was doing at that moment. Was she dancing? Was she in the arms of some young soldier, twirling around the ballroom, spiting him, angry with him for not being there – thinking he'd let her down?

He pushed the thought away, then began to edge forward again. It wasn't far now. Another ten minutes and he'd be there. Just another ten minutes.

And if they set the house on fire before then?

"Kim?"

He froze, his eyes searching the darkness in front of him. Then, with a jolt, he realised that the voice had come from inside – from the implant in his head.

"Who is it?" he whispered.

"It is I," the voice answered. "The Machine."

Kim felt a chill go through him. He had not known that it had access to the implant. Always, before now, he had spoken to it in the air – insisting on it. But all the while it had been there – silent, observant, like a ghost inside his skull.

"What do you want?" he asked, the words so softly spoken they were barely formed. But it heard him perfectly.

"You must go back. Now. You must make your way back to the room you were in when they came."

"But they'll find me."

"No. There are only two of them in the house now, and they are in the control room."

"Then they'll see me."

"No. For there will be nothing to see."

"Ah..." He understood. It was talking about manipulating the images on the screen – of showing an empty room when the room was not empty.

"Who are they?" he asked.

It was silent a moment, then – "You must start to go back. There's little time. She will be here very soon now."

"Who?"

"Jelka... She's coming for you."

"No!" He said it too loud, then repeated it more quietly. "No. She mustn't come. They'll kill her."

"Only if they see her, and even then..."

"Even then what?"

It ignored his question. "You must begin. Now. The rest I'll see to."

"Machine?"

"Yes?"

"Make sure nothing happens to her."

"I'll try."

"And Machine?"

"Yes, Kim?"

"Thank you."

The reality of it was worse than she'd imagined. Seeing the women's skins hanging there on the rail of the cool room, padded out by their plastoform inserts, their owners' eyeless faces staring lifelessly ahead, Emily felt the bile rise in her throat and had to turn away, leaning over the sink in the corner to retch, until there was nothing left in her stomach.

For once the files hadn't prepared her. For once she had let the sheer nastiness of it get to her.

They called it 'shelling'. Five years ago it wouldn't have been possible, but new research had found a way of keeping the flesh of a human alive without the bone or blood or muscle. These – these skins – had once been 'worn' by living human beings; by young women from the Lowers, the kind of women who, even if they were missed by those they loved, would never have been traced, never accounted for, because they were too poor, too unimportant in the scheme of things to be bothered about.

Kidnapped by special teams, they were taken to a special lab and drugged. There the operation was performed, the surface layer of skin and fat carefully removed, to be preserved in a vat of nutrients until required. The rest – the living being, stripped like a bloodied skeleton – was given to the Oven Man.

She shivered, thinking of it; trying to imagine the kind of person who would find this kind of thing *attractive*; who would pay a thousand *yuan* a time simply to wear one of these skins.

Of course, the skin was the simplest part. The really 'clever' bit was the part that brought the skin to life – that allowed the wearer to tap in to the skin's nervous system and experience exactly what it experienced. A fine mesh of ice was sewn into the inner layer of the skin, feeding to a series of artificial ganglions at the base of the spine, beneath the sex organs and at the base of the neck, which rooted pain and pleasure signals to the brain of the recipient.

By this foul means a man could wear the body of a woman and make love as a woman. He could feel what it was like to be possessed by another man, to have his breasts stroked and fondled, the nipples kissed. It was an ancient dream come true. Shelling made it possible. But at a cost.

She forced herself to look again – to sear it into her memory. This was what human beings could do to each other. This. She reached out to touch one of the skins, surprised by its warmth, a shiver of pure anguish passing through her at the thought that this had once been a living woman like herself, with dreams and hopes and memories, perhaps with children of her own – children who missed her, crying themselves to sleep at night for want of her. But now... Emily shuddered. Now it was a mere sense-matrix, a flesh-pad for some rich, uncaring cunt!

A shock of the purest, blackest hatred passed through her like an electric bolt. Inhuman, some might call this. Obscene. But she had her own word for it. *Evil*.

These bastards were truly evil.

She pulled on her gloves then stood before the mirror, taking long, deep breaths, trying to prepare herself. The attack had been an unqualified success. Despite the heavy security of the place, they had achieved almost complete surprise. The guards had been overwhelmed in the first thirty seconds, the alarm system shut down. The rest had been easy.

As for the clients, they were in the next room, lying face down on the thickly carpeted floor, naked, their hands tied behind their backs.

She had intended to gut the place: to set fires at all the doors and let the bastards burn to death, or suffocate, but that would be too kind. Having seen these awful mementoes, she was of a mind to take the bastards back with her; to take them down level and keep them; to torment them, the way these poor women had been tormented.

Yet even as she considered it – even as her blood sang at the thought – she knew how impractical it was.

Torment. Yes, they deserved to live in everlasting torment for what they'd done.

She looked about her one final time, then turned away and, drawing her knife, stepped out into the other room.

I'll cut your balls off, that's what I'll do, she thought, looking about her at the dozen men who lay spread-eagled on the floor in front of her. *And I'll make you eat them, you evil fuckers. Every last tiny morsel.*

And afterwards?

She reached down and grabbed the first of them by the hair, pulling his head up so that he could look at her – at the winking, razor-sharp edge of the knife in her hand - and smiled.

Afterwards she would have them skinned. *Without* anaesthetic.

The young Han crouched in the shadows beyond the broken lamp, watching them come from the lift. He had known something was going on; had heard the screams from up above when he was working in the shaft and had known they would come this way. What he hadn't known was what would happen next.

He was smiling, his deformed face pulled to the right, when the guns opened up. Two of the Hand went down at once, dead. The others scattered, finding whatever cover they could, but it was pretty hopeless. In a minute it was over. He waited, his heart threatening to burst from his chest, his legs weak from the shock of what he'd witnessed, keeping his eyes closed, thinking he'd be next.

After a while he opened his eyes and looked.

Gone. They were gone.

He stood, putting a hand out to steady himself against the wall, almost falling as his legs gave. He waited, letting his strength come back, then forced himself to walk over to where the bodies lay, forced himself to look.

They were dead. All eight of them were dead.

There was a faint noise, a hint of movement. He turned, his mouth forming a silent cry of fear.

His heart was pounding, he shuffled across, then stooped, listening, studying the fallen woman, seeing the faint rise and fall of her chest. She was alive. He leaned over her, studying the wounds to her head and her shoulder. They were bad. She was losing a lot of blood. If he left her here she would die for certain.

And if he took her?

He swallowed drily, then, knowing he had no other choice – that he was compelled to help her – he moved round and took her legs. Then, slowly, inch by inch, he began to drag her – away from the scene of death and into the shadows. Away... a snail-like trail of blood smeared on the dusty floor of the corridor. Away... the weight of her seeming to grow with every step he took.

As the lift slowed, approaching the top of the stack, Jelka moved to the side, pressing herself against the wall. The feeling that something was wrong had grown and grown in her until by now she was jumpy, her nerves on edge.

This was stupid – common sense cried out against it – but right now she couldn't help herself. If Kim *was* in trouble, she had to help.

And if he wasn't?

Well, she had to know that too. So that she could get on with her life.

The camera eye over the door swivelled, following her every move. She closed her eyes briefly, trying to keep control. No doubt they were watching her from the control room and laughing; laughing because she didn't have a chance.

The lift stopped abruptly. She was there. She waited, expecting the doors to hiss open, but they stayed closed.

"Open the doors," she said quietly, looking up at the camera, "Why don't you open the doors?"

Nothing. Just the underlying hum that was everywhere in the City.

Jelka hesitated then stepped across and, slipping her nails beneath the control panel's rim, popped it out. Beneath it were a number of panels. She pulled one out and, taking a second to remember the override sequence, punched in the code.

Nothing. It was as if the thing was dead.

She smacked her hand against the mirrored wall. "Shit!"

"I wouldn't do that," a voice said softly. "You'll only hurt yourself."

It sounded like a woman's voice, mature and well-modulated, the intonation somewhere between Han and *Hung Mao*.

"Who are you?" she asked, staring up at the camera.

"Never mind who I am. Just listen. The Mansion has been taken over by intruders."

"Intruders?"

"Your father's men. They have instructions not to hurt anyone, but the situation might change at any moment. If it does, this whole thing might escalate into something much nastier."

"And Kim?"

"Kim is safe, but only for a while. If they decide to make another physical check of the Mansion..."

"So what do you want me to do?"

"Just do exactly what I say. Take the audio unit from the control panel and carry it with you. I'll speak to you through that."

Jelka nodded, then went to the panel again and removed the tiny, dice-like unit.

"Okay," it said, its voice suddenly tiny, coming up to her from within her palm. "You must pretend you are invisible."

The masked man stepped from the gaping metal of the outer air-lock and shook his head.

"He's not there. The dome is empty."

"*What?*" Von Pasenow's face registered shock. "But that's not possible. He *has* to be there!"

The man lifted his mask, wiping his face with the back of his hand. "Maybe we should check the house again..."

"Quiet! Let me think!"

A second man joined the first, glancing at him, a faint amusement in his eyes, then both looked to Von Pasenow.

There were only two ways into this place and they had watched them both. Kim hadn't come out, so he had to be there still, inside.

Von Pasenow paced back and forth, punching his left fist into his right palm again and again. Convinced that Kim was inside the dome, he had dismissed the majority of his men. To search the Mansion again with only five of them would take too long; and besides, they had done a thorough job first time around.

"Tolonen," he said quietly, stopping dead. "I'll speak to Tolonen."

He spun around, then began to run toward the house.

The two men watched him a moment, then, shrugging, began to walk after him.

Tolonen closed and locked the study door then went back to his desk and sat, trying to control the trembling in his arm.

"Put him on!" he said irritably, glaring at the screen.

Von Pasenow's face appeared. He bowed low then made to speak, only Tolonen cut him off.

"What in the gods' names do you want? Don't you realise how *dangerous* this is? Do you have him?"

Von Pasenow lowered his eyes. "I... I can't find him, Knut. He's here somewhere, only..."

Tolonen stared back at him in disbelief, then slowly shook his head. "Then you had better find him. And quick."

"But Marshal..."

Tolonen cut contact and sat back.

Aiya! First that awful scene with Jelka in the ballroom, and now this!

He put his hands to his face, groaning. It had all seemed so simple. So straightforward. But now...

He gritted his teeth against the memory of the things she had said to him – of the words he'd let fall from his own lips. Words that could never be recalled.

"*Kuan Yin* preserve me..." he said softly. "Jelka... my pretty little Jelka. I never meant..."

But it was done. Broken. And no way back.

He shuddered, then, laying his head upon his folded arms, began to sob. *I never meant...*

She moved through the great house slowly, silently, her feet making no noise, as if invisible, moving from light to shadow like a ghost, while on screens in the control room, the watching cameras showed only empty corridors, untenanted rooms.

At the back of the great house, in a small room on the upper floor, she found him, seated on a low stool, waiting.

"What's happened?" he asked, surprised by the pain that was in her face, but she only shook her head.

He stared at her a while, noting her clothes, the simplicity of her appearance, then reached out, taking her hand. It seemed the simplest thing, yet it had taken seven years – seven long years – to achieve.

She looked down, her hand lying passively within his, then smiled, a strangely wistful smile.

"I didn't think..." she began before her face creased up once more, as if she were about to cry.

He understood at once. Her father. She had broken with her father. He held her to him, the difference in their heights making it an awkward first embrace, yet in an instant all awkwardness was forgotten. He slowly kissed her face with tiny, delicate kisses, exactly as he had dreamed of doing, then moved back, staring up into her eyes, surprised to find her looking back at him; surprised by the awe, the love, the expectation in her eyes.

"Is it a dream?" he asked, his voice barely a whisper.

She shook her head. "We must leave. The Machine..."

"I hear it," he said, touching the access slot beneath his ear. "It speaks to me. Inside. It told me you were coming."

He reached up, his fingers touching her mouth, her nose, her cheeks, checking to see that she was real.

Kim smiled. "We'd best go," she said. "They're running out of time. Any moment now they'll come and look for us."

He nodded, but still he was reluctant to go, afraid to lose this moment. He could feel a faint trembling in him, as if he were a bell that had been struck and still resounded, long after the hammer's blow had fallen.

"Where are we going?" he asked when the silence in his head extended; when no answer came.

"To the island," she said and smiled, the pain momentarily forgotten. "To Kalevala."

CHAPTER 130

THE FLESH OF KINGS

Tsung Ye was kneeling, his head pressed to the floor in front of the Chancellor. Nan Ho looked down at the young secretary in astonishment. He had known something was going on – who hadn't? – but as long as it was being kept discreet, it was not his business to interfere. Now, however, Tsung Ye had made it his business.

He groaned inwardly. This was the last thing he needed right now. In fact, he was tempted to send Tsung Ye away and tell him not to be so ridiculous – that sleeping with the Empress was no great crime, so long as he did not rub the T'ang's nose in it. But Tsung Ye was determined to be absolved, the great burden of his guilt taken from him.

Nan Ho sighed heavily. He felt a great pity for the young man, but he only had himself to blame. No doubt it had been flattering to be pursued by his Mistress. But it seemed she had taken things too far. Nan Ho listened, embarrassed, as Tsung Ye spelt out – in some detail – just how far she had taken them.

It would not have been so bad had Pei K'ung kept to her original agreement with Li Yuan. Then, at least, he could be certain that, should any issue come of the liaison, it was at least no son of Li Yuan's, but the one night she had spent with her husband complicated matters. If she were pregnant...

He turned away, suddenly impatient with it all. For a time he had thought her different from the rest – had thought he'd found a woman above all of that business – immune to it all. But underneath it all she was just the same.

Sex. Why could they not be free of sex? For all the trouble it caused – all the unhappiness and blighted lives – there seemed little enough reward.

"Enough!" he yelled, facing Tsung Ye again. At once the murmur of the young man's voice fell silent. "You will go to your rooms and lock the doors. You will take pen and paper and write down all you have told me, then you will return and give the document to me. Meanwhile I shall ensure that the Empress does not come near you again."

"Thank you, Master Nan," Tsung Ye said with pathetic gratitude, beginning to crawl backwards, away from the Chancellor. "I am *pu ju pen fen*."

Nan Ho watched him go, then went to the window. *Pu ju pen fen.* One who has failed in his duty.

And when his duty was to serve his Mistress without question? What when her instructions conflicted with his duty to his T'ang?

The old man pulled at his collar which had been chafing him, undoing the button on the right-hand side of the neck. He was glad, for once, that he did not have to make a decision. It was an issue only Li Yuan could rule upon.

And what would be say? Well done, Tsung Ye? You do well to keep the old girl from my bed?

Nan Ho almost laughed, thinking of his Master's predilection for young maids. Why he had let Pei K'ung into his bed that once he would *never* understand. And then to banish her again!

He shook his head, then returned to his desk. Matters were pressing. If he judged things correctly things were coming to a head. The reports of his spies were ominous. They spoke of large movements of men and supplies. They hinted at secret meetings and of deals done in shadowy rooms. But nothing certain. Nothing absolute. When it came it would come suddenly. And he must be prepared.

Nan Ho sat, the image of Tsung Ye naked, his buttocks rising and falling between Pei K'ung's open legs haunting him a moment, making him frown. Then, pushing the matter aside, he picked up the tiny hammer and rang the bell on his desk, summoning his secretaries.

Tolonen made to get up from his chair, but the abruptness of Rheinhardt's entrance into the room caught him by surprise.

"Knut! What the fuck are you up to?" he demanded, leaning over the old

Marshal aggressively, his face burning with anger. "I've five men in my cells and, were it not you, Knut Tolonen, I would gladly make it six!"

Tolonen looked down, embarrassed. "You don't understand..."

"*Understand?* What *is* there to understand? That you hired a disgraced Major and his team of tin-pot mercenaries to kidnap one of this City's most important – and *valuable* – men?"

Tolonen's head came up. "*Important!* That ragamuffin!"

He made to get up, but Rheinhardt pushed him down savagely; the first time he had ever dared to touch the old man. He leaned close, speaking the words into Tolonen's face as if addressing the most lowly of his officers and not the man who had been general even before he himself was born. "*Important.* You understand me, Knut? As in *indispensable.* If he's been harmed... If in any way..."

"I gave strict instructions," Tolonen began, but Rheinhardt glared at him once more, making him fall silent.

"You've done many things in your time, Knut Tolonen. Some of them were... well, impolitic is to put it mildly. Some of them weren't strictly within the rules. But *this!* Did you... well, did you even *think?*"

Tolonen stared back at him, his natural defiance tempered by the fact that he knew Rheinhardt was right. He had been stupid.

"What will you do?" he asked quietly.

Rheinhardt straightened up then shook his head with exasperation. "There's nothing I *can* do. Li Yuan will have to know. If Ward presses charges..."

Tolonen sat forward, some of the old fire returning to him. "Let him press charges! But he will never marry my daughter!"

Rheinhardt stared at the old man with a mixture of dismay and pity, then spoke to him, more gently than before.

"Jelka is of age now, Knut. Don't you understand that? She can choose for herself now. And if she chooses Ward..."

Tolonen stood abruptly, pushing his chair back as he did, his golden hand bunched into a fist. "He won't! I won't let him! Why, I'd rather see him dead!"

Rheinhardt drew himself up rigid, pained to hear the old man reduced to this. "I would be careful what you say, Knut Tolonen. I am empowered to uphold the law in City Europe. Your words..."

"Are no more than the truth," the old man said defiantly, his grey eyes piercing Rheinhardt's. His voice boomed now with all its ancient power. "Arrest me, if you dare. Go tell Li Yuan. But you will not stop me. Whether I lose my daughter or not, *he* shall not have her! Do you understand me, General Rheinhardt? I won't let him."

Rheinhardt stared back at the old man a moment, then came to attention, clicking his heels and bowing his head smartly.

"You will hear from me, Marshal," he said, stepping back. "Until you do..."

But Tolonen was not listening. The old man turned and, crossing the room, disappeared into his dressing room, slamming the door behind him.

Rheinhardt closed his eyes, letting out a deep, audible sigh. Then, feeling a sadness that was beyond expression, he turned and left, knowing that the old man had given him no choice.

Li Yuan stood at the top of the landing ramp, looking out towards the silent stone walls of T'ai Yueh Shan palace, his mood despondent.

It was a grey, cheerless day, the wind whipping off the water of the lake, the calling of the geese like the cries of lost souls.

I should not have come, he thought. *I should have left her here to rot.* But now that he *was* here he would see it through. Besides, he had to know. To purge himself of this so he could move on and be strong again.

He turned, calling for another, warmer coat. At once a servant brought one.

The past few weeks had been a torment. In his mind he had constantly pictured her with Tsu Ma. Whereever he went, there they were, leering at him and laughing, their nakedness taunting him. 'Little Boy!' they had called him, mockingly. 'Such a silly little boy to love his brother's wife!'

The pain he felt at such moments was intense. No less intense for being of the mind. Two souls they said each person had – the earth soul and the spirit soul, *p'o* and *hun* – and at such moments he had no cause to doubt them, for while his body was untroubled, his spirit ached. Ached like a rotting tooth that could not be pulled.

Well, so it might be, yet he would try to rid himself of it. Here, today, he would face that inner pain and try to find surcease.

He went down, walking between the lines of kneeling, bowing guards, and on along the path that led to the great West Gate.

Eight and a half years ago he had given her this place, for her and her bastard son. He had divorced her on the day of his coronation and she had had the child two days later, on his wedding day.

Li Yuan slowed his pace, looking to his right, across the grassy slope towards the ornamental bridge, remembering.

His wedding day... It had been a day much like this, with the wind whipping off the lake. The nineteenth day of the nine month it had been. The week before *Chiu Fen*, the Autumn Equinox.

He sighed. And now those three he married that day were dead.

And she still lived...

How strange it was that, after all that had happened, it was to her he was returning. Always to her.

But no more. After today.

Fei Yen was waiting in her rooms. She greeted him with a cold civility, kneeling and pressing her head three times against the cold stone floor before she straightened.

"How are you?" he asked, yet a single look told him far more than she could have ever said. There was a darkness behind her eyes that had not been there a month ago, a tightness to her mouth. Whatever madness had compelled her to fly to Tsu Ma's palace that day, whatever hotness of the blood had urged her on, it had congealed in her now. Eyes which had burned with an angry passion now stared back at him with a frigid insolence.

Her words, when they came, were, like the formality of her greeting, only a mockery,

"I am very happy here, *Chieh Hsia*. You do me great honour, visiting me."

He felt the pain rekindled; felt that familiar tightening of his stomach muscles. Why was it thus? Why did she still have this power over him, after all these years?

"I came to clarify things," he answered. "Much was left... *unstated* last time we met."

She laughed bitterly. "Unstated? Why, forgive me, *Chieh Hsia*, but I thought I expressed myself quite eloquently. Your cousin fucked me. Not once, but many times. Would you like to know *where* and *how*?"

Her eyes searched his, as if trying to gauge how best to inflict pain. "It would be no trouble, if you've the time. I can recall each and every occasion."

She smiled. "He may have been a bastard, but Tsu Ma was a memorable fuck. He..."

"Enough!"

He turned from her, smoothing out his gloves, trying not to show the intense hurt, the agitation he was feeling, but her voice went on, ignoring his command.

"We would ride up to the ruins of the old monastery, up in the hills above Tongjiang. Inside, in the oldest of the temples, he would lay down his riding blanket and we would strip and lie on it. And then..."

He turned, staring at her, compelled, despite himself, to know.

"And then..." Her voice, her face slowly changed, softening. "And then he would make love to me." She sighed. "So fierce and yet so... so gentle, he was. As if he could feel what I was feeling. As if..."

She looked away, all of the anger in her transmuted suddenly to pain, then met his eyes. He stared at her, for that briefest of moments understanding her.

Yes. For the very first time forgiving her, understanding just what had driven her.

Aiya! he thought. *To feel that and yet to be tied.*

"I understand," he said quietly. "It was not your fault. Tsu Ma..."

He choked off the sudden surge of hatred he felt for the man.

She came across and stood beside him, her dark eyes looking up at him, the sweet scent of her filling his senses.

And if he were to reach out...

Slowly he put his arms about her and bent his face to hers. Her mouth opening to his, her lips warm and moist. It was the thing he had missed most all these years: being kissed by her.

He broke from the kiss and moved his head back, staring at her, suddenly afraid of what he'd done.

"Make love to me, Yuan," she said softly, her eyes pleading with him. "Now, before the moment passes."

He shivered, then, unable to help himself, nodded, letting her lift the cloak from his shoulders then begin to unbutton his robe, a boy again, the veil of years torn aside.

"Fei Yen," he whispered, his hand reaching up to caress her neck, her cheek, his fingers smoothing the side of her head as it pressed back against his touch. *"Fei Yen..."*

She drew him down onto the bed, her soft warm kisses on his neck and shoulders blinding his senses, making him groan with sweet delight. She fumbled at his loin cloth, her hand brushing intimately against his fiercely swollen sex, and then he was inside her, thrusting into her, the pain of longing in her face inflaming him, making him spasm and come immediately. And still he thrust, and still he met each thrust, her cries of pleasure keeping him hard.

" Yes... oh, yes... oh, oh..."

He felt her reach up, holding herself tightly, intimately against him, felt the great shudder of release that rippled through her, and then she fell back, as if she'd fainted. As she did, he felt his penis slip from her and gave a tiny groan. At once she reached for him and eased him back inside her, then cradled his head against her with one hand while the other smoothed his buttocks.

He felt a shuddering sigh escape him, then closed his eyes, conscious of the hard length of his flesh within her, linking them, binding them as no words or ceremonies had ever managed.

If it could always have been thus. But the flesh was weak, that connecting warmth illusory.

They made love again, this time beneath the blankets, his face above her own, watching her, savouring every moment, using all his skills to bring her to her climax long before he let his seed flow into her.

"I had forgotten," he said afterwards, facing her, his hands tracing the contours of her body. "All these years..."

She watched him lazily, like a cat, all of the hardness, the resentment washed from her; purged, it seemed, by his love-making.

"Do you think..." he began, then sighed, shaking his head.

"You can always visit me," she said, teasingly. "You could tie me up!"

"Is that what you like?"

She gave a soft grunt then looked away. "You do not know the half of it, Li Yuan. The men I've known. The years... Ach! Each year has seemed like ten. Like those years I spent in exile in the floating palace, mourning your brother's death."

He sighed, pained by this insight into her. All these years he had blamed and hated her.

"I have been blind. I never understood you, did I?"

"No." She looked back at him, then smiled. "So what now, my husband?"

The words sent a strange thrill through him – a shock of recognition, of *rightness*. He smiled back, feeling as if it were the first true smile – the first honest, open smile – he had ever given her.

"So now... well, now we start anew."

He reached out, drawing her to him, cradling her above him and kissing her.

"Once more and then I have to go. But I'll be back for you, I promise. We'll start again, Fei Yen, and damn the world. I'll divorce Pei K'ung and make Han Ch'in a prince. I'll set things right, I promise you. I'll make things better than they were."

Then, rolling her onto her back, he climbed above her and entered her again, like an exiled king, returned to his kingdom.

"Fei Yen," he whispered, her movements matching his perfectly, Yin to his Yang. "My darling wife, Fei Yen..."

Tsu Kung-ch'ih was drunk. He stood there, red-faced, facing his uncle's Master of the Inner Chambers, Hwa Kwei, and shouted angrily.

"You incompetent fool! Can't you do *anything* right? I pay you a fortune and you mess things up! I mean, what now?"

He tore at his rich bright yellow silks in anguish, then turned away sharply. Behind him the embarrassed Hwa, his head bowed, kept his silence. Tsu Kung-ch'ih was right. He had failed miserably. Tsu Shu-sun was pregnant and he had failed to prevent it. His potions had made her sick, certainly, but still, somehow, she had conceived.

The young prince turned, one foot up on the low wall that surrounded the inner courtyard and its shallow pool. His disappointment was clear in his face. His sallow lips quivered and his eyes were moist, but he spoke more softly now, trying to control himself; struggling against the sudden impact of this news. He had learned of it only today – only an hour past. Tsu Ma had kept it to himself until now.

Shuddering, he looked to Hwa Kwei again.

"Was it so difficult? You said it would be easy. You *assured* me!"

Hwa Kwei gave a small nod, then bowed even lower. It *should* have been easy, but who would have known that Shu-sun would conceive on her wedding night? Who would have thought that Tsu Ma would change his mind and go to her?"

Kung-ch'in glared at him a moment longer, then turned away, a noise of sheer exasperation escaping him. He felt betrayed. As if his uncle had been toying with him. And though he had pretended otherwise, it was clear that Tsu Ma had enjoyed telling him the news. Salt in the wound. As if he didn't know what it meant to him.

He laughed bitterly, dismissing the middle-aged servant.

What good was it, trusting in others? No, this was something he would have to do himself.

He looked around. Hwa Kwei had gone. "Good riddance," he said quietly, but the words did not begin to express the turbulence of what he had felt this last hour. Now, however – now that he was alone at last – one thing seemed to surface, rising above all others, vast, bloated, obscuring the rest in its dark and awful shadow. Tsu Ma had known! He had known all along. And Hwa Kwei...

Tsu Kung-ch'ih closed his eyes, a faint nausea overcoming him momentarily. They had toyed with him. Played him like a fish on a line. And now they would reel him in.

"No-oooh..."

He opened his eyes slowly. No one had heard his cry of anguish. He turned and looked about him, making sure. But no, he was alone.

"What then?" he said softly, talking to himself now. "Should I go to him and tell him what I've done? Go down on my knees before him and beg forgiveness?" He shook his head. "No, I'll not do that. Not after what he's done to me!"

Which left him but a single choice.

Smiling grimly he stared down at his reflection in the mirror of the pool.

"So be it, then."

Li Yuan swept down the grand corridor at Tongjiang, his entourage almost running to keep up with him, servants – surprised by the haste with which he came upon them, dropping quickly to their knees and lowering their heads as he hurried past. The T'ang was more than three hours late and had missed several important meetings.

As the door to Nan Ho's study burst open, the Chancellor looked up from his desk, then hastily came round his desk, kneeling before his Master.

"*Chieh Hsia!*" he said, looking up at Li Yuan. "I am delighted to see you well. I was worried that something had happened."

Li Yuan waved the concern for his health aside, moving past his kneeling Chancellor to study the papers on his desk.

"What has been happening, Master Nan?"

Nan Ho got up slowly, grunting from the effort, then went to his Master's side.

"Minister Chu is in the Eastern Palace being... *entertained*, let us say. The *San Shih* I saw myself. I felt it best not to keep them waiting, considering recent events."

Li Yuan nodded, yet he seemed distracted. "And the matter with Tsung Ye?"

Nan Ho blinked. "Tsung Ye?"

Li Yuan glanced at him. "He came to see you this morning, I understand. About the Empress's demands on him."

The old man's mouth opened, then closed again. He nodded.

"So what do you suggest, Master Nan? Should I have the young man castrated? Or should I make him a member of my Advisory Council? After all, to find a man who is both a dedicated servant and yet a man of honour... that is not to be discarded lightly, neh?"

Nan Ho's mouth worked without sound. He looked in shock. Finally he found the words. "I... I did not know that you knew, *Chieh Hsia!* I... I have had him draw up a full confession. It is..."

Li Yuan shook the sheaf of papers at him. "I am reading it, Master Nan. An interesting document, neh? One we could use, if we wished."

"Use, *Chieh Hsia?*"

There was an urgent knocking at the outer doors. Li Yuan looked to Nan Ho. "Are you expecting anyone, Master Nan?"

"No, Master."

"Well... we had best find out who wants us, neh?"

Master Nan bowed, then went across. Opening the door a crack, he exchanged a few words with his secretary, then turned back. "It is General Rheinhardt, *Chieh Hsia.* He wishes to speak with you urgently."

Li Yuan folded Tsung ye's confession and pocketed it, then nodded. "Send him in. I will see him here. And master Nan... please stay. There is something I need to arrange with you."

Nan Ho studied his Master a while, noting the strange smile he wore, then turned away. A moment later he was back, leading in the Marshal.

"Helmut..." Li Yuan said, greeting his General, holding out his ring for him to kiss, then watching as he knelt and touched his forehead to the floor before him. "How can I help you?"

Rhienhardt looked to Nan Ho, then got to his feet again. "It is Marshal Tolonen, *Chieh Hsia*. He tried to have Ward kidnapped."

"Tried..." Li Yuan laughed, surprised by this latest news. "You jest, surely, Helmut? Knut kidnap Kim? Why on earth would he do that?"

"To prevent him from marrying his daughter."

Li Yuan went very still, his face suddenly severe. "Am I to believe my ears, Master Nan? You mean there was a relationship between Ward and the Marshal's daughter and I was not told of it?"

Nan Ho bowed low. "It was long ago, *Chieh Hsia*. I... I did not feel it was important."

"*Important? Aiya*, Master Nan! Nothing is more important than these personal matters. Nothing! Surely you of all people understand that?"

"Forgive me, *Chieh Hsia. I am pu ju pen fen.*"

Li yuan stared at him, surprised by the formality of the phrase – 'one who has failed in his duty' – then turned to Rheinhardt again. "So what happened?"

"It seems the Marshal hired mercenaries to kidnap Kim at his mansion, to prevent him from attending his daughter's Coming-of-Age party, but for some reason Ward eluded his attackers. Now both he and the Marshal's daughter have gone missing."

"Together?"

"That's the strange thing, *Chieh Hsia*. We can find no camera records of their movements. It's as if they vanished."

Li Yuan sucked in his breath. If he had lost Ward...

"And the Marshal? What does he say of all this?"

Rheinhardt looked down. "I am afraid the Marshal is unrepentant. He says that Ward will never marry his daughter. That he would kill him first."

Li Yuan went to the window and stared out. "Why now? Why now of all times?" He half-turned. "We must find Ward, Helmut. We simply must. He is vital to our plans. As for the Marshal..." He sighed heavily. "You will place

Marshal Tolonen under house arrest. You will give orders to the guards to use the minimum force to restrain him if need be, but restrain him they must, if it proves necessary. As for his honorary rank, he is stripped of it until this matter can be investigated. From henceforth he is considered no more than any other private citizen."

Rheinhardt looked down, saddened that it had come to this. "I am sorry, *Chieh Hsia*. To bring such news..."

Li Yuan went to him. "It is not your fault, Helmut. Sometimes even the best of us lose our way, neh? The Marshal is an old man. He was always inflexible. Old age has made him more so."

He stepped back, making a gesture of dismissal. Rheinhardt bowed low, then backed away.

When he was gone, Li Yuan looked to his Chancellor and let out a long breath. "*Aiya...*"

Nan Ho came across and knelt at his feet. "Forgive me, *Chieh Hsia*. If I had known."

Li Yuan reached out and touched his head gently. "It is alright, Master Nan. I forgive you this once. But..."

Unexpectedly, he laughed.

Nan Ho straightened up, staring at his Master. "Are you alright, *Chieh Hsia?*"

The young T'ang smiled. "Never better, Master Nan. Never, in all my life, better."

The old men filed in silently, their shaven heads lowered modestly, their saffron robes whispering on the ancient stones of the Great Hall. When all seventy-eight were seated, the three *San Shih* made their way to the centre of the great circle of chairs and stood, their arms crossed before them, concealed within the silken folds of their robes.

Luo Ye, the eldest and most senior of them, looked about him at the patiently watching faces, then bowed. "*Ch'un tzu*," he began, "we have come to report to the *Pa shi yi* concerning our meeting this morning with Li Yuan."

The old man hesitated, then, drawing himself up straight, he raised his right hand from within his robes, the crooked index finger pointing to the ceiling high above. As he did, his voice rang out, the perfectly intoned

Mandarin filling the ancient hall.

"I am afraid to tell my revered brothers that the T'ang was not there. It appears he was... *delayed.*"

A great hiss of disbelief went out at the news. Luo Ye waited a moment, then continued.

"Instead we spoke to the *Ch'eng Hsiang,* Nan Ho. He advised us to wait; to let our grievances until a better time. To... well, in brief, to go away and do as we were told."

The hiss became a buzz of anger. On all sides old men looked to each other, animatedly discussing this new development.

"*Ch'un tzu...*" Luo Ye said, calling them to order. "It may be that the great Li Yuan was indeed delayed. That, knowing that we wished to see him on a matter of the first importance, yet allowed himself to be detained elsewhere. However, it was my feeling that this was a deliberate insult; a snubbing of the *Pa shi yi,* indeed, of the great New Confucian movement itself. Since we failed his son, he has, it seems, had little time for us. Like a sulking woman, he has sought to avenge us in petty ways. But this..."

Luo Ye drew himself up straight, the grave authority of his voice echoing amidst the stone pillars of the Great Hall.

"Since the time of the great sage, Meng Tzu, it has been agreed by all men that to govern Chung Kuo a Son of Heaven must have Heaven's Mandate, and that to be in possession of the Mandate, such a one must be a man of virtue and benevolence. Similarly, it has been agreed that any Son of Heaven found lacking in these qualities forfeits his right to the dragon throne. In such a case the Mandate is broken." He paused significantly. "For some time now the actions of our Master, Li Yuan, son of Li Shai Tung, have caused this Council great concern, but this... this wilful disregard for other men... does this show virtue? Are these the actions of a benevolent man?"

"No!" came the cry from all sides. "No!"

"Well, brothers," Luo ye said, folding his arms within his robes once more, a smile of satisfaction on his lips now. "Then it seems we must debate a brand new matter. It seems it is time for the *Pa shi yi* to act. To teach this wilful young man from whence his power derives!"

Tsu Ma's face was blanched, like a mask of shocked anger, the muscles of his neck taut. He sat there, his hands clenching the carved arms of the throne, his whole body held rigid, listening as his Master of the Inner Chambers, Hwa Kwei, made his confession.

Hwa Kwei was sprawled below the raised dais, his forehead pressed against the stone floor, his arms thrown out before him in supplication, his whole attitude one of abject apology. When he had finished, Tsu Ma gave a small grunt and leaned forward.

"Is that all, Hwa Kwei?"

"It is all, *Chieh Hsia.*"

The T'ang shuddered violently, then stood, looking past his servant at the great doors. They were alone here in the audience chamber. Tsu Ma had dismissed the guards, trusting his old retainer. But now? For a moment his anger spilled out. He raised his voice.

"*Why,* Hwa Kwei? What have I done to deserve this of you?"

But his anger was seasoned with the knowledge that Hwa Kwei had come to him. Dishonoured and a traitor he might be, but he had acted honourably at the last. Tsu Ma sighed and, making his way down the steps, raised Hwa Kwei's chin with his foot.

"I shall spare your family, Master Hwa. I promise you that."

The retainer took the T'ang's foot and kissed it, then returned his forehead to the floor. For himself, he knew, there was only death, but the T'ang had been merciful. Hwa's family, at least, would live.

There was a hammering at the door. Tsu Ma stepped past Hwa Kwei, frowning, then glanced back at the servants.

"Enter!"

It was Yung Chen, one of the eunuchs from the women's quarters. He was breathless. His eyes stared wildly at the T'ang as he bowed low, then straightened.

"What is it?" Tsu Ma said quietly. His stomach had tightened, his whole body gone cold. He had the sense that something dreadful – something utterly irreparable – had happened.

"It is Kung-ch'ih, *Chieh Hsia!* He has gone mad. He holds Shu-sun at knifepoint and calls for you to come. Tan We is dead and two others!"

Tan We was the Chief Eunuch, Tsu Ma's mentor from his childhood. The news was like a physical blow. For a moment Tsu Ma faltered, not understanding what was happening. Then, stumbling forward, he pushed past the eunuch and began to run.

In the corridor outside the guards fell in behind their T'ang, astonished to see him in such a state. Out into the courtyard they went, into bright sunlight, then through the water gardens and across the narrow bridge that led to the women's quarters.

And as he ran, Tsu Ma was thinking, *And Tao Chu? Is Tao Chu in on this too? Can I trust no one?*

The first three rooms were empty. Beyond them was a small courtyard with cherry trees in blossom and a small pool. Beyond that were Shu-sun's rooms. Two servants stood on the far side of the pool, turning towards him and bowing as he came out into the courtyard.

"Where is he?"

One of the servants turned, pointing inside. Tsu Ma strode across, but he had only gone a few paces when two figures appeared in the far doorway.

Tsu Ma gasped. Kung'ch'ih held Shu-sun before him, the long, deadly knife held lengthways beneath her chin. He could kill her before Tsu Ma took another step.

The T'ang halted, glaring at the young prince. "Are you mad, Kung-ch'ih?"

"Never so sane, Uncle."

Shu-sun looked terrified. Her silk wrap was spattered with blood and her small white hands were clasped together in front of her. She seemed close to fainting and looked to Tsu Ma with imploring eyes. Seeing her so, Tsu Ma felt his stomach turn; felt an emptiness, a fear, he had never felt before. Even so, he kept it hidden from his face; kept all his love, his weakness tight inside, steeling himself to deal with his nephew.

"Why this?" he asked, taking one step towards his nephew.

"No further, Uncle," the youth warned, tilting the blade slightly so that it nicked the flesh and made Shu-sun cry out.

Tsu Ma gritted his teeth then let a breath hiss out between them. "What do you want?"

Kung-ch'ih's hand was steady, his whole manner dangerous – far more dangerous than Tsu Ma would have expected. He had thought him weak. In that too he had been wrong. He waited while the youth considered his reply; appraising the situation, his eyes straying to each side and to above, trying to assess what might be done. Shu-sun's body shielded Kung-ch'ih's. If his guards shot at Kung they would probably miss and Shu-sun would be dead.

"I'm tired of games," Kung-ch'ih said finally, ominously.

"*Games?*" Tsu Ma was puzzled. He made to take another step, but saw how the muscles of the hand that held the knife tensed, and so he relaxed, letting his hands open at his sides.

"You have toyed with me, Uncle. Played games with me. All along you have mocked me. I know. Hwa Kwei told me."

This puzzled him more. What could Hwa Kwei possibly have told him to make him think that? Then, suddenly, he understood. It all fell into place. The announcement of Shu-sun's pregnancy! *That* had precipitated all this!

"No," he said softly, almost tenderly, as if he understood the hurt the boy was feeling. "I have played no games with you, Kung-ch'ih. Until today I..."

The boy's cold laughter cut his words short. "I do not believe you, Uncle. Even now you think to trick me. To keep me from what I want."

"And you want this?"

Tsu Ma had gone cold again. He saw no way out of this. No way but death.

"I wanted what was mine. By right."

By right? But Tsu Ma said nothing, only bowed his head slightly, as if acknowledging what had been said.

Kung-ch'ih spoke again. "For years you led me to believe I would be T'ang one day."

Did I? Tsu Ma thought. Well, maybe he had. Even so, nothing justified this.

"What do you think this will achieve, Kung-ch'ih?"

Again the young man laughed. But his eyes gave nothing away. He had killed three times already; perhaps those deaths had changed him.

"I could kill your son, perhaps, Tsu Ma. Kill the heir you think to have."

Tsu Ma was silent a moment, simply watching the boy, trying to control the sudden violent hatred he had felt hearing those words, remind himself that this was his brother's child, his ward. Yet when he spoke again he let nothing of that hatred show, steeling himself to be calm and unemotional.

"I can wed a dozen wives, Kung-ch'ih. One of them will give me a son."

For the first time the knife wavered slightly and a look of doubt crept into the prince's eyes. But it was an instant's hesitation only. The look of cold determination returned. Kung-ch'ih slowly shook his head and laughed.

"No, Uncle. You do not fool me with your act. I've *seen* you with this woman."

Once again, Tsu Ma felt a hot flush of rage pass through him. He wanted to kill the boy; to tear him apart with his bare hands. And yet he had to stand there, calm, his hands open at his sides, his face clear of the anger he felt. For Shu-sun's sake. Because to show what he was feeling would mean her certain death.

He laughed and let the laughter roll on for longer than its normal course. Again there was a moment's uncertainty in the young man's eyes. Tsu ma let the laughter spill over into his voice.

"So you think you *know* me, boy?"

This time no words, only a curt, uncompromising nod. The knife was held steady beneath Shu-sun's chin, the sharp blade dark with others' blood. Shu-sun had closed her eyes, her chest rising and falling heavily. Kung-ch'ih's left arm was locked about her shoulder now, keeping her from falling.

Tsu Ma, watching, wondered what she was feeling; whether it was one part as dreadful as the fear he felt for her.

"What now, then?" he asked, keeping his voice steady.

They had come to an impasse. There was nothing he could offer. No deal could come of this. No compromise. He sighed heavily, suddenly weary of all this, then, with an anger he had concealed until that moment, he yelled – a high-pitched, blood-curdling yell - and threw himself forward.

Surprised, Kung-ch'ih's instincts took over, and for one brief moment the knife moved outwards in a wide arc, as if to meet the oncoming threat. Then it jerked back and Shu-sun fell forward, screaming.

Tsu Ma stopped, horrified, looking down at his fallen wife. Then his head jerked up.

Kung-ch'ih was on his knees. The knife had clattered to the floor. From the centre of Kung-ch'ih's chest a long steel pike protruded. Kung-ch'ih coughed once, blood dribbling from between his lips, then fell onto his face.

Behind him, in the huge, arched doorway, stood Tao Chu. His silks were drenched and his hair slicked back and wet. He looked down on his brother in surprise, a dreadful look of pain – of sheer loss – on his face, then looked across at Tsu Ma.

Shu-sun was scrabbling forward, whimpering with fright. Tsu Ma met his nephew's eyes a moment, then stooped down and held his wife to him, his big frame shivering uncontrollably as he comforted her.

After a moment he looked up at Tao Chu again. The boy was still standing there, looking down at the brother he had killed. Tears rolled down his cheeks, one after another, and, even as Tsu Ma watched, the boy knelt and kissed the dark-haired head of his brother, one hand gently touching and stroking the yet warm neck, as if he merely slept.

Nan Ho sat at his desk, staring into space.

"Kuan Yin preserve us!" he murmured.

"Master?"

He looked to his secretary, Hu Chang, and shook his head. "I said Kuan Yin preserve us. This business... it is an ill day's work. The Empress Pei K'ung is a good woman, and if she has needs... well, we all have *needs*, neh, Hu Chang?"

Hu Chang lowered his head. He was not going to be drawn on such a personal matter.

"I tried to talk sense into him," he went on, "but he would not listen. It is just as before. He is obsessed with her. Infatuated by the she-fox. She has cast her spell over him again and we must all suffer for it."

Hu Chang looked up. "Master?"

"Yes, Hu Chang?"

"Perhaps we should try to delay matters and let time cure our Lord of this... this *strangeness*."

Nan Ho turned to him. "*Delay?*"

"Yes, Master. If we could find some... distraction, perhaps, to keep him from pursuing the matter. Some..."

Nan Ho raised a hand. Hu Chang fell silent, bowing his head.

"He wants it done tonight. The divorce document is being drawn up even as we speak. Tsung Ye's confession... achh!" He heaved a great sigh of exasperation then stood, his restlessness taking a physical form. "I should have ignored my conscience and had the woman killed while I could."

Hu Chang's eyes followed his Master, appalled by what he was hearing. Never had Nan Ho spoke of killing anyone. Always he had been the voice of reason. But this matter, it seemed, had stripped all rationality from him... or revealed it?

Hu Chang swallowed, then spoke up. "To kill her... it would solve nothing, Master Nan."

"No?" Nan Ho turned to him. "You do not know this woman, Hu Chang. Such deviousness..." Again he shook his head. "And this time she will not be so easy to dislodge. This time..."

The summons bell rang. Nan Ho stared at it, then grimaced. "That will be him. Go to him, Hu Chang. Tell him that I am sick and have taken to my bed. Tell him..."

Nan Ho stopped, lowering his head, genuine pain there suddenly. "My boy... my poor, poor boy. How could he do this to himself a second time? How can I bear to stand by and watch it happen?"

The bell rang again.

"You want me to go, Master?"

Nan Ho looked at him, then smiled sadly. "No, Hu Chang. It is my duty to attend. My duty to serve, whatever my Master asks of me. It is the way, neh? Wherever it leads."

Hu Chang bowed his head, relieved to see his Master returned to his former self.

Nan Ho came across, touching his arm gently, then went from the room, making his way towards Li Yuan's rooms, ready to serve his Master – *whatever* was asked of him.

"You summoned me, *Chieh Hsia?*"

Li Yuan looked up from his desk and waved Nan Ho across. "Have you heard, Master Nan?"

"Heard, *Chieh Hsia?*"

Li Yuan handed him the single sheet of paper. "It arrived a moment back. Copies are being posted throughout our City even as we speak."

Nan Ho read it through, then looked up, his face blanched, his eyes bewildered. "But this says..."

"The Mandate is broken, that's what it says. The *Pa shi yi* have declared my government invalid. They have sanctioned open rebellion."

Nan Ho stared back at him. "*Aiya!*"

"*Aiya* indeed. Yet not unexpected."

"Master?"

"We have known for some while now that the New Confucians were dissatisfied with things. And your meeting this morning... well, did you not sense this in the air, Master Nan?"

Nan Ho shook his head. It seemed he had foreseen few of these developments. "But what shall we do?"

"Do? Why, have them all arrested. Arrested and executed."

Nan Ho swallowed, clearly uncomfortable. "But that would mean..."

"War? Possibly. But this..." He took the paper back from his Chancellor. "No, Master Nan, I cannot have this."

There was a knock. Li Yuan raised an eyebrow. "Enter!"

A messenger bowed his way into the room, then, kneeling, offered a sealed letter to the T'ang's secretary who unfurled it, read it, then brought it across.

Li Yuan took it and read it, then turned in his seat, calling for the screen to be lowered.

"Watch," Li Yuan said, then, speaking to the air. "Show me the latest scenes from Weimar!"

At once the screen showed a picture of the great House. Drawing back, it focused on a group of men outside the huge entrance gates. Media remotes hovered about their heads like bugs as one of them, recognisable as the Leader of the House, Representative Kavanagh, was speaking.

"... yet such an unprecedented statement by the New Confucian hierarchy can only be read as a recognition by those within the T'ang's government — those who know him best, let it be said — that things have reached such a pass that only the most extreme action can remedy the situation. It is therefore with great reluctance but with a sense of duty that we have taken a vote on the issue and offer the full support of this House to the *Pa shi yi*. Further, we urge the citizens of City Europe to reject the rule of the despot Li Yuan and accept Li Min as Son of Heaven and our new T'ang."

There was a gasp from all those in the room. Nan Ho turned, expecting to find his own shock mirrored in his Master's face, but Li Yuan was smiling.

"*Chieh Hsia?*" he asked, astonished that at this worst of moments the T'ang should be amused. "Are you alright, Master?"

"Never better, Master Nan."

Li Yuan stood, then came round his desk, stopping before the image of House Leader Kavanagh.

"Arrest them!" he said, the confidence in his voice surprising them all.

"All of them. And then burn the House. We must teach these *hsiao jen* a lesson, neh, Master Nan?"

"*Chieh Hsia?*"

Li Yuan turned to face him, the smile slowly fading from his face until, in its hawk-like seriousness, it resembled his father, Li Shai Tung's.

"You heard me, Master Nan. Arrest them. Triad members, New Confucians, Representatives and all. All who oppose me... It has begun," he said, his voice a strange mixture of fear and relief. "The gods help us, Master Nan. It has finally begun."

At the cliff's edge stood a ruined chapel, its roof open to the sky, the doorway empty, gaping. It was a tiny building, the floor inside cracked and overgrown with weeds, one of the side walls collapsed, the heavy stones spilled out across the grass.

Kim stopped beside her, looking up at the lettering cut into the stone lintel.

"It's Latin," he said. "From The Revelation to John."

Jelka looked to him, surprised, as he began to read.

"I saw an angel standing in the sun, and with a loud voice he cried to all the birds that fly in middle heaven, 'Come gather for the great supper of God...'"

He turned to her, finishing the quote, "to eat the flesh of kings, of all men, both free and slave, great and small."

He smiled, then looked about him. "Is this it? Is this your special place?"

"No. Not this." She looked out at the sea beyond the ruin, then walked on.

It was an old path, worn by many feet. Near the bottom, where the way grew steep, steps had been cut into the rock. She picked her way nimbly between the rocks and out beneath the overhang. Kim followed. There, on the far side of the shelf of rock, was a cave.

She turned, smiling. "This is it. My special place. The place of voices."

Kim went halfway across the ledge then stopped, crouching, looking down through the crack in the great grey slab. There, below him, the incoming tide was channelled into a fissure in the rock. For a moment he watched the rush and foam of the water through the narrow channel, then he looked up.

She was watching him, amused.

"Can't you hear it, Kim? It's talking to you!"

"Yes, I hear it."

He stood, wiping his hands against his thighs, then went across and stood there at the edge of the rock, looking out across the rutted surface of the sea, feeling the wind like a hand on his face, the tang of salt on his lips.

"Here," she said, drawing his attention again.

There on the wall behind her, were the ancient letters, a hand's length in height, scored into the rock and dyed a burned ochre against the pale cream of the rock, their stick-like, angular shapes bringing to mind the shape of yarrow stalks.

Kim frowned, recognising them as runes, as a name. Tolonen. And yet they were what? Fifteen hundred years old?

He shuddered then narrowed his eyes, watching as she stooped, making her way further in, towards where the ceiling sloped down to meet the floor of the cave.

"It was here that I saw the fox," she said, turning back to him, her blue eyes staring out at him from the half dark. "Later I dreamed of it... and thought of you."

A fox. He went inside, taking her hand.

"So wild it was," she said, kneeling, then pulling him down beside her. "Erkki wanted to shoot it, but I wouldn't let him."

He stared back at her, bewitched, the dark scent of the place awaking something in him.

A fox...

He drew her face to his and kissed her, a savage fox's kiss, then pushed her down, the brightness slipping from her.

Back in the house, he walked about the rooms, disturbed by what had happened, wondering just what it said about himself. Yet Jelka seemed happy. He could hear her in the kitchen, singing to herself as she prepared a meal for them, her laughter strange and unexpected. He had thought her so cold and regal.

At the door to the study he stopped, lifting his head and sniffing the air, then stepped inside, his eyes widening at the sight of so many books.

"Books!" he cried, carrying one out to her. "Real books!"

"Kalevala," she said, taking it from him. "My uncle lent me this. It was the first real book I ever read. Here..." She handed it back to him. "You must read it. My people..."

"Your people..." He looked at her sadly. "You should contact him, you know. Let him know that you're safe. He'll be worrying."

"Let him worry!" she said angrily. "He deserves it. But aren't you angry at him?"

"Angry?" He laughed, then, putting the book down, took her hands. "How could I be angry? Without him there would be no you. For that... well, forgive him everything."

He smiled, trying to coax her to his viewpoint, but he could see she was not to be brought round. Not yet, anyway.

"Let me help," he said, looking past her at the pans on the old-fashioned stove. "I like to cook for myself."

In answer she beat his hands away. "That was when you were on your own. Now... well, now you're mine. If it worries you, we'll take turns. But tonight... tonight I want to cook for you. Please. I've dreamed of it!"

He smiled. "You dream a great deal, Jelka Tolonen."

"Yes..." Her eyes grew serious. "I dreamed that you would come for me and save me from the world of Levels. I dreamed..."

She stopped abruptly, a sudden fear growing in her face. "Something's happened," she said. "Something..."

She moved past him, heading for the great living room. He followed, intrigued by the change in her, by the sudden intuitive leap she'd made. As she crouched before the big screen, trying to tune it in, he looked about him, surprised, constantly surprised to find himself there on the island, in this strangest of houses. Had she dreamed this? And was he, even now, trapped within her dream of no more substance than Caliban's?

> "Sometimes a thousand twanging instruments
> Will hum about mine ears; and sometimes voices,
> That, if I had then wak'd after long sleep,
> Will make me sleep again: and then, in dreaming,
> The clouds methought would open, and show riches
> Ready to drop upon me, that, when I wak'd,
> I cried to dream again."

She turned, looking at him, even as the screen came to life behind her.

"What is that? It sounds... *familiar.*"

"Just words," he said. "Something that no longer exists except in the mind of a machine."

"Words?" but already her attention was being drawn by what was on the screen. There, framed by dense black smoke, was the House at Weimar, its great windows smashed, its levels licked by flames. Long lines of shackled men were being led away by visored guards. Then the image changed, to scenes of rioting and rule, of screaming men and crying women.

"What's happening?" he asked, stepping up beside her, then crouching, taking her hand. "What in the gods' names is happening?"

"It has begun," she said, a tremor passing through her. "The gods help us all. The War's begun."

CHAPTER 131

THE RIDER THROUGH THE AUTUMN WIND

You must talk to him, *Chieh Hsia*. You simply must!"

"*Must*, Master Nan?" Li Yuan turned from the great map, stoney-faced, to confront his Chief Minister. "Will you tell me also who I must sleep with?"

Nan Ho lowered his head, chastened. All around the War Room others – more than forty in all – did the same, recognising that tone in the great T'ang's voice. At such times he was at his most dangerous – or so it had proved these past five days.

Nan Ho glanced at his Master from beneath his lashes.

Five days... was that all it had been since war had been declared? A mere five days?

It seemed like an eternity.

"They say he is dying, *Chieh Hsia*," he said quietly, risking his Master's wrath; knowing he would never forgive himself unless he attempted some kind of reconciliation.

"Dying?" Li Yuan turned, surprised. "I had not heard that. I thought..."

"Poisoned, *Chieh Hsia*. Or so I am told. It is... well, difficult to know the truth. Our usual channels are not as reliable as they were."

Li Yuan nodded, understanding. All was in chaos. And information – *reliable* information – was the hardest thing to come by. Li Min had seen to that.

We did not know, Nan Ho thought, looking at the map of City Europe and noting how the dark areas – those that denoted Li Min's territories – had grown in the last two days. *We failed to realise just how big he had become – how powerful. We thought what Visak told us was all lies, but it was true.*

To be blunt, they had totally underestimated their enemy. They had thought he had delayed – had issued his famous Statement of Loyalty – because he was too weak to fight them. But now they knew. Li Min had delayed only because he wanted to be certain before he acted.

And now Li Min was a day from victory. Two days at most. And still Li Yuan refused his cousin's help.

He watched his Master, seeing how the young T'ang studied the map, as if it were a board, the whole thing a massive game of *wei chi* in which he might find some flaw in his opponent's strategy, some previously overlooked weakness he might exploit. But there was nothing. Li Min had planned his campaign well. The game was his. He had only to place the last few stones.

Li Yuan turned back to him. He had not slept in three days now – kept awake and alert by special drugs – and his eyes were heavy from lack of sleep. "All right," he said softly, nodding to his Chancellor. "Arrange for us to speak."

"*Chieh Hsia!*" he gasped, relief flooding him.

While Li Yuan pored over the map, Nan Ho made contact with the palace at Astrakhan, yet when the screen lit up it was not Tsu Ma's Chancellor who faced him but his young nephew, Tsu Tao Chu.

The young man's face was tight with anguish. Everything about him spoke of loss. Even before he said a word, Nan Ho knew.

"My uncle, the great Tsu Ma, is dead. He..." Tao Chu lowered his head, a tear trickling down his cheek. "He passed away this morning."

Li Yuan, standing beside his Chancellor, stared mutely at the screen.

"It was a great relief," Tsu Tao Chu said after a moment. "He suffered greatly. If he had not been so strong..." He shuddered, then, noting Li Yuan's presence, gave a bow of recognition.

"I am sad to hear the news," Li Yuan said, waving Nan Ho away so that he could speak to Tsu Tao Chu alone. "As you know, we had not been speaking these last few weeks, yet his passing comes as a great blow to me. I feel as if I have lost a brother."

Tsu Tao Chu smiled tightly, a deep sadness in his eyes. "Thank you, cousin Yuan. I know that he always considered you his brother."

Li Yuan returned his smile. "How are things in your City, cousin?"

Tsu Tao Chu grimaced. "Not well, cousin Yuan. Each hour brings more bad news. Things look bleak for us all, neh?"

"That is true, Yet if we stand together..."

"I would like that. I..." He paused, looking round, speaking to someone off-screen, then faced Li Yuan again. "Forgive me, cousin, but it strikes me that if you were to come here, to Astrakhan... If we were together in one place, then perhaps we might coordinate our efforts and therefore fight our enemies more effectively. Tongjiang is a fortress, true, yet Tongjiang is a long way from your City. If you were here..."

Li Yuan considered that a moment, then nodded. "I would like that, Tao Chu. I would like that very much."

"Then come, cousin Yuan. Come now, without delay."

The news was good. Tsu Ma was dead, and Wei Tseng-li too, in all probability. Asia was in chaos and Europe... Europe would be next to fall. It needed but one last push.

Lehmann stood there, looking down at the great map of City Europe, studying the shape of things, the white that denoted his territory clearly in the ascendant.

This was the end game. A time of sacrifices and captures. A time when shape was all-important, when the all-connectedness of his schemes would matter more than the bravery of soldiers or the skill of generals.

In his right hand were the five white stones that represented his reserve forces. Five battalions of his best troops, held back until now. He rattled them in his hand then looked about him. His men watched him silently, awaiting his decision with a confidence – a certainty – which mirrored his own. They were almost there. Just one more push.

He leaned across, placing a stone in Stuttgart. That would reinforce his forces there and help keep the supply corridor open to the army that was besieging the Mannheim garrison. A second stone he placed in the far west, in Nantes. Again it was a defensive move, to safeguard the capture of the great spaceport.

Which left three.

Lehmann hefted the three white stones, feeling their weight, then leaned right across the map and slapped them down at Bremen.

"There!" he said. "Right to the heart!"

There was a deep murmur of satisfaction. Bremen. It was Li Yuan's chief stronghold, its name alone representative of the power and strength of the seven generations of the Li family who had ruled Europe. Take Bremen and the rest would follow.

"Get me Soucek," he said, looking to his Financial Strategist, Cao Chang. "I want to know what the situation is."

In seconds Soucek's long, ox-like face appeared on the giant screen to the left of the room. Lehmann went across and stood beneath it.

"Well, Jiri? How goes it?"

Soucek's face was black with smoke. He rubbed at one eye, then answered Lehmann. "We're making headway, but slowly. Resistance is fierce. The Mannheim garrison is a proud one and well disciplined. Not only that, but Karr has taken over the command."

"Karr?" Lehmann nodded thoughtfully. "Well, press on, Jiri. Karr or no Karr, I want you in Mannheim by the morning. Understand me?"

Soucek bowed his head.

"And Jiri. I've defended your supply line at Stuttgart. But look for news from Bremen. It's there the final battle will take place. If I'm right, Li Yuan will withdraw some of his forces from Mannheim to defend Bremen. When he does, press home. And Jiri?"

"Yes, Master?"

"Take no prisoners."

Karr sat on an ammunition case, resting, the sound of gunfire coming closer by the minute. Each time they would draw a defensive line and each time it would be overrun. Hour by hour they were being pressed back, the number of their dead and wounded mounting steadily, until finally...

Finally we'll all be dead.

He looked up, studying his young equerry. The boy – for he was little beyond seventeen – had been posted on him only yesterday when he'd taken this command, yet he already felt he knew him well. Right now the boy was looking to his right, towards the gunfire, a strange calm – or was it shock? – pervading his gaze. Then, realising that Karr was watching him, he blushed and turned to face his colonel, bowing his head smartly.

"It's okay," Karr said. "There's no ordinance against thinking."

"No, sir. It's just…"

Karr smiled, touched by the boy's shyness. "Go on. Say what you're thinking, lad. I grant you permission this once."

Barlow looked away, his whole manner awkward. "I was thinking of a girl, sir."

Karr smiled. "Me, too. Two of them, in fact."

"Sir?"

"My wife, Marie, and my daughter, May."

"Ah…" The cadet laughed, then felt silent, serious again.

"You know, it's much harder on them," Karr said. "They carry the burden of not knowing what's happening to us. The burden of imagination. Whereas we… Well, we only have to worry about the unseen bullet, the sudden pain and the darkness that follows."

Barlow met his eyes and nodded, no sign of fear in his own.

Good, Karr thought. *He understands. It's far simpler when you understand. Death, when it comes, is easy. It's the waiting that's hard.*

Karr stood, then reached down for the big automatic rifle he had been using, picking it up by the strap and slinging it over his shoulder.

"Sir?"

"Yes, Barlow?"

"Why is this happening, sir? I mean… why didn't Li Yuan crush the White T'ang when he could?"

Karr sighed. "A good question. But not one for us to ask. We are but our Master's hands, no?"

Barlow stared at him briefly, surprised by the tone of his words.

"Have we… lost, sir?"

"Lost? No, lad. Things aren't *that* bad." But it wasn't what he believed. News had come only an hour back of Tsu Ma's death – news he had kept from his troops, lest it demoralise them. Closer to home, it was said that the old Marshal was sick. On his deathbed. Soon there would be no one left. Soon there would only be the darkness – darkness and ghosts.

And as for Marie and May… well, maybe they *would* be safer in Astrakhan, but the news of their evacuation from Tongjiang had troubled him far more than he'd believed possible.

Safe? No. No one was safe any more.

In any case, it doesn't really matter, he thought. *For this is the end. All this... this drawing of lines... we're only going through the motions. Filling our own territory with stones, for the truth is he's already won.*

"Sir?"

He looked to Barlow again, then reached out and brushed the hair back from his eyes, as if it were his son. "Yes, lad?"

"How long do you think we have?"

"Daddy?"

Tolonen stirred in his bed, then turned his head, looking across the darkly shadowed room towards the door.

"Jelka?" he asked weakly. "Is that you?"

She went across and knelt beside the bed, clasping his good hand – the hand that was flesh and blood – between her own.

"Oh, Daddy... what have you been up to now?"

He laughed softly; laughter that quickly degenerated into a hacking cough. She waited, looking anxiously at the doctor who hovered silently on the far side of the bed.

It's okay, he mouthed, smiling reassuringly.

She looked back at her father. He was old – that was a fact – yet never before now had he ever *looked* old. He had always been so healthy, so... *robust.* To see him like this pained her, and for all that Kim had argued with her about it, she still saw it as her fault. *She* had done this to him. She and her bloody-mindedness.

"How are you?" she asked, reaching up to smooth his brow.

"Just fine," he said, his grey eyes watching her. "Not a day's sickness in all my life and then suddenly..."

She pressed his head back gently where it had come up from the pillow. "They say you must rest. They say you must take things easy and not worry."

"Worry?" He laughed bleakly. "Did you hear? They're talking of evacuating Bremen... Bremen! Aiya!"

"Daddy... *please.* It will do no good. You have to forget what's happening. You can do nothing."

"You think I do not know that?" He turned his head aside, then sniffed deeply, a look of bitter shame on his face. "I have never let him down. *Never.* Until now."

She squeezed his hand lightly, touched by this display of loyalty. It was true what he said. Whereas she...

"Is *he* here?"

Jelka sighed. "No, Daddy. I came alone."

He closed his eyes and nodded, then placed his other – the hand of golden metal – over hers. She stared down at it, trying not to flinch away from that unnatural contact – from that part of him it had always seemed to represent – that cold, inflexible part of him.

"I've come to stay," she said quietly. "I've come to nurse you, Daddy."

His head turned slowly, his eyes flicking open. "For good?"

It was hard to meet his eyes and disappoint him, yet she knew she must. "Until you're well again. Kim says..."

"Damn you, girl!" he yelled hoarsely, lifting himself up from the pillow. "Don't even speak his name in my presence! I..."

He gave a sudden shudder, as if he were about to have another fit, then lay back again, glancing at his doctor. "I'm sorry, I... I forgot myself there. I must rest, I know."

She moved back slightly, letting the doctor fuss about him a moment, checking his pulse and his blood pressure, then leaned close again, giving him a smile.

"Let's not fight, neh? Let's be friends."

"You're all I have, Jelka. All the others... they're dead. Klaus Ebert, Hal Shepherd, Li Shai Tung... Dead, every last one of them. The world... it's like there's nothing here but ghosts. Excepting you, my love. Excepting you."

She felt her stomach muscles tighten, felt the tears begin to well in her eyes; yet at the same time she knew what he was doing; knew that this too – true as it was – was another battle for him. To win her, that was his aim. And to defeat his enemy, her lover, Kim.

"I love you, daddy," she said, the tears beginning to trickle down her cheeks. "Never doubt that. But I love him, too, and I have to be with him."

He stared at her, silent, his eyes accusing her.

"Can't you see? Don't you see how easy it would all be if you just stopped this silliness? Why can't you just accept him? Then we could together... all of us. We could take you Kalevala and..."

"No!" he roared, sitting up, his face suffused with a sudden anger. "You'll not have him! You won't..."

She saw the surprise in his face, the look of shock that came into his eyes, the way his hands clutched at his chest.

"Oh, gods," she whispered, frightened. "Please, no..."

Then there was shouting in the room and doctors urgently hurrying about. In a daze she found herself lifted to her feet and led away.

"It'll be alright," someone was saying reassuringly. "He needs rest, that's all. All this excitement..."

But even as she was led from the room, she could still hear his murmuring.

"You won't have him! You *won't!*"

Li Yuan embraced his cousin, then turned, introducing the senior members of his staff who had travelled with him from Tongjiang.

"I am glad you came," Tsu Tao Chu said, when they were alone again. "The situation..."

Li Yuan touched his arm, understanding. Tao Chu had not been born to rule. The deaths of his half-brother and his uncle had come as a double blow. Nor had he been given any time to prepare himself for such a mighty responsibility. All of this was new to him. Even so, he was a good, upstanding young man. If anyone could shoulder such a burden, Tsu Tao Chu could, surely?

"It's okay, Tao Chu. Together we will make sense of this, neh?"

Tao Chu smiled. "I have prepared the Northern Palace for your people, Yuan. If that is insufficient..."

"It will be fine," Li Yuan said quickly. "But before I do anything else, I must pay my last respects to your uncle."

"Of course."

Tao Chu led him through, past grieving servants and into a dark, cool hall in which the funeral bier had been set up, the casket open to the air.

Li Yuan went across and stood there over it, looking down at his old friend, finding it hard to believe that he was dead. The poison had left its mark on Tsu Ma. His face seemed much older than Yuan remembered it, and the hair... the hair was almost grey.

Li Yuan sighed, then turned to Tao Chu again.

"Have you found out yet who did this thing?"

"I have the man. I racked him, made him sing."

Li Yuan stared at Tsu Tao Chu, surprised by the unexpected hardness in his voice and face.

"And his Master?"

"You know his master well, cousin Yuan. Your armies fight him even now."

Li Yuan gave a tiny nod, then looked back. For some reason the memory of an evening years before came back to him – of Tsu Ma and he in a boat on the lake at Tongjiang, with Fei Yen and her cousin, Yin Wu Tsai, the lanterns dancing in the darkness. What a night that had been. What a beautiful, entrancing night!

He grimaced then turned away, torn between the jealousy he felt – the anger at Tsu Ma's betrayal – and the love he'd had for him.

You were like a brother to me, he thought, as if addressing Tsu Ma in his head. *Why, then, did you take my bride from me?*

As if in answer, the words from Ch'u Yuan's "Heavenly Questions" floated into his mind.

Dark Wei followed in his brother's footsteps and the Lord of You-yi was stirred against him...

In a sense it was true – he had taken his brother's wife, and in turn his brother – Tsu Ma – had done the same to him.

But now it was done with. Death had paid all debts. Now he could let that matter go and remember his cousin with affection.

Li Yuan turned back, bowing deeply to Tsu Ma, his hands pressed together, palm to palm, as he offered his respects, then looked to Tao Chu and nodded.

"There is much to do, cousin Tao. We had best begin at once."

Karr had been expecting the order for some time; even so, as he unsealed Rheinhardt's handwritten letter and read its contents, he felt his heart sink, the spirit go out if him. He was to abandon Mannheim and go at once to Bremen, taking whatever forces remained at his disposal.

This is it, he thought sadly, folding the letter and slipping it into his tunic pocket. *Another day and all is gone.* On whim, he took out the picture he carried and looked at it, studying the smiling faces of his girls. He kissed it fondly then returned it, and, calling his duty captain to him, began to issue orders.

"It is no good," Li Yuan said, pointing to the southern half of the map, indicating the five remaining tiny islands of black around Bordeaux, Lyon, Turin, Ravenna and Belgrade. The rest was solidly white now – more than two-thirds of the City; almost everything beneath the ancient Loire and Danube rivers – while to the north, Li Min had made encroachments in at least a dozen places. "We shall have to let them go. Issue the order now, General Rheinhardt. I want all of our forces pulled back above the Seine in the west and the Danube in the east.

"But *Chieh Hsia*," Rheinhardt began, appalled by the thought of relinquishing so much.

"You have your orders, General. Now do it. And get Karr on the screen. I have a use for him."

Rheinhardt bowed and left the room, leaving Li Yuan alone with Nan Ho and Tsu Tao Chu.

"Was that wise, *Chieh Hsia?*" Nan Ho asked quietly. "Rheinhardt knows what he is doing, and those garrisons... well, they have served to tie up a great number of Li Min's troops."

"And a great number of ours, too," Li Yuan said, leaning across the map and drawing an imaginary line from west to east with his finger. "No, Master Nan, it is time for drastic measures. What's lost is lost. We must conserve what can yet be saved. Li Min's new forces have swung the balance heavily against us. Yet all is not lost. Until now we have been hampered by the need to hold down a vast area, to try to police it even as we wage a war. But now that responsibility is Li Min's. he must now subdue those parts of the City he has conquered. That will tie up more and more of his forces, while our own will be freed to defend what remains. Moreover, if we keep our forces here in the north, in this section," he indicated a swathe of territory less than a quarter of the City's total size, then we also have the advantage of keeping our supply-lines short."

Nan Ho studied the map a moment, then shrugged. "Even so, *Chieh Hsia...*"

Li Yuan snorted. "Aiya, Master Nan! Must I constantly be held back by you and your 'Even sos'? We have no option. We must draw a line and fight to preserve it. If we fail..."

Tsu Tao Chu stared at the map a moment, then nodded. "A line, cousin? Why not a *physical* breach... some kind of gap?"

Li Yuan looked back at him and smiled. "Why, yes! A gap! As about Tunis! We could destroy a line of stacks... here." He drew the line again with his finger, this time more definite, his eyes shining with excitement. "We could make a break two *li* wide and defend it... as if we were fighting a fire."

He looked to Nan Ho. "Have we still got those stocks of ice-eaters that were confiscated that time?"

"We have, *Chieh Hsia,* but..."

"No buts, Master Nan. The idea is an excellent one. And Karr... Karr's the man to implement it, no?"

Nan Ho looked to his master, imploring him with his eyes to drop the idea, but Li Yuan was adamant and, after a moment, Nan Ho bowed his head.

"Very well, *Chieh Hsia.* It shall be done."

Tsu Tao Chu sat in the window seat, chewing a thumb nail, while Li Yuan paced the room in front of him, reading the latest reports.

That evening Tao Chu was to be appointed T'ang of West Asia in an official ceremony in the Hall of Celestial Virtues. But by then, it seemed, West Asia would be gone and he would be T'ang of nothing. Nothing but these ancient stones.

After two hundred years of peace, Asia had fallen into darkness once again. Warlords had divided the great continent between them, reacting to the scent of blood like sharks in a feeding frenzy. The twin cities, once the jewels of Chung Kuo, now burned and tens of millions died each hour as darkness fell.

"Is it bad?" Tao Chu asked, looking up to him, a youthful innocence in his eyes.

Li Yuan sighed. "It could not be worse, Tao Chu. It is all slipping away from us. It might be best if we prepared to take our courts... off planet."

"Off planet?" Tao Chu looked alarmed. "As bad as that?"

Li Yuan nodded.

Tao Chu got up suddenly, then, with a polite smile and a curt bow to Li Yuan, he made to go past him to the door, but Li Yuan held his arm.

"Cousin? Where are you off to in such a hurry? I thought we might talk."

Tao Chu looked down, embarrassed. "Forgive me, Yuan, I..."

Li Yuan smiled. "I remember the first time we ever met. It was after your grandfather Tsu Tiao's death. You were..."

"I remember it well."

Tao Chu nodded thoughtfully, then looked to Li Yuan with a smile. "Yes. I remember that I gripped your arm, I was so afraid. I thought that my uncle..." he shivered, a look of pain in his eyes. "I thought he had killed Tsu Tiao. I did not know it was only a GenSyn copy."

"Was that the first time you had encountered death?"

Tao Chu nodded. "I remember you explained it all to me. Why my uncle Ma had to kill the image of his father to become his own man. Yet I never really understood. Not deep down. To kill one's father..." He shuddered.

Li Yuan reached out and held his shoulder gently. "The first of the crafts from TongJiang will be here shortly. Perhaps you would like to come and greet them with me?"

But Tao Chu shook his head, his eyes avoiding Yuan's. "I... I would prefer to get some rest, cousin. I... It has been a very trying day for me."

Li Yuan bowed. "I understand. The times take much from us, neh?"

Tao Chu bobbed his head in response, then, with a strangely pained glance at his cousin, went to the door and out.

Li Yuan stood there a while, staring at the open door, wondering if there was anything he could do to ease his young cousin's suffering. Then, with a heavy sigh, he went out to meet the incoming craft.

The five craft came in from the east in tight formation. Li Yuan, watching from the parapet above the eastern gate, saw the faint wisp of smoke that came from the exhaust of the central craft and at the same time heard the slight difference in the tone of its engines, and knew at once that something had happened.

He hurried across, lifting his silks so he could run, the honour guard exerting themselves to keep up with him. As he came to the hangars, they were already disembarking. Li Yuan made his way through until he stood before the Commander of the flight, who was busy examining the damage to one of his craft.

"What happened?" he asked, staring past the Captain at the smoke-blackened flank of the cruiser.

The Captain span round, surprised, then bowed low. "Forgive me, *Chieh Hsia*. We were attacked coming over the Uzbek plantations... three ships out of Tashkent. We gave the imperial codes, yet they attacked all the same. Deliberately, it seems."

Li Yuan nodded, sobered by the thought. Before today it would have been unthinkable that an imperial cruiser would have been attacked by security forces, but today the unthinkable was finally happening.

"We lost two ships, *Chieh Hsia*, but none of the transporters were harmed. Not in any serious way, that is."

"And the attackers?"

"We destroyed them, *Chieh Hsia*."

"Good. You will be rewarded for your actions, Captain. You and all your men."

Li Yuan turned, looking around him, seeing at once the face of his son, Kuei Jen, staring down at him through the portal of one of the other cruisers. He went across, greeting the boy at the bottom of the ramp, picking him up and hugging him, relieved that he was safe.

In the hatchway beyond the boy stood his wife, Pei K'ung. He stared at her then nodded, strangely pleased that she had survived.

"What is the news from Tongjiang?" he asked, setting his son down and facing her.

"Tongjiang has fallen. A thousand dead, so they say. The news was full of it as we flew across. Another half an hour and we ourselves would not have escaped."

"Ah..." He felt a heaviness descend on him. A thousand dead. And Tongjiang itself... gone. He felt like weeping at the thought. But at least his family had survived.

Cling on to that, Li Yuan, he told himself. *For many men this day have emerged from this with far less than you. Millions are dying even as you stand here with your son, your wife. So give thanks to all the gods you know!*

He shivered, then stretched a hand out to her. She hesitated then came down the ramp and took his hand, surprised, for it was the first gesture of kindness he had shown to her since that night weeks ago when she had shared his bed.

"Forgive me, Pei K'ung," he whispered, drawing her close. "I have not been myself."

She drew back slightly, meeting his eyes. "Husband... there is nothing to forgive."

"And my cousin, Wei... is there any news of him? The rumours..."

"Wei Tseng-li is dead," she said, the solemnity of the words filling him with dread. "We taped all of the newscasts as we flew over. The pictures..." She shuddered physically. "They are most disturbing. They strung him up, like an animal. That lovely man..."

He grimaced and closed his eyes, then reached out, holding the two of them to him – his wife, his son. After a moment he looked up again, meeting her eyes. There were tears there, as in his own. "Then there are just the two of us now. Tsu Tao Chu and I. Two T'ang and but a single City. That is, if my own City survives the night.

"And if it falls?"

Li Yuan looked away, his left hand gripping his son's shoulder fiercely, a muscle in his cheek twitching. "Then we must leave Chung Kuo and go elsewhere."

He had seen the demonstrations. One moment the ice was a solid thing, the next...

Karr shuddered. They were hovering above the City's roof, the hold of the cruiser packed with cylinders of the stuff. Two hundred and forty cruisers in all – more than half their remaining strength – had been loaded up and flown into position along a line from Le Havre in the west through Nurnberg and Dresden to Stettin in the north-east. Now he had only to give the order and the spraying would begin.

There was no time to evacuate. No time to give the people down below any chance to escape, for to do so would be to tip-off Lehmann. And if he knew...

"Okay," he said, leaning forward towards the cockpit's control panel. "Let's get this over with. Begin spraying."

Karr turned, then clambered up, going to the left-hand portal to look out as the chemicals began to fall like a mist of fine rain onto the City's pure white roof. And where it touched...

He caught his breath, then groaned. It was unbearable to watch. He could see them far below him, jumping as the levels slowly melted. As in a dream... the ice melting beneath the fine spray that fell from the heavens, the levels vanishing.

As if they'd never been...

He sat down heavily, closing his eyes, trying not to imagine it, but it was no use. He could see them still – all those people – thousands of them, hundreds of thousands, falling through a dissolving mist of ice, like stones, falling downward to the earth.

He groaned. He had done many foul things in the service of his T'ang. He had killed and lied and sold his soul a hundred times, but this... this was the nadir.

Karr stood, forcing himself to watch once more, to bear witness. Behind them a great space had opened up, like a canyon between two smooth plateaus of ice, a cross-section of the levels exposed by the acid-like mist. And where the mist still fell the City seemed to sink into the earth as layer after layer shimmered into nothingness.

Like earth in a sieve, he thought, trying to find the words to describe what he was watching – trying not to go crazy at the thought that each of those tiny black shapes was a human being.

I gave the order, he thought, stunned by the enormity of it. *Yes, it was I who gave the order.*

For a moment longer he watched it, then, swallowing down the bile that had risen in his throat, he went back through and sat, staring out at the whiteness that stretched ahead of him, trying hard not to think of all those down below who, in a blink of an eye, were about to learn what their Master, the great T'ang, had decided for them.

The cruiser descended slowly, sinking into the space between the Cities. Below, a vast army waited in the late evening gloom, rank after rank, their bright red uniforms standing out against the forlorn silver shapes of what had once been the City's supporting columns. The great mass of men stretched out into the distance, their number filling the two *li* gap between the massive walls. Ten thousand brightly-coloured banners fluttered in the wind that blew down that vast, artificial canyon. Torches flickered in the twilight, then, at a signal, drums rolled and trumpets blew. As one the masses came to attention.

Looking out through the cockpit of the cruiser, Lehmann studied the host below. Eight hundred thousand man there were. To the west, in the shadow of Rouen, a further million waited, while to the east, at Eberswalde, a smaller force of four hundred thousand were gathered.

In an hour it would begin. As darkness fell he would make the final push; would hammer the final nail into the great T'ang's coffin.

He turned to Soucek. "So here we are, Jiri. A few hours more and all is ours."

Soucek – recalled only an hour past from his labours in Bremen - bowed respectfully.

"I never doubted it, Master. From that first moment until this, we have walked an iron path."

The albino's face was like a waxwork, devoid of all emotion. Yet men followed him in their millions, bled for him, laid down their lives for him.

"That was a bold move of Li Yuan's," he said, a grudging respect in his voice, "but it will not save him. Drawing a line is one thing, defending it another."

The engine noise changed, intensifying as they dropped below the last level of the City and into the semi-darkness beneath. Soucek looked out and shuddered. The ice-eaters had done their work mercilessly. They had stripped the levels bare.

The craft touched down onto the Clay.

As the door hissed open, a great cheer went up from all sides. For a moment the hatch was silent, empty, and then Lehmann – Li Min, the White T'ang – stepped out, dressed from head to toe in white, his left hand raised in a triumphal salute.

At once the cheer became a roar. Helmets were thrown in the air, guns thrust toward the heavens.

Lehmann half turned, his face a blank, his eyes cold like glass. "You see, Jiri? They have a need of kings."

He walked down the ramp to a tumultuous reception. It was like the roar of a great storm. Soucek stood at the head of the ramp a moment, watching him descend, then looked out across that sea of eager, exultant faces, seeing no sign of doubt – only an ecstatic adulation.

We walk as in a dream...

Soucek stepped down, taking his place behind and to the right of his Master as the senior officers presented themselves. Glancing down, he noticed for the first time that the ground underfoot was hard and glassy where the aerated ice had reformed. Bodies were embedded in it.

As Lehmann went up the line, inspecting the honour guard, he walked over the upturned faces of the dead. Overhead tiny remotes hovered like carrion, catching each word, each gesture for posterity.

History, this was. A turning point. The day the White T'ang came into his kingdom.

Soucek shivered at the thought, a strange thrill of love passing through him. Visak had failed the test – had faltered at the final hurdle – but he had remained true, and now he would live to see his Master crowned, seated upon the dragon throne itself, king of the underworld no more, but king of all.

At the head of the second line, Lehmann turned and looked across at him, then nodded. At the signal, Soucek went across and, walking behind Lehmann, began to make his way through the crowd to where a platform had been set up. There Lehmann was to address the masses; to rally their spirits before the final attack. Yet even as they passed between the ranks, the deafening sound of cheering rolled on and on, he sensed something was happening. On the platform up ahead a group of officers were gathered about the mobile transmitter, listening anxiously, their faces troubled.

"What is it?" Lehmann asked unceremoniously, as he mounted the steps onto the platform.

Soucek, coming up behind Lehmann, saw how they looked to one another, a shock of fear passing among them, then how the most senior of them stepped forward.

"There are rumours, Master..."

"Rumours?"

"Reports... from Malaga, Toulon, Taranto... and other places."

Lehmann lifted him from his feet, one hand tight about the man's neck. As he did, so the cheers slowly died, until the whole space between the Cities was silent.

"No babbling, man," Lehmann said quietly, his face only a breath from the other's, his steel-like grip almost choking him. "Give me no rumours. Tell me what you know."

He let the man fall, then stepped past him, pointing to another.

"Tell me! What's happened?"

"We have been betrayed, Master," the man said, his voice trembling. He fell to his knees, staring up at Lehmann, his eyes wide with fear. "The Mountain Lords have come against us, Master. They have attacked us in the south. Five great armies have come against us."

"There are reports?"

"Coming in all the time," another offered, also falling to his knees. "They began twenty minutes back. At first we discounted them. But in the last few minutes..."

"Enough!" Lehmann said, raising his left hand abruptly. He looked to Soucek. "Jiri... find out where they are attacking and what strength they have, then gather my generals south of here, in the captured garrison of Milan. We must hold a Council of War."

"And *this*, Master?" Soucek said, pointing north, towards what remained of Li Yuan's City.

"Another day," Lehmann said, turning to face the south, his eyes burning coldly in the glass of his face. "First I must give my African cousins the welcome they deserve."

Karr jumped down from the cruiser and began to run up the slope of the lawn towards the palace, laughing to himself at the news he brought, imagining the face of his Master when he told him. But as he approached the Eastern Gate, he slowed, hearing bells from within the ancient palace.

Had someone else beaten him here with the news? One of Rheinhardt's young officers, perhaps?

He waited impatiently at the gate while the guards double-checked his ID and ran hand-held scanners over him, then went through, ducking beneath the low lintel and into the grounds of the inner palace. He expected to hear laughter, the sound of celebration, but there was nothing – only an ominous silence, in which the sound of the bells seemed suspended as if in glass. He jumped down the steps in threes and began to make his way along the path to the centre, heading for the Northern Palace, then stopped dead, the breath hissing from him.

From beneath the great arch of the Southern Palace, a procession was emerging, his Master, Li Yuan, leading it. Behind him, on an open bier carried by thirty bearers in white silk robes, lay Tsu Tao Cho. His face had been made up as if in the perfect bloom of life, and he wore the dragon robes – the imperial yellow with the nine dragons, eight shown and one hidden. Beneath him the rich furs of the bier were strewn with white petals.

Karr made his way across, to join the procession, then, some twenty *ch'i* from his Master, fell to his knees, touching his forehead to the earth.

The procession stopped. Li Yuan looked to him, his face ashen. "Is it over, Gregor? Has the White T'ang taken my City?"

Karr lifted his head. "No, *Chieh Hsia*. We are saved. The Mountain Lords..." He looked beyond Li Yuan a moment, appalled by the sight of the young prince. "Fu Chang and his cousins... they kept their word, *Chieh Hsia*. They came!"

Li Yuan nodded, but it seemed that even this news had no power to raise his spirits. He sighed heavily, a bitterness in his eyes. "Then my cousin's life was truly wasted, neh?"

"*Chieh Hsia?*"

Li Yuan stared at Karr bleakly. "We found him an hour back, in his rooms. He had locked the door, then hung himself."

Karr felt the shock of that pass through him. A Son of Heaven, dead by his own hand. It was hard to believe.

"But your news..." Li Yuan gave him the ghost of a smile. "Your news brings us some small comfort in these dark hours. We live to fight on, neh, Gregor Karr? We who survived."

"*Chieh Hsia.*"

Karr bowed his head, trying not to think of what he had seen that very day. Of the levels misting into nothing. Yes, he thought, for now they were safe. For a time. The Seven had gone. Li Yuan alone had survived. A single man. A Son of Heaven, true, and yet a single man.

Li Yuan put out a hand, gesturing for him to get up.

"Cone, Gregor Karr. Walk with me. The time will come to celebrate your news, but now we must place my cousin Tao Chu beside his uncle."

He paused, gathering his full dignity about him once more, then nodded. "It is time to observe the rituals. Time to grieve the dead and see that their souls are welcomed in the other world."

The Night-Coloured Pearl

AUTUMN 2217

"The Yellow Emperor went wandering
To the north of the Red Water
To the Kwan Lun mountain. He looked around
Over the edge of the world. On the way home
He lost his night-coloured pearl.
He sent out Science to seek his pearl, and got nothing.
He sent out Analysis to look for his pearl, and got nothing.
He sent out Logic to seek his pearl, and got nothing.
Then he asked Nothingness, and Nothingness had it!
The Yellow Emperor said:
"Strange indeed: Nothingness
Who was not sent
Who did no work to find it
Had the night-coloured pearl!"
—Chuang Tzu, 6th century BC (*Writings*, xii, IV)

THE NIGHT-COLOURED PEARL

The cockpit was packed, all nine of them trying to crown into that tiny space to watch the screen.

Below them lay Chung Kuo, bright in the sunlight.

Ebert, in the pilot's seat, frowned, then spoke to the air.

"What's happening, Master Tuan?"

There was a moment's hesitation, then the old man's voice sounded in the cabin, as if from every side.

"Much has changed since you were last here, Hans. The Seven have become One, and the world..." He laughed gently. "Some say the world has shrunk. I see it differently. To my eyes the world is a much bigger place these days."

Ebert stared at the world below him, shaking his head. The great shapes of white that had once covered every continent had now diminished to a patchwork. In some places – in the Southern continents particularly – it was gone entirely. Only in Europe was the City still dominant, but there too it was split – a great, jagged line, like a crack in the surface of a frozen pond, running from west to east.

"I didn't realise," Ebert said. "There's been a war, neh?"

"War was the least of it," Tuan Ti Fo answered, placing images on the screen before them. "War is but the prelude to disaster. After War there is Pestilence and Starvation, and always – *always* – there is the darkness."

"The darkness?"

It was Aluko Echewa who spoke. All about him the young Osu murmured, their discomfort evident. They had never been off Mars until three months back. Now they were to start a new life on the planet below, alone, cut off from their loved ones, preparing the way for others of their kind.

"The darkness within," Tuan answered. "Hatred and fear and evil."

Dogo, the strongest and biggest of the young Osu, laughed. "Father Aluko thought you meant us, Master Tuan. With us the darkness is visible, no?"

There was general laughter at that. Eight dark faces grinned, showing pearled teeth like polished stones. But Ebert seemed distracted.

"What is it, Efulefu?" Echewa asked, laying a dark hand on his shoulder. "Why the long face?"

"What happened here..." He looked up at them, real pain in his eyes. "I was much to blame for it. The things I did..."

He turned, looking back to the scene of horror that continued to fill the screen.

"Where should we go, Master Tuan?" Ebert asked. "What does your friend, the Machine, suggest?"

"We shall go south," Tuan answered. "We shall..."

There was a sharp buzz of noise and then a rapid clicking.

"What is it?" Echewa asked, leaning forward, suddenly anxious.

"I don't know, I..."

"Leave the cabin," Tuan Ti Fo said faintly, his voice almost inaudible above the static. "Now... before..."

Ebert was facing the screen as it lit up. The others were more fortunate: they had turned away, making to obey Tuan's voice.

The light from the screen was fierce, like the light from the heart of the sun. It flooded the cabin, seeming to scour every pore, every cell of their bodies. The Osu were screaming, the pain in their heads – in their eyes – like nothing they'd ever experienced. But their blindness would prove temporary. For Ebert it was different. Ebert had taken the full force of the light. He sat there in the chair, groaning, his face blistered and steaming, his eyes burned from their sockets.

The light faded, the clicking stopped. Echewa, on his knees in the doorway, turned blindly.

"Efulefu? Are you all right?"

Ebert groaned again.

"What happened?" Echewa asked, beating down his fear. "What was that?"

"It was a light-mine," Tuan Ti Fo answered. "Our presence in its air-space seems to have triggered it."

"But I thought..."

Echewa fell silent. He had thought Tuan's 'Machine' would have anticipated such a danger and dealt with it. He'd thought...

"Efulefu?"

"It's okay," Ebert said weakly. And then, strangely, he laughed.

"Efulefu? Are you alright?"

"I'm... blind," Ebert said, then laughed again.

Echewa struggled to his feet, then turned, trying to see, but his eyes were still too painful. All was a blur; a blur of pain and confusion.

"But Efulefu... why are you laughing?"

"Blind... the Walker in the Darkness, blind!" And for a third time he laughed. Then, just as unexpectedly, he groaned. "Gods," he said quietly. "All those things I did. All those people I hurt. All that darkness..."

"Is past now," Tuan Ti Fo said, his voice warm and reassuring in the air surrounding them. "Now sit quietly, *Tsou Tsai Hei*. The Machine will see you down."

CHARACTER LISTING

MAJOR CHARACTERS

Ascher, Emily — Trained as an economist, she was once a member of the Ping Tiao revolutionary party. After their demise, she fled to North America, not merely to settle there, but to pursue her life goals – which are change and the downfall of the corrupt social institutions that rule Chung Kuo.

DeVore, Howard — A one-time Major in the T'ang's Security forces, he has become the leading figure in the struggle against the Seven. A highly intelligent and coldly logical man, he is the puppet master behind the scenes as the great 'War of the Two Directions' takes a new turn. Defeated first on Chung Kuo and then on Mars, he has fled outward, to the tenth planet, Pluto.

Ebert, Hans — Son of Klaus Ebert and one-time heir to the vast GenSyn Corporation, he was promoted to General in Li Yuan's Security forces, and was admired and trusted by his superiors. Secretly, however, he was allied to DeVore and was subsequently implicated in the murder of his father, Klaus. Having fled Chung Kuo, he was declared a traitor in his absence. After suffering exile, he had found himself again among the lost African tribe, the Osu, among the desert sands of Mars.

Karr, Gregor

A Colonel in the Security forces, Karr was recruited by General Tolonen from the Net. In his youth he was a 'blood' – a to-the-death combat fighter. Physically a giant of a man, he is also one of Li Yuan's most trusted men, working alongside his sidekick, Kao Chen.

Lehmann, Stefan

Albino son of the former Dispersionist leader, Pietr Lehmann, and one-time lieutenant of Howard DeVore, he has, by brutal conquest and guile, become the ruler of City Europe's "underworld", its 'White T'ang', and – as Li Min – the principal enemy of Li Yuan.

Li Yuan

T'ang of City Europe and one of the Seven. As second son of Li Shai Tung, he inherited after the deaths of his father and brother. Considered by many to be old before his time, he nonetheless has a passionate side to his nature, as demonstrated in his brief marriage to his brother's wife, the beautiful Fei Yen. His subsequent re-marriage ended in tragedy when his three wives were assassinated. Despite his most recent re-marriage to Pei K'ung, his real concern is for his young son, Kuei Jen.

Pei K'ung

Fifth wife of Li Yuan, she is eighteen years his elder and a rather plain, straightforward woman from a Minor family background.

Shepherd, Ben

Great-great-grandson of City Earth's architect, Shepherd was brought up in 'The Domain', an idyllic valley in the south-west of England, where he pursues his artistic calling, developing a new art form, the 'Shell': a machine which mimics the experience of life.

Tolonen, Jelka

Daughter of Marshal Tolonen, Jelka was brought up in a very masculine environment, lacking a mother's love and influence. Yet her attempts to re-create herself – to find a balance in her life – have only brought her into conflict, first with a young soldier, and then with her father, who – to prevent her having a relationship with the Clayborn, Kim Ward – despatched her on a tour of the Colony Planets. Returned, she bides her time, awaiting the day when, at twenty-five, she will come of age and can decide her own destiny.

Tolonen, Knut   Former Marshal of the Council of Generals and one-time General to Li Yuan's father, Tolonen is a rock-like supporter of the Seven and their values, even in an age of increasing uncertainty. In his role as a father, however, this inflexibility in his nature has brought him only repeated conflict with his daughter, Jelka.

Tsu Ma   T'ang of West Asia and one of the Seven, Tsu Ma has thrown off a dissolute past to become Li Yuan's staunchest supporter. A strong, handsome man in his late thirties, he had yet to marry, though his secret affair with Li Yuan's former wife, Fei Yen, revealed a side of him that had not been fully harnessed. Now, in his middle years, he wishes to lead a more settled life.

Ward, Kim   Born in the Clay, that dark wasteland beneath the great City's foundations, Kim has survived various personal crises to become Chung Kuo's leading experimental scientist. Hired by the massive SimFic Corporation as a commodity-slave on a seven-year contract, he is a staunch supporter of Li Yuan.

THE SEVEN AND THE FAMILIES

Li Kuei Jen	son of Li Yuan and heir to City Europe
Liang K'o Ting	Head of the Liang Family (one of the Twenty-Nine Minor Families) and father of Liang Shu-sun
Liang Shu-sun	Minor Family princess
Pei K'ung	Wife of Li Yuan
Pei Ro-hen	Head of the Pei family (of the Twenty-Nine) and father of Pei K'ung

Tsu Kung-chih	older nephew of Tsu Ma
Tsu Ma	T'ang of West Asia
Tsu Tao Chu	younger nephew of Tsu Ma
Wei Tseng-li	T'ang of East Asia
Yin Fei Yen	"Flying Swallow – Minor Family princess and the divorced wife of Li Yuan
Yin Han Ch'in	son of Fei Yen
Yin Sung	elder brother of Yin Fei Yen and Head of the Yin Family (of the Twenty-Nine)
Yin Wu Tsai	cousin of Yin Fei Yen

FRIENDS AND RETAINERS OF THE SEVEN

Autumn Snow	maid to Pei K'ung
Barlow	young equerry to Gregor Karr
Chiang K'o	private secretary to Tsu Ma
Chu Shi-ch'e	*Pi-shu chien*, or Inspector of the Imperial Library at Tongjiang
Ebert, Pauli	bastard son of Hans Ebert and Golden Heart and heir to the GenSyn Corporation
Golden Heart	one-time concubine to Hans Ebert and mother of Pauli Ebert
Haavikko, Axe	Major and Commander of Security for the 'Western Isle'
Harrison	AAD Project Director
Hoff	member of the *Shen T'se* elite security squad
Hu	Surgeon, AAD Project
Hu Ch'ang	Principal Secretary to Nan Ho
Hwa Kwei	Chief Steward of the Bedchamber to Tsu Ma
Karlgren	Lieutenant in Security, Astrakhan
Karr, Gregor	Colonel in Security
Lao Kang	Chancellor of West Asia
Lo Wen	Master of *wu shu* and fight instructor and tutor to

	Li Kuei Jen
Lu	surgeon at Tongjiang
Luo Ye	most senior member of the *San Shih*, the 'Scholar Princes' of the New Confucian movement; also a Minor Family prince.
Munk	Captain in Security, Astrakhan
Nan Ho	Chancellor of City Europe
Needham	captain of *Shen T'se* elite Security guard
Rheinhardt, Helmut	General of Security, City Europe
Shepherd, Ben	son of the late Hal Shepherd; 'shell' artist
Tan We	Chief Eunuch at Tsu Ma's palace in Astrakhan
Tiny Jade	maid to Pei K'ung
Tolonen, Jelka	daughter of Marshal Tolonen
Tolonen, Knut	ex-Marshal of Security; acting Head of the GenSyn Corporation
Tsung Ye	private secretary to Pei K'ung
Tu Fu-wei	private secretary to Tsu Ma
T'ung	Surgeon to Tsu Ma's court
Wang	Steward at the Astrakhan palace
Ward, Kim	Clayborn scientist, employed as a commodity slave by the SimFic Corporation
Ye	Senior Steward at Tongjiang
Yi Ching	Colonel of Internal Security to Tsu Ma at Astrakhan
Yung Chen	eunuch from the woman's quarters in Tsu Ma's palace in Astrakhan

OTHER CHARACTERS

Ascher, Emily	ex *Ping Tiao* terrorist, late of City Europe and known as 'Rachel'
Ashman	henchman of Pasek
Bartels, Emil	young First Level bachelor
Beinlich	ex-Security lieutenant, working for Von Pasenow

Berrenson	Company Head
Blaskic	henchman of Pasek
Cao Chang	Financial Strategist to Li Min
Chang, Hu	agent with Supernal Property
Chang Mu	servant at the Ebert mansion
Cheng Lu	Lehmann's ambassador to Fu Chiang's court
Chou Te-hsing	Head of the Black Hand terrorists
Cui	Steward of Marshal Tolonen's household
Curval, Andrew	experimental geneticist, working for SimFic
DeValerian, Rachel	pseudonym of Emily Ascher
DeVore, Howard	ex-Major in Li Yuans' Security forces
Dieter, Wilhelm	Black Hand cell leader
Eyre	henchman of Pasek
Fox	Company Head
Fu Chiang	"the Priest", Big Boss of the Red Flower Triad of North Africa
Fung	*Wu*, or Diviner to Yin Fei Yen
Grant	henchman to Pasek
Hart, Alex	Representative at Weimar; Dispersionist and friend of Stefan Lehmann
Heng Pang-chou	wife of Minister Heng and childhood friend of Jelka Tolonen
Hooper	Senior Engineer aboard DeVore's craft
Hsueh Chi	Big Boss of the Thousand Spears Triad of Southern Africa
Hsueh Nan	Warlord of Southern Africa and brother of Hsueh Chi
Hu Lin	Red Pole of the Red Flower Triad of North Africa
Huang Peng	Steward at the Ebert mansion
Karr, Marie	wife of Gregor Karr
Karr, May	daughter of Marie and Gregor Karr
Kavanagh	Representative at Weimar and Leader of the House

Lehmann, Stefan	"The White T'ang", Big Boss of the European Triads
Li Ho-nien	servant at the Ebert mansion
Li Min	"Brave carp"; an Alias of Stefan Lehmann
Lo Chang	Steward at the Ebert mansion
Ma Ch'ing	servant at the Ebert mansion
The Machine	an artificial intelligence
Meng Tzu	'Mencius' Chinese philosopher
Mo Nan-ling	"the Little Emperor", Big Boss of the Nine Emperors Triad of Central Africa
Neville, Jack	Head of Product Development for SimFic
Pasek, Karel	Head of "The Sealed"; religious fanatic and senior member of the Black hand terrorists
Peng, Madam	matchmaker
Peters	cell leader in the Black Hand
Ravachol	the 'second prototype'; an android created by Kim Ward
Reiss, Horst	Chief Executive of SimFic
Ruddock	Minor Official employed by Lehmann
Sheng Min-chung	"One-Eye Sheng", Big Boss of the Iron Fists Triad of East Africa
Shepherd, Meg	sister of Ben Shepherd
Shih Chi-o	servant at the Ebert mansion
Soucek, Jiri	lieutenant to Stefan Lehmann
Stewart	henchman of Li Min
T'ai Cho	friend and ex-tutor of Kim Ward
Tan Sui	White paper Fan of the Red Flower Triad of North Africa
Ting Ju-ch'ang	Warlord of Tunis and frontman for The Mountain Lords
Ts'ao Wu	cell leader in the Black Hand
Tsou Tsai Hei	"Walker In The Darkness"; another name used by

	Hans Ebert
Tuan Ti Fo	Master of *wei chi and sage*
Vierheller, Jane	Black Hand member
Visak	lieutenant to Stefan Lehmann
Von Pasenow	ex-Security Major
Ward, Kim	Clayborn scientist
Yang Chih-wen	'The Bear'. Big Boss of the Golden Ox Triad of West Africa
Yen Fu	North African Warlord
Yi Pang-chou	Jelka's schoolfriend, married to Minister Heng
Yin Fu	African warlord
Yu I	proprietor of the Blue Pagoda tea-house

THE OSU

Dogo	one of 'The Eight'
Echewa, Aluko	Head Man and one of 'The Eight'
Efulefu	"Worthless Man"; chosen name of Hans Ebert among the Osu
Hama	Osu wife of Hans Ebert
Jaga	*ndichie* or Elder of the Osu on Mars
Nza	"Tiny bird" an Osu child, adopted by Hans Ebert and one of 'The Eight'

THE DEAD

Aaltonen	Marshal and Head of Security for City Europe
Althaus, Kurt	General of Security, North America
An Hsi	Minor Family prince and fifth son of An Sheng
An Liang-chou	Minor Family prince
An Mo Shan	Minor family prince and third son of An Sheng
An Sheng	Head of the An family (one of the Twenty-Nine Minor families)
Anders	a mercenary
Anderson, Leonid	Director of the 'Recruitment Project'
Anna	helper to Mary Lever

Anne	Yu assassin
Bakke	Marshal in Security
Barrow, Chao	Secretary of the House at Weimar
Bates	leading figure in the Federation Of Free Men, Mars
Beatrice	daughter of Cathy Hubbard, granddaughter of Mary Reed
Bercott, Andrei	Representative at Weimar
Berdichev, Soren	Head of SimFic and later leader of the Dispersionist faction
Berdichev, Ylva	wife of Soren Berdichev
Bess	helper to Mary Lever
Big Wen	a landowner
Blofeld	agent of the special security forces
Boss Yang	an exploiter of the people
Brock	security guard in the Domain
Brookes, Thomas	Port Captain, Tien Men K'ou, Mars
Buck, John	Head of Development at the Ministry of Contracts
Chang Lai-hsu	nephew of Chang Yi Wei
Chang, Li Chen	junior dragon in charge of drafting the Edict of Technological Control
Chang Yi Wei	senior brother of the Chang clan; owners of MicroData
Chang Te Li	"Old Chang", Wu (Diviner)
Chang Yu	Tsao Ch'un's appointment as First Dragon
Chao Ni Tsu	-computer genius; friend and advisor to Tsao Ch'un
Chen So	Clerk of the Inner Chambers at Tongjiang
Chen So I	Head of the Ministry of Contracts
Chen Yu	steward to Tsao Ch'un in Pei Ch'ing
Ch'en li	associate of Governor Schenck
Ch'eng I	Minor Family prince and son of Ch'eng So Yuan
Ch'eng So Yuan	Minor family Head
Cheng Yu	Member of the Seven, advisor to Tsao Ch'un Cherkassky, Stefanex-security assassin and friend of DeVore
Chi Fei Yu	an usurer
Chi Hu Wei	T'ang of the Australias; father of Chi Hsing
Chi Lin	legal assistant to Yang Hong Yu
Chih Huang Hui	second wife of Shang Mu and stepmother of Shang Han-A

Ch'in Shih Huang Ti	the First Emperor of China; ruled 221-210 BC
Ching Su	friend of Jiang Lei
Chiu Fa	Media commentator on the Mids news channel
Cho Hsiang	Hong Cao's subordinate
Cho Yi	Master of the Bedchamber at Tongjiang
Chu Heng	"kwai" or hired knife; a hireling of DeVore's
Chun Hua	wife of Jiang Lei
Curtis, Tim	Head of human Resources for GenSyn
Chun Wu-chi	head of the Chun family (one of the twenty-nine Minor families)
Chung Hsin	"loyalty"; bond servant to Li Shai Tung
Clarac, Armand	Director of the 'New Hope' project
Coates	security guard in the Domain
Cook	Duty guard in the Domain
Cornwell, James	Director of the AutoMek Corporation
Cutler, Richard	leader of the "America" movement
Dag	a mercenary
Dawson	associate of Governor Schenck
Deio	Clayborn friend of Kim Ward from 'Rehabiliation'
Donna	*Yu* assassin
Douglas, John	Company Head and Dispersionist
Duchek, Albert	Administrator of Lodz
Ebert, Gustav	joint head of GenSyn; brother of Wolfgang Ebert
Ebert, Klaus	Head of the GenSyn Corporation; father of Hans Ebert
Ebert, Ludovic	son of Gustav Ebert and GenSyn Director
Ebert, Wolfgang	Joint Head of GenSyn; brother of Gustav Ebert
Ecker, Michael	Company Head; Dispersionist
Edsel	Agent of special security services
Egan	Head of NorTek
Einar	a mercenary
Ellis, Michael	assistant to Director Spatz on the Wiring Project
Endacott	associate of Governor Schenck
Endfors, Pietr	friend of Knut Tolonen and father of Jenny, Tolonen's wife
Erkki	guard to Jelka Tolonen
Eva	friend of Mary Lever
Fairbank, John	Head of AmLab
Fan	fifth brother to the *I Lung*

Hua Shang	lieutenant to Wong Yi-Sun
Hubbard, Cathy	daughter of Tom and Mary Hubbard
Hubbard, Meg	daughter of Tom and Mary Hubbard
Hui	receptionist for GenSyn
Hui Chang Ye	Senior Legal Advocate for the Chang family
Hui Tsin	'Red Pole' (426, or Executioner) to the United Bamboo Triad
Hung	Tsao Ch'un's spy in Jiang Lei's camp
Hung Mien-lo	Chancellor of Africa
Hwa	Master, 'Blood' or hand-to-hand fighter, below the Net
I Lung	"First Dragon", the Head of The Thousand Eyes, the Ministry
Jackson	freelance go-between, employed by Fairbank
Jiang Ch'iao-chieh	eldest daughter of Jiang Lei
Jiang Lei	also known as Nai Liu ('Enduring Willow'); General of Tsao Ch'un's Eighteenth Banner and foremost poet of his age
Jiang San-chieh	youngest daughter of Jiang Lei
Jill	principal helper to Mary Lever
Joan	Yu assassin
Judd, Drew	actor; star of UBIK
Jung	steward to Tobias Lahm
Kan Jiang	Martian settler and poet
K'ang A-yin	gang boss of the Tu Sun tong
K'ang Yeh-su	nephew of K'ang A-yin
Kao Jyan	assassin; friend of Kao Chen
Karl	a mercenary
Kemp, Johannes	Director of ImmVac
Kennedy, Jean	wife of Joseph Kennedy
Kennedy, Joseph	Head of the New Republican and Evolutionist Party and Representative at Weimar
Kennedy, Robert	elder son of Joseph Kennedy
Kennedy, William	younger son of Joseph Kennedy
Kennedy, William	great-great-great grandfather of Joseph Kennedy
Krenek, Henryk	Senior Representative of the Martian Colonies
Krenek, Irina	wife of Henryk Krenek
Krenek, Josef	Company Head
Krenek, Maria	wife of Josef Krenek

Kriz	senior *Yu* operative
Ku	Marshal of the Fourth Banner Army
Kubinyi	lieutenant to DeVore
Kung Wen-fa	Senior Advocate from Mars
K'ung Fu Tzu	Confucius (551-479 BC)
Kurt	Chief Technician
Kustow, Bryn	'American'; friend of Michael Lever
Lahm, Tobias	Eighth Dragon at The Ministry, "The Thousand Eyes"
Lai Shi	second wife of Li Yuan
Lehmann, Pietr	Under Secretary of the House of Representatives and first leader of the Dispersionist faction; father of Stefan Lehmann
Lever, Charles	Head of the giant ImmVac Corporation of North America; father of Michael Lever
Lever, Margaret	wife of Charles Lever and mother of Michael Lever
Li Chang So	sixth son of Li Chao Ch'in
Li Chao Ch'in	member of the Seven and advisor to Tsao Ch'un
Li Chin	"Li The Lidless"; Big Boss of the Wo Shih Wo Triad
Li Ch'ing	T'ang of City Europe, father of Li Shai Tung and grandfather of Li Yuan
Li Fu Jen	third son of Li Chao Ch'in
Li Han Ch'in	first son of Li Shai Tung and one-time heir to City Europe; brother of Li Yuan
Li Hang Ch'i	T'ang of City Europe; great-great grandfather of Li Yuan
Li Kou-lung	T'ang of City Europe; great grandfather of Li Yuan
Li Kuang	fifth son of Li Chao Ch'in
Li Pai Shung	nephew of Li Chin; heir to the Wo Shih Wo Triad
Li Peng	eldest son of Li Chao Ch'in
Li Shai Tung	T'ang of City Europe, father of Li Yuan
Li Shen	second son of Li Chao Ch'in
Li Weng	fourth son of Li Chao Ch'in
Lin Yua	first wife of Li Shai Tung; mother of Li Han Ch'in and Li Yuan
Ling	steward at the Black Tower
Ling Hen	henchman for Herrick
Liu Chang	brothel keeper/pimp

Liu Tong	lieutenant to Li Chin
Lo Han	tong boss
Lo Wen	grand-daughter of Jiang Lei
Lu Ming-shao	"Whiskers Lu"; Big Boss of the Kuei Chuan Triad
Luke	Clayborn fiend of Kim Ward from 'Rehabilitation'
Lwo Kang	Li Shai Tung's Minister of the edict
Ma Shao Tu	senior servant to Li Chao Ch'in
Maitland, Idris	mother of Stefan Lehmann
Man Hsi	tong boss
Mao Liang	Minor family princess and member of the *Ping Tiao*, "Council of Five"
Mao Tse-tung	first Ko Ming emperor (ruled AD 1948-1976)
Matyas	Clayborn boy in Recruitment Project
Melfi, Charles	Genetic father of the Shepherd males
Meng K'ai	friend and adviser to Governor Schenck
Meng Te	lieutenant to Lu Ming-shao
Mien Shan	first wife of Li Yuan; mother of Li Kuei Jen
Milne, Michael	private investigator
Ming Hsin-fa	Senior Advocate for GenSyn
Ming Huang	sixth T'ang Emperor (ruled AD 713755)
Mo Yu	security lieutenant in the Domain
Moore, John	Company Head; Dispersionist
Mu Chua	Madame of the House of the Ninth Ecstasy, a brothel
Mu Li	"Iron Mu", Boss of the Big Circle Triad
Nai Liu	'Enduring Willow', the pen name of Jiang Lei, as a poet
P'eng Chuan	Sixth Dragon at the Ministry, the "Thousand Eyes"
P'eng K'ai-chi	nephew of P'eng Chuan
Pan Tsung-yen	friend of Jiang Lei
Pao En-fu	Master of the Inner Chambers to Wu Shih
Parr, Charles	Company Head; Dispersionist
Pavel	young man on the European Plantations
Peck	lieutenant to K'ang A-yin (a *ying tzu*, or 'shadow')
Pei Ko	member of the Seven; advisor to Tsau Ch'un
Pei Lin-Yi	eldest son of Pei Ko
Peskova	lieutenant of guards on the Domain
Ragnar	a mercenary
Raikkonen	Marshal in Security

Reed, Jake	web-dancer in futures market in London and father of Peter Reed; husband of Mary
Reed, Mary	wife of Jake Reed; mother of Peter Reed
Reed, May	sister of Jake Reed
Reed, Tom	son of Jake and Mary Reed
Reed, Peter	son of Jake Reed; executive employee of GenSyn
Rheinhardt	Media Liaison Manager for GenSyn
Ross, Alexander	Company Head; Dispersionist
Ross, James	private investigator
Rutherford, Andreas	friend and adviser to Governor Schenck
Sanders	Captain of Security at Helmstadt Armoury
Schenck, Hung-li	Governor of Mars Company
Schwarz	lieutenant to DeVore
Schwartz	Aid to Marshal Aaltonen
Seymour	Major in Security, North America
Shang	"Old Shang"; master to Kao Chen when he was a child
Shang ch'iu	son of Shang Mu and half-brother to Shang Han-A
Shang Chu	great grandfather of Shang Han-A
Shang Mu	Junior Minister in the "Thousand Eyes" or Ministry
Shang Wen Shao	grandfather of Han-A
Shao Shu	First Steward at Chun Hua's Mansion
Shao Yen	Major in Security; friend of Meng Hsin-fa
Shen Chen	son of Shen Fu
Shen Fu	First Dragon; Head of The Ministry
Shen Lu Chua	computer expert and member of the *Ping Tiao* "Council of Five"
Shepherd, Alexandra	wife of Amos Shepherd and daughter of Charles Melfi
Shepherd, Amos	great-great-great-grandfather (and genetic 'father') of Ben Shepherd; Chief Adviser to the tyrannical Tsao Ch'un
Shepherd, Augustus	'brother' of Ben Shepherd
Shepherd, Beth	daughter of Amos Shepherd
Shepherd, Hal	father (and genetic 'brother') of Ben Shepherd
Shepherd, Robert	great-grandfather (and genetic 'brother') of Ben Shepherd
Shu Liang	Senior Legal Advocate
Shu San	Junior Minister to Lwo Kang

Siang	Jelka Tolonen's martial arts instructor
Si Wu Ya	"Silk Raven", wife of Supervisor Sung
Song Wei	sweeper
Spatz, Gustav	Director of the Wiring Project
Spence, Leena	"Immortal" and one time love of Charles Lever
Ssu Lu Shan	official of the Ministry
Steiner	manager at ImmVac's Alexandria facility
Su Tung-p'o	Han official and poet of the Eleventh Century
Sun Li Hua	Wang Hsien's Master of the Inner Chambers
Sung	Supervisor on the plantation
Svensson	Marshal in Security
Tai Yu	'Moonflower', maid to Gustav Ebert; a GenSyn clone
Tarrant	Company Head
Teng Fu	Plantation guard
Teng Liang	Minor family princess betrothed to Prince Ch'eng I
Tewl	"Darkness", chief of the raft people
Tolonen, Hanna	aunt of Knut Tolonen
Tolonen, Helga	wife of Jon Tolonen; aunt of Jelka Tolonen
Tolonen, Jenny	wife of Knut Tolonen and daughter of Pietr Endfors
Tolonen, Jon	brother of Marshal Tolonen
Tong Chu	assassin and "kwai", a hired knife
Ts'ao P'i	'Number Three'; steward at Tsao Ch'un's Court in Pei Ch'ing
Tsao Ch'i Yuan	youngest son of Tsao Ch'un
Tsao Ch'un	tyrannical founder of Chung Kuo
Tsao Heng	second son of Tsao Ch'un
Tsao Hsiao	Tsao Ch'un's eldest brother
Tsao Wang-Po	eldest son of Tsau Ch-un and heir to Chung Kuo
Tsu Chen	member of the Seven and advisor to Tsao Ch'un
Tsu Lin	eldest son of Tsu Chen
Tsu Shi	Steward to Gustav Ebert; a GenSyn clone
Tsu Tiao	T'ang of West Asia; father of Tsu Ma
Tu Ch'en-shih	friend and adviser to Governor Schenck
Tu Mai	security guard in the Domain
Tu Mu	Assistant to Alison Winter at GenSyn
Tung Cai	a low level rioter
Vesa	a Yu assassin
Virtainen, Per	Major in Li Yuan's Security forces

Visak	lieutenant to Lu Ming-shao
Wang An-Shih	Han official and poet of the Eleventh century
Wang Chang Ye	first son of Wang Hsien
Wang Hsien	T'ang of Africa and father of Wang Sau-leyan
Wang Hui So	member of the Seven and advisor to Tsao Ch'un
Wang Lieh Tsu	second son of Wang Hsien
Wang Lung	eldest son of Wang Hui So
Wang Sau-leyan	T'ang of Africa
Wang Ta-hung	third son of Wang Hsien; elder brother of Wang Sau-leyan
Wang Tu	leader of the Martian Radical Alliance
Wei	a judge
Wei Chan Yin	T'ang of East Asia
Wei Feng	T'ang of East Asia; father of Wei Chan Yin
Wei Hsi Wang	second brother if Wei Chan Yin and heir to City East Asia
Wei Shao	Chancellor to Tsao Ch'un
Weis, Anton	banker, Dispersionist
Wells	Captain in Security, North America
Wen P'ing	Tsao Ch'un's man. A bully
Wen Ti	"First Ancestor" of City Earth/Chung Kuo, otherwise known as Liu Heng; ruled China from 180-157 BC
Wiegand, Max	lieutenant to DeVore
Will	Clayborn friend of Kim Ward from Rehabilitation
Wilson, Stephen	Captain in Security under Kao Chen
Winter, Alison	ex-girlfriend of Jake Reed; Head of Evaluation at GenSyn
Winter, Jake	only son of Alison Winter
Wong Yi-sun	"Fat Wong"; Big Boss of the United Bamboo Triad
Wu Chi	AI (Artifical Intelligence) to Tobias Lahm
Wu Hsien	member of the Seven and advisor to Tsao Ch'un
Wu Shih	T'ang of North America
Wu Wei-kou	first wife of Wu Shih
Wyatt, Edmund	Company Head; Dispersionist
Yang Hong Yu	legal advocate
Yang Lai	Junior Minister to Lwo Kang
Yang Shao fu	Minister of Health, City Europe
Yi Shan-ch'i	Minor Family prince

Yin Chan	Minor family prince and second son of Yin Tsu
Yin Shu	Junior Minister of the "Thousand Eyes", aka, The Ministry
Yin Tsu	head of the Yin Family (one of the Twenty-Nine Minor Families and father of Fei Yen)
Ying Chai	assistant to Sun Li Hua
Ying Fu	assistant to Sun Li Hua
Yo Jou Hsi	a judge
Yu Ch'o	Family retainer to Wang Hui So
Yue Chun	'Red Pole' (426, or Executioner) to the Wo Shih Wo Triad
Yun Ch'o	lieutenant to Shen Lu Chua
Yun Yueh-hui	"Dead Man Yun"; Big Boss of the Red gang Triad
Ywe Hao	"Fine Moon"; female *Yu* terrorist
Ywe Kai-chang	father to Ywe Hao

GLOSSARY OF MANDARIN TERMS

Most of the Mandarin terms used in the text are explained in context. However, as a few are used more naturally, I've considered it best to provide a brief explanation.

ai ya!	common exclamation of surprise or dismay.
ch'a	tea. It might be noted that *ch'a shu*, the Chinese art of tea, is an ancient forebear of the Japanese tea ceremony *chanoyu*.
chang shan	literally 'long dress', which fastens to the right. Worn by both sexes. The women's version is a fitted, calf-length dress, similar to the *chi pao*. A South China fashion, also known as a *cheung sam*.
chan shih	a fighter.
Ch'eng Ou Chou	City Europe.
ch'i	a Chinese foot; approximately 14.4 inches.
chih chu	spider.
chieh hsia	term meaning 'Your Majesty', derived from the expression 'Below the Steps'. It was the formal way of addressing the Emperor, through his Ministers, who stood 'below the steps'.
chi pao	literally 'banner gown'; a one-piece gown of Manchu origin, usually sleeveless, worn by women.
Chou	'state'; here the name for a card game based on the politics of the state of Chung Kuo.
chung	a lidded serving bowl for *ch'a*.
ch'un tzu	an ancient Chinese term from the Warring States period, describing a certain class of nobleman, controlled by a code of chivalry and morality known as the *li*, or rites.

<table>
<tr><td></td><td>Here the term is roughly, and sometimes ironically, translated as 'gentlemen'. The ch'un tzu is as much an ideal state of behaviour – as specified by Confucius in the Analects – as an actual class in Chung Kuo, though a degree of financial independence and a high standard of education are assumed a prerequisite.</td></tr>
<tr><td>erhu</td><td>two-stringed bow with snakeskin-covered sound box.</td></tr>
<tr><td>fen</td><td>unit of money (a cent); one hundred fen make up a yuan.</td></tr>
<tr><td>han</td><td>term used by the Chinese to describe their own race, the 'black-haired people', dating back to the Han Dynasty (210 BC – AD 220). It is estimated that some ninety-four per cent of modern China's population is racially Han.</td></tr>
<tr><td>hei</td><td>literally 'black'; the Chinese pictogram for this represents a man wearing warpaint and tattoos. Here it refers to the genetically manufactured (GenSyn) half-men used as riot police to quell uprisings in the lower levels.</td></tr>
<tr><td>hsiao jen</td><td>'little man/men'. In the Analects, Book XIV, Confucius writes: 'The gentleman gets through to what is up above; the small man gets through to what is down below.' This distinction between 'gentlemen' (ch'un tzu) and 'little men' (hsiao jen), false even in Confucius's time, is no less a matter of social perspective in Chung Kuo.</td></tr>
<tr><td>hsien</td><td>historically an administrative district of variable size. Here the term is used to denote a very specific administrative area; one of ten stacks – each stack composed of thirty decks. Each deck is a hexagonal living unit of ten levels, two li, or approximately one kilometre in diameter. A stack can be imagined as one honeycomb in the great hive of the City.</td></tr>
<tr><td>Hsien L'ing</td><td>'Chief Magistrate'. In Chung Kuo, these officials are the T'ang's representatives and law enforcers for the individual hsien, or administrative districts. In times of peace, each hsien also elects a representative to the House at Weimar.</td></tr>
<tr><td>Hung Mao</td><td>literally 'redheads', the name the Chinese gave to the Dutch (and later English) seafarers who attempted to trade with China in the seventeenth century. Because of the piratical nature of their endeavours (which</td></tr>
</table>

<table>
<tr><td></td><td>often meant plundering Chinese shipping and ports) the name has connotations of piracy.</td></tr>
<tr><td>Hung Mun</td><td>the Secret Societies or, more specifically, the Triads.</td></tr>
<tr><td>hun tun</td><td>'the Chou believed that Heaven and Earth were once inextricably mixed together in a state of undifferentiated chaos, like a chicken's egg. Hun Tun they called that state' (from 'Chen Yen', Chapter 6 of The White Mountain). It is also the name of a meal of tiny sac-like dumplings.</td></tr>
<tr><td>jou tung wu</td><td>literally 'meat animal'.</td></tr>
<tr><td>kan pei!</td><td>'good health' or 'cheers'; a drinking toast.</td></tr>
<tr><td>Ko Ming</td><td>'revolutionary'. The T'ien Ming is the Mandate of Heaven, supposedly handed down from Shang Ti, the Supreme Ancestor, to his earthly counterpart, the Emperor (Huang Ti). This Mandate could be enjoyed only so long as the Emperor was worthy of it, and rebellion against a tyrant – who broke the Mandate through his lack of justice, benevolence and sincerity – was deemed not criminal but a rightful expression of Heaven's anger.</td></tr>
<tr><td>k'ou t'ou</td><td>the fifth stage of respect, according to the 'Book of Ceremonies', involves kneeling and striking the head against the floor. This ritual has become more commonly known in the West as kowtow.</td></tr>
<tr><td>Kuan hua</td><td>Mandarin, the language spoken in mainland China. Also known as Kuo-yu and Pai hua.</td></tr>
<tr><td>Kuan Yin</td><td>the goddess of mercy. Originally the Buddhist male bodhisattva, Avalokitsevara (translated into Han as 'He who listens to the sounds of the world', or 'Kuan Yin'), the Han mistook the well-developed breasts of the saint's for a woman's and, since the ninth century, have worshipped Kuan Yin as such. Effigies of Kuan Yin will show her usually as the Eastern Madonna, cradling a child in her arms. She is also sometimes seen as the wife of Kuan Kung, the Chinese God of War.</td></tr>
<tr><td>li</td><td>a Chinese 'mile', approximating to half a kilometre or one-third of a mile. Until 1949, when metric measures were adopted in China, the li could vary from place to place.</td></tr>
<tr><td>min</td><td>literally 'the people'; used (as here, by the Minor Families) in a pejorative sense (that is, as an equivalent to 'plebeian').</td></tr>
</table>

Ming	the Dynasty that ruled China from 1368 to 1644. Literally, the name means 'Bright' or 'Clear', or 'Brilliant'. It carries connotations of cleansing.
niao	literally 'bird'; but here, as often, it is used euphemistically, as a term for the penis, often as an expletive.
nu er	daughter.
nu shi	an unmarried woman; a term equating to 'Miss'.
pai nan jen	literally 'white man'.
pau	a simple long garment worn by men.
Ping Tiao	levelling. To bring down or make flat.
p'i p'a	a four-stringed lute used in traditional Chinese music.
san kuei chiu k'ou	the eighth and final stage of respect, according to the 'Book of Ceremonies', involves kneeling three times, each time striking the forehead three times against the floor. This most elaborate form of ritual was reserved for Heaven and its son, the Emperor.
shan shui	the literal meaning is 'mountains and water', but the term is normally associated with a style of landscape painting which depicts rugged mountain scenery with river valleys in the foreground. It is a highly popular form, first established in the T'ang Dynasty, back in the seventh to ninth centuries AD.
shao lin	specially-trained assassins; named after the monks of the *shao lin* monastery.
Shih	'Master'. Here used as a term of respect somewhat equivalent to our use of 'Mister'. The term was originally used for the lowest level of civil servants, to distinguish them socially from the run-of-the-mill 'Misters' (*hsian sheng*) below them and the gentlemen (*ch'un tzu*) above.
Siang Chi	Chinese chess.
tai	'pockets'; here used to denote Representatives bought by (and thus 'in the pocket of') various power groupings (originally the Seven).
t'ai chi	the Original, or One, from which the duality of all things (*yin* and *yang*) developed, according to Chinese cosmology. We generally associate the *t'ai chi* with the Taoist symbol, that swirling circle of dark and light, supposedly representing an egg (perhaps the Hun Tun), the yolk and the white differentiated.
T'ai Shan	the great sacred mountain of China, where emperors

	have traditionally made sacrifices to Heaven. T'ai Shan, in Shantung province, is the highest peak in China. 'As safe as T'ai Shan' is a popular saying, denoting the ultimate in solidity and certainty.
Ta Ts'in	the Chinese name for the Roman Empire. They also knew Rome as *Li Chien* and as 'the Land West of the Sea'. The Romans themselves they termed the 'Big *Ts'in*' – the *Ts'in* being the name the Chinese gave themselves during the Ts'in Dynasty (AD 265–316).
T'ing Wei	the Superintendency of Trials. See Book 3 (*The White Mountain*), Part 2, for an instance of how this department of government functions.
ti tsu	a bamboo flute, used both as a solo instrument and as part of an ensemble.
tong	a gang. In China and Europe, these are usually smaller and thus subsidiary to the Triads, but in North America the term has generally taken the place of 'Triad'.
ts'un	a Chinese 'inch' of approximately 1.44 Western inches; 10 *ts'un* form one *ch'i*.
wan wu	literally 'the ten thousand things'; used generally to include everything in creation, or, as the Chinese say, 'all things in Heaven and Earth'.
wei chi	'the surrounding game', known more commonly in the West by its Japanese name of 'Go'. It is said that the game was invented by the legendary Chinese Emperor Yao in the year 2350 BC to train the mind of his son, Tan Chu, and teach him to think like an Emperor.
wen ming	a term used to denote civilisation, or written culture.
wuwei	non-action; an old Taoist concept. It means keeping harmony with the flow of things – doing nothing to break the flow. As Lao Tzu said, 'The Tao does nothing, and yet nothing is left undone'.
yamen	the official building in a Chinese community.
yang	the 'male principle' of Chinese cosmology, which, with its complementary opposite, the female *yin*, forms the *t'ai chi*, derived from the Primeval One. From the union of *yin* and *yang* arise the 'five elements' (water, fire, earth, metal, wood) from which the 'ten thousand things' (the *wan wu*) are generated. *Yang* signifies Heaven and the South, the Sun and Warmth, Light, Vigour, Maleness, Penetration, odd numbers and the Dragon. Mountains are *yang*.

yin — the 'female principle' of Chinese cosmology (see *yang*). Yin signifies Earth and the North, the Moon and Cold, Darkness, Quiescence, Femaleness, Absorption, even numbers and the Tiger. The *yin* lies in the shadow of the mountain.

yu — literally 'fish' but because of its phonetic equivalence to the word for 'abundance', the fish symbolises wealth. Yet there is also a saying that when the fish swim upriver it is a portent of social unrest and rebellion.

yuan — the basic currency of Chung Kuo (and modern-day China). Colloquially (though not here) it can also be termed *kwai* – 'piece' or 'lump'. One hundred *fen* (or cents) make up one *yuan*.

yueh ch'in — a Chinese dulcimer; one of the principal instruments of the Chinese orchestra.

Ywe Lung — literally, the 'Moon Dragon', the wheel of seven dragons that is the symbol of the ruling Seven throughout *Chung Kuo*: 'At its centre the snouts of the regal beasts met, forming a roselike hub, huge rubies burning fiercely in each eye. Their lithe, powerful bodies curved outwards like the spokes of a giant wheel while at the edge their tails were intertwined to form the rim' (from 'The Moon Dragon', Chapter 4 of *The Middle Kingdom*).

AUTHOR'S NOTE

The transcription of standard Mandarin into European alphabetical form was first achieved in the seventeenth century by the Italian Matteo Ricci, who founded and ran the first Jesuit Mission in China from 1583 until his death in 1610. Since then several dozen attempts have been made to reduce the original Chinese sounds, represented by some tens of thousands of separate pictograms, into readily understandable phonetics for Western use. For a long time, however, three systems dominated – those used by the three major Western powers vying for influence in the corrupt and crumbling Chinese Empire of the nineteenth century: Great Britain, France, and Germany. These systems were the Wade-Giles (Great Britain and America – sometimes known as the Wade system), the Ecole Française de L'Extrême Orient (France), and the Lessing (Germany).

Since 1958, however, the Chinese themselves have sought to create one single phonetic form, based on the German system, which they termed the *hanyu pinyin fang'an* (Scheme for a Chinese Phonetic Alphabet), known more commonly as *pinyin*, and in all foreign language books published in China since January 1st, 1979 *pinyin* has been used, as well as being taught now in schools along with the standard Chinese characters. For this work, however, I have chosen to use the older and to my mind far more elegant transcription system, the Wade-Giles (in modified form). For those now used to the harder forms of *pinyin*, the following (courtesy of Edgar Snow's *The Other Side Of The River*, Gollancz, 1961) may serve as a rough guide to pronunciation:

Chi is pronounced as 'Gee', but *Ch'i* sounds like 'Chee'. *Ch'in* is exactly our 'chin'.

Chu is roughly like 'Jew', as in *Chu Teh* (Jew Duhr), but *Ch'u* equals 'chew'.

Tsung is 'dzung'; *ts'ung* with the 'ts' as in 'Patsy'.

Tai is our word sound 'die'; *T'ai* – 'tie'.

Pai is 'buy' and *P'ai* is 'pie'.

Kung is like 'Gung' (a Din); *K'ung* with the 'k' as in 'kind'.

J is the equivalent of r but slur it, as rrrun.

H before an s, as in *hsi*, is the equivalent of an aspirate but is often dropped, as in Sian for Hsian.

Vowels in Chinese are generally short or medium, not long and flat. Thus *Tang* sounds like 'dong', never like our 'tang'. *T'ang* is 'tong'.

a as in father
e – run
eh – hen
I – *see*
ih – her
o – look
ou – go
u – soon

The effect of using the Wade-Giles system is, I hope, to render the softer, more poetic side of the original Mandarin, ill-served, I feel, by modern *pinyin*.

This usage, incidentally, accords with many of the major reference sources available in the West: the (planned) sixteen volumes of Denis Twichett and Michael Loewe's *The Cambridge History of China*; Joseph Needham's mammoth multi-volumed *Science and Civilisation in China*; John Fairbank and Edwin Reischauer's *China, Tradition and Transformation*; Charles Hucker's *China's Imperial Past*; Jacques Gernet's *A History of Chinese Civilisation*; C. P. Fitzgerald's *China: A Short Cultural History*; Laurence Sickman and Alexander Soper's *The Art and Architecture of China*; William Hinton's classic social studies, *Fanshen* and *Shenfan*; and Derk Bodde's *Essays on Chinese Civilisation*.

The Luoshu diagram, mentioned in the Prologue, is a three-by-three number square

```
4   9   2
3   5   7
8   1   6
```

and was supposedly seen on the shell of a turtle emerging from the Luo River some two thousand years before Christ. As can be seen, all the numbers in any one row or column or diagonal add up to fifteen. During the T'ang dynasty its 'magical' properties were exported to the Muslim world where they were used – as here – as a charm for easing childbirth.

Wu Shih's mention (in Chapter 1) of 'the three brothers of the Peach Garden' is a reference to Lo Kuan Chung's classic Chinese novel, *San Kuo Yan Yi*, or *The Romance of the Three Kingdoms*, in which the three great heroes, Liu Pei, Chang Fei and Kuan Yu swear brotherhood.

The translation of Ch'u Yuan's *T'ien Wen*, or 'Heavenly Questions', is by David Hawkes from *The Songs Of The South: An Anthology Of Ancient Chinese Poems*, published by Penguin Books, London, 1985.

The quotation from Jukka Tolonen is from a song on the album, *Lambertland*, by the Finnish band, Tasavallan Presidentti, and the lyrics from the song 'Last Quarters' are reprinted with the kind permission of Sonet Records.

The passage quoted from Book One [V] of Lao Tzu's *Tao Te Ching* is from the D. C. Lau translation, published by Penguin Books, London, 1963, and used with their kind permission.

The quotations from Rainer Maria Rilke's *Duino Elegies* are from the Hogarth Press fourth edition of 1968, translated by J. B. Leishman and Stephen Spender. Thanks to the estate of Rilke, St John's College, Oxford, for permission.

The translation of Tu Fu's 'After Rain' is by Sam Hamill from his wonderful anthology of Tu Fu's verse, *Facing The Snow, Visions Of Tu Fu*, published by White Pine Press, Fredonia, New York, and is reprinted here with their kind permission.

Once again, I find I have quoted extensively from Samuel B. Griffith's translation of Sun Tzu's *The Art Of War*, published by Oxford University

Press, 1963. I reprint the four passages used herein with their kind permission and only hope I have directed a few readers to this most excellent work.

Finally, for those of you unfamiliar with the pidgin Cornish used in Part Two of the book, here are translations of the relevant passages. First, the utterances of the Clay-men:

> *Avodya!* Get back!
> *A-wartha!* Up above!
> *An chy. Kerdhes! Tenna dhe an chy!* The house. Go! Take the house!
> *Ena ... Ena ha ena!* There ... There and there!

And Ben's whisperings:
> *Of ancow.* I am death.
> *Gwelaf why gans ow onen lagas.* I see you with my one eye.
> *Ow golow lagas dewana why!* My bright eye pierces you!
> *Ow enawy a-vyn podretha agas eskern ...* My light will rot your bones.
> Furthermore, when the hologram of the Ox-faced angel says 'Dyeskynna!' ('Come!') there is a faint echo of the Revelation to John (6:1).

ACKNOWLEDGEMENTS

Major thanks this time to Brian Griffin who, as ever, put in long hours trying to work out - for my benefit - just what I was up to in the text. Thanks also to to my original editors, Carolyn, Jeanne and Alyssa for their encouragement and guidance, and to good friends Andrew Muir, Mike Cobley and the late Robert Carter for their unswerving support.

And of course, huge thanks to my darling wife, Susan, for making all this possible, and to my beautiful girls, Jessica, Amelia, Georgia and Francesca, without whom none of it would be worth doing.

Autumn 2022